The Book Of Seconds

The Ruach Saga
Volume Two – Second Edition

Mark A. Cornelius

THE BOOK OF SECONDS

THE RUACH SAGA
Volume Two – Second Edition

With Illustrations by
Shay Cavender

Table of Contents

INTRODUCTION

"Why are you writing about what happens after the Rapture?" a friend and fellow believer asked me, the question almost an accusation. I could hear in their voice the true issue: *If you really believe in that scenario, you won't be here. Why go to the effort?*

Why indeed? After writing *The Singularity*, a pre-End Times thriller, I thought I was done too. Still, a question kept nagging at me. Did the writers of Scripture just write for the moment? Were they not also peering beyond the horizon, preserving their work on parchment for the benefit of generations far in the future?

Not that this manuscript, or any of my writings for that matter qualify as Scripture. But this fictional representation does weave in Scripture already recognized. The details, I pray, are representations based on a long study of God's message, warnings and the hope He provides us in His word.

To the point then: Why am I writing this? It has to do with something my Lord and Savior once said:

> "And then many will fall away and betray one another and hate one another.
> And many false prophets will arise and lead many astray.
> And because lawlessness will be increased, the love of many will grow cold.
> But the one who endures to the end will be saved.
> And this gospel of the kingdom will be proclaimed throughout the whole world as a testimony to all nations and then the end will come."
>
> *(Matthew 24:10–14)*

It would be typical human self-centeredness to suggest that, after the rapture, our responsibility to future generations will have passed. We are taught that even as we are going, we need to teach all nations what has been done for us. My hope is that *Seconds* will not only resonate with the world as we know it now, but also with those seeking hope when they discover they remain after the *Gathering-Up*. Of course, some may argue, such an event will never happen. Regardless, I hope you'll find this an entertaining and compelling piece of fiction.

B'rukah,

Mark A. Cornelius

THE BOOK OF SECONDS

"So they shall fear the name of the LORD from the west and his glory from the rising of the sun; for he will come like a rushing stream, which the wind of the LORD drives.

"And a Redeemer will come to Zion, to those in Jacob who turn from transgression," declares the LORD.

"And as for me, this is my covenant with them," says the LORD: "My Spirit that is upon you and my words that I have put in your mouth, shall not depart out of your mouth, or out of the mouth of your offspring, or out of the mouth of your children's offspring," says the LORD, "from this time forth and forevermore."

—Isaiah 59:19–21

The Book of Seconds is a collection of histories and diaries discovered in the aftermath of the worldwide holocaust resulting from the *Gathering-Up*, when Christians vanished from Earth.

Although scribed separately, these writings appear connected, not only through the language and insights of the writers, but also by their consistency related to biblical prophecy. This is remarkable in itself considering the conditions under which they were written. When *The Dark* began, immediately after the Gathering-Up, no consistent communications bridge such as the Internet, radio or television existed. Electrical and nuclear power ceased to operate at any level. Transportation reverted to horses (until they became food), bicycles, steam-driven vehicles, water travel and walking. Intercontinental exchange, even between countries, states and tribes was inconsistent and perilous, as were trust relationships.

Those who could get their message out and convince others of the truth of it held dominance. Falconers, pigeon trainers and pony riders became nobles and legends of the community. Local government took the form of feudal kings who held territory and traded favors in turn with other self-titled "princes". For the price of fealty, these provincial rulers provided whatever food, technology, weapons and protection still existed.

PROLOGUE

He thumbs through the pages, eyeing specific phrases that seem to repeat, even though the authors of the testimonies had been scattered across the globe and were not in communication with one another during most of the writing. Captions like "spiritual presence," idioms such as "faith," actions suggesting first-hand sacrifice and willing compassion appear in contradiction to civility's complete extinction. The contrast of what was to what now is—instantly haunting.

Have I missed something? Surely this is a work of fantasy. Even as he makes the indictment, he knows the fallacy of it. This time he speaks audibly, looking up to a once-unrecognized source to whom he now pleads with a sense of awe woven with fear. "Please tell me it's not too late. Please show me how to love you."

The silence in response crushes his heart, yet still the muscle pounds in his chest. Amos BenMadai wants nothing more at this moment than to rip out the useless organ and throw it aside. It serves to remind him that he chose his own imprisonment within the confines of this life. He struggles to feel love; faith—unfamiliar territory: *is hope all that is left?* Can he rely on that alone? Exhaustion overwhelms his body and he faints into a depressed sleep of tortured dreams. Darkness seems the victor. Amos the victim, or perhaps worse—a contributor to his own condemnation.

In the void of his nightmare, a pinprick of light—a voice? Someone or something…*calling* to him? BenMadai awakes with a start, taking up a reasonably clean rag from his meager desk to wipe his brow. *Why am I sweating?* Lighting another precious candle, he picks up the manuscript for a second time and starts again to read from the beginning—persisting without food, taking just the occasional break for water and necessities— but with a different objective, one spoken into the night as a request: "Lord, show me what I must do."

The Witness of Fitzgerald Elijah Hindeland

The shrieking alerts me to their approximate location before I can make them out through the hurricane darkness. The fact that I can hear them at all from the other side of the heavy glass and over the roaring wind is a good indication of the agony they experience. I have no choice; in moments they will be no more.

Donning every piece of clothing I can find, I also grab a rag, quickly wetting it with a few precious drops of water and wrap it around my head before exiting from the protective cocoon of my office building.

Immediately I am hit with the heat and the ferocity of the gale, my legs striving against its fury. I fight to catch a glimpse of those in distress, moving in the vague direction of their shadowy images. I yell out to them and quickly realize my mistake. By drawing that robust breath, I have sucked in the toxins raging in the air. They turn to lava in my nostrils and tear at my throat. But it is the strange sensation in my stomach that doubles me over. A building pressure quickly works upward past my esophagus forcing its way past the fire that used to be my tongue, erupting as bloody red soup through my mouth and into the cloth mask I wear. Falling to my hands and knees in agony, I squint desperately toward the victims I wished to save. I am too late and they are too many.

Now I can see them also fallen and writhing. Their skin melts and parts of their bodies sail past me. Finally they evaporate and I too begin to wither in the storm. The last thing I sense, as I perish, is a hand held out from a loving voice. It speaks away all of the torture, heals my agony. Three words are all I hear as I crave to catch the hand.

"Come up here."

The hand grasps mine and I am awake.

Yes, a dream. The same dream, the one I dread to revisit because its complexion is so life-like in its unfolding. Comet-like I orbit helplessly back on a collision course with the beginnings of the tribulation. Again I want no part in it, yet knowing in its completion, You Lord God, are there. You are asking me to share something boundless with what is left of this decaying world. All I have is what You give me to offer: A living history transcribed into the written word.

This scripting is by no means an attempt at a new gospel or a book of wisdom. You have inspired other such texts and have already revealed Your good news for those with the moxie to read and believe. This is a testament to the end of it—what was to come—is now. I have heard Your calling. I am Your messenger, my disclosure coming from a source beyond my understanding. Others who read these pages will have to consider the text. They will find it best to use the filter that I utilize—faith in the One unseen. That must be their touchstone. Without faith, these words will be empty.

Who am I to even attempt this? I am a servant and an adopted child of the Most High. I have been known as Professor Fitzgerald E. Hindeland. I recognize He has called me to remain for a time. I accept this opportunity, unworthy as I am, to warn and encourage those lingering and those yet to be born. I write on these pages what is already known by God. I do so for the purpose of witnessing to eyes that might read and be opened, to spiritual hearts that might hear and believe at the telling.

For a moment let me remember back to what seems a better place. They were the thriving times when even the poor seemed blessed—not like today when all seems dead. That past consisted of so many as spoiled naïve children—all claiming to be chosen, all claiming needs and superiority at the same time. It was the age of building, what I will refer to now as

Old Culture, when mankind thought itself unrivaled; when towers and technology aspired toward the heavens.

Then, one day, a sound in the air unlike any sound before or since. The atmosphere was shaken and then, a change. They were gone—the special ones—the ones who seemed to care most and who were best at sharing and seemed most easily taken advantage of. They had been, in some ways, very predictable and uninteresting—keeping to their provincialism and encouraging others in temperate behavior. In other ways they were exciting, having unusual abilities and skills which set them apart, made them seem strange to the rest. And as You understand all too well, Lord—to strange people, happen strange things.

They vanished in a breath, just as some of them had predicted would happen. Just as I warned would happen and on the day that You Lord said it would happen: the day called by Jews around the world as the Day of Trumpets or *Yom Teruah*—translated literally "The Head of the Year".

What was not known was the reaction and aftermath of the unexplained disappearance of a billion people from all walks of life. Almost immediately, society fell apart. Those remaining who had power titled themselves *masters*. Those who hungered for power, but had little, conspired for opportunity.

It is difficult to extrapolate when and what was the final breath before Old Culture's demise. Many have blamed the portent, now referred to as the "Dark Blue". Some of us had known it, still understand it for more than that; a singularity in space designated by scientific nomenclature as V4641. This strange anomaly incredibly shifted neighborhoods, from the center of our galaxy to a patch very close to Earth. V4641 now can be observed in the night sky, not by brilliant light, but by its astrographic signature, the strange cobalt-tinted void absorbing the light of any mass near enough to enter its irresistible pull.

I still am in awe of its placement, far enough from our solar system to avoid complete disintegration, but close enough to alter our planet and lives, alerting us to Your presence in all that has taken place and all that will take place. The most drastic of changes so far has been what some of us refer to as the Gathering-Up, when God-believers vanished before the very eyes of those who denied or marginalized His existence.

Of course, problems had started well before the appearance of V4641. Expansion of warfare beyond anyone's comprehension, earthquakes on a scale unparalleled, strange weather patterns, floods, and pestilence—all this and more—contributed to a catastrophic death toll that no one was willing to define in real numbers. The losses were too large for our feeble minds to comprehend. And yet that auditing became small in comparison to the devastation after the Gathering-Up. Since that moment, the world has known only chaos—hunger, strife and disease have become the absolutes of survival. Because of the strange effects of V4641, the magnetic poles reversed and…something else. I remember it well; not even I as an astrophysicist could have predicted the possibility. Energy died. No, not all energy, but the ability of electrical current to conduct from one terminal or location to another…failed.

I had just completed a cell phone call with my close colleague and mentor, Rabbi Moses Folzman, instructing me to find my way to Jerusalem. That is when the lights in my facility at the University of Texas shut off. I thought the backup generators had run out of fuel. We had been running them continuously due to the failure of the utilities network in our Austin, Texas location where my group had obtained sanctuary. Since I was alone (the rest of my group having been "gathered-up", I refer anyone reading to my earlier epiphany about my remaining for a purpose), I tried making another call on my cell phone and found the device useless. I groped for and clutched a flashlight, but it also had no power. When daylight came, I hunted for anything that might have a battery or stored power. Every facet of electrical mechanics was and remains now, dormant.

By my continued research, limited in scope as it is, I am convinced that electricity has not ceased to exist. But its ability to travel—through solids, liquid, gas; by any means—has somehow been inhibited. Had an electromagnetic pulse bomb been set off by some world power? A nuclear device set off at maximum altitude would render everything electronic or electrical inert or overloaded. The strategy would disable all communications, computer use, most transportation and all electric convenience…temporarily.

The true dilemma revealed itself days after. I was able to make contact with some local authorities. The power reduction could not have been caused by any known earthbound device because no electrical power could be restored whatsoever. Not even a hand crank generator would function.

How then, if electrical power and communications have caved, do I know so much about the disharmony apart from my own area? God has supplied an incredible spirit of stamina and resourcefulness to those remaining. Though the methods are primitive at best, word still travels. There is the element of exaggeration and misinformation to be considered, but repetitive reports from diverse sources validate what I already knew to be escalating prior to the Gathering-Up.

As for determining any scientific explanation for our new environment, without the assistance of sophisticated instruments, that is more the challenge. After reviewing all my notes, the only empirical answer continues to dazzle me:

The matter-antimatter reaction purposely set off within V4641 by the minions of Darius Mede, then chairman of the Green Order Government, initiated an energy reaction. V4641 had already consummated some kind of kinetic bond with earth—a phenomenon that my group had been researching. I believe the rocket sent to destroy the singularity caused instead a permanent static transfer disruption (as best as I can define it), so that nothing, not even a simple electric current will now move from one point to another. Not wirelessly or along more outmoded wired lines. The lingering capability we appear to still have is simple friction—the ability to cause a minute spark by flint or friction allowing the generation of flame. Thank You Living God for this remnant; otherwise I believe mankind, for that matter all life, might have perished.

Do you readers of this account, in whatever time you now abide, doubt me? What if flame were rendered inert? What if the basic function of fire combusting fuel and producing heat had been disabled by the stupidity of those who had thought themselves all-powerful? What if our very sun had been doused by the folly? Who or what would be left to complain? But here we are, still existing, still surviving. For what purpose? The same purpose as always: there are others to be gathered to the love of the Creator.

Many will question my choice of words: Creator? Love? Of whom do I speak? And if He loves so much, why is the world in this state of affairs? Rather than try to justify His plan, I will simply expose the obvious: we have been deserted here, not because of God's errors, but because of our own.

I am chosen to remain to shine a light on these times at the beginning of the *Messianic Age,* what may be called the *New Advent.* My writings offer on His behalf, one final overture for all remaining humanity to return to Him—to worship YHWH, my God as Creator and to accept His Son as Messiah of this fallen world.

Most will scoff at the existence of God. I ask those doubters now: *how is that doubt working for you?* If any of you do recognize Him as reality, why strike out angrily at Him, indicting Him rather than yourselves for what we now endure? Why do you persist?

The world is red-hot with rage and overwhelming hopelessness—ideal times for redemption. But there must be a willingness: a want for greater, not just better things.

I am finally beginning my journey to Jerusalem—I can wait no longer though the traveling is difficult at best, dangerous as well. I plan to record my daily encounters, detailing my experiences with those I meet on the road and the results of my witness. Mine is a message that I first had to accept in my heart, one I resisted because of my academic upbringing.

It is that same scholarly rearing that has helped prepare me for my journey. I know I must travel light, but also effectively. Most would think a simple compass all that is necessary for navigation along the road. But the fact that the earth's axis has shifted combined with the apparent radical deviation of the magnetic poles' make such a device practically a relic. Still, it will prove valuable for other purposes, so it comes along. Additionally, I will be carrying a sextant, chemical wands for emergency lighting, several firearms and possibly my most valuable apparatuses— seven telescopic lenses and specialized filters. These I can use—even with the continuous cloudiness we now experience—to observe the stars, measure the lunar cycles and perhaps equally important Lord, for continued observation of the Dark Blue and its effect upon us. I will also be bringing along a rather unusual ally who I hope will help guarantee even greater protection along the trail.

The trick with all of this is finding some method of transit away from my university offices which have been surrounded for a mile in every direction by water from the up-welling of the Edwards Aquifer. I have to take the risk and swim to other nearby buildings to find something I might use as a boat. Thank You Lord that the current is not unmanageable for one of my advanced years. You have given me good health and a strong stroke for the task.

Incredibly, a boat is exactly what I find—likely the one dumped by a deceiver from among our group who used it for escape after a failed attempt to kill another of my colleagues. What happened to that thespian? Lord, I leave her circumstances in Your hands. I confess I care not other than gratitude for her abandonment of her craft. I have managed to port all my traveling goods to drier ground where my trek is to begin.

But enough about my equipment and minor challenges; I will also need counseling by my Master. I hunger for Your teaching and am learning that primordial hope still throbs within those who weary of this age. God willing, I will arrive at my destination a changed man who accepts his task of being used to change others.

Let my obedience in making this dangerous journey be acceptable to Your needs.

Lord, keep Your plan before me. Remind me that there is still an opportunity to discover new life; a life of hope beyond these most tragic of times, in this most horrendous of ages. I refer to Your future hope, not hope in this life (who in their right mind would be satisfied to continue on in such indigence?).

My odyssey eastward reveals rampant despair; a constant grey pale that saturates the shambles of cities and towns I have observed along the way.

I am certain it is the same throughout the world—a smoldering overcast left by the chemical fallout contributing to the oppression of these times.

I speculate that, if the global electrical matrix has shut down, then so has the ability to satisfactorily cool and contain the nuclear cores of reactors on land and in sea vessels. Meltdowns and hotspots will have caused millions to die. Some will have drunk untested water polluted from the radioactive aftermath. Others will be exposed by proximity to the affected areas. Countless more will be victims of wind currents that carry the deadly residue indiscriminately.

So few humans are left…so little of anything is left and what survives now competes aggressively. Former canine pets are no longer trusted companions. They have reverted to traveling wolf-like, in packs. I have seen the results; the remains of mangled bodies and scattered bones tell the forensics: loners, ill-prepared or naïve to the realities of the new landscape. Woe to the unsuspecting; nature knows no mercy. So also rats, coyotes, badgers and other once-timid cohabiters are now considered "contact risks." They want as we want and if they are engaged in larger and stronger sizes, we become competitors or possible meals.

What *used to be* is now but a story told at night in protective huddles. Tales of glories past sound magnificent around a campfire, even the most humble histories. But, the words do not comfort; they are meant to remind—*what we are, is changed; we are less.*

Many used to speak of the goodness of man, but no longer. We have seen that splendid performance played out and it was a ruse. Men are cleansed of any veneer and appear now as a dangerous blight to the world and to each other. There is little loyalty; less mercy.

It is broad daylight. I think nothing of the place and time. There are plenty of others on the road…well, I count fourteen at least, spread out over a quarter-mile's distance who are heading east, as I am.

Everyone on the road independently picks and weaves their way through the snarl of abandoned cars, trucks and refuse. There is no inclination to share the discovery of a tool, useful clothing, or preserved foodstuff that might help one to survive along the way. Each person, even if traveling in what looks to be a family unit, seems to keep their thoughts and intents insulated from all others—a sign of the times. Not even blood relatives watch out for one another, much less strangers. Should one be eliminated, the rest benefit from the spoils.

So when the gang of six men appears from the woods to the side of the cluttered road, it is a solitary confrontation on my part.

It is a foolish moment. I am distracted by the wanderings of my own mind, neglecting the fact that I have outpaced my comrades and am now quite a distance ahead of any of them. Not that it matters; none of the others are concerned for me. Thank You my Savior, that You are not calloused in this new age and so continue to concoct means for us to receive Your mercy and protection.

There is no doubt of the intent of the six. Emerging from the forest, they draw out their guns, not aiming them at me yet, but advertising they are well armed. Their leader boasts with his two Browning pistols, one in each hand. I am laden with travel goods: a large backpack, a pull-cart and of course my Winchester. Looking around to affirm that no assistance from the others is coming my way, I decide that I don't have enough firepower (nor the will to use it) to curb an attack. Diplomacy will not work either. They appear to be approaching aggressively with no interest in creating community.

So I do the thing I can do. As they near, I begin to sing at the top of my lungs, "I saw the light, I saw the light. No more darkness, no more night. Now I'm so happy, no sorrow in sight. Praise the Lord…" As I chant, I start taking things out of my pull-cart, throwing them back from the way I had come from. This stops the culprits dead in their tracks at first, obviously wondering what this mad man is doing. My antics buy me a little time which I spend continuing to sing, scattering my cargo down the road. The gang actually takes one step backward when I suddenly stop singing and turn rapidly to look at them. I could take a shot at the one who seems to be the one they heed, but the risk is excessive. What if I miss? What if I were to kill or maim someone who is not culpable? How could I live with myself as an attacker of others?

My better judgment prevails and my hasty plan starts to pay off. The first ones of those I have been traveling with now catch sight of my antics. Like my would-be attackers, these folks can only gawk at my behavior. The sight of packaged food, clothing, shoes, bedrolls and other prized paraphernalia tumbling toward them causes an equal, but opposite reaction. Instead of hesitating, they start charging forward, as I had suspected they would, in hopes of acquiring loot.

The adversaries blocking my path however perceive the advance differently, thinking the stragglers might now be coming to my assistance. More of my supposed compatriots start running in my direction and the ambushers choose to abandon their quest, hightailing it back for the woods. This is a turning point and I have to follow through with the rest of my strategy. I cannot risk the rascals darting into the trees, then turning around and firing on us from a protected vantage point.

I reach behind me to a small pocket on my backpack and extract a metal cylinder which I open—immediately out flies a creature: It is one that the world is not yet widely acquainted with, but will soon come to dread, as Bible prophecy has already predicted. This winged beast is three inches in length and literally looks to be made of metal, an aberration caused by the breeding that spawned it—an experiment-gone-bad in the depths of a mine beneath the Midwestern United States. Abaddon, as I have christened it, is equipped with golden spikes encircling its head and razor-sharp teeth. Its appearance is made stranger by the humanlike hair flowing beneath the crown of spikes. The attribute that demands immediate attention when encountering the beast is its tail which is barbed with a myriad of stingers. The stingers contain venom that is not deadly to humans, but one who is stung will wish for death until the lacerations heal. Add to all this, the sound of its beating wings; like glass being broken and scraped across metal at the same time. The noise makes rational thought nearly impossible and easily generates frenzy.

Lord, You well know the origins of this strange creature. I was introduced to its berserk makeup when it was captured for examination just a short time before the Gathering-Up. My research team discovered then that those who have chosen to believe in Christ are miraculously protected from its aggressive fiber. On the other hand, to the *non-believer*—be warned!

So I let loose hell on our would-be attackers; Abaddon aims straight for the woods and soon screams, more grating to the nerves than Abaddon's winged racket, can be heard fading into the distance as the bandits run for safety.

Now my concern is for my fellow wayfarers who are confused and are starting to come unglued. "Quickly," I urge, "everyone come close to me if you want to avoid being attacked."

Most everyone obeys without hesitation, drawing into a tight circular unit with me at the center. I can hardly move and have to push out with a yell, "Let me through!"

As this is happening, Abaddon returns and seeks out four slower trekkers who have not yet reached our clique. It lands on their exposed skin, even the tiniest fraction that is showing, thrashing again and again with tail and teeth, drawing cries of terror and injury from its victims. When I am able to free myself from the crowd, I open another container that holds my other outlandish asset immediately recognizable to all within the area, human excrement, purposefully allowed to decay. Through experimentation, I had derived this concoction as an extra-special treat for Abaddon. My terrifying pet mutant immediately turns away from the stragglers and flies back toward me. I quickly insert the fetid contents into the metal tube and Abaddon dives into the receptacle without hesitation. I fasten the cap back on tightly and then turn to beseech my daunted audience.

"You have just witnessed the wrath of God and His mercy displayed in the same instant. You don't know me, but I hope you will learn to trust that I and the God I bow to, mean you no harm. As a matter of fact, I and He would like you to know us better. I am traveling east on a long and purpose-filled journey. Some of you may also have destinations in mind; others may be drifters just trying to survive. Whichever you are, I invite you to continue with me on my quest as far as you care to follow. I have other endurance skills and I know that you also have abilities to share. Together we will travel more safely."

I go immediately to each of those wounded by Abaddon, asking, "Do you want to know God?" All four plead "yes," and so I follow Jesus's s example, laying my hands gently on each, praying to God and watching His Love repair their sores and stings. I acquaint them with my Savior's tenderness by a simple statement, "Your faith has healed you."

I let Your Spirit, Lord, continue to guide me in the next words I speak. "I also offer to teach you, from specific knowledge I have been given, about the true meaning of what has happened to our world over the last months. Join me for as long or as short a time as you wish and I assure you, greater things than this you will see."

I turn and begin walking east without looking back, continuously praying in my heart one phrase, "Thy will be done. Thy will be done…"

And You answer! Soon I can hear and sense the presence of others who have chosen to follow—fifteen from that first group. As we make our way toward the coast, others join. The story of my journey not only attracts those already heading on a comparable course, but somehow telegraphs outward. We walk through towns and people come out of buildings or houses to fall in line without question. It is as if they had been told ahead of time about the strange singing sojourner and his troupe, ready to travel wherever I am leading. You are indeed an awesome God!

But most are not ready to make such a commitment and treat our ragtag lot suspiciously, peering from behind windows or positioned prominently with weapon in hand—announcing to us our unwelcomed status. It saddens me because I remember the time before the Gathering-Up when a voyager coming through a town would be greeted, possibly even invited to stay and take a meal, especially in rural communities. At one time, migrants brought news and told stories of other places that offered towns and homesteads a broader view and perspective, but these are not those days.

On our trek, we continue to be on guard and occasionally run into other bands who have less goodwill. A feudal system seems to be emerging and leaders of these tribes want to ratify their newfound power. I am noticing two consistent approaches that such groups make in espousing their dominance.

One group might see our trespass (or we might spot them first) and will send out scouts to determine if we are hostile, if we intend to settle in the area, or if we are just passing through. These types of groups might even try to extort payment for passage or strong-arm some sort of guarantee that we are not invading. Most of the talk is bluster because none demonstrate any true capacity to defend the land. It is just too soon after the Gathering-Up for there to be cohesive garrisons or codified armies of any size. Once these groups realize that we are merely moving "through," they frequently stand down without further provocation.

Master, thank You again for Your protection over us. Several more times we encounter the "other kind" that attacks us unprovoked. These are dangerous and appear to have no other purpose than to overpower and take whatever tangibles we are carrying. Because of these groups, we have to systematically appoint guards at the front, rear and sides of our body. Their duty is basically to telegraph warnings at any sign of trouble, at which point I release Abaddon who somehow distinguishes friend from foe and quickly scares away our would-be attackers.

Occasionally, a flamboyant chieftain, a desperate community starved by mediocre planning, or a colony plagued with disease will show itself. Even the threat and sting of Abaddon are sometimes not enough. The collapse of convention is pitiful poetry, sung to the tune of envy and hatred by those who have nothing, to those who have little. It is a grim chorus to which we reply: *our perpetuation or theirs?* It is a response I justify only through being appointed as Your attendant over those whom You have given me to direct.

Many are too flagged to fight and join our ranks in silent subjection. Rarely, the crazed continue to attack until tortured into submission by my bug or are chased off by the raising up of our sticks and weapons. Never once have we taken a life, but some are undeniably ravaged by spirits other than Yours, Lord God: some live already in an earthly hell, hoping we will help them on to the next.

Amazingly, we suffer not one casualty by contact with outsiders. In this new age, there is little if any trust. Each cloaks himself in a heavy darkness—hiding underneath it for protection rather than seeking strength in semblance. Any conversation between us I consider, a small victory. When someone does speak, it is mostly for immediate need.

"Where will we stop next?"

"The weather is shifting."

"There's a stream to the left."

All are impaired and guarded because of their past experiences—to them it is best not to be known, not to risk giving away their most precious commodity: themselves.

I have learned from carefully listening to sparse comments the group offers as we journey, that most have decided to follow because they recognize me. I have to keep reminding myself that I am, for all intents and purposes, the last person seen by a viewing audience on a television or computer screen. That is because of the unusual activities associated with the Gathering-Up, the time I was formerly used as a communications vehicle by you, Lord.

Being a reader of history myself, I realize how, over the course of time, meanings and definitions can become confused. Cultural, technological, even geological changes may someday cause people to muse, "What is a television? What Gathering-Up is he speaking of?" I pray You Lord will be visible in this short telling of these events. Only You know how long into the future these scribblings of mine might testify to others.

I should probably explain more of my recent experiences, so that the world may know of Your great power to enable and disable.

In the weeks preceding the Gathering-Up, a former assistant and my most gifted protégé, a young man named Daniel Adamson, came to visit me. He and another trusted colleague, Brandon Lader, had been working on a research project and had discovered the correlation of the now famous V4641 singularity with all of the happenings that have so drastically altered Earth.

At that time, we had no idea what was truly behind those amazing days. Now, it is quite clear to me that a crossroads of biblical prophecy had been reached. Danny (an affectionate name for my friend) and others were gathered-up as was predicted in Scripture. But a few of us have been willed, by You, to carry on the work begun by our Savior during his ministry on Earth, preparing for his inevitable return.

That is why I journey east. That is why I must reach my journey's end, no matter the time or risk involved.

A peculiar phenomenon has left many of the remaining men and women who had been parents, depressed. At the time of the Gathering-Up, children—all under or near the age of twelve to fourteen years—all vanished. Of course Christ followers from the former age would have understood readily that anyone under the *age of reason*—that time when most young adults become aware of their choices in the world—would be called to the heavenly kingdom. They had no accountability. Praise You God for granting them immediate grace.

My faction however is not comprised of believers in Jesus, so they are having great difficulty with guilt and separation from their families. I am spending much of our travel time delicately advancing the idea that there is still hope of reuniting with their loved ones…in a different way…in a different time and place. Even so, there is reluctance on their part to let out their feelings and thoughts. I am starting to feel depressed myself at what I consider a futile effort. Who can blame them for resisting my efforts to reach out? Who wouldn't be loath to siding up with a six-foot-two, singing, baldheaded physicist who carries a monster insect in his backpack?

Deviations occur—You Lord have always seasoned Your plan with nuance. We are somewhere near the northern border of what had been Georgia and South Carolina, part of what is now called by the locals. I appreciate the day for its unusual beauty. There is a pristine blue sky, very little wind. It is mid-morning with the temperature in the 60 degree Fahrenheit range and the birds are in full song. There are very few days like this anymore. The weather has been influenced dramatically by the advent of V4641. Also, this day reminds me so much of another, years past, that started out in the same way and ended up so terribly different— that day was the eleventh day of the ninth month of the old Gregorian calendar in the year 2001. I remember on that September day long ago, another peculiarity of the times—there had been absolutely no jet airplane contrails to be seen in the cloudless heavens that morning. For those of you who have only heard tall tales of such things, contrails were the vapors expelled by aircraft exhaust at soaring altitude, which looked like cloud trails that could be seen behind the jet for many miles.

Perhaps I have over-simplified this explanation for those reading this in a distant future—unfamiliar with such craft—*Jet planes* were amazingly fast mechanical transporters that flew in the air! They were built at the apogee of the Old Culture. Jets and contrails were quite ordinary sights in the skies through-out the world back then and their absence on that September day had caused many to ask the foreboding question, "Where are all the planes?" even before knowing what had happened.

The rest of that story is now the stuff of legend. Now the most accurate calendar is kept once again by following the phases of the moon and by counting days from after the Gathering-Up. By my extrapolation, which is challenging due to the clouded conditions, I have been on the move for three complete lunar phases. For me all this is a harbinger that again causes me to wonder, *what is to come?*

I have a dilemma to consider on multiple levels. Near the end of our traveling day, we crossed a creek and decided it was a good place to water-up and clean our cooking utensils. Using sand to scrub a pot only goes so far and this water appeared to be as uncontaminated as we would find anywhere. Good stream-sources have become few and far between.

As I washed my cookware and some of my soiled laundry, I noticed an unusual piece of natural slate wedged into the tall creek-bank. Upon inspection, I identified lettering, but it appeared to be in some other dialect, possibly of Cherokee or some other native origin. Being lodged firmly and apparently deep into the side of the incline, I could not get a clear read on the script. Employing the assistance of several of the stronger men of our group, I was able to dig around and then remove the slate. When we pulled the object away from the earth, along with it came a human skull, some bones and a few other ancient trinkets too weathered to identify. The slate stone was in decent condition and indeed, its writing was in a different cuneiform. Some of the strange glyphs interfered with a complete message. The beginning looked more like Native American writing interwoven with something else strangely familiar…

ᎠᏓᏅᏯᎩכ ᏂוᏯᏓל

—But, then I examined the next portion and the strangely familiar became shocking to me. The inscription was no-doubt in Hebrew! I know because it is my tongue of birth and I had no trouble reading much of the message…

בשנה הבאה בירושלים…
next year Jerusalem

—There are more symbols located in seemingly random locations on the slate. They do not appear to be linked in any way to one another. The entire piece seems inclusive; there is no immediate indication that it is broken off another larger manuscript.

I have not informed the others that I understand at least part of the inscription. For all I know the tablet may be some elaborate hoax or an accident of recent historical culture-mixing. There is little use in generating false interest in an artifact when our very survival is in jeopardy. This much is certain; I must carry and protect this relic during our journey, so that it may later be professionally examined. And there lay the challenge. Its weight is approximately fifteen to twenty pounds, not a load I would normally consider burdensome, except I am already hefting seventy pounds upon each of my animals and any addition means more strain to the steeds. For the meantime, I will carry the treasure in my personal backpack, along with my more valuable belongings and hope the weight will not tax me too greatly.

YHWH, I sense that this stone is a gift from You, I have not yet discerned its value or purpose. But I will trust You to reveal that in Your time and to provide the ability for its transport.

We have tried to skirt the more rugged mountain areas to the north (keeping to the river paths for need of water on our trip, but making sure to avoid any that have possibly been contaminated by failed nuclear facilities). We come to the small town of Citation: the roadside sign reads, "Population 607." Citation appears to be uninhabited but for one person. A young man sits on the side of the road in a fold-out lawn chair—sawed-off shotgun and a long pistol resting in his lap.

He seems very much at ease there, not indicating by any overt action that he is after my provisions (even traveling with a convoy, I am still a well-marked target—a man with two horses, one-loaded with booty). If my demise is at hand, so be it, yet I walk in the confidence that YHWH's presence continues to be my armor.

As we approach, the sitting man speaks. "Ah'd hate to impair such fine animals with a missed shot," he muses, eyeing my mares, "so why don't you come off your filly and let me just take both of them off your person. Ah might even let you live."

It is a fair offer from a man who looks as if he could follow through on such a proposal. Even in his reclined state I can tell he is tall and well-muscled, probably around twenty-five to thirty years old. The Marine signet ring on his finger also tells me this one is not to be trifled with, though he has no idea of our safeguarded weaponry or of my pernicious pet confined in my backpack. This man-boy might have friends cloaked within the timber; his audacity suggests as much. But why then ask me to dismount? They could easily pick me off my mount with a clean shot. No, he is alone and is putting on a front for his own protection.

I choose to take an alternate path with him, replying, "We are just passing through and mean no harm. Actually, you are welcome to join us if you would like. I am leading this caravan group to Israel."

The smirk on his face says he thinks I have landed on the wrong planet—certainly the wrong continent. Not knowing his name or the condition of his soul, I decide it best to make an introduction. Extending my hand along with my warmest smile, I offer, "My name is Fiz Hinde…"

—Just then, my horses and all those beasts held by our group, neigh, refuse their reins and take off running. As they disappear into the landscape, the ground erupts. This is a "big one" as we have come to know them. Earthquakes have become commonplace, but most are small, regularly reminding us of the new constants we must survive. This one wants to take us out. I am catapulted from the ground and land against an old car, which is dancing from wheel to wheel. Rolling to avoid being run over, I hear a loud "crack" above the noise of the quake's rumble and see a telephone pole begin to topple in my direction. The shaking will not let me gain my feet and I prepare myself to be crushed by the pole.

At the last moment, a hand grabs my arm and pulls me aside as the pole crashes and rolls in the other direction. Still the earthquake is not done. A house to my left implodes and it apparently has an old functioning propane tank. In another instant, the tank—now leaking gas—is ignited by a random spark and rockets into the air. I lie on the ground and watch in amazement as its trajectory will clearly bring it upon me.

A command slaps me to fresh alertness. "Get up!" and again a hand pulling at my arm. This time I find my footing and am able to dive away as the flaming tank lands where I had a tick ago lain prostrate.

The quake slowly subsides over the next few minutes; no other wreckage comes my direction. I survey the main street of Citation, which has already been littered with neglect. It is a picture out of the Holocaust. Storefronts and homes have collapsed onto a terrain that now has dips and juts, reminding me of a military-style obstacle course.

Several structures are in flames and I become worried that some of our traveling group might have tried to dive for defense into the damaged buildings. I begin looking around for two things: the owner of the hand who saved my life and survivors.

I don't have to search far for the first. The young man to whom I had been introducing myself, is just to my right and is brushing the dust off his clothing. He is otherwise unscathed.

He also seems to be scanning the vicinity and then turns, reaches out his hand to me and artlessly says, "Jason Billards. Let's see who else needs help."

I am shocked at the quality this man has just displayed. He actually seems to care about the predicaments of others. I don't dwell on the matter, but for a moment. He is right; there are others who might need immediate ministration.

Of the forty-three who have been traveling with us, not one has sustained major injury. Even so, treating the various cuts and bruises takes some doing—our horses had run off at the beginning of the quake and with them, most of the bandages, iodine and antiseptic that we had scavenged. Along our journey there have been other cuts and injuries. We have learned that rubbing moss and dirt into the wounds is at least a temporary solution until we can find an unharvested drugstore or an apothecary.

Once everyone is treated, I turn to Jason and say, "Thank you." But I can't help being curious and follow up with, "What inspired you to help me? It's not a common trait these days."

"Why shouldn't it be common?"

What a simple yet knotty question. How should I answer? Is there an answer? After witnessing the strength of humanity called away to another realm, there seems little left to save of mankind. Certainly traces of goodness, random acts of kindness and civility still exist, but as the exception. Why Lord, have You not just wiped clean the face of the earth instead of leaving this patchwork of dysfunctional survivors who mostly look after and fend for their own narcissistic needs? Is there hope for even these? This brave soul beside me deserves an answer.

"Your act is one of a man seeking a loftier purpose," I reply, carefully choosing my answer and praying silently for the right words.

My God, You are not satisfied with my statement. In my heart of hearts, I know this man should be given more than an answer; he needs a question to pursue and Your Holy Spirit provides one for me to ask. "Who taught you such behavior?"

At this, Jason looks puzzled. He leans back on the heels of his boots, crosses his arms and seems to ponder the query fully. Then he gives me a crooked smile and I am amazed by his response. It is in the form of another question, challenging mine.

"Do you have to learn to do good things?"

And the lesson has begun. I smile back and am about to share a parable taught to me by Rabbi Moses. At that moment, my backpack starts buzzing. Jason looks at me with his quizzical smile again, but I have no response. Abaddon is doing something very odd indeed. Usually docile in his metal habitat, he is now sending out signals. With each passing moment, his buzzing and shaking become more frantic.

Instead of trying to explain to my new friend, what is in my backpack, I sense the higher priority. My pet bug is in a furor for a reason. Is it trying to warn me? The earthquake has already happened. What else can possibly follow worse than that?

Oddly, it is Jason who answers the question. "Something bad's gonna happen—real bad. The air's all wrong." I look at him and realize he is actually sniffing the surroundings as a hunter or an animal does to determine evidence of prey or an enemy. He glances at the sky carefully in all directions with a look of sober analysis on his face. "Get everyone together, we've got to git."

Having lived in Texas as long as I have, I am very familiar with the term *git* and its true meaning *leave and that means NOW.* I assume it means the same thing in South South, so I quickly pass the mandate among our group and Jason gives a sign for us to follow him. He turns and begins to trot, not looking back or seeming to care if we comply.

"Hurry," I repeat and follow the young man, not quite understanding why Your Spirit is urging such trust in him.

Jason heads for an outcropping that is at the base of an imposing cliff face. He runs around a huge boulder into what seems to be a dead end. When I round the boulder, I stop cold—he is gone. Vanished like a vapor. I look around and then hear to my left, coming from behind a large holly bush and toward the base of the escarpment, "In here old man!" A strange thought comes to mind—*talking bush?* I then peer around behind the holly and see an unsealed hatch that serves as a cover to a ramp leading into the cliff face. It is doubtful that I would have ever discovered the ingress without Jason's steering.

There is enough room to maneuver past the bush, so I mime for the others to hurry through the entrance which transitions to another doorway. At this portal, Jason is busy working a complicated set of mechanisms. Apparently, when dialed in the right succession, access will be gained. The doorway reminds me of one to an old bank vault.

"Took me a while to figure this one out," the young man mumbles as he rivets on the correct sequencing.

Finally I hear a loud mechanical "click" and Jason pulls the door open. "Everybody-in," is all he says before again disappearing ahead of me. I remain at the doorway and encourage everyone to hurry through as best they can.

As some jostle to get their trappings and carts full of supplies into the cave, the sky begins to darken and there is a rumbling from somewhere overhead unlike anything I have heard before. People naturally turn to see what is causing the noise and change, so I continue encouraging them to move into protection.

How do I know it was protection and not a trap of some kind? Those of you who do not know the powerful ability of the Spirit of God to communicate good and evil intentions, would not understand. By Your power Lord, I know and my sensing of Your presence is all that matters. In the cave is good; topside, death is approaching.

I squeeze past the progressing gypsies so that, from the entrance, I can examine the western horizon. There seems to be a different tint to the sky—not dust or cloud-created—I now pickup on what Jason has already sensed—the air itself is changing. Taking a slim breath—indeed there is a sour burn on tip of my tongue. As the sky continues to darken, the sun also dims as if it is being eclipsed by another orb. My scientific mind discredits this notion for I have been tracking the circumgyration of the moon and Earth and have spotted no other celestial substances affecting the light of the star.

Others who are waiting in line to enter the cave also notice the difference and the stew begins to boil; those at the rear of the line attempt to hurry those in front through the passage. Shoving and cursing increase and then I see the first fist fly. This is going to get out of control—at least half the group is still trying to gain entry and the progression is slow. I have to think of something fast and from my pack I pull out the cylinder containing Abaddon.

The banshee noise of the vibrating container reverberates through the entryway, drawing everyone's attention to me. I snag the moment. "Any of you who want to live: steady yourselves. Those who wish to witness hell unleashed, continue this foolishness. We have little time and we need to work together to get inside right now."

"Ah got a better ideer," a burly man adorned in a stained white T-shirt and torn blue jeans interrupts. I cannot help but notice that every part of his visible body from the neck down is covered in tattoos. I remember him being a recent arrival to our group. He literally stands out from the rest—at least six and a half feet tall, flaunting what looks to be an equally large elephant gun that he now has pointed directly at me. I do not know which appears more menacing: the owner, who has obviously been a weight lifter at some recent time in life; or the weapon he wields. Both inspire me to pray. His inflection is calm, but his intent is clear. Still, he lays out his proposal rather eloquently for all, especially me, to consider. "How 'bout Ah blow ya to hell and that creepy varmint 'long with ya? Then maybe whatever bad spirits is plannin' on takin' us will go away and…"

—To his left comes the sound of a blast and I see the man's head disappear in a spray of blood. The rock-face behind where he had stood is painted wet crimson and in seeming slow motion, his body collapses to the ground. There is a bewildered moment before I can force my head to turn to the left, tracking the explosion to the barrel of an even larger rifle-cannon. It is held in the hands of another new member, a stocky weatherworn woman. Her hair is capped by a bandana and she too is tattoo clad. She wears a simple gingham dress, stands all of five feet tall and sports a backpack that is nearly as big as she. Her age is impossible to tell. She looks directly at me without emotion and explains, "He'd had it comin' fer a long while now. Him aimin' at you, Preacher, is just a good excuse. Now can we all get back to work, so's we don't all die out here?"

I have no words for her or the others. I manage to motion and help direct those in front to resume an orderly procession into the cave. The whole time I keep shifting my gaze to the roiling sky above and then over to the fallen body of my former nemesis. I want to be sick, but the increasing rumble in the distance and my concern for protection of the others keep me in control.

Finally they are all through the narrow gate. Jason reappears from inside the cave.

"Everybody in?" he asks.

"Everybody who's coming," replies the woman who saved my life. I still have not found my voice.

Jason looks at her curiously before running to secure the farthermost entrance. He returns to the portal door and motions for me to help him. Together we grab the metal handle attached to the large cast-iron wheel on the door and pull it shut. He spins the wheel and the metallic clicking seems to assure him it is secured.

Lord, give me strength to overcome the slight case of claustrophobia starting to overtake me, there is no time to be self-absorbed: almost immediately after the door has been locked in place, the rumble from the world rises to a nearly deafening crescendo. The bosom of the cavern shakes and dust from the ceiling sifts over us all. My bones feel like they are oscillating against some dissonant chord and Abaddon buzzes as I have never heard before. There are some in the room who trill in fear, but most are frozen silent waiting for an unknown end. At this curious moment I ask myself, *How can I see in here? There are lights! How is that possible?* The questions remain unanswered for the moment as something else suddenly draws my attention. Silence. As rapidly as the threat mushroomed, it is gone. Abaddon continues to buzz, but at a greatly subdued cadence. Then even he settles.

I turn to notice everyone else looking at me. I can read the bidding in their eyes—*tell us what to do next.* Being new to our man-made womb, I too need to gather my bearings and turn immediately to Jason. He responds without my having to ask the question. "Guess this'll be your new home for a while. Ah might as well show you 'round."

You are amazing, Lord God,

You provide when I don't even know of the need,
You heal wounds I don't even think exist.

You protect those who call on Your name and reach
out a hand to those who do not even acknowledge You exist.

But for how long, Lord will You continue to show mercy?
The earth is alive with death

The fields wither, the air is becoming poison
Darkness is the new day

Your light is hidden from the world
In my spirit and my soul, I know these
signs to be only the herald

How long, Oh Lord, before Your terrible day?
How long before Your longsuffering will cease
and Your loving-kindness is taken away?

Give me strength to endure and wisdom
to proclaim You to others. Let their eyes be open,
let their ears hear so they may know and believe

You are the Everlasting God
and Your Son is returning in glory

—Fitzgerald Elijah Hindeland

The cave we have entered turns out to be more than just a simple enclosure. Apparently, the U.S. military had built an undisclosed installation in this area, so vast that its predetermined entrance was on the South Carolina side of the border and the townspeople of Citation had no inkling of what existed beneath them until after the Gathering-Up. One of the many recent earthquakes changed that. Jason and two others had been out on a hunting expedition when they were caught in the alcove by a tremor and bombarded by shale from the cliff above. Each received multiple injuries and one was fatally wounded. After burying the victim, the two others returned to the alcove because they had heard a metallic sound during the earthquake. That's how they found the well-disguised hatch behind the holly bush. It took several days to figure out the unlocking sequence. When they did and discovered the hideaway, they entered to thoroughly explore their find. After a discussion with the remaining fifty-three people of Citation, it was decided to abandon the town and take up permanent residence in this secured bunker. Several of the men devised the crude, but effective stone gate that hid the townspeople and their new domicile.

The mystery is why this place had been vacated. Or had it ever been inhabited? The interior is in spotless order and even has ingenious mechanisms for atmospheric circulation and water containment that do not require electricity. Compressed gas, kept in an array of cylindrical containers and a thermal heat exchanger, provide power and heat. There are even portable breathing units and small gas and oxygen containers that if necessary may be ported on a long and extreme journey. It is as if whoever built this structure, well in advance of the actual happenings, knew what essentials, would be apt.

No records in any file drawers, no names, no identification of any kind can be found to reveal the purpose or the intended occupants of this place—this concerns me. People don't tuck away something this well without great purpose.

Ein Gedi, as we have come to call our protective enclosure, is well furnished and amply reinforced. Even continued ground tremors and an occasional more cataclysmic quake do not affect it—no ruptures in the exterior walls or inner facilities have been detected. The design of this sanctuary is truly an architectonic wonder. Still, there are other obvious maintenance issues that must be contemplated.

A subterranean spring under this geologic formation provides us ample water and so far the changing geology has not cut off that source (praise You, Almighty). The storage bay has been well stocked including food— enough for a small army—to last perhaps a year or more. There is a kitchen with additional tanks of low-pressure…LP gas that can still be ignited to produce flame for cooking.

There are semi-private sleeping quarters with room and beds enough in each compartment for ten tenants. Other compartments are set up as office locations, meeting rooms and even designated "seclusion areas", obviously to be used on a reserved basis as the need for isolation is determined.

Oh yes, the lighting! It is another scientific marvel to behold. The system is entirely fluid based and looks to be a combination of LED and tubular lighting containing some undeterminable inert gas. It cannot be fluorescent or neon—those require electrical current to operate. The connecting tubes have been built modularly. They are each, five feet in length, so that if one intersection breaks, it can be replaced with spares kept in the storage bay of Ein Gedi. The mystery is how luminosity can be self-sustaining in a light-emitting chemical diode when no electrical current is present. The designer has solved this problem by having two types of reacting gas converge at the LED junction. The charged particles cause a low-impact, but sufficiently bright light in the LED. Irrespective of the annoying red tint reflected through the compound, it is an elegant, minimal-energy solution that reminds me of the endeavors of a former colleague. Perhaps I am digressing from the details of Ein Gedi in explaining that relationship, but I sense an important connection, so please forgive the following side story.

In days far past, while I was working on a NASA propulsion system project for long-distance space travel, I was introduced to a brilliant mind. He was a European chemist who had also somehow beguiled his way into the government fraternity. His work on chemical relationships and biotronics—especially in the area of plant and animal reproduction in the hostile environs of space—made us ideal partners for the project. So well did our expertise mesh that we were awarded a Nobel Prize for our work together. That was where our camaraderie ceased however, for I soon discovered this man's passionate interest in social engineering—a discipline my faith and my Jewish heritage would not let me encourage.

At first I reached out to my associate, hoping to encourage him to utilize his skills toward a greater purpose, but he grew more and more arrogant in his belief that mankind's maturation was in his hands.

Lord, at that time, You convicted my spirit to be vigilant about this man's errand and to be a watchman on behalf of others in an effort to stymie his efforts. It would continuously pit us as adversaries in the scientific and the political arenas, even to the time of the Gathering-Up.

At the discovery of this lighting system which closely mimics his work, I pondered whether Darius Mede had something to do with the construction of Ein Gedi.

Regardless of its origins, this place is an incredible blessing that I believe you Lord have allowed us to discover to save our very lives. Yet there is a growing concern on Jason's part and mine, that the preordained dwellers of this place might eventually knock at the door and evict us. Additionally, most of those in my group were on journeys to other places before finding asylum here—some of them seeking family members to connect with, others on solo quests. After just a few weeks within the confines, I detect a sense of "cabin fever" among them. No one desires to make this place a permanent home.

Exterior conditions have worsened. In addition to the pervasive wind and seismic activity, darkness prevails. We have one window to the world. It is an ingenious piece of flex-glass contrived into the lithic cliff. When we approached Ein Gedi from the periphery, I did not see the window at all. Just like the outer hatch, it had been magnificently curtained. From the inside we can climb to the second-story observation deck to see anyone or anything encroaching from the west—the singular point of entry into the alcove. Of course, amidst the storm, little to nothing can be seen. If a giant meteor were to blitz our location, we would be oblivious until the moment of impact.

Through this looking glass we peer out powerlessly as the perpetual tumult assails. There is no rain, but nature deflates us with other unexplainable phenomena. Vicious lightning will temporarily illuminate the dismal vista, striking sizzling pits into the infertile ground. Such events remind us (as if it is necessary!) that we are not welcomed outside of these walls. The discharges intrigue me more than a little. I find myself studying them for hours in amazement. It is the most powerful evidence of all that electron charges are still possible. But Your hand seems to be withholding what we once took for granted as ours to do with as we pleased—the generating and harnessing of electrical current by mankind.

And another more somber question comes to my awareness. Will I ever see a blue sky again?

Within our safe haven, we discover parts and equipment that allow us an antiquated means for testing the peripheral chemistry. Special pressure filters in Ein Gedi cleanse the air conveyed from out-of-doors—I do not need to examine the filters' mechanics; they are the brainchild of a dear friend, my mentor and the most renowned micro-biophysicist to live, Moses Folzman! I recognize his structural signature within the setup because Moses was the director for the same aforementioned NASA project. Yes, Lord what a sense of humor You have to put a brilliant biblical scholar on a team for deep-space exploration. The filter discovery serves as confirmation that indeed, Darius Mede, or someone with access to all our patented projects, has been involved in the construction of this facility.

Thank You God that someone has had the foresight to utilize those past skills, for the filters do not require any electrical current to run. But run they do! From this, one of my most disconcerting questions emerges: *to whom else have You revealed Your plans?* Was someone used as nothing more than a tool, not understanding Your ultimate outcome, to construct this place? Or are there others that You are working through even now to conduct Your superior spiritual engineering?

Occasionally we fit a glass vial, complete with a live insect (unfortunately these still seem to be thriving as well as we are) over one of the filter units, turn the "filter" switch off briefly. The behavior of the insect reveals the inherent breathability factor. In each case, the aggrieved creature quickly dies and in some cases actually wilts before our eyes. For the time being, this will be our home and I pray the protecting equipment continues to function accordingly.

Over the first three months of staying here, I have begun to hold—for lack of a better term—class. It is more than that of course, but education appears to be of great interest to everyone and there is plenty of down-time. Because of my background, I have decided to take the lead.

The material we cover seems innocent enough—geography, history, literature, even math and yes, science. There is an actual library of paper-bound books assembled here for us to draw from. And to keep my charges on their toes, rushing to the available resources for reference, I use my typical technique of challenging each morsel with questions. For instance:

Was cross-evolution between species a provable concept?

If the theory of evolution was only a theory, why are so many other theories bred from it?

Why did the Greek and Roman cultures collapse if they were so sophisticated?

Why was Frodo such an exceptional choice to carry the ring of power?

But most amazing to me is the fact that among all the tomes and volumes archived in Ein Gedi, not one Bible, Qur'an, or any book directly referencing *any* spiritual matter can be found. Fortunately, the study Bible I have ported with me (large and cumbersome as it is), remains my most prized and useful asset.

My assignments include having the students (most of the now ninety-five adults consider themselves such) take a topic from whatever book or interest area attracts them. In each session, I elect one "researcher"—typically the one who appears to choose the most intriguing study of the moment—to find a parallel connection within the pages of my Bible. It has become a tournament to see who can discover the most revealing or the most debatable point of the week.

I know from experience how powerful the Spirit can be when working with an inquiring mind, but I was not prepared for what is happening because of these sessions. It was the twelve-year-old named Ben who first made his own decision. In class one day, he raised his hand tentatively and asked, "Is this place we're in…an ark? Like Noah's?" I invited any in the class to offer an opinion and was amazed at how many were scarcely aware or not at all familiar with the story. For that matter, none seemed to recognize a significant quantity of the stories from the greatest book ever written.

So begins my greatest educational opportunity ever: to inspire my ambitious students to explore the Word of God, having only one copy of the text from which to share the experience. After a good deal of prayer on the matter, I have borrowed a page from history, using the monastic model as my guide. I have offered anyone interested their own copy of my personal Bible, including the markings I have made in the margins. All they have to do is either hand-copy or type (amazingly, the builders of this place even thought of providing fifty old-style manual typewriters, ten of them portable models!) the text, word for word, exactly as it has been presented to them. I do require that I be able to oversee their work and each student is allowed one book of the Bible at a time to transcribe.

Anything I have written in the margins they are required to mark in blue ink and any quotations from Jesus, in red. The provided typewriters are equipped with tri-colored ink ribbons and a special key lock that easily allow for this operation.

A conundrum presents itself in what I do to allow the work to begin. My Bible—a gift given to me forty years prior by Rabbi Moses—has to be somehow disassembled so that multiple people can be typing out multiple sections at any one time. This requires me to use a box-cutting straight-edge to slice away the pages from the binding. This is more an emotional than a tedious chore, but I know the outcome is worth the inferred desecration.

Equal numbers of pages are given to each person. Once they duplicate those pages, the students are given the next pages in succession. My hope is that eventually, each person will keep one entire copy of the text. Consequently, by their efforts, they will absorb significant understanding by what they have copied.

The work goes surprisingly quickly—the time some spend waiting on others to finish hand-copying is being used to further study the text. I am amazed at how attuned the student writers and typists have become to their efforts. One strong example is when Ben (fast becoming my favorite) asks me, "Is what's happening outside, Wormwood?"

Wormwood: the legendary star in the book of Revelation that plunges to Earth from out of the heavens. It poisons a third of the waters, thereby killing a bulk of the population. I have also wondered what destruction is being wreaked globally, but have not dared to put *that* name to it.

At Ben's question, I have everyone pause from their work as an opportunity to begin one more thought-provoking teaching moment.

"My young friend here is copying from one of the most challenging excerpts of Holy Scripture and has unpeeled a question that I'm sure is on all of your minds in one form or another. 'Is God destroying Earth?'

"I encourage you to look back through your paragraphs and I suspect you will find multiple inferences to God's plan for the completion of His work. Some will read of havoc, others of you will find passages of hope and mercy. The restoration of what El Shaddai began in the Garden is not a harmless process. We must suffer, just as He willingly suffered for us. There is a name for this plan—a very familiar name that is used often and yet is routinely misconstrued. The name is *love*, ciphered from the Hebrew, *awhab*, or the Greek *agape*. The word defines devotion beyond understanding, God cherishing and desiring a relationship with His creation so badly that He is willing to offer a way for us to be forgiven if we admit our faults and desire to change."

"…Why would a god do that?" The woman's name is Betty. She is the one who had shot my attacker outside of the Ein Gedi entrance and she asks the question from the back of the room. Everyone in the room turns to look at her. She stands up and continues to question. "Why would someone who is so friggin' big 'n' mighty, who can beat ya down whenever they want and who can do anything they want, why would they wanna be so nice?"

Her question is acerbic, contrasting and very real. *Lord, You are so strongly present in this moment.* Although no electricity is evident in the world, the air in the room is charged with Your Spirit, more conspicuous than the tingling of the atmosphere from the prevailing lightning storms. I look around at the others and see most nodding and grumbling. Betty is their voice, their conscience. This is their lost souls' song of the times—a mournful collective dirge of despondence. All of the "good ones" are gone. These who are left know they have been left. They want to know why, if God is so good, they have been discarded.

"Why are we *Seconds* still here?" Betty drums the question more as an accusation of abandonment.

Seconds, what a perfect term, I think to myself. *Lord, give me an equally perfect explanation for them.* "A very real and honest question: To answer it, I have to know something first. Do you believe in God?" Now I have their attention. If Betty is just throwing out an argument for argument's sake, then there is no point in moving forward. But Your Spirit is attentive to her covert wrestling; I know it as it were my own. How? Lord, that is the mystery of Your work. People in the room are indeed being convicted to seek an answer. This is the start of a new and great awakening. I pray silently, waiting for a response.

Betty hesitates and then speaks. "If there is a god, then—"

"—That is *not* my question!" Maybe I am reacting a little too harshly to her avoidance, but I sense the opportunity slipping away. "Do *you* believe in God? Yes or no will do quite nicely."

This time it is a full, agonizing minute before she responds. At first she stares at me in a way that makes me think I might be her next victim for target practice. Then her visage softens slowly, as tears creep down her cheeks. Finally she opens her mouth. It is still several moments before the hushed antiphon comes out, "I want to, but…I don't see a god out there worth loving. Look…just look at what we've been left with. How can He do that, take away children and…husbands and…how can ya speak of love when ya look at what's left!"

Now she is weeping a shower of enraged tears, her wounds fully exposed and the memories overwhelming. Betty is not the only one. The room is awash in grief. All, not just some, are broken open and their contrition takes flight to the unknown. It is this moment I have prayed for and now speak over.

"I have lost most everyone I cared for too. So how can I dare stand here and tell you about a loving Creator? I can only do this because He has invited me to know Him and I have accepted the invitation.

"Do not misunderstand me, this is not *free* love. It cost me everything to receive it. And this is not the type of love we have understood in the past, it is infinite. God too has lost loved ones He is aching for—all of you. It cost my Savior God everything to offer his love. Both He and I had to be willing to die. You must also be willing to give everything, your very life included, for this love.

"But those who remain may not be willing to surrender the last of what they have left for the One who loved them first. To them…to us, it seems like God doesn't care, because we don't care.

"In fact, He cares so much that He is waiting, waiting sorely and patiently for us to care just enough to allow Him to enfold us. Unless we are willing to be overwhelmed, soon there will be another change…God will stop waiting."

"What does that mean—God is going to get tough on us or something? Aren't things bad enough for us?" This comes from a young man, Pavoli, probably in his early twenties. He has not spoken much in class, but I have noticed that he takes copious notes whenever I speak.

"Just the opposite: God, at some point, will stop being anything at all to those who spurn Him. He will stop calling out, He will stop answering. He will not offer mercy or love and He will stop filling the emptiness of broken lives as He does now." It is time to bring the point home. "But let us get to the real question that everyone asks in the darkness. If there is a Supreme Being out there, what hope is there of getting His attention anyway? Why try at all—we will never be flawless—frankly, perfection is too hard. Why bother? Why not just live and let live?"

Now everyone is nodding in agreement, so I press on. "That's the way we've tried to do it in the past, isn't it? Each man and woman for themselves—everyone free to do their own 'thing'. So do you like your freedom? Are you fully satisfied? How is all that 'me first' working for you? Can you honestly blame your quandary and the decay of the world on God? You are free to trudge through life without Him."

No one will look at me. No one will look at anyone else. They know the truth of it—they have chosen to ignore God and now they are paying for their own mistake brought about by their own hand, not the hand of God.

"So from what you just said, Ah got two choices, not three like Ah thought Ah had." It is Jason, standing by the door. He usually doesn't attend the classes and I hadn't seen him until he had spoken. He wears the grin that I remember first seeing upon our first meeting. I have seen it often in our months together, Lord. I have determined that his disarming smile is a symptom of Your Spirit at work in this man. Even when he is unaware, You are helping him to fill in the missing pieces of his life's puzzle.

"What are ya talking about, Farm-boy?" It is Betty again. She has taken an obvious liking to the modest protector of the town and has shown it in her own peculiar way by giving him a nickname.

"Well, seems to me, Ah can choose to believe in God, full throttle, pedal to the metal, or Ah can turn 'round and say, 'no way, Jose,' and make like Ah'm the one in charge. The thing Ah can't do is say…'maybe.'"

"Maybe?" I echo his question, thinking I know where he is going. The fact that Jason has taken up the torch is amazing. I don't want him to lose momentum.

"Maybe Ah will believe and maybe Ah *won't*—depends on the time and place. Do Ah want what God wants? OK, then Ah *will* believe. Do Ah want somethin' that He don't? Like a light switch—on when ya need it, off when ya want some spiritual shut-eye."

The analogy is so simple; I just let them all consider it in the silence of the room. Betty reacts first. She walks from the back of the room and comes up to look me straight in the eye and asks, "Ya believe in this God that strongly—like Farm-boy said?"

"With all my heart and all—"

"—Yes or no, Preacher, we don't need no sermon."

What else is there to say? "Yes."

Betty actually starts counting out points on her fingers. "Well, yer actions say it and yer words say it and…well, the bug thing is weird, but I can't argue with what I see happening. OK."

"OK?" I parrot. I have to know what that means to her.

"Ohhh kaaay. Are they just slow where ya come from? That means I buy it. God *is*." She looks up at the support beams and around and then back at me and asks, "Now what?"

I have to think about that question. I believe she expects a heavenly choir to sound or blinding light to explode into the room. I smile and ask her, "Betty, do you believe that God can do anything?"

She nods her head mistrustfully.

"Do you believe He loves you—not the kind of love that men have disappointed you with—*real* love that never changes?"

Betty's confusion about the definition of love plays on her face, so I elaborate.

"Imagine God loving you enough to allow His son to die for your failures and to then be brought back to life, just as your dead life can be brought back to life?"

"I never heard it put that way, but—"

"—Yes or no, Buckshot Betty, don't need no double talk." My retort to her causes everyone to crackup with laughter. Everyone except Betty, who is looking at me with another curious expression on her face—fear? Rebellion? Whatever turmoil is bubbling up inside of her causes new tears to stream down her face. The room again quiets—all of us wait for her to resolve her conflict.

Finally, she looks up from the floor and nods at me with a surety I have not seen on her face before. "Yes," she says and seems surprised by her answer. "No turning back now. Ah have lied and slept with lots of men, even kilt me one and…well, there's lots more than that. If Jesus died for all that and God can forgive me, there's nothing on this planet can't be done through Him."

I couldn't have expected what happens next. A unison cheer goes up in the room and everyone rushes in to hug Betty. As each person makes contact with her, they then come to me and say something like "me too," or "I believe." Apparently someone has gossiped to the rest of Ein Gedi of what is happening and additional people begin to flood the classroom, each one coming to Betty, then to me, many confessing indiscretions and even blatant sins. For over an hour the conversions continue. At the end, I don't even try to count how many are saved that day.

A strange new spirit is in the room. These, who have demonstrated a very visible disregard for one another, for any other, are suddenly hugging and conversing, asking for prayer and…for care. It is what I had not been able to put a name to before—a missing ingredient—as on the day of September 11, 2001 when no jet contrails were evident. Now, as had not existed since the Gathering-Up, I see communion reborn.

The last person to comment is Jason. "Guess that's 'bout it," he states, not going into any other explanation, assuming I know his meaning. I do not and say as much.

"Ah mean, everybody's committed now. They've all joined the club."

"Everybody?"

"Not all, but most. The rest'll come 'round."

I am not satisfied with Jason's casual approach, seeming to avoid his own commitment. He is an excellent reader of body language and this moment proves no different.

"Don't worry 'bout me, Preacher, Ah'm with you on this. God and me had a chat a while back—Him doin' most of the chattin'—and Ah'm on the right road now. Ah may keep things close to the chest, but Ah ain't no fool…least, no more."

Then he reaches his hand out and I take it in mine in a firm handshake, now trusting that we are brothers in the Faith. I know what has to happen next. "Everyone, please listen." The buzz in the room immediately ceases. "Jason has just brought up a great point. All here in what we have dubbed the Unity Hall, have apparently committed their lives to Messiah Jesus, but there are still those of Ein Gedi who remain uncommitted. We cannot nor should we try to force anyone to make such a decision. Yet we are asked by our Savior to reveal to others the change within us."

Everyone looks confused. I can almost read their thoughts. *Have they not already done that?*

"We have confessed to one another, but that is the first step of many. Now we need to demonstrate by an outward sign to nonbelievers of what has convicted our spirits within. I suggest you all follow me to the storage bay. Get everyone else in the compound to join us there."

This is another opportunity to witness on behalf of God—I am being spiritually encouraged to lead the way. We all gather around the one large water tank that has a drain valve and, next to it, a quality-testing tank about the size of two large cast-iron bathtubs put together. Without asking permission, I open the valve to fill the testing tank and murmurs begin to germinate in the room.

"Please do not be alarmed." I speak loudly so that everyone can hear. "The amount of water I am drawing is my concurred ration for a month. I am willing to offer this for the community in order to complete a vow I have made with my God."

Everyone, including the new believers, is befuddled and Betty issues a verbal cautioning to me. "Whatever yer planning, Preacher, ya can't live without water for that long. I'll split my cut with ya."

Others in the room also offer the same and I know my life is in their hands. A critical lesson—*do unto others*—has been played out and the remaining nonbelievers have to be asking themselves why anyone would possibly want to dismiss the *everyone for themselves* mode of life.

"I appreciate your love and will offer all I have to you as well. That includes this moment. I also want everyone in this room to know you are taking these steps at great peril. In this new age, you will be hunted and ridiculed, brutalized and most likely killed for speaking the name of Jesus as your Savior. Do not doubt me on this."

That brings absolute silence to the room except for the running water, which I bend down to turn off. When I look back up, an incredible sight meets my eyes. All in the room are holding the hands of the person next to them. Young Ben puts words to the moment. "I guess we'll all live and die as Seconds together then, won't we?"

Now it is I who cannot contain the flood of tears. Motioning to Betty, who comes and stands by my side, I whisper instructions into her ear and then she turns and looks at me in utter amazement.

"You want me to do what?"

I do not try to explain again, instead looking toward the now full tub. Betty shrugs her shoulders and then climbs into the tub, fully clothed and sits down. I also enter the basin, kneeling beside her and ask, "Betty, do you believe that you are a sinner and do not deserve the presence of God in your life?"

"I do," she says without hesitation.

"Do you believe that Jesus, the Son of God, willingly gave his life for you so that you can reclaim a relationship with the Maker of the universe?

"I do." She is blubbering once more. An odd thought crosses my mind. *She might be able to fill the tub with her tears and if not, we can all contribute.*

"And, do you testify to the change within you, that your old life is dead and gone and that Jesus, Messiah, has saved your soul and is now alive within you?"

"I tell you it's the truth, Jesus is my Savior!" She shouts this at the top of her lungs and all the new believers in the room are now applauding and hooting.

I place my hand on her back, as I had told her I would. I use my other hand to gently pinch her nose shut and speak, "Betty, I baptize you in the name of the Father God, the Son Jesus and the Holy Spirit," while simultaneously leaning her back down into the water. I bring her back up and she gasps.

Betty responds for the whole room and beyond to hear. "I don't know about the rest of you, but I'm proud to be a Second! That's what we should all call ourselves from now on. God didn't forget us. He needs us to be here at this time."

The group agrees loudly now, so Buckshot Betty bellows again to be heard. "The rest of you Seconds, hop in. The water's fine!" This former "biker chick" is not only baptized, she is clearly ready to tell the whole world what and Who has happened to her.

When all is said and done, eight have not converted. I actually admire their honesty and cannot fault them for being open with their doubts. In my humanity, I am still frustrated—have I not been compelling enough, have I left something out or said too much? The realization hits me that none of these people's conversions are my doing anyway; the Spirit of God is at work here. I need to rely on that alone. And I am learning that God is not through, either. As our community grows closer and our lives display the difference due to the community of faith, three more are converted.

But one has become markedly agitated and spiteful of the changed lives around him. Kendal is popular, but seldom participates in group activities. He has attended several of my classes, always debating my teachings, but has ceased coming when I requested that he support his arguments with source material from the library. He stated to me on his last visit, "I enjoy argument for the sake of argument. You need to get used to that—there are others like me in the world."

Perhaps that was his best argument of all. I couldn't disagree and indicated to him I had run into many such people in my academic life. We used to call them university students. But argument without substantiation was not a method of learning that I would continue to engage in. I welcomed him to choose another method or cease participation. He chose the latter.

I had not realized, nor could I anticipate, the impact the new converts' zeal is having on those who have chosen another route. One day, Kendal and a group of five others approach me. He stands in front of me with his arms crossed—the others gather behind him for support. When he speaks, it is with obvious frustration. "Look, you've got to stop this nonsense," he says in a polite but discontented voice. "The others are driving us nuts, singing in the halls, offering to help with our chores and always wanting to talk about this *Jesus* thing. I don't want to talk about nor do I want anything to do with your god."

The others behind him shake their heads in agreement. So I ask, "What happens when you tell them to leave you alone?"

"Well, they...leave me alone," Kendal grumbles. "But that's not the point. We can't go anywhere in the compound without hearing this stuff. Our freedoms are being violated and I'm offended by their attempts to win me over."

"I thought you said they were leaving you alone now, how can they be trying to win you over?"

Catching him in a contradiction seems to frustrate him even further. Instead of answering me, he becomes more demanding. "You tell them to stop or I'll—"

I was not about to accept threats or ultimatums so I cut him off. "Kendal, before you say something we all might regret later, know that I have no intention of forbidding anyone, including you, from expressing their beliefs. As a matter of fact, I'm very interested in what you consider to be precious in your life."

Kendal and the others stare at me for what seems a full minute. Then he speaks/mumbles, not able to defend his position, "Just leave me alone, that's all I've got to say."

And they walk away. The same night, another of his group comes to me to offer his life to Messiah Jesus.

I've been using the Ein Gedi facilities aimed toward a new purpose. There are many spare parts, wiring and all the compounds necessary to wire together a dynamo—basically a simple hand-cranked electric generator. If successful, we will be able to then find a flowing water source and construct a hydro-electric system. That depends on when or if the world becomes habitable once again, but Your word, Lord God, suggests the eventuality, so I press forward.

Young Ben is serving as my laboratory assistant and today we are both excited, for it will be our first attempt to create a sustained electric field. I've taken every precaution for safety and so feel confident in allowing my new protégé to initiate the experiment. I direct him to connect the wires to an outlet containing an incandescent light bulb fixture. Then he begins turning the crank on the contraption we have so lovingly constructed together.

A whirring noise indicates that the conducting brushes within the dynamo are making contact with the copper wiring so carefully wrapped and ready to transmit current. As Ben studiously cranks, a slight glow begins to emit from the bulb. Encouraged by the reaction, he begins to increase the velocity of his motion and I warn him to be steady. But he is a boy, still prone to the excitement of the moment. He ignores me and increases further his gyrations. For some odd reason, I cannot move to stop him. Is it my own excitement? Suddenly the intensity of the light increases and then becomes blinding. I hear an explosion, but cannot see its source or the results.

Then I smell it: the unmistakable pungency of broiling flesh. I choke as I desperately try to find Ben to save him. Now I realize it is my own flesh melting in agony. My throat is drowning in flames—there is no elixir to ease my wounds. I try to find the water tub in an effort to baptize away the flames that now annihilate me and all of Ein Gedi.

It is my own verbal scourging that awakens me and I quickly realize that no such experiment has taken place, because no such inquest is possible. I know this because I had tried all options before vacating my lab at the University of Texas. Thankfully, Ben was fine; all of Ein Gedi is still and fine. Even my brief anguished noise has gone unnoticed, for all are asleep. As for me—I am not fine. My startling dreams continue—what spiritual warfare might be going on within the depths of my being?

You Lord have given me great skill which I used to help build an astronomic and technological empire. Whether by the trickery of demons or somehow for Your purposes, the ragged dreams remind me that all my wondrous work of the past has gone up in a cosmic Armageddon. I realize it will never return by my hands and I look at those hands in the dim chemical light. Am I just to be an old nagging reminder to the world of what mankind had been, how we had overreached in our arrogance? *What will You have me do now, Lord? I am nothing.*

Kudos to the work of the steadfast Seconds: the copying of my Bible speeds forward. This presents another opportunity to distract me from my recent melancholy associated with the nightmares. There are more and more questions rising from the ranks that itch for solid answers:

> "Why are each of the gospels so different—shouldn't they be the same?"

> "What had Moses been doing for forty years before he killed the Egyptian and had to leave?"

> "What changed Jesus's disciples from an assortment of frightened fishermen/boys into the eloquent spokesmen they became in the book of Acts?"

These are but a few of the queries emerging and I know I will need help in explaining the interwoven abstracts of Scripture. So, I follow your model, Jesus and choose twelve out of the group who, like you, are passionate. They seem excited about serving others and about study of the Scripture, researching and sharing their faith openly with the community. Buckshot Betty, Jason, Pavoli and young Ben are the first I invite (and who enthusiastically accept!). Then I approach eight others who have displayed interest in "digging deeper" and offer to walk with them on their journey.

There is plenty of time to study and discuss, as well as time to whet their skills, offering whatever resources they have to others in the community. I advise them not to force themselves on the remaining five nonbelievers but to be ready to assist if ever asked.

Interestingly, after another month, Kendal and his flock accost me again.

"Your 'do-gooders' are a bunch of hypocrites! They go around helping people, but never approach us. What happened to the old 'love thy neighbor' stuff?" Kendal appears to be very proud of his scriptural reference.

"You told me to advise others to stay away from you. Have you changed your mind?"

Kendal reacts with an edge-sharpened argument. "Look, we just don't want them preaching to us, but if we have a need, just like anyone else, we want the same treatment, that's all."

I smile inwardly, thinking, *All the benefits and none of the responsibility.* Then I re-approach the confrontation. "Kendal, I think we may have started off on the wrong foot. I'd love to better explain how my faith and its actions are..."

Before I can finish, Kendal grabs the lapels of my shirt and pushes me up against the wall. "I'm telling you right now," he yells. "I don't want to hear anything more about your damn faith! I'm sick of your almighty crap and you need to shut it up. All of you."

Others come around corners to see what is happening. What Kendal does not know is that I excelled at one time as a tae kwon do student, thanks to an extracurricular class taken at the University of Texas. One simple move and I could easily incapacitate him. My next actions will define for my new brothers and sisters what being like the Messiah is all about. Instead of physical retaliation, I reply. "Be sick."

"What?" Kendal loosens his grip and appears suddenly unsure of his vigor.

"You said you are sick of my actions. I can't stop you from being sick because my actions aren't going to change. So—be sick." I stare him straight in the eye and suddenly his face turns from the bright red patina of outrage to a pasty white. He hiccups once, releases me and turns back toward his pack. Before he can say anything else, he throws up on the two immediately in front of him. He bends over, holds his stomach, then hurls again, this time with a groan.

I speak in a loud firm tone to make sure everyone can hear. "I want desperately to tell any of you who will hear that I worship the One True God Jehovah, knowing that He loved me enough to offer a special gift on my behalf. I recognize that gift to be my Messiah, my Savior, whose name is Jesus, the only Son of God. I serve only him. I am through being polite and I will no longer tolerate disrespect for the name of the Living God. I have chosen and those of you who chose as I have, I call my family."

Now I look directly at Kendal's covey. "The rest of you are free to choose whatever you want to worship and you are welcome to remain here. What you will not do is dictate who I will serve."

Kendal continues to heave and his friends all jilt him, choosing to sulk away and avoid the humiliating moment. All but one, that is. One of those that Kendal has thrown up on, in his early twenties by my guess, looks down at the retching man, then at me. "Can you help him, please?"

I read real compassion and maybe even pleading in his eyes—something is changing within the boy. I reach down a hand to Kendal and say, "Get up, you will feel better." Kendal brushes away my hand and continues to cough as if something is trying to escape from him.

"Dad, please!" the boy pleads and suddenly I understand the connection.

I reach out again and this time softly implore, "Kendal, get up."

Kendal looks at his son, who nods and then, without looking at me, takes my hand and stands. Immediately he seems to bounce back, but instead of turning to me, he looks at the boy and says, "Let's go." Then he walks toward the bunk quarters.

His son hesitates a moment, glances at me and says, "Thank you." I can somehow actually feel his gratefulness. But then he too turns and obediently follows his father's steps.

At first, the other Seconds who have witnessed the showdown remain frozen in place. I suspect they are afraid I might make one of them sick. I smile and shake my head in assurance that they are safe. Then, Pavoli speaks up and says, "Are you…OK?"

I nod in reply and then he speaks to the others. "OK, don't just stand there, let's get some buckets, water and mops and clean this mess up."

I have put the chemical lab and library to a new use, purposefully waiting until our survival and cultural issues have been adequately addressed: Now, a bit of research to stimulate my curiosity. Today I have pulled out the stone slate that I had found in the nearby creek-bed. It is time to validate or debunk the existence of this piece. To do so, I have carefully cleaned the slab, making sure to avoid removing the algae and other growth that has imbedded itself into the etched surfaces of the symbols. Protecting this material is crucial to my research, having learned that this matter grows at a very specific rate, depending on environmental causes and surface texture.

If we still had the resources of the previous age, I would now simply flip on my electron microscope and examine the exact growth patterns. Combined with electro-chemical analysis, this would allow me to quickly measure, almost to the year, the age of the writings. But we no longer have those abilities and I am relegated to stone-age (forgive the pun) methods.

For this example, the slate was protected from direct sunlight when buried. Taking algae type, average temperatures, soil content and rainfall factors of this region into account, the algae on the buried object in this area would develop at a very specific rate and produce a byproduct known as carbonic acid, which would actually deepen the scoring of the symbols over time. Observing the progressive coloration of the plant material while measuring the depth of scoring has given me a very rough idea of the age of the inscriptions.

I estimate that these writings were created in the range of 1200 BCE (Before Common Era) to 600 BCE, suggesting the impossible to now be reality. There had been a Jewish presence on this continent for possibly a thousand years before the birth of Jesus.

The questions and implications this information suggests are boundless. How did middle-eastern travelers, in a time before any worthy sea-vessels existed, make the journey to this place? How did they manage to unite with the indigenous tribes, then create a new language and culture?

There are many myths, legends and even cults that have suggested such a melding. Other artifacts had surfaced, but their authenticity was questionable. In recent modern times, DNA research suggested the possibility of such cultural intercourse to be high. But that was all speculation. Now I am the bearer of a rewritten history. In the course of time, prior to the Vikings or the Europeans, at least one of the tribes of Israel settled the Americas.

Recalling the fresh look to the strata of the creek-bed, it appeared that one of the many recent earthquakes had opened up the channel, allowing me to discover the buried treasure. This would suggest that the tablet had purposefully been buried with the occupant of a grave.

The next morning, Kendal's son finds me in the hallway. At first he seems insecure, looking behind him as if worried that he is being followed. Apparently satisfied that all is safe, he comes up to me and says, "I believe."

I understand his meaning and the possible danger in which this proclamation places him. I invite him into a side room and there, he pours his heart out, describing how his mother had been gathered-up and that his father, who had gone to church dutifully with her, became incensed at the idea that he had not been good enough to be taken as well. Nate (the son's given name), describes how his father started to drink, cursing at God for making good on the warnings of Scripture. He would even pull out the family Bible, sit his son down and rave about specific prophetic events and passages that should not have been allowed to be fulfilled. Then he would rip the pages from the book, pour part of the gin he was consuming on the paper and light it with his cigarette, watching with a twisted smile on his face as the text blackened and shriveled to ashes.

Nate explains the two effects of these sessions. First, his father's anger seemed to increase rather than decrease with each passage he "terminated," with no apparent concern for his son's loss of his mother. Second, by reading the passages to his son, Kendal actually inspired the boy to consider his own viewpoint and fate. Nate, it seems, came to a different verdict than his dad; maybe God wasn't the one at fault and maybe, if he could learn more about how this "God thing" worked, there was a chance for mother and son to one day be reconciled.

Understandably, he has kept his thoughts from his father—from anyone in fact, up until this moment and his next claim amazes me. "I've met Jesus. I want to die for him."

"I'd rather see him live in you," I reply, assuming he is speaking metaphorically and spiritually. Just the same, I make a mental note to watch him and make sure he isn't suicidal.

"Do I need to be baptized like the rest?" The boy sounds eager to participate.

I think through the scenario before replying and then explain, "Water is not necessary for salvation—you have obviously already received the fire of the Spirit. The fundamental reason for a water baptism is to show others what has changed within you, in hopes that they also might be inspired to change."

We talk more about those within Ein Gedi who have not come forward to advocate Jesus as Lord. And then we pray together concerning his father's discord and their relationship. My next statement sounds extremely brash coming out of my mouth, but I feel led to explain, "Nate, I cannot encourage or discourage you from witnessing to your father at this time, that is between you and The Spirit. I will advise you to pray much more before you come to that decision. This has to be something you are led to do, not an act of wishful hope sprung from selfish desires."

The young man sitting in front of me looks downward with his hands clasped, obviously taking my input to heart. Lifting his head back up, he nods and replies, "It's not time, but can we continue to meet and pray together?"

You Lord, have placed a strong spirit in this young man, wise beyond his twenty years. I encourage another meeting, but advise that we be discreet. I don't want to have his father thinking I have somehow coerced the son into faith as some sort of retaliation. Again, Nate nods and then stands up, walking to the door without a word. He peers both directions down the hallway to double-check he is not seen and then slips away.

Sitting in silence thereafter, I offer up a private petition regarding the incredible moment that has just transpired.

The incident with Kendal has pointed out a glaring gap in the system at Ein Gedi, which we have strangely overlooked. Who is in charge? At first, the "townies" from Citation naturally recognized Jason as their authority—but when we interlopers showed up, some would tend to seek me out for advisement. I have discussed the situation with Jason and we both agree that it is time to set up some basic form of government so that people will know who to see about what.

The obvious model would be something taken from municipal records in the town, but those records are obviously not immediately accessible.

There are some helpful resource books in Ein Gedi, but you Lord have inspired us toward another solution. The Bible is full of governmental models, some that worked very well and others that failed miserably. After reading and praying over some examples, I conclude that this should not be something I set up but a system in which the whole group takes ownership.

We ask for volunteers to further research the scriptures for a practical solution and five step forward. After a week, one of the volunteers comes back with a strange proposal.

"We need to cast lots."

"Are ya tetched?" Betty is, as always, vocal. "We live in a democracy, not a gambling casino! This is the United States of America!"   I   am surprised that these people have any slant (even if an incorrect one) on the ancient method of affirmation by rolling spiritual dice. First, Jason clears up for Betty and the others that we had actually lived in a republic, not a democracy and that since the Gathering-Up, we no longer live under any national control whatsoever. I nod at the irony that most of our members still have in their minds, a pledge of allegiance to a country extinct except in geographical terms—that oath, the Old Culture and all they represented is gone. It seems a good opportunity to explore daring alternatives.

"Just for a moment, let's wipe the slate clean," I press. "Imagine we are characters in some science fiction novel and we have somehow been placed on a new planet with no rules or laws or history. Let's say that we recognize one leader—very powerful, but we've never met him in a physical sense, we just know he exists because of all the evidence around us suggesting he has been at work readying this new place for us."

They all nod—obviously making the connection that we are now in that new place.

"Now, if everyone trusts this great leader as being smarter and vastly more experienced than ourselves and has proven on multiple occasions that he has their best interests at heart, even when making unpopular and difficult decisions, wouldn't it stand to reason that we should defer our sense of propriety to that of the leader?"

"Depends," one of the new converts offers. "If the leader tells me to go jump off a cliff, I might have second thoughts."

Everyone chortles, including me and then I respond, "Of course you would. So would I. Whatever is asked of any one of you, or of this group, needs to be verified scripturally. That's why we need to be as familiar with God's written professions as is possible—it is our obligation to one another. Just because one of us says we have heard a word from God doesn't mean it applies to everyone. We need to examine and test what we believe we are receiving."

"Romans 12!" It is Julie who touts this verse.

"Yes and there is one more factor that's important—the *Watchmen*." I have my students right where they need to be, curious and ready to learn.

"The Bible gives frequent examples of something we choose to ignore in modern times. One person is given a very specific message or warning to pass on to others. The message is scriptural, but seldom does it match up with the wont and wisdom of the time. The Jews recognize this as *Ipcha Mistabra*. It is an Aramaic term popularized in the Jewish Talmud which means 'On the contrary' or 'It appears different'."

As a former university professor, I know I am in danger of lecturing this group to death, so I try to better frame the idea. "Moses told the people they were going to be freed from slavery and conquer another land. Jonah preached repentance to a nation that did not recognize God. Jeremiah told Israel to capitulate to Babylon. How do you think these ideas initially seat with those whom God was trying to reach? It just wouldn't have made sense at the time…so why did they listen?"

"They trusted the messenger?" Out of the mouths of babes…it is Ben who best fathoms the cultural thought behind the 'Watchmen-Prophets'.

"Sometimes, yes. Sometimes the Watchmen were killed for bringing messages the people did not trust," I elaborate. "The trust factor is vital because of confusing situations in this age which will be surfacing soon. Rather than delving into prophecy myself, I'll follow my Savior's example and illustrate with a parable.

"Let's say the wise monarch we are all considering following has a family member who we have met or heard about. Say this principal asks this close relative to jump off the cliff so that we won't have to. Let's suppose that the relative does take the plunge, dies a terrible death and then the wise ruler is able to bring his relative back to life. Would you follow that ruler?"

Everyone nods. It seems unnecessary to connect the dots that You, my God, are the wise One and Your Son, the sacrificed relative. I take the reflection one step further by quoting Leviticus 18:

> "You shall not do as they do in the land of Egypt, where you lived and you shall not do as they do in the land of Canaan, to which I am bringing you. You shall not walk in their statutes. You shall follow my rules and keep my statutes and walk in them. I am the LORD your God. You shall therefore keep my statutes and my rules; if a person does them, he shall live by them: I am the LORD."

And then Deuteronomy 6, what the Hebrews dutifully call the "Shema":

> "Hear, O Israel: The LORD our God, the LORD is one. You shall love the LORD your God with all your heart and with all your soul and with all your might. And these words that I command you today shall be on your heart."

I outline how You had instructed Your human family to trust in You completely and without question. At first there were no kings or suzerains. As a matter of fact, it is now obvious, Lord, that You intended governance to mirror the direct relationship between You and Your people. But the people of the Old Testament were much like us and wanted control over their circumstances. So You patiently appointed judges and kings to allow Your subjects to see how difficult and complex it would be to trust in human dictates. Disastrously, instead of recognizing that You were the better choice, mankind kept seeking more ways to control their lives.

Even the best attempts—which resulted in the constitution and branches of government of the United States—became corrupted. We all wanted control misnamed as freedom rather than recognizing that the only one capable of honorably ruling is You, King of the Universe. I look at this group, so fresh in their faith and pray that they (and I) are ready for my next statement.

"Until we turn completely back to recognizing Jesus as the overlord of our lives and totally trusting in his ability to govern us—not us governing him—we will never be free from our selfishness. We have to become slaves to God in order to free our spirits."

There is a very uncomfortable silence after I am finished. Then, young Ben raises his hand. I defer to him with a smile and again the child leads us. "But how does that fit with what you just said about one of us hearing something from God that's different from what others believe?"

"A great question!" I respond and then I pray silently. I do not want to give these incredible new believers a false or misleading message. "There were a select few times when God made Himself physically present. Otherwise, He chose and still chooses at very special moments, to present us with His desires through His delegated messengers."

"Are ya one of those?" God bless Buckshot Betty—always to the point.

"I believe I have met several of His messengers," I reply. "God's purpose for me? That remains to be seen. To a great extent, all of us must be watchmen, any believer might be a voice crying in the wilderness. The rest of us need to be convicted according to the message offered by that one voice. To do that, we should accept what we do know, admit there are things we may have misinterpreted and study together in order to improve our understanding of God's word.

"How will we recognize these prophets and their messages? Diligent scriptural study, prayer and *iron sharpening iron*—the constant open-ended discussion with other like-minded believers who want nothing more than to walk in unity with Jesus as their King."

"So the Bible might be wrong?" Jason scratches his head, looking very puzzled.

"Scripture is spiritually right—it is we who miss or misinterpret the message. Would you like an example?" Everyone nods, so I continue. "Who can show me a passage in the Old Testament that clearly states that the Messiah will be resurrected from the dead?"

To their credit many come up with very good scriptures, including Isaiah 52 and 53; Psalms 16, 22, 69 and 110; Job 19. Some start quoting pieces of the New Testament and then as quickly apologize, realizing what I had asked for. What amazes me most is that just several months ago, this group would not have even known the difference between the two testaments of the Bible, much less be able to quote specific segments from its pages. You are indeed amazing, Spirit. Still, I sense there is another message You want me to impart to them.

"All of those are good, some even use the word 'exalt' or the phrase 'lifted up'. Some prophesy the actual suffering and plan God has for repossession. But none actually say that God's elect, His Messiah, was to die and then would be resurrected in a 'first coming'."

There is absolute silence in the room. I bow my head to listen for Your wisdom and then begin hearing something interesting. The rustling of pages—the sound of seeking: These special ones will not be content with my words; they, like I, hunger for better answers. I wait until I see everyone in the room shaking their heads in confusion and then ask, "Now do you see why it said in John 20 that Jesus's disciples still didn't understand that he would be revived after the crucifixion, even after He had told them it would happen? If I had been one of them, or a Pharisee, or any well-versed Jew at the time, I too would have scoffed. My champion would have come galloping into Jerusalem on a stallion and would have turned all my enemies to dust with one word!"

"So how do we know Jesus is the right messiah?" This from Julia. The right question at the right time, Spirit, thank You.

"You tell me?" I am not about to spoon-feed them. They are quite astute in their studies. Still, there is a long silence before anyone speaks. And then, it is the newest believer of all: Nate, risking persecution even from his father, leads from innocence.

"The miracles behind."

Everyone, including me, gives him quizzical looks, so the young man continues to develop his thought. "They couldn't see before the resurrection and we couldn't see before the Gathering-Up, because we may have had faith, but didn't trust our faith. Just some trusted, though there are plenty of scriptures pointing to Jesus as the obvious Chosen One. The ones that have real faith—they're in a super special place now.

"The rest of us, we need the dots connected. To look ahead, we first need to look behind us to see God's work already completed and the prophecies that are now being fulfilled. They didn't recognize Jesus, because he needed to live out…uh, die out and then live out…the plan. Maybe that's why Jesus said to Thomas, 'Blessed are those who believe though they have not seen'?" With all my book learning and supposed genius, I could not have penned such a heartrending portrait of our condition. Lord, I am humbled that You would place me in the presence of one so great as this. Now help me to "connect the remaining dots," as Nate so aptly put it.

"With that understanding in mind, we need to be aware that God is still revealing things to His stiff-necked people. In this very difficult age, we are going to need to be preparing for a new government upon the shoulders of Jesus and it is not going to be what we are used to. What have you read in the Bible about theocracy?"

Silence and scratching of heads follow my question. And of course it would. Until a few years ago, such a concept was foreign to me as well. No offense, Lord, but I still have to read between the lines to understand what You had in mind from the beginning of Your plan.

"As the old United States currency used to affirm, we are finally going to know what it means to trust in God."

Ben asked, "So instead of us messing things up anymore, you want us to vote for God as president?"

We all laugh again and then I reply. "Something like that, except, God doesn't need a vote, all we have to do is obey what is already in place. The tough part will come when each of us has to choose to give up things we really enjoy, recognizing those things are bad for us or the community. And we are going to have to trust in leadership that God, not mankind, puts in place. Those new prophets will not speak or look like anything most of the world would expect."

Betty stands up and declares, "If God says it, I'll do it. Nobody better try to stop me!"

We'll see, I think to myself. *We'll see.*

The first trial of our "New Way" government comes immediately, unexpectedly and harshly. Most everyone has assembled in the Unity Hall to discuss our recommitment to theocracy. I ask Buckshot Betty and Jason if they will go find the missing residents. The absentees should be made aware of this decision and their roles in it—especially because of who the missing parties are: Kendal and two of his hangers-on.

At the same time Julia, one of the more vocal Seconds, is suggesting how easy it would be to follow the basic commandments found in Scripture, but how difficult it would be when those in the world wanted to have "their way".

"I've been reading some history," she explains, "and it's not that the world has changed any, it's that Jewish and Christian believers compromised their beliefs and morals in order to try to fit in. Now this new age heralds God's desire for us not to compromise anymore. There will be a lot of risk…"

The door slams open to reveal Kendal and his cohorts brandishing automatic weapons. Kendal saunters into the stunned silence and pronounces, "You're right about that, lady, there will be risks—starting with you, Preacher Man."

I can clearly gauge the bore of the weapon now aimed in my direction—.45 caliber. Its holder demands, "Before I take you from this Earth, I want your apology."

"My apology for what?" I ask—my fear in this moment carefully concealed.

Instead of answering directly, Kendal reaches with his free hand into his back pocket and pulls out a folded notebook. He slings it between us, onto the floor and points at it with his machine pistol. "Go ahead, pick it up. It'll be good for you to know why you're gonna bleed all over it," he says through a wicked smile.

I am about to walk forward to fetch the pages when Nate stands up. He turns to his father, but speaks to me. "You don't need to pick it up, Professor Hindeland, I can tell you what it says."

Kendal's attention is diverted for a moment by his son and I am tempted to rush him, but Nate comes forward and purposefully stands between his father and me. He continues to speak toward his father, never facing me. "I wrote in that notebook—my notebook, actually—my thoughts and prayers to God. I told Him that I love Him and that I think what is happening here is a good thing. I also wrote how much I love my father and how I want to do anything I can to introduce him to my Savior, Jesus."

"Shut up!" Kendal's head tilts toward the ceiling, his eyes bulge and the veins in his neck swell into purple ropes that look as if they might burst at any moment. His whole body quivers and twitches as he speaks to some unseen accomplice. Then he takes a huge gulp of air and brings his gaze to me. He inspects me as an exterminator would a bug—there is momentarily no emotion showing from him, just the professional gaze of someone about to eliminate a nuisance.

"Do you see what you've done to him?" The man's words spit past the revolver while he completely ignores his son's presence. "You fed him your false hopes and damn lies and now he's…he's…"

The man is barely able to control his faculties, struggling to find words for the change in his son. Nate tries to help him. "Dad, I'm right here and I'm fine—better than fine. I've been saved. Just like Mom. For the first time in my life, I'm alive!"

His father's face turns an even more vibrant crimson and his trembling increases—tears trickling down his face. For an instant, he gazes at his son, then toward his own feet. Kendal looks up again and states flatly with a gauzed hue in his eyes, "No, you're not," and he fires five rounds into his son's chest. As Nate's lifeless body crumples, Kendal swivels his fury, wordlessly leveling the pistol at my head and pulling the trigger.

Nothing but a single "click" emits from the gun. He looks at the weapon, manually re-cocks and fires again. "Click, click," We are all so fuddled that no one moves. I think Kendal might try to charge me, but instead he looks down at his son's corpse and says, "You deserved better." Chucking his useless weapon, he turns and walks out the door, unstopped by anyone.

Immediately, Jason and I rush to Nate along with several others, but he is gone. Several Seconds quickly turn and take the weapons from the unresisting followers of Kendal. His aides seem as dazed as everyone else by what had just transpired. I moan a prayer, "Yahweh, Yahweh! Show mercy to Your servant Nate!" Jason gets up off his knees and runs out the door. I cannot bring myself to leave the body. Holding my brother in my arms and rocking, my own tears mix with the blood now pooling all around us. Oh, YHWH, You alone understand the depth my grief coming out in convulsive sobs as I close his eyes in final rest.

"Now child, you are in a super special place."

Jason comes back into the room and quickly to my side. "Ah know you're grievin', but we got a situation at the airlock and Ah think you're the only one who can help." He makes sure I look at him as he says the words and I hear the calm reason in his voice.

"Yes," I hear myself speak mechanically, standing up with his help—someone else stepping in to tend to Nate's body. Jason and I exit the room.

Jason immediately fills me in. "He went into the receiving compartment and right to the portal door. Now he's in the airlock itself at the outer hatch. He's locked himself in and said he wants to talk to you."

What is he talking about—there is a deceased brother I need to attend to—whatever this is cannot, should not, override that. Wrangling in my emotions, I realize he is referring to Kendal.

Through the small window of the portal door I see a tortured man—pacing back and forth, wringing his hands, shaking his head, raging exclamations which, even deadened, pierce the heavy metal aperture. "It should be you, Hindeland! I didn't kill him, you did. You're the one, you killed him and you should die!"

He continues his rant and then suddenly turns and looks straight at me. "I'll kill you yet. I know how! It's even written in your stupid book, 'you have to die to the self to live'."

I suddenly realize his intention and howl back at him, "Kendal, don't! There's another way!"

He stands statue-still for a moment, then shakes his head and speaks calmly through a sigh, "No other way." Then Kendal turns to face the exit, cranking the mechanism that allows the outer hatch to swing out to the world beyond. The noise of rushing wind and turbulence inundates the receiving compartment—a shuddering subdues his body. He turns back to attempt opening the portal door which proves an impossible effort. There is the bubbling of skin on his arms and then he is sucked outward, rolling and half-flying into the unforgiving void. For a fleeting moment, Kendal catches his footing and leans into the sheering typhoon, trying to force his way back toward the entryway. Flashes of lightning measure his meager progress for our eyes—futile, awful steps, each weaker than the next.

My reoccurring dream has come to life, except that I am not rushing to this man's rescue. Not that I don't try, but Jason easily holds me with his strong arms from racing after Nate's father.

My efforts would be too late anyway, of course. As we watch, pieces of Kendal seem to randomly vaporize in a wisp of dust—an arm here, an ear there. Then, in one flashing moment, we witness the gale-force winds pumice his writhing body as one would blow a flickering candle flame into a wisp of smoke, never to be lit again.

There was one other difference from my dream. Kendal has not made a sound from the time he exited; at least not one we can hear.

In the end, Jason is the one who finds his voice. He somehow chooses and utters the exact scripture that is permeating my mortified brain. "All are of the dust and all turn to dust again."

God of Heaven and Earth, I have been extremely depressed for several days since the deaths of Nate and his father. You have Your ways, but it is so difficult sometimes to trust when tragedy steals away a part of those things we cherish in life. You know I trust Your ways, but that does not mean I am not frustrated by those lost to us.

Leaving my room to exercise my legs, I come upon LaShandra, wife of Pavoli, our first to be blessed with a new pregnancy. This is a great joy to all of us because their young son and daughter were both called to You in the Gathering-Up and she has since suffered with depression, far greater, I imagine, than what I am now feeling. The promise of new life within her has given her new purpose.

LaShandra is sitting on the floor of the hallway with her back against the wall when I turn the corner. She is looking down at her swollen belly and is talking to her unborn child. My presence seems inconsequential as she continues the conversation.

"I don't know how, but I could hear you tell me in my tummy *'I want peanut butter'* the other day. And I ate some just for you," she giggles. "Or at least peanut butter-flavored crackers—that is all we have!"

The loving mother notices and turns her head to look at me with hope in her eyes. With those pleading eyes I can hear her inner voice, wanting me to pray with her that hers will be a successful labor and delivery. Then LaShandra looks upward, perhaps to Another—to You, her Keeper, whom she hopes is listening and speaks again. "Sometimes, babies can do that. Tell their mom—even their daddy—what they want and we can hear them. What a joy it will be to hear my child's real voice!"

My dreariness of the last days disappears and, along with Lashandra's, my hope is reborn.

I alluded that the test of our theocracy came at the moment of Kendal's attack, but we didn't realize until later what had really happened. When my assailant's discarded pistol was inspected, all remaining rounds in its magazine proved to be good. The firing mechanism was also functioning within normal operating parameters. Someone even evaluated the gun—no misfires, no problem. There could be but one explanation—supernatural intervention. You, Lord of Hosts, have graced me to still be writing these pages. All but the two who followed Kendal believe that You are now fully active in our lives and that spiritual trust has been very visibly shown to be our greatest weapon.

As for the two, another decision has to be made. Pavoli suggests that we pray as a group for the right way to handle the matter. While this occurs, the culprits are held in a guarded room. Neither of them seems to want to cause trouble; in fact, they have both apologized for their behavior, but there is no point in taking chances.

"Should we somehow make examples of them?" This question comes from Betty after our prayers at the group meeting. It is subtle, but I note that instead of her immediately wanting to judge the attackers, she is asking a question, as if mercy might be the preferred option.

"They appear to be very docile without a stalwart to influence them," I say. "My suggestion is to let them go."

"Just like that? Without punishment?" It is Julie's question.

"What did they do other than make bad choices and follow lousy counsel? Have they harmed anyone?" Jason asks this and everyone nods.

It is decided that the two will have limited access to most areas and that no retribution should take place. What better witness to God's grace?

It seems so simple, so easy for everyone to agree—what has happened? This is not the way of the world we once knew.

Jason holds young Ben's hand. They look at me and ask, "Are you getting brighter? I look around and then go over to them. "It's not just me," I reply, pulling them both close to me. "It's you too—all of you." That's not exactly true, because Kendal's two cohorts are not registering on the blue glow meter at all.

Moses Folzman, my mentor and great friend, has miraculously found his way from Israel to our sanctuary at Ein Gedi—I am still waiting for him to explain how he managed it. But in his usual method, he is more focused on the future than the past. "The moment has come," he says simply, looking at me more somber than excited. "Anyone care to lead us in a song?"

"Here's a tune for you!" It is our two nonbelieving residents who have responded. Somehow, they have found automatic weapons and begin firing them at everyone in the room. I see the spray coming my way and cannot move away in time. The bullets pierce my body, and my last vision is of Moses crumpling to the floor.

Blackness turns to a red glow. I open my eyes, realizing I am laying on my bed, staring up at Ein Gedi's strange lighting system. Another very different dream has begun to disturb me. What are you trying to tell me, Lord? Is this a warning of things to come? What is your will for me and how must I prepare?

Imagine the idea of committing to a well-defined spiritual mindset, consistently acting on that mindset in the physical world and observing the physical world respond in kind! It has happened as I am a witness.

It is the day, the very moment, we have granted Kendal's friends their freedom and the weather is changed. Everybody realizes it at once; the consistent gales, the unlit skies, the unceasing rumbling of the ground beneath, all immediately diminish, as if their chorus of terror has reached its finale.

How long have we been sequestered in this place? It is difficult to tell; time has been a vague integrant during the storms. Ein Gedi has its supply of windup clocks and watches, convenient for scheduling meeting times—but as timekeepers? Even traditional calendars have become useless, because Earth's rotational period seems to be in flux. Before we entered Ein Gedi, it appeared to me that the apex of the sun had even changed, suggesting a shift in Earth's axis. Who but you Lord, can count the days now? Has the revolution of the planet slowed down or sped up? Is it even necessary to track such things when eternity might soon be at hand? The guess we have is to rely on what we once knew and that loose reckoning suggests eight long months have passed.

Because of the cramped interior, we take turns, in small groups, observing the new local conditions from the second story. It is a surreal still-life. The sun fights to puncture the cloud canopy—noticeably lighter—we can debatably call it daylight. But there is nothing green to be seen; no animal life is apparent. There is a tubular mercury thermometer fixed to the outside rock-face indicating a temperature of 92 degrees Fahrenheit—warm, but survivable. A barometer on the same wall reveals high pressure with 10 percent humidity—strange for this typically humid area of the country, but again, adequate. Yet, who knows if the equipment is functioning properly? Is this just a lull? Are the storms finished? What will happen to any who venture out? I see the same questions almost visibly pronounced on the faces of each of the Ein Gedi residents.

Finally Jason, several others and I apprehensively open the door and enter the receiving compartment where the portal door to the airlock is located. Kendal made his farewell deliberately leaving the outer hatch opened. We are left with the portal door and retaining wall as our sole protection. Had that somehow been breached, we would have had no way to keep the poisonous fog from consuming our sanctuary. We had actually sealed off, as best we could, the receiving compartment, but truth be told, it had been more for psychological reassurance.

The sum of Ein Gedi once more assembles in the Unity Hall to discuss the situation. It is decided that we need to qualify the ecosphere with live subjects. Conveniently, there are plenty of insects and rodents that have joined us (not by invitation!) in Ein Gedi and we have rounded up a passel just this hoped-for moment. The trick is how to expose our animals, not just to an air sample, but to all tropospheric elements, without endangering ourselves.

The solution comes from Jason who has been rummaging through the stored supplies and has come up with one complete HAZMAT suit. Why there was a single one and whether it will protect its wearer from whatever contagion awaits are questions unanswered. The immediate question is: *Who will volunteer for the duty?*

The duty? To carry specimens out through the portal door and outer hatch. It is amazing how many step forward, willing to take the risk. We actually have to draw straws to choose. In the end, Buckshot Betty picks the short stick and wants to take the task on immediately. "All I ask," she says, "is that, if things look good, then I get to be the first human guinea pig to go out without the silly suit."

I don't know why, but I am also compelled to bring my container holding Abaddon with me to our initial staging point—the hallway junction in front of the receiving compartment entry leading to the portal door. The closer I come toward the sealed entrance, the more frenzied his buzzing becomes. I do not know whether it is anxiousness to escape or a warning of danger that agitates him. We will soon find out.

Betty dons the HAZMAT suit and I think how strange she appears— neither from our Ein Gedi world, nor of the remaining world. She is separated and alien to both. In her left hand she carries a container occupied by a field mouse and also a pill bottle filled with several roaches. Betty does not want a large crowd of witnesses associated with her excursion, so Jason and I are the chosen two who accompany her to this point.

"Now you gotta secure the receiving compartment door when you go out, then close the portal door once you're in the airlock and then… depending…try to seal off the hatch when you're outside." Jason does not elaborate on what he means by "depending." But I understand and I believe Betty does too—depending on whether or not she suffers the same fate as Kendal. She nods and reaches her right hand out to touch Jason's arm. He responds and I realize there is a relationship between them I am not privy to.

Betty then speaks to both of us. "Now will you please let me work?" With that, she turns and faces the door to the receiving compartment in silence.

I cannot let it go at that, however. I place a hand on her shoulder and on Jason's and pray out loud. "Father, Your servants are willing, but we are nothing without You. Give Betty, give all of us, aspiration to persist. Protect us from any evil that would try to undo Your plan. In Jesus's name, we ask it. Amen."

The woman inside the suit visibly shudders, but does not otherwise respond. I know now she is ready. She purposefully turns the handle without hesitation and proceeds through, then closes it behind her. The portal door is heavy but cantilevered to allow easy movement by one person, so she has no problem with its negotiation to entering the airlock. Without any signs of discomfort, Betty turns in our direction and holds up the container with her left hand and also lifts her right hand with three fingers raised indicating three creatures—the one mouse and two roaches. There is a microphone in her suit, but it is electrically powered and therefore nonfunctional in our new world. So she shows us a thumbs-up with her right hand, signifying, according to our prearranged code, that all three are still alive. Without another word, Betty sets the container down in the airlock, allowing her to use both hands to securely reseal the portal door. She then gathers up her cache, continues through the airlock and outer hatch and closes it behind her. All we can do now is continue to pray.

Our point of reference does not allow us to follow her movements. So on a gamble, we open the receiving compartment door and then quickly reenter. Jason and I do a quick visual check of one another, monitoring our respiration to verify Ein Gedi has not been compromised. Everything seems good, so we rush to the observation deck to better audit Betty's pace.

According to plan, Betty is to stay out no more than a brief moment to allow for any reactions of the examinees. Then she is to bring them back so that we can perform a more thorough examination, to classify any residual effects. Apparently, she has other ideas. She turns and looks left, then right and then pauses with her eyes closed. We can see her mouth moving and presume she is saying a prayer. Then without warning she raises her hands to her helmet, unfastens the clips and removes it. "No!" Jason bays as he slaps both palms of his hands against the glass pane that separates us from the outside.

Betty takes a terse breath, coughs twice, closes her eyes and inhales intensely, then appears to exhale slowly. She remains in that stance for what seems an eternity. She opens her eyes and bends down to the ground, unlatching the doors on the containers holding the mouse and the roaches. Shaking them out, Buckshot Betty reveals her sensitive side, encouraging the creatures to scurry away. Then she walks purposefully back to the airlock and goes through the procedure to reenter.

"What was you thinkin'?" Jason had almost flown down the stairs and now charges toward her upon reentry. I can't distinguish if his tone is irate or elated, but there are tears flooding down his face. He embraces her and holds on as if she were his life preserver in a stormy sea.

"Simmer down, Farm-boy, I was fine. He said I would be," Betty says very pointedly.

"He?" I ask both as a question and as encouragement for her to explain.

"Jesus," she continues. "I can't tell you how I knew it was him, but it was. He told me to volunteer and he explained what I should do. I didn't want to tell you because I know you'd think I'd lost my marbles."

"Ah still think you lost your marbles," Jason responds. "What would have happened if…well, you know what Ah mean…"

I know what he means. What if Betty had vaporized like Kendal? But I point out to my friend that Betty didn't die. She was asked to trust (and did!) the One we are told to trust. Her act was one of unbridled faith. Would I have been so bold?

And then there is the other fragment of her comment. I have to ask her to elaborate. "You actually heard the voice of The Messiah?"

"Who? Oh, you mean Jesus. Well, I…yes, it was his voice. I heard it as clear as if he were talking with us right now."

After she says these words, we are all silent for a moment, as if inviting a continued spiritual conversation, but there is no auditory response. I had heard of this kind of direct dialogue once before, from a younger friend, now most definitely called to be with You. It reminds me of how much I miss those I knew, who have been gathered up.

Enough sentimentality—there is work to be done! If the air is breathable, I have to continue eastward and the others now at Ein Gedi have choices to make: stay or leave.

"This be home fer me. Think Ah'm goin' to keep it that a way fer a time." Jason vocalizes the sentiment of at least half of the population at Ein Gedi—many heads nod when he makes the statement in a general meeting called to discuss our options.

"There is a risk," I add. "The builders of this place may come to reclaim it. We can't predict if they'll be friends or foes."

More discussion follows, but in the end, those who wish to stay are willing to accept the risk. And so, it is just a matter of reluctant separation. We carefully measure out the needs for those of us who will be leaving. There is no way to foresee the conditions outside of our region—we have sent out some scouting parties that determine there is not a lot to forage for at least thirty miles to the east. The temptation is to "overload" those who are leaving, but the more we pluck out, the less will be available for those staying behind. There is also the consideration that we will be expending a great deal of physical energy carting our luggage with us.

After balancing the variables, we arrive at a decision. Since we no longer have any horses or pack animals to help lug the load, each traveler will carry their own six days' allotment, including water. Fortunately, along with nourishment, the creators of Ein Gedi have also stocked freeze-dried meals, backpacks, tents, cooking utensils, small butane tanks, lanterns, first aid kits and such items that we now find invaluable in allowing us to continue our trek.

In the Ein Gedi stores, we have also discovered collapsible pull-carts ingeniously tethered to quick-release harnesses. These can be attached easily to each person who wears the gear. When they move right or left, the cart wheels match the motion and allow for minimum stress when carrying the extra load over difficult terrain.

There are seventy-two of us who will move on. I speak to the group about the biblical irony, this number being the same as the group Jesus sent out to witness. "We've already been blessed by this house providing for our continued journey. Personally, I'm not concerned about future protection; God has already proven faithful and in that I trust. I encourage you to do the same."

That last conversation takes place on the morning of our planned departure, but there is one more key task to be undertaken—the wedding of Jason and Betty. They have both decided to stay and their devotion to one another is obvious. I have been asked to officiate and I can't think of a prouder moment in my life. Two who have come to know You while in my company are now mirroring Your love to Your bride, the Church, by their commitment to one another.

We all gather just before sunrise for the last time in the alcove beyond the holly bush. This is a tender and moving moment of sacrament in a time of hardship and uncertainty. The sun can actually be seen—a dim and hazy red sphere that has begun its contest for recognition on the horizon, peaking over the eastern mountains—an extreme event. Still the star's presence is already increasing the temperature toward uncomfortable levels. I ignore the heat and the barren backdrop, speaking of hope for a future in a land full of lush green pastures and ripened fruit that You promise to all Your faithful.

After the ceremony, it is time to say our goodbyes and for me to lead the seventy-two into the new wilderness. Jason speaks a simple benediction over us, reminding everyone how we have arrived at this parting. His simple and distinctive Southern country drawl encourages us on.

"God put us all together not just to survive but to learn. The Almighty used Doc Hindeland to teach us how to love Jasus, 'cause he, Preacher, is living the way Jasus lived. He's taught me"—here the young man tenderly clasps the hand of his new bride—"taught us all, not just to say or read the Bible, but to trust the words like they're real…like they're tools for fixing mah life. Thanks, Preacher. You've showed us something way different."

Unbeknownst to me, LaShandra, who has given birth to our newest member (whom she named Geraldine in honor of me!), has taken the liberty of borrowing a song sheet I protected in the pages of my now decimated Bible. Cradling her child in her arms, she sings, teaching the notes and lyrics to the rest of us. I am the only other who knows the piece by heart, but its message speaks to me in an entirely new way at this moment:

> Lord of all creation, of water, earth and sky
> The heavens are Your tabernacle, glory to the Lord on high
>
> God of wonders beyond our galaxy
> The universe declares Your majesty
> And You are holy, holy
>
> Lord of heaven and earth, Lord of heaven and earth
>
> Early in the morning, I will celebrate the light
> When I stumble in the darkness, I will call Your name
>   by night
>
> God of wonders beyond our galaxy
> You are holy, holy
> The universe declares Your majesty
> And You are holy, holy
> Lord of heaven and earth, Lord of heaven and earth
>
> Lord of heaven and earth, Lord of heaven and earth
> Hallelujah to the Lord of heaven and earth
> Holy…holy…holy God…
>
> God of wonders beyond our galaxy
> You are holy, holy
> The universe declares Your majesty
> And You are holy, holy
> Lord of heaven and earth, Lord of heaven and earth
>
> Precious Lord, reveal Your heart to me…
> Father holy (Lord God Almighty)…
> The universe declares Your majesty
> You are holy, holy, holy,
> Hallelujah to the Lord of heaven and earth

All are anxious and excited about the journey. No one wants to separate what has become a true spiritual family—*clan,* as we call ourselves. But we can delay no longer. Those who are remaining at Ein Gedi hug, kiss and encourage us. I try to offer a promising statement for those staying behind and for those moving forward into the unknown: "Next year in Jerusalem!" And then without further fanfare—other than one final gift that I pass privately to Jason—we head out.

Pasha Sumje's Pilgrimage

The coals never stop simmering, the air is putrid with desperation, but we do not dare leave. Away from this place—beyond the distant shore of the river stenched with the unending flotilla of dead bodies drifting to the sea—prowls Vidhvansaka, the destroyer. He waits patiently as one with no concern for time. Time is his partner—she invites the anxious ones to visit him.

The *kita-kingsas*, vile things that they are—flying and swarming in every direction—also pen us in. Stray too far and they sting us back into our baking bastille. We have become nearly deaf; the flying beasts' roar is louder than the screeching of those they prey upon. Trapped in Naraka between two greater hells; even the escape of madness is punished. Some hostages, in mindless irrationality, flee through the gauntlet canyon in which we have become trapped; as they run the winless race, the attacking insect army teaches the escapees the path to their river graveyard. There, the nearly dead dive into its oozing waste. If they survive to the other side, we hear their final wails as Vidhvansaka impales them.

We know what becomes of them from the sickness we undergo until the time our own madness finally overtakes us. In the night hours, the birds—now minions of Vidhvansaka —transport the broken flesh of those we once called *bhai* and *beham*—brothers and sisters—and drop the escaped refuse back into our camp. Our family is now one with us again for we must feed on them to survive.

Buddha is gone, Krishna is gone. Only our fire-prison remains. We thought Kali Yuga, the age of strife, was ending. It has now just begun— all other ages of man are done away by it. And another surprise! Lord Kalki has come discreetly and taken his chosen with him, leaving the rest of us reborn to this nightmare. We are left to wonder at the cause of our misfortune. Were we truly unfaithful to be punished in this way? I fight the insanity of it by reflecting on three mysteries. These have become my life; all else is *mauta*—living death.

The first mystery is how we all arrived in this torturous place. Thousands of us, families upon families, washed up here in the early days after the disappearance of Lord Kalki's chosen ones. The earth was angered at their leaving and swallowed another half of our people. Then came the wind with darkness to teach the remainder of us fear and loneliness.

Finally, when all food and hope had perished, the river rose beyond belief. All of resplendent Vadodara, including our homes and sacred fortunes, was carried away. I was a scribe and scholar for the holy temple. I was a son, a husband and a father. When the waters stopped rising, I was a castaway, orphaned without family, stature, or even an understanding of my destination. My dwelling place became the top of a large metal storage container, bobbing in the enormous torrent.

Many others skim with me on the wash. Some climbed upon my crate while others sought similar containers and other rafts of isolation. Many had no other choice than to tread water or hold on in fear to any refuse available until at last they fatigued and became the drink of vengeful gods.

By karma or whatever other powers might be at work, many of us survivors were carried on a current that deposited us at this sweltering place. By then, we all had experienced the continuous stings of the strange insects, what I now call the kita-kingsas. Many refugees had been so tormented that they chose to seek the bottom of the murky depths, committing ātmahatyā in hopes of obtaining a better life to come.

The remainder of us endured that torture; then to encounter the fire, my second mystery to consider. The smell of it suggests rot and decay, yet it does not seem to ever be quenched—its flames seeming to reach ever higher.

What feeds it? What can purge its blistering heat? These things are unknown, but its origins are unmistakable. Preceding the flooding there was a terrible light that crossed our skies. A meteor or some other off-world demon crashed upon the boundaries of once-fair Vadodara. It was immediately after this event that the earth became tumultuous beyond anything experienced before. The location where we have been floated to imprisonment is without doubt at the edge of the crater made by that flying catastrophe. How cavernous is the pit? Could it have opened to the heart of the earth, which now pours out smoke and fire in anger for our past indulgences? I am no closer to answering this puzzle than I am to escaping its attack.

So I rest my hopes on the third mystery—the gifts entrusted to us, one of those being the tools allowing me to write these words. The very storage container on which I survived when the river rose broke open upon landing at this place. In it we discovered a stockpile of water jugs, each sealed and waiting to quench our undying thirst.

The fear in many convinced them to attempt hoarding the precious liquid, but it was for naught. Others forced the greedy ones, by murder if necessary, to share the drink. Some drank hungrily and much too quickly and were taught the terrible price—the very heat they tried to suppress caused them to spew forth their ill-gotten gains. These ruffians perished from the fatigue of it. Others took their own lives rather than face the futility of learning to endure their anguish in moderation.

To me and most others, the water is a gift gratefully guarded, offered by a source unknown. Along with that gift was another, fathomed it seems, particularly by me. Within the container was a supply of pens and paper—enough to allow these volumes of description and more. No one else seems interested in documenting this perdition. I honestly can't explain my own fascination with it. Perhaps it stems from my talent, which now is the one thing keeping me from joining those running to Vidhvansaka. My choice of language for the task before me will be English. It is not my native tongue, but it is more universal. If any beyond the putrid place in which I now dwell, discover and read of our ordeal, then chances are they will more likely understand that language.

As for the present, three other mysteries remain: light in the midst of darkness, endurance that survives anguish and hope for new life to come. The greatest to me, that on which my karma is balanced, remains hope.

There is no good cipher for the passage of time. That dimension has vanished with darkness. But I still think! My powers of reasoning have not been scorched away as I have seen it cleansed from others. Concerns? Hah, many! Not the least being the measuring of the water. Although we have learned to consume in meager sips, our pool of life is quickly ebbing. Instead of measuring the days by clock or rising and setting of sun (which will not show itself above the inferno), we look toward one inevitable outcome: when the water is gone. Each liter drained measures our demise more explicitly. Yet another illness feeds our hope in a sick way. For when one of us gives into the madness of meeting Vidhvansaka on the other side of the river, we who remain are only slightly delayed from our inevitable death sentence. And so the inner kernel of our purpose is slowly nibbled away. A time will come when even hope will vanish, no matter our conviction to it. I am beginning to think that Vidhvansaka's call to me is a flattering one. Why should I refuse the invitation?

It has begun to rain. Not the refreshing drops of water that waken life from the ground—this is a torrid acid that pours down on us. I think the fire and the bugs might be better, but both are gone. The conflagration is quenched. The bugs? I don't know and no longer care where they have gone or if they might return. The clouds still don't reveal the sun or moon, so all we have is a dim proposal of daylight and the blackness of the underworld for our night.

I've taken up refuge within the protection of the container that transported me here in the first place. Others have also crowded in. The smell and the heat of all the bodies is nearly unbearable—nearly, I say, because the poison rain that has eaten my skin is the worse choice. I have managed to annex the corner front edge of the container so that I might use the meager illumination from outside to pen a snippet more.

The birds have also ceased to visit, so we are without the dead for our food. It is better this way—when we cease this life and pass into the next, at least we can do so in humble dignity. We still have bottles of water, but those too will soon disappear. The darkness grows, stealing the strength of my hand and my hope. The tide outside is rising again. I watch in morbid horror as one decrepit graybeard crawls to the edge of the container, pausing briefly before casting himself into the murkiness. My fluster is not at his action, but at my inaction. Neither I nor any of his bhai or behan try to save him. There is no bellow from the old one as he smolders away. There is simply a simmering steam as his flesh evaporates into the heavens. This is also better. His suffering is shorter than my own. I think about joining him. Instead I watch as two men stronger than me pull at the doors of the container to close them. I know not if their action is to keep the acid away or to entomb us for a more dignified transition toward *bhaviṣya jīvana*. The men are succeeding no matter their motives. I am ready for the end of this emptiness. Let the darkness take us.

A fourth mystery? How can it possibly be? We live, we eat and there is light. By a miracle I have yet to understand, our container coffin was again heaved into the great river. Sealed inside, I was ready for us to all suffocate or experience a leak that would sink us into the depths. Instead, I passed into unconsciousness and, stranger yet, dreams. An enormous man with a long bushy beard invited me in these visions to walk into the light. How could there be any more light? It had been swallowed along with the dead by Vidhvansaka.

Yet after uncountable days of drifting, our repository landed once more—no one within was awake for our arrival. But from the outside the doors were reopened to flaring brightness. Even then, we had no strength to praise the sunlight. Our rescuers had to pry our bodies out of the hold to distinguish the living from the perished. And a delightful punctuation to the fourth mystery—none perished! Indeed, all had survived our strange sailing trip.

As I was carried out of the container, my voice returned—whisper as it was—to beg of my saviors, "Please, find my diary."

Those carrying me seemed confused by my speech. *Perhaps they do not speak Hindi in Nirvana*, I remember thinking, so I tried my second tongue of English. Then a man appeared before me—no, not just a man but the very giant I saw in my dreams. The giant kneeled by me and smiled radiantly. Then he spoke to me in another language—familiar by my extensive studies. It was Hebrew! "Shalom ha-chavera sheli." *Peace, my friend.* And then in adept Hindi he surprised me with, "Mera nam Moses Folzman hai. Apa naya jivana mila gaya hai." *My name is Moses Folzman. You have found new life.* He slid something onto my chest and then gently lifted my arm from beside me, moving it to rest on the vellum cover. I recognized the feel of it immediately: my lifeblood, poured out on pages of excruciation. And I knew I was in *Svarga*—heaven's sanctuary.

All right then, this is not paradise, but it is also not the bedlam once known. The people are different; the mood is different; the air is different. Those who pulled us from death appear so much more alive than I was even before the time of calamity. There is hope in their attitudes and confidence, though the world around us continues to tremble and sear. They seem to want to invite us into their *nirvana*…their well-being, with each of us. Don't they realize we are all perishing? Perhaps they know something I do not. I thirst for what it is that they drink in that I do not. I hunger for their hope more than any other nourishment they may offer.

Shikshak, Teacher Moses has now revealed a great truth to me. Correctly, I should call it *The Truth,* or at least a result of The Truth. As I walk together with this giant man—who is clad in a simple goatskin garment— toward *Yaruushaleem,* he reveals his God's scriptures to me—the writings of ancient prophets who predicted our recent happenings with incredible accuracy. Names like Daniel, Isaiah, Jeremiah, Joel, Micah and John are now becoming familiar to me.

I am reading from one now and the words cause my heart to sing:

> "As the rain and the snow come down from heaven and do not return to it without watering the earth and making it bud and flourish…so is My word that goes out from My mouth: It will not return to me empty, but will accomplish what I desire and achieve the purpose for which I sent it."

This passage comes from one of my favorite writers so far, Isaiah. It is as if he knew in his time that I would need to cling to the power of these words in my own time.

As much as I am coming to hunger for the writings themselves, one name has become most interesting of all. His sagaciousness appears to contain the essence of Kalki and the promises of Siva. His name I was familiar with only in passing, but of which I am now making a strict study. It is the one name that all the other names seem to be pointing toward—those of the Hindu, those of the Hebrews, Islam—all seem to be completed in this name. And so, as I speak the name, the power of it draws me into hefty meditation and greater humility. I am learning to pray to the name and to obey it. It is the name of my new love, *Jisu.* Many call him *Isa,* others *Yeshua;* some call him Jesus. To me, all the names now tell that he is Savior to the broken world.

Apparently, the route we are taking to fair Yaruushaleem is close to that taken by Gaspar, the great Hindu sage. It is said that in ancient times, he converged with Melchior and Balthazar, each a great and wise magi in and of themselves, seeking answers to the message. They divined by the stars, the heralding of a new and different king who would soon manifest himself to mankind. This story had been a pleasant legend to my Hindu culture. Now my heart quickens as I seek the reality of this same king. I am told by Shikshak Moses and others traveling with us, that Messiah Yeshua is soon to return centering His kingdom in the holy city. He will rule for all time over all other kings.

Shikshak Moses and others throughout the world have been on a mission of single purpose to gather together those who would worship Yeshua. I am longing to bow at my Savior's feet, but the journey is a difficult one. Just today, we experienced another earthquake in which two of our party lost their lives, being swallowed by Prithvi's greedy stomach. Strident winds rise up to meet us and we cannot stay in the open lest the sand of the desert we traverse scour away the very skin of our frail bodies. Thankfully, we are guided by Shikshak Moses, whom I have discovered has physical knowledge to match his spiritual understanding. He somehow is aware before any fury attacks us, guiding us as to what we must do.

I have borrowed the Shikshak's holy text and have been studying one book that characterizes another such man. In that book called Exodus, a great prophet is given spiritual insight and leads a large group of victimized people to a new homeland. It is that same homeland toward which we now travel by another route. Our challenges are the same as those early journeyers. How do we eat along the way? Who among the group can we trust and who might be enemies within trying to break apart our unity? What molestation might we face each day and night and how might we protect ourselves?

The hordes of kita-kingsas surround us. We watch helplessly as they attack other pioneers we see along the way. Yet the creatures do not molest us. I'm told that the God of Abraham intends them to educate those who have not chosen to believe in Him. Remembering my own trauma from these beasts, I would say it is a powerful education indeed.

We have been avoiding the old highways and better roads because of the thieves that still manage to survive at the expense of peaceful excursionists. Choosing the rugged paths as our route slows the journey, but decreases the risk of an unwanted encounter. Our caravan crests a rise and there to our amazement, is a vast herd of camels! Not just any such creatures, but great snow-white dromedaries. What a rarity to come upon them grazing casually on the slope before us—hundreds of the sterling animals which I have only read about before this moment. Shikshak Moses becomes very excited and motions for a few of our cadre to pull ropes from the carts in which we carry the scraps we have scavenged along the way. These people are apparently well-acquainted with the camels. They walk casually up to the brutes, speaking in soothing tones and genially improvise muzzles about their heads. The animals resist not at all and seem to be accustomed to human contact. In fact, several of our party immediately mount what I am told are called "ships of the desert."

Gradually, we are each handed the reins to one of the animals and taught how to first lead and then ride. This exercise is very comical. Most of us take at least one fall and find ourselves having to chase our steeds across the landscape. After a good hee-haw over our antics, Shikshak Moses teaches that "honey is better to draw the fly." He gives us each a measure of grain from a sack he has produced. The camels immediately stop their flight and become our best friends, each greedily licking the seed from our outstretched hands.

Within two days we are suddenly blended into the terrain as nomads, no longer appearing as awkward and paltry vagabonds but riding comfortably on our strange charges. So at ease am I in my makeshift saddle that I am able to compose as we sojourn! I even find myself having time for an eccentric thought: *this is not India!* Such a simple observation, but I was not able to make such comparisons while immersed in the torturous time of my old life. I'm able to make another correlation as well, looking to my past without Lord Jisu and to my future with Him. It is an incomprehensible bridge I have crossed over. Looking back over the lightless gulf I have swum, I now understand just how misguided and superfluous my existence had been. It makes me frustrated in a way—why could I not see before this time what I was being offered? Why did we have to suffer so and now have to mourn those who did not know? Was the choice not there all along? Of course it was and that is the most vexing scrutiny of all. Why did I not pursue the Truth of it far earlier? Shikshak Moses helps with this consideration:

"To delight in new food, we must first choose to taste."

We are making much improved time in our quest to reach Yaruushaleem. The southern route we travel is through a wilderness that is difficult to describe. Our desert mounts are taking us through a sea of rocks. Forgive me—that image suggests a smooth expanse, but it is not so. No two stones are the same size, shape, or composition. It is as if God became bored with gravel in other regions of the world and decided to fabricate freakish new minerals, storing them here for some special use later on.

I had thought before that a desert would be relatively flat with more sand than anything else, but we are more often in canyons and climbing crags.

Thank Lord Jisu for camels, they thrive in this climate and are marching us ever closer to the most holy city on Earth. Somehow they find nourishment nested in slender cracks beneath the surface slab and because they carry their own water, we hardly have to care for them. I am counseled by Shikshak Moses that these animals use their highly developed sense of smell to detect water sources and if they do become thirsty, no physical being dare stand between them and their quest. As he speaks the words, the camels all start grunting in unison and make a sudden left-hand detour. Two hours later they have led us to an oasis in a desolate place.

Shikshak Moses looks carefully around him. He walks up to the stream that feeds this place, kneels and swirls his hand in the waters, pulling a draft to his mouth, first to smell and then drink. Suddenly he stands erect and belly-laughs, his dulcet bass voice making bright the dimming day. "The Jordan!" he chuckles. "I hardly recognize it. At one time I feared its crossing. But now? So shallow, such a trivial little trickle! We are not long for home!"

We camp here and I say, on my honor, I watched the camels drink into the night without pause. I fall asleep and cannot say when they stopped their intake!

We awake to what should be sunrise, but instead encounter the fiercest sandstorm of all. To avoid losing my eyesight by its sting, I wear goggles supplied by my new friends. Still I can see nothing at all and must trust that others know what they are doing. I suspect them mad for not burrowing in. Instead Shikshak Moses speaks close to my ear, so that I can hear him over the thunderous wind. He tells me we must be in Yaruushaleem by the next day for a fantastically significant feast which will begin at the setting of the sun.

Shikshak says that to our right lies the most ancient city known to exist—Jericho. All I can differentiate in the direction he points is a granular curtain. Shikshak points ahead and explains that we will now climb in elevation over a thousand feet and travel over the wilderness mountains where Lord Jisu fasted for forty days and then had a spiritual clash with the devil once known as Lucifer. That former angel is now known as Satan and I believe he is at this moment still in this place, trying to keep us from our destination. I yell to Shikshak Moses, asking him what feast could be this important. I have trouble understanding his reply and then see him pull a piece of paper from his pocket. He somehow finds a pencil and scratches the festival name upon the writ. I do not recall having heard of it before. But by the fact that we press stubbornly on, directly into the gale, I deduce it must be an extremely sacred event. I look at the paper and mouth the word written there, inviting it to become a part of my karma.

Passover

We have traveled through the dismal night to ensure arrival in the Holy City on schedule. The dust caked in my lungs challenges each breath. My brain must be starved for oxygen. In brief moments when the gusts of grit wane, I catch glimpses of—it cannot be, but is—a fearsome rider, not on a camel, but bridling white horse of enormous size. With the deluge, it is difficult to resolve features, but I think the rider has some sort of crown and decorative garments—impossible. What would they be doing out here? What are we doing out here!

I convey the images I am seeing to Shikshak and he appears concerned. "Time is short," he urges on and we all quicken our pace. This is a challenge, as we are walled in on both sides, navigating the floor of a vast canyon. The howling wind is a belligerent defender, doing its best to keep us from progressing. Its cutting force is agony to any exposed body part, but even in our bloodied condition we press on. At that moment a rockslide from the canyon wall attacks. The camels need no persuasion to gallop forward and only one, a man who was in the container with me, is caught by the collapse. The amount of fill is so vast that we are not able to retrieve his body and the cliffs surrounding us continue to rumble their threat of doom. We are forced to move on and I pray for my lost cousin. I suspect each of us is wondering who will be next to pass into eternity.

In another hour we have exited the gauntlet and the tempest appears to be gradually abating. I look out ahead of us, but there is no sign of the White Rider. As we round a mountain curve, two amazing things happen. The wind stops completely and the sky shifts to a yellow hue. It is sunrise; the golden beacon appears clearly behind us, not shrouded in dusky haze as has been the new normal. It illuminates before us—a magnificent sight. We stare in halted silence for uncounted moments. Shikshak Moses exclaims our recognition and joy of what we behold: "Jerusalem!"

I know now what I have never known before. A peace I cannot paraphrase, a home where I have never lived, but now know to be the sanctuary where I will dwell until I am called to heaven's gate. This is all I need to write. I have come from the bondage of worldly religious rituals to a place where I am one with a God who loves me so much, He would make Himself known to me (and anyone hungry for relationship with Him). He knows I am not able to love Him enough and so He does the loving, even loving to His death, even loving in resurrection. Not a reincarnated life where we must keep striving for some ambiguous attainment. This is new. He makes me and all who call His name, complete in Him—a concept difficult to describe other than with the image of a marriage. I am a new being and I thank Him now for inviting me to the holiest city of all. Now only the greatest question of all remains…

—Lord Jisu, our Savior, what would you have us do?

The Confessions of Jason Billards

I wet myself. Maybe more, but this wasn't no checking time. It was a running or a kneeling time. My legs chose for me—I collapsed to the ground on my face.

"Who are you?"

"I…my name's Jason."

"Your name is already known, but who are you? What purpose do you serve?"

"I'm a…actually, I used to be a store clerk, sold…gas and stuff. Now that the world's gone to hell in a hand basket, I guess, uh, I serve no purpose at all, or, didn't until…"

"Until you discovered life?"

"I think it's more like realizing I was dead…really dead, not just my body. That's when everything began to change."

"So you are a Second."

"Yeah, that's a saying for it. I'm a Second."

This conversation happened one day after Doc Hindeland, known to us as Preacher and seventy-two others left our clan, headed for Israel. Our "clan" is a group holed up in a bunker in the mountains of South South. We found this place because God wanted us to find it and I'm writing this because God wants me to. Preacher said that after he left, we should keep a record of what's going on, but I'm not much for writing. He said to just listen and the words would come. He was right, as usual. I've learned a whole lot about listening and writing lately.

The strange thing is, when I read these pages, I don't hear me. I mean, it doesn't sound like me talking—I have a real thick accent and you just can't write that. Of course, no good English teachers are hereabouts, so I might be just thinking I'm writing better than I talk. No matter—because of the "other thing". I'm hearing voices—actually *a* voice. As crazy as it sounds, that voice is telling me most of what I'm writing. Guess that makes me more of a pencil than a writer. Maybe the pencil should just get busy doing what it's supposed to. Here goes.

I had just married my wife, Betty—amazing woman, she—and I was trying to figure out what to do to improve the morale of our group. Everyone was kind of down since Preacher left, so I exited the cave to send a question into the dusty morning sky. "God, what do we do now?"

That's when the surprise hit me. I got an answer: The answer that still makes me dizzy and crazy when I think of who was doing the answering; the answer that was not just an answer but a jar to my whole system. There were a thousand questions more in the answer.

"You are a Second."

I think I knew what that meant at the time. It's what Betty nicknamed us and what Preacher started calling us, because…well, because it just fit. But hearing *The Voice* of the Questioner telling me made it sound like a new word, more like there was something I needed to be doing because I was a Second.

You may be thinking right now, "Telling you? You was having a conversation?" That's right, *telling* me. I didn't meet The Voice, but we was talking up a storm—no question. It was kinda one-sided, but that was OK. I was all ears.

What's the job description of being a Second? What now? Wasn't that the question I had been praying to get an answer for?

I didn't have long to ponder because, as I stood outside in the heat of the morning, I caught sight of a strange cloud to the west. I had brought along a pair of binoculars and raised them to see what was causing the commotion. Not but a couple miles off was some new folks headed directly toward Ein Gedi, the hideout we had moved into months back.

"This feels like trouble," I said to myself and to The Voice—He didn't answer back and I took that for agreement, so I ran back into our compound. The entrance was disguised to look like—well, like nothing special, so that no one unwelcome would get curious. I slipped in through the outside hatch and shut it behind me, pulling tight the special locking mechanism. Fortunately for us, we could still look out towards the approaching cloud through a special camouflaged window on the second story that we thought of as our observation deck. We found this place by accident, built inside a cliff face, but that's another story and not real important right now.

I found Betty, told her to clue everybody in about the excitement and then I hustled up to the window to make sure whatever was coming wasn't somehow dangerous. I was hoping it would just pass us by and head toward the nearby hole-in-the-wall town of Citation. That wasn't to be, though. The "whatever" was coming straight for us.

The next few hours seemed like a replay of something we used to call an action movie—of course, movies can't be played no more; least not like they used to be. I guess anyone reading this will just have to picture it real good in their mind.

The cloud off to the west was a strange one, keeping to the ground, hard to tell from far off what such a dark moving thing might bring with it. As it blew closer, we figured it wasn't a cloud at all but a swarm of… something. It didn't veer course at all, but beelined right toward Ein Gedi—no doubt about it.

We warned everyone and soon, as many as could cozied in for a view of the coming threat. Slowly it seemed to boil toward us—hot with intent. Finally, when it hovered within yards of Ein Gedi, we could tag figures within the swarm. There was thirty of them, all decked out in special HAZMAT suits which looked just like the one we had in our storage bay. I remember because my bride Betty had risked using it to test the outside air after the brouhaha with the weather had died down.

I warned the clan to start hiding our valuable stuff, like we had drilled. We always knew there might be the possibility of a return someday of the original builders of Ein Gedi: looked like this was that day.

Whoever they was, it were a good thing they was wearing the HAZMAT getups, because that swarm was all on them. It was bugs like the one Preacher had kept as a pet. But these was no pets. They attacked over and over, trying to sting and bombard the suited ones. What would make the things so contentious? Why was they so persistent? The fact that the bugs didn't like them told me we shouldn't like them either.

Still, to leave them outside didn't seem right—we had weapons and at least as many folks as them—plus, they began working on ways to open the special outside hatch, so it seemed right to let them in under our terms, not theirs. The trick, we thought, would be getting them inside without the bugs following. Strange as it seemed, The Voice told me exactly how to fix the problem. We all went down to the entry leading into the receiving compartment. I told everyone to stay in the hallway with the door closed, having their weapons ready, in case…well, I didn't know in case of what. Then I entered the compartment and went into the airlock alone through the portal door to officially welcome our guests.

Without really thinking about the ramification, I opened the outer hatch and just walked outside—no protective suit, no nothing—to greet our guests. All of them looked real perplexed when I appeared and all the bugs suddenly flew away. One of the HAZMATs stepped toward me, pressed a button on the side of his helmet and I heard a metallic voice crackle in my ears.

"We have some wounded ones with us." The man sounded urgent—his statement seeming more an order than a request for entry. An old movie came to memory at that moment, *The Day the Earth Stood Still.* I didn't feel good about these foreigners, but again The Voice encouraged me to be friendly, so I invited them in.

Interestingly, they didn't seem surprised to know we was inside and didn't appear threatened by our pointing guns at them. We could see their faces through the clear bubble helmets they wore. The one who had spoken to me seemed to have authority over the others. They wouldn't make a move unless he either motioned or told them to do so. He seemed real at ease and somehow I got the sense that this was almost a homecoming. When he spoke again, my suspicion was vouched.

"Good, you've kept our little hideout in great condition, thanks. We brought some extra supplies and more will be coming. Meanwhile, it's best that we get acquainted and settled in as quickly as possible. It looks like a dust-storm is headed this way. Let me be the first to introduce myself. My name is Jonathan Trimble."

Now anybody who's anybody knows who Jonathan Trimble is, or was. He had been the owner of the largest media and news corporation in the world. Sure, Preacher is famous as being the last televised face on the planet, but this guy, Trimble, had something else—power. His kind of power made me feel pretty uncomfortable, kind of like having a tiger on a leash. We only thought we had control. There was one other thing about the man that was confusing. Although he was intimidating, the man also had charisma and seemed real nice and relaxed. So when he stuck out his hand in greeting, I shook it without a thought.

Trimble and his people moved in quickly and the training from my army days reminded me that this looked an awful lot like an occupying force, swooping in to take control before anyone had sense enough to ask questions. Our folks appeared confused and disoriented and I thought it would be a good idea to get everyone in our group on the same page.

I passed the word around and we discreetly gathered in one of the secondary supply rooms. Trimble's group was real focused on their work and not a one of them seemed concerned with our movements.

"What's going on?" asked Julie. "Where did they come from and what gives them the right—?"

"I think they may be asking the same question about us," I interrupted. "That posse is heavily armed, seems to know all about this place and I think we need to be careful about how we react to them. Did y'all hide the Bibles and the letters?"

Before Preacher and the seventy-two left, we had been making copies of his Bible—the only one we knew at the time to still exist. We didn't want to take any chances with those copies getting into bad hands, so we put together a hiding plan just in case something like this happened.

After deciding our new guests weren't an immediate threat, we all ambled about. It was tough for everyone, trying to appear as if as if we wasn't interested in the outsiders' busyness. We stayed watchful to see what they was up to, passing messages to one another when we saw the others doing something suspicious. It seemed better to watch, learning rather than reacting.

It didn't take long for Trimble to show his hand. I was walking down a hallway when he sidled up to me and said, "I've been told by others on your team that you're *the man*. I just wanted to let you know that we've brought extra food and some seeds to plant that we think should grow in these settings."

Well, maybe I had a wrong feeling about this guy. This was a mighty generous thing he was offering. But then he hit me with the bombshell.

"Of course, since you've been using the facilities, we'll need to figure out some compensation for the reserves you've already used up. We can find a simple way to have you pay the cost back in labor."

My bad feelings came right back to me. What kind of labor? Why should we be singled out for finding this place? We came in and kept it up. There was no sign on the door saying "No Trespassing," and Jonathan Trimble had no mortgage papers for Ein Gedi. I vented my feelings, with maybe a little too much *cock*, as I tend to do.

"Well, we're more than happy to co-op the place with you, but I think we come in even to the game. As for your haul, we'd be obliged to let you store it here as long as you're willing to share them—no cost. If that doesn't work for you, you're welcomed to leave at any time and we won't charge you rent or nothing."

Trimble gave me a long, even look. It was like the tiger was deciding which claw he was going to use to slit my throat. But then he seemed to become bored with the thought and he spoke out, real nice like. "You're absolutely right, we appreciate being invited in. For the moment, let's see how we can best help one another rather than who has control over resources."

For the moment? The hair on the back of my neck went up at his comeback, but I showed calm. There would be time enough to figure what Trimble really wanted. Another storm was brewing outside and we sure didn't need one inside at the same time.

As Mr. Trimble and his brood continued to organize, our clan talked about what we should and should not reveal to them—primarily, we all agreed that they didn't need to know anything about our stash of Bibles, nor about Preacher and the seventy-two that had left with him. Funny, since we had all snubbed our egos and received Jesus as Lord, everyone in our group appeared to have a strong connection to the presence of the Holy Spirit and now we also seemed to be able to tell when an ornery spirit was hanging around. One was definitely hanging in this place now.

We decided the best idea would be to keep observing and we planned to meet in small groups every day, appointing a leader for each of those groups to be the communicator to the larger body. The leaders would meet every other day to make sure we was all kept up to speed on what was happening. This way, we hoped not to make the other crowd suspicious.

After our strategy session, I headed toward the storage bay to see what Trimble's troupes was up to. But before I could get there, the man himself came my direction.

"Jason, I'm glad to see you. I wanted to let you know what we've been doing."

I had a pretty good idea that whatever they really was doing wouldn't even be close to what he would confide to me. I played it cool and told him I'd be very interested in hearing his take on things.

"Of course, you know that there appears to be no way to sustain electric current," Trimble began by stating the obvious. "What you may not be aware of is that some of us are learning how to harness other powers that may replace electricity and may even be more powerful."

Now he had my attention. I didn't say anything, hoping he would continue. The man loved an audience.

"We noticed that, since the global plague that took so many of our loved ones…"

Really? That's what his group called the Gathering-Up—a plague?

"…some of us have attained a strange power to change atmospheric conditions. Not anything large, mind you…increasing the temperature of a room by a degree or two, we're getting better. And by joining efforts—more than one person fixated on any object—we can even increase the temperature around larger structures, say the size of a human body."

Prince of the power of the air came to mind as I listened to Trimble. I tried to remember the chapter in the Bible where Preacher showed me that…1 Corinthians 2. Yup. Now I became real alert as to whom this guy was answering to. I stalled with a question while trying to work out the thoughts set off by my inner-radar-alert. "How's that going to replace electricity?"

"We're not close yet," Trimble responded, seeming a little defensive, "but we believe that soon we will be able to *think* anything into a source of fuel or energy."

I hoped I had misheard him because he had talked about moving and heating up a human body and then he mentioned thinking things into fuel. Was he planning on toasting some of us to keep warm in the winter?

"Don't worry, we want this ability to be available to everybody," he said, seeming to read my mind. "We also want to share another gift."

Again I just looked quizzically at him, waiting for him to continue.

"We're able to communicate with one another telepathically."

"So they can read our minds?" Betty was pacing and fidgeting with her hands like she always done when she got anxious.

I told her and the other leaders that I didn't think so. Trimble explained that two people had to be brain-pointing in the same way they would have to when cooking stuff. It was more like they could *move thoughts* between themselves. I also told the group that I tried a real quick quiz with Trimble, thinking real bad thoughts about him to see if he'd react. Preacher would have been proud of my little experiment—Jonathan T., the well-dressed buzzard, was spiritually deaf as a post.

I even got to thinking that Trimble was using the suggestion they could heat things up as a ploy to mess with us psychologically, purposefully trying to distract us from our trust in God and our wholehearted worship of Him. So after our meeting, I went back to Trimble with the idea of trying to get him to play his hand. I found him sitting in the observation deck, peering calmly out the window at a looming sandstorm. He spoke as I entered.

"You're concerned because you want to make sure I can't read your mind. I assure you I can't."

I didn't know whether or not to be reassured by his statement. My thoughts as I had been searching for him in the compound had been exactly what he just described. "I'm more concerned with what you're planning to do with your new powers and if you're a threat to my folks."

A fanciful smile crossed his face and he responded almost immediately. "If we were a threat to you, we wouldn't even be having this conversation. Actually, we want…need…you and your group's cooperation and I'm excited about the prospect of working together."

"Glad to work with you too, but let's take it slow and easy. My history has taught me to be a little suspicious of gift horses."

Trimble replied, "Jason, I have every intention of winning you over and your prudence is actually meritable. Let me ask you, though: if I can show you that I want the best for your people and will offer them everything I have to keep them safe and satisfied, will you support me?"

I decided honesty was the right recipe. "That depends. I've been learning a lot lately, mostly from some words of an old friend. He told me, 'Understanding what God has done by offering His son for us is not rocket science'." As I see it, God's doing a work right now and we've got to be real sure whoever we're dealing with is on God's side too. So, are you?"

"That's a powerful question—the idea of a supreme being having something to do with our destinies is intriguing. I like to think that God gave us the ability to handle our own problems and that we do better at that when we're all working together." Trimble paused for a moment and then casually stretched his arms over and behind his head, yawned and at the same moment asked, "By the way, which friend laid that idea on you?"

I don't know why I did it, probably because I thought Preacher and his wagon-train was safely away now. And, well what harm would it be if I dropped his old nickname? "Oh, you wouldn't know him. He went by the name Fiz."

An immediate stiffness seemed to attack Trimble and instead of the temperature increasing, as Trimble said he was able to make happen, the room felt like it went down to freezing. The man tried not to show concern, but his voice faltered when he asked, "Fiz? Fiz Hindeland as in Fitzgerald Hindeland, the notorious scientist? You…know him?"

I knew right away I had given away some kind of privileged information to the enemy and I tried to cover my tracks. "Knew him? He was a family friend. Couldn't tell you where he is now."

Trimble brushed the comment aside, looked at me with new interest and spoke words that sent a chill colder than the room down my spine. "I'm sorry, then, to be the one to tell you the news. We found Dr. Hindeland dead on the side of the road as we were nearing Citation.

An unjust man is an abomination to the righteous, but one whose way is straight is an abomination to the wicked.

—Proverbs 29:27

Now I had a real problem. I was real broken up about the news of Dr. Hindeland's death. After Trimble let me know, I had to excuse myself and run to the bathroom to throw up. What was I supposed to do? Should I tell everyone else? If I did, they'd all probably get real upset like me and then Trimble would know there was some kind of connection between all of us and the late professor. He'd sure want to snoop around about that and sooner or later, he would find the Bibles. What would happen then would be anyone's guess. Would it be right to hold back such crucial information from my clan?

I prayed hard about it and it was The Voice that told me what to do next. Honestly, I should have figured it out myself, but I was not in the best frame of mind.

Betty was by herself in one of the seclusion areas. I came in quietly and saw her sitting on a wooden bench, hands folded, eyes closed and seemingly oblivious to my intrusion. I turned around to leave and she spoke. "Don't go away."

Immediately she rose up, came over, gave me the tenderest hug ever and said, "Tell me what's wrong."

Betty and I talked and prayed about what to do some more and she came up with a larruping good thought.

"What proof do we have that Trimble Toes is telling the truth, not just about Preacher but about anything? Seems like he's squawking an awful lot, trying to confuse and scare us. Plus, I saw him talking real kindly to Kendal's two buds—the last unbelieving ones. I'm thinking he may be trying to get the goods on us through them."

She was right and her questions hammered the last nail into the coffin. My opinion of the man was that he couldn't tell the truth if he wanted to and I didn't actually think he wanted to.

We decided to tip off everyone in our clan of our sense as to what Trimble was doling out. He was probably whispering in the ears of some of the others anyway, so why not nip the problem in the bud?

I passed the word on to the clan leaders—even the possibility of Preacher's demise—and they took it well. They had also suspected Trimble to be a false prophet kind of guy and they each agreed to warn all the clan.

After finishing up with everyone, I decided to browse around the storage bay. It was The Voice again making the suggestion and it made sense. We had never eyeballed what Trimble and his entourage had brought in with them. Their gear was minimal—had to be, under the conditions. But there was two boxes, both about the size of a suitcase that might be used on a long trip, which caught my attention. That was because they was both making noises. And it was a noise I knew—birds. More exactly…

"Pigeons," came a voice from behind me. I flinched a bit, have to tell, but kept my cool as I turned to face Jonathan Trimble. He went on to explain. "My livelihood has always been communications, so, since the power grid stopped working, we've been trying to experiment with ways to send messages over long distances." He smiled that crooked grin of his and continued, "Sometimes the old ways are the best."

Who was he trying to communicate with? This time he didn't appear to read my mind, but went with a friendlier approach.

"Jason, I need your help. For some reason, it seems you and your group have no difficulty going outside. Those terrible bugs don't attack you."

His questioning look told me he was fishing for my explanation. The Voice said to go ahead and tell him. "For You bless the righteous, O Lord; You cover him with favor as with a shield."

"Hmm, part of Psalm 5. I believe the rest of it talks a lot about doing away with enemies."

Got to admit, I didn't expect Trimble to know that.

"Don't look so surprised, son. We communicators have to be familiar with all types of resources in order to make our points. The Bible is one of many good tools for influencing people."

I was ticked because I didn't want to let him see I was surprised, I did my best to play my cards close. More than that, I was concerned about what kind of plans he might be cooking up to influence our clan. Trimble had found a bone to gnaw on and was sinking his teeth in.

"Jason, I'm honestly trying to understand your relationship with God. Are you telling me that anyone who says they believe in Him is somehow protected?"

I hesitated, not knowing the answer, just the source. "I can't rightly say. If we was totally protected, I'd say nothing could hurt us, but I bleed just like the next man. Still, there's some things that seem meant to get the attention of those who don't recognize Jesus as Lord."

Did I just see the great communicator wince? His smooth voice paved over what I reckoned to be his true reaction. "The God of love doesn't love everyone? He hands out special exemptions to some?" Trimble asked this in a way that sounded a tad sarcastic. I'd never heard him irked before, not even a tad. It caused a real strange reaction in me. I wanted to get my gun and put the cur out of his misery before he got worse and attacked. I thought it might be a good idea to move the conversation along.

"So how can I help you?"

Trimble smirked again. He wasn't going to draw me into a biblical fist fight and he knew it. "Several ways," he said. "I'd like to get some messages out to some friends using my pigeons. But that means someone has to set them free. I think you probably understand why my people may have some difficulty doing that."

I understood real well. "Sure, them bugs just plain don't like y'all. Do they like your birds any better?"

"They…the insects…seem interested, more than anything else, in humans…"

"Some humans," I reminded him—I was enjoying this. "Sure, we'll help you with that. What's the other way we can help?"

Trimble didn't answer for a piece. I think he was trying to figure out the best way to pitch his idea. "We have seeds that can be planted—corn, barley, beans—but again we…our group can't do the planting—"

"Or the tilling, or the harvesting," I interrupted. "Yeah, that's a lot of work you're asking of us. I know you'd share the crops with us, but it sounds like we'd be doing all the heavy lifting."

"Yes, you would be," Trimble admitted. "But we are providing the seeds. That should count for something. You have no idea how much work was involved in getting them here." Trimble saw that I was thinking it over, so he tried to sweeten the pot. "There might be additional ways of compensating you."

Compensation? What in the world would this man have that I would want? This time, my thoughts was easy to read. Trimble just kept on talking.

"Remember what I told you about our new abilities? We'd be willing to teach you those skills."

On the one hand, I didn't believe this flimflam man had any such skills. On the other hand, this might be a great chance to find out what they was really up to. The Voice agreed, so I took the bait. "What if it doesn't work—your skill teaching?"

"Oh, I can assure you it will. But if not, you have my oath that we will find other ways to incentivize you."

That statement worried me more than anything else he had said. Yet the idea of real food, instead of the dry packs we was all tired of, was incentive enough. I just didn't think Jonathan Trimble needed to know that. "Tell you what," I answered. "We'll help you out and see what your skills are all about."

Trimble stuck out his hand. I just looked at it and said, "Sorry, but old habits die hard. I don't take nobody's hand without it being earned. We ain't quite there yet." The Voice was telling me to be ready for anything with this one.

No one else in the clan was buying what Trimble was selling either. We had followed through with our commitments: first helping with the pigeon lob and then we tilled a half-acre plot outside to plant the seeds. Neither of these tasks was as simple as they seemed. The birds looked to be disoriented. We'd set them free, they'd circle about and then come right back to us. I believe I understood their problem.

I remember Preacher giving me one of his scientific explanations about how the earthquakes and other crazy stuff caused by the singularity had shifted the planet's axis by two to three degrees. He also taught me how to make a homemade compass using a magnetized needle in a cup of water. Then he showed me the end of the needle that should have been pointing north was pointing south. Preacher explained that Earth's magnetic poles had reversed. He had said it was affecting everyone's personalities too. I believe it; I have not felt right since all the shaking around. It might even explain my hearing His Voice bouncing around so strong in my head.

No wonder the pigeons was confused. After five or six tries, they finally seemed to catch on that we wanted them to *get* and *get* they did. Oh yeah, did I mention that I took an extra precaution with the birds? It seemed like the right thing to do and The Voice didn't argue with me. While I was holding the first bird we was going to let fly, I turned facing away from the observation window so that curious eyes wouldn't see my next moves.

I opened the plastic capsule holding Trimble's penciled message to his friends and read it:

CITATION SITE AQUIRED, BUT POSSIBLE
RESISTANCE. ASSIST ASAP

I didn't like the sound of that, so I signaled Betty to come over, making like I needed help getting the bird ready. Still facing away from the window and pointing at the western sky, I showed her the note. I love that girl; she knew just what to do. Taking her own pencil and pad that she carried with her, she quickly wrote a new note and popped it in the capsule. We released the bird and that's when it flew straight and true. We went through the same actions with each of the other four birds. Each time we changed the message, the hen took off with no problem. Imagine that. Of course, how the pigeons was going to manage avoiding being attacked by all the bugs out there was between them and God.

As I said, planting the seeds was no small chore either. The ground was dry and hard and working the loam was backbreaking. On one occasion, we all came in for some water. There in the receiving compartment was one of Trimble's female followers. I remember someone calling her Roxanne. She came up to me looking uneasy, put her hand to my shoulder, looked around—I reckon to make sure someone wasn't watching—and then whispered into my ear, "I believe."

I turned to talk to her, but she backed away, looking a little afraid. "Nothing to fear," I said in a quiet voice. "It can remain between you and me and God for now if you want."

She shook her head and told me she no longer wanted to hide. Matter of fact, she wanted to help. She looked real hungrily toward the portal door. I took her meaning and said, "That's risky. I'd like to ask you a few questions before we go out there."

"Anything," she said restlessly.

As we talked, The Voice kept nagging at me, warning me of the danger of the conversation with this girl. I knew it was dangerous, of course it was. We was talking faith. That meant Trimble would blow a gasket if he heard of it. But there was something else The Voice was trying to tell me and I just couldn't hear it right.

"Do you understand that you're a sinner and that only God has the power to forgive you?"

She nodded quickly, focusing her stare over my shoulder at the portal door. I looked at her profile, thinking, *This is one who would stick in my mind for sure.* Bright red hair, tattoos just about…everywhere and her nose decked out with rings. Pretty, for sure, but not my type, just too decorated. And yet I knew that I knew her. How? I decided that there was more onerous things at the moment. I could think on it later.

"Do you accept Jesus as your Lord and Savior?"

"Yes, yes!" Did I hear impatience in her voice?

"This is a great thing," I said. "How about we greet our Lord together with a prayer?"

Roxanne gave me a blank stare. I could almost hear the gears in her brain working through what I had just offered. Finally she said, "Thank you for the offer, but my faith is still a very intimate thing to me. I need to get used to the idea of praying with others. But I really do want to help. Can't we just go out there?" She looked hopefully toward the door. "You wouldn't stop me from going out, would you?"

I was not liking what I was hearing. She didn't want to hide anymore, but her faith was exclusive? She didn't want to pray, but she did want to leave this place in a bad way? I waited for The Voice to say something more, but I heard nothing. It seemed like I was being checked out in some way and I didn't have a clue what to do. I asked her to wait a minute and I went over to Betty and some of the others. After explaining what just happened, we decided that Roxanne was a big girl and that if she wanted to go outside, we wasn't going to stop her. I suggested that I'd take her to the garden alone and that some of the others should be ready in the airlock to come out just in case.

"In case of what?" she asked.

That was a great question.

Roxanne and I walked through the airlock and when we was in the open, I watched her close her eyes, take an extravagant inhale of air and then smile at me. "Thank you," was all she said.

I nodded in reply and then surveyed the landscape for any signs of danger. It was a rare day in rare times. The sun could actually be seen through the dust and clouds. The wind was not bad and the temperature was tolerable. Might as well come clean, I was looking for an excuse to be outside again. Ein Gedi was my safe-place, but the outdoors was and always will be, my home.

As we walked toward the field, I noticed something different. The bugs was riled up and flying every which-way. They wasn't attacking, but they sure didn't seem to like what we was doing either.

Roxanne drew in closer to me, putting her harm around mine and said, "I'm a little scared. Will you protect me?"

"No need to protect you, they would have already come after us if there was a problem," I replied, referring to the buzzing swarm.

When we got closer to the crops, she leaned even closer and asked, "What's that over to our left?"

There was nothing but a pile of small boulders in the direction which she had pointed, as near as I could tell.

"I thought I saw a small animal or something," she said, trying to lead me her way.

This was all raising my hackles, making me real uncomfortable and I told her it was better that we just stick to the plan. Roxanne pleaded with me and was so insistent that I finally gave in, deciding to find out what she was so worked up about. We headed toward the jumble and she whispered huskily as she stroked my arm, "Your biceps are so powerful—I'm glad I'm a Christian girl with a Christian boy right now. Otherwise you might take advantage of me and I might let you."

Now I knew for sure this was bad idea. I stopped and said, "We need to head back right now."

"I didn't mean anything by that," she said with panic in her voice. "Please, let's just go a little farther." She tugged at my arm, encouraging me toward the boulders. I shook my head—something was awful wrong here and now The Voice was saying, *Get her back inside!* I reached with my left hand to take hers, but she broke away from me, ran toward the rocks.

With one very athletic crouch and kickoff, she dove over them, shouting over her shoulder to me as she vaulted into the air, "I'm sorry!"

At that moment I heard a terrible noise—or more like noises—sounding like breaking glass, metal grinding against metal, the gnashing of dying things. All those things at once was coming from up, down and everywhere—the bugs was on the warpath. They completely ignored me and headed for the boulders—for Roxanne.

All of this happened so quickly that I was able to see the creepy things actually rendezvoused in mid-air with the leaping girl, attacking her all at once before she disappeared on the other side of the heap.

Then there was a new noise, even worse than that of the bugs. Roxanne's screams rose higher than her physical act. The air itself seemed to break into fiery shards at the sound.

I got my legs working and galloped to the outcrop, climbing over to see something plain awful. I couldn't see Roxanne. There was just a squirming cocoon of noisy bugs, all crawling and jabbing their scorpion tails and biting with their ferocious teeth.

Options was scarce—only one thing to do. I reached in to push the hateful things away from the withering body. Apparently these pests had just gotten some new flying orders about it being OK to bother believers. They crunched and jabbed on me just as well. I went blind with the burn of it. The last thing I could think to do was more of a reaction than anything else. I fell on top of Roxanne, protecting her body with my own. The bugs all decided to give us both a final goodbye stab and then they blitzed away. At least, I think they all left. I don't remember much more at all, other than wanting to meet Jesus in person right then and there.

Bugs and blinding lights; horses with funky riders: I didn't cotton to these dreams at all. Then an angel's wings wrapped me up and my jitters was gone. Like when I first heard The Voice: I was dead, only this time, my body was dead too. Sure felt that way, at least. And it was OK—I really loved being there. I could have lived with that kind of dead.

But I wasn't at all dead, not even close. Funny, I remember hearing stories about folks having accidents and seeing a bright light and even heavenly images—never gave it much thought till now. Even so, I didn't meet Jesus or the Father or nothing like that. I wasn't ready for that—*His Voice* told me so real clear like.

His Voice is what I used to call "The Voice", but now it was even stronger and more dazzling and…everything right. His Voice was simple and uncomplicated. How do I know whose voice it was that I'd been hearing? I knew. Anyone could have heard the difference between that voice and any other voice. He told me I had a couple of things to say and to do. He whispered most of those things to me, like the best of secrets. Some other things He said He'd have to tell me some other time—when I was ready, whatever that meant. He kissed my forehead and that was it—I woke up. Oh yeah…it was Jesus's Voice…no doubt. I can still hear it singing to me.

Betty was right there when I opened my eyes. We held each other tight for a long while. I wanted to tell her everything that had happened, but I was crying too much—Niagara Falls bawling—like a baby…but a tickled one. It probably doesn't make sense to anyone else; it didn't to Betty. She asked if the bug bites still hurt that much. I wanted to tell her it wasn't the bugs at all that was making me all weepy. It was the kiss. I had been touched and given something I just thought I knew before—God's true love.

It was about an hour before I could stop the outpour. Then I spilled to Betty the most uncomfortable things His Voice told me to say to her. "You're next."

She stood back away from me and gave me that *tell me what in the world you're talking about* look that she could do better than anyone. I explained what I had seen and heard while I was "out". Then Betty nodded her head and said, "I got the same message, but in a real strange way."

Strange way? Stranger that what I just went through? Now she had me curious. My gorgeous bride explained. "When we brought you and the she-devil over there…"

I looked where she was pointing and for the first time since I woke up, realized there was another person in the room with us. Least I think it was a person lying on the other bed. It looked more like a swollen mummy all wrapped in bandages. But this mummy groaned like a dying moose. I figured from Betty's "'she-devil'" comment that the body probably belonged to Roxanne. Betty kept on with her story.

"I was asked to help put the bandages on. Ya know the bugs don't kill, no matter how many pokes and chomps people get. I think I even remember reading something about that in John's book of Revelation. They're just lucky I didn't stuff the bandages down her throat after what happened to you."

Betty could hardly finish the sentence. It was her turn to cry in my arms for a short stretch. Then she went on explaining.

"When I turned her over to treat her back, there it was, clear as could be—a message spelled out in bug stings. It read 'You're next'."

She was right, that was about as strange as me having a table talk with Jesus.

"I asked everyone else in the room if they saw the lettering, but no one else did. They thought I was tetched. I thought I might be too, but I even placed my fingers on the area and could feel the stamp on the skin. It was creepy. What am I next for, swelling up like...like that?"

She cried again. OK, we both did, I'm proud of it now. Betty told me she didn't know what the message meant, but she did know Who sent it. In typical Buckshot fashion, she said to me, "Whatever *next* means, I'm ready."

Now came the real hard part. Maybe Betty didn't know what was next, but from my chat with the Son of God, I knew exactly. So I told her, "Roxanne needs to be healed."

My bride reacted. "Oh, she'll heal alright, just enough so I can—"

"Heal her," I filled in.

"Like I said, she'll—"

"Betty, you heal her," I said as tenderly as I could, with all the love I could muster for her. "You can revive her now—right now. You know you can. You're next."

She just kept shaking her head back and forth as I said the words. Tears streamed down her face while I kept talking. "I know you're vexed right now and want to blame someone for what happened to me. It was my choice to help her—mine. If you're going to take it out on someone, take it out on me."

Betty shook her head even more vigorously, but didn't say a thing. Then she closed her eyes, drew in a lavish breath and released it slowly. Her lips whispered what I guessed was a silent prayer, eyes still closed, tears still pouring out. Then Buckshot Betty's eyes suddenly opened—least I think they was her eyes. There was a…shine, a sparkle in them, on her whole face that I'd never seen there before. I'd never seen anything, anyone, so…incandescent. At that moment I fell in love all over again—with Betty; with Jesus.

And there was another change. I can't explain it real well, but His Voice explained it well enough for me. He said, "Betty has died, what you see now is me in her."

And I did. I saw and I fell to my knees, I could do nothing else. Betty could, though. She turned to the body on the bed. As if in a trance, she spoke in song.

"Your faith has healed you. Jesus is Lord of your life."

I'd never heard Betty sing before. It just wasn't her thing. But, now it was. It was the sun rising over a new morning in the mountains with a crystal spring river flowing down from the peaks. There was birds there and a sky so clear that I could see the beginning of…forever. That light and all those images filled the room. It was almost the same as my trip to heaven, except this was heaven's trip to me. I couldn't do anything but sing back one word, "Yeshua!" And then it was done. Time started up again.

I know I'm babbling. That's the best way I can describe that moment—other than to say that when Betty sang her song, when time left, it felt real familiar. It was a warm home on a cold night where I had once lived, but couldn't recall.

I realized my eyes was still closed. When they opened, there was Betty and Roxanne hugging one another. Both was boohooing again, both saying to one another, "I'm so sorry, please forgive me," over and over.

Then Betty, with her new sparkly eyes, turned to me and said, "All I had to do was what I had done for you about five minutes ago."

Of course, I thought. *That's why I wasn't also swollen up like a giant marshmallow.* God had taken care of me the same way He had Roxanne. He had made Betty a healer!

The door opened noisily and Jonathan Trimble made a dramatic entrance. Following him into the room was four of his tallest, strongest men; each sporting automatic weapons pointed straight at us.

"Roxanne, are you alright?" This was Trimble's only greeting. I thought to myself, *You should have seen her about fifteen minutes ago.* His henchmen came right to Betty and me. Without explanation, they bound our hands behind our backs. "Fortunately, your wellness training kicked in," Trimble pronounced to Roxanne. "It saved you."

Funny, I thought *Someone* else saved her, but she wisely remained silent. Trimble turned to me and became a criminal detective like I used to watch on TV. "We've been monitoring your activities, Jason. I am very disappointed. The reason we had Roxanne risk her life was because, from the observation deck, one of my other people visually tracked the pigeons you released. One of them was struck by one of your vile locust creatures and fell behind some boulders."

Then Trimble flamboyantly produced a small piece of paper in his hand. I recognized it as one of the notes Betty had written and that we inserted in the plastic capsules for the pigeons to carry off. But this so-called communicator wanted to make sure his point was being communicated, so he read the words out loud, "The King is coming back. Watch for Him!"

Ah-ha, it all came clear to me then. That's why Roxanne was so anxious to get over the rocks. Her job was to grab the bird and get it back to Trimble, even at the cost of her own life. I had to admire her. Even with the convulsing she was going through, somehow she managed to find the fowl and then must have stuffed it in the pack I now remember her wearing. They must have offered or threatened her with something mighty big. His Voice told me exactly what to say at that moment.

"Thank Jesus she's OK, I can't imagine what would have happened if you had taken the responsibility to go out there yourself instead of putting someone else in danger."

Trimble's face turned all kinds of purple. He didn't respond to me, but motioned his security detail over for some confidential chitchat. Apparently, they didn't think we was a threat and that was right. His Voice said to relax, so I did. Betty seemed to know what to do too. They also ignored Roxanne, who took the opportunity to turn subtly toward us, turning her head away from the others and winked with a half-smile on her face. Betty and I both nodded, understanding.

Trimble then whirled back, walking to Roxanne and putting his arm around her in a very friendly way. He whispered something to her; she nodded timidly and the two left the room without a word. Two of Trimble's remaining boys pointed Betty to the door. She looked at me and I spoke. "It's OK, I expect these gentlemen to treat you with honor and courtesy." My bride glared at the two "gentlemen," cocking one eyebrow, questioning their intentions. They both grudgingly nodded with their eyes looking toward the ground. Then the three of them also left the room.

I was about to ask the remaining guards, who were standing behind me, what was going to happen next. Then I saw the shadow of something playing on the wall in front of me. *Was that a raised arm holding something in its hand?* Before I could turn, there was a blinding jolt to the back of my head and then, darkness.

I woke up with the worst headache ever, but that quickly became the least of my problems. I was tied to a chair in the Unity Hall filled with Trimble and "Trimblites" and I was thinking about suits. Not the ones Trimble and his admirers was wearing when they showed up. I was thinking about the kind of suits my daddy would talk about. The high-dollar kind, made with silk so that there was a shine to the fabric. In the old days in our town, the lawyers and salesmen wore the suits and that was, for the most part, all you saw them in. So that, after a while, the suits became their identity. Folks would see one of the big-league attorneys walking their way and would comment, "Here comes a *Suit*," as if it was a proper title.

By the looks of the meeting I was involuntarily invited to, the Suits still existed. Not the clothing, I'm talking about the people. No cufflinks or power ties, these Suits was worn on the inside, woven not of silk or fine cotton, but of confidence and bluffed power—people trying to impress— old-time techniques.

One of Trimble's assistants, I hadn't learned his name, walked to a wooden stand that someone had found in one of the Ein Gedi equipment closets. A cloth with some kind of logo inscribed on it was draped over its front to give an impression of "bigwigness" to anyone who stood behind it.

Our clan had attended two other "Energy Builders", as Trimble liked to call these wingdings, but I had never seen the symbol displayed before this. It was a silhouette of a man bowing to a sideways "8"—what did they used to call that, an infinity loop?

After the first two EB meetings, everyone in our clan had figured out that this group's tattle about being able to heat up the temperature in a room and their googly-eyed reading of each other's minds was all show. It was at the very first session that the image of Suits came to my mind. I don't think His Voice was much impressed with Suits either.

On the clan's behalf I had gone to Trimble and politely turned down any more VIP seating for future hoopla. That's what made the event I was at now, so bothersome. Not only was I here, tied to my seat as I was, but so was the rest of the clan, all sitting tight in the front rows, surrounded by guards with automatic weapons at the ready. This was serious stuff, so I got to praying seriously.

Trimble's man—I was thinking of him kind of like a Master of Ceremonies, all pumped up—leaned tall, out over his pulpit. His rabid followers guzzled the last of their water glasses, knowing they was supposed to be zeroed in on their host. "MC" told a joke or two and then subtly launched into a story about a man. A life story of mishaps and amazing fortitude resulting in substantial success was presented; a history that seduced the others to pay attention, be amazed and want what this man had. The man was then introduced, but I don't think he needed an introduction—we all knew the setup, we was all familiar with the story, his ballad had been sung before. Into the room, greeted by thunderous applause, charged Jonathan Trimble.

Jonathan Trimble actually did have the nice suit—the physical kind. He wore it now, tailored for him and him alone, sporting gold diamond-encrusted cufflinks and a blue-and-gold silk tie, complimented by a superbly matched handkerchief in his left breast pocket. His suit also touted the man-bowing-to-infinity emblem, a duplicate of the one on the podium, subtly embroidered onto the kerchief pocket. The man was a piece of work—ever the strutting peacock.

The "Master of Suits", Jonathan Trimble, looked to his MC who had ushered him in. MC began a chant; a cheer, to be more exact. "Do you want it or not?"

The response from his followers was unanimous: "We want it all! We want it all!"

MC encouraged, "What do you want so much? What do you want so bad?"

"ENERGY!"

MC raised the bar. "Can you taste it? Can you smell it? Is it bright in your brain?"

The volume of the crowd rose with the excitement. "Bright, bright, bright…"

"You already have it. You don't need to ask for it—use it," commanded the MC.

"En-er-gy, en-er-gy, en-er-gy!"

Over and over they crooned, Trimble putting on a lousy act of attempting to quiet the crowd, but everybody knew what he really wanted and the volume of their assents increased. He smiled as his minions gathered confidence in the repetition and then at just the right moment, he lifted his arm high and made a fist. Everybody recognized the gesture and at that precise moment, the engine of excitement driving the room crashed, as if hitting a concrete wall. The Master of Suits opened up his hand and the crowd exploded in a single cheer. Another moment and he clamped his fist tightly shut again. The cheer was shut off like an old light switch would turn off a lamp. Silence. The spotlight was now on Jonathan Trimble. He controlled all.

"I am humbled by the excitement and potential displayed in this room," Trimble began. "If only we could harness what you exude in drive and determination…On the other hand, perhaps we can!"

"We can, we can, we can…" Trimble let the mantra go on for a full minute. There was even some more "Energy, energy" that rang out. Then with another hand motion, he silenced the room and went on.

"As you know, my burgeoning empire was decimated by the failure of governments, such as the former United States, to competently gauge the physical abuses and neglect enacted upon our planet. This resulted in the cascading degradation and our near destruction. Only now are we able to see what should have been—a redefining of order and authority that would have saved us from what we now endure. But, now that we know what should have been done, is it too late to do it? What can we do now to ransom and resurrect our resources?"

The crowd was familiar with this question, having been asked the same question by Trimble at countless Energy Builders. Their response was automatic and resounding. "Heal the sun, heal the sun, heal the sun."

There's no doubt what this pomp was for. It was all a dog and pony show, scripted to inform us who was better, who was stronger, who was more… energetic. I had heard it before, we all had. The idea was that, through groupthink, Trimble, his followers and others like them throughout the world could revive the ecosystem. To their way of thinking, it was mankind's fault that energy had disappeared and that the sun was now mostly shrouded in darkly clouded skies. Right before and at the time the singularity showed up, there was even a world government movement headed up by some clown named Darius Mede and a "new age" type called Brenda Anders. They formed some kind of coalition, "GAG" or something like that, which attempted to unite all the nations and people behind the idea of giving total global power to one small group that supposedly had Earth's best interest in mind.

It was this group that designed and fired the rocket straight toward V4641, hoping it would stop all the earthquakes and geophysical imbalance that had started increasing. The rocket-thing didn't work out so well. At the same time it exploded, all the Christians, except for a few, just up and disappeared. Blip, like that. Then things got utterly worse and…here we are.

So when I hear the kind of talk that was going on in that room, it makes me a little crazy. I should have kept my mouth shut, but I didn't and His Voice didn't seem to want to stop me.

There was a brief lull in the excitement and that's when I started chanting real loud, "En-e-ma, en-e-ma, en-e-ma!"

There was stifled laughs around the room, mostly from our clan, but also in some of Trimble's rank and file. Mr. Suit himself came over to stand in front of me, wearing that cockeyed grin of his. He kept grinning at me, but he spoke to the crowd. "Does this not typify the condition of the world? Is there any doubt"—at this point, Trimble stretched his arm out toward me, palm up, like I was some kind of critter in a display case—"that the world needs our oversight, our power and wisdom, our energy more than it has ever needed anything!"

Then the big man put on a real sad face and said to me in a pity-party voice, "Jason, let me take away your conflict." Trimble closed his eyes, waved his hands slowly over my head and hummed to himself like he was trying to fix my brain or something. After a time, he dropped his hands to his side, dropped his head and sighed big-time, as if he'd just tried to lift a ton of bricks.

Another lull, no one else dared to say a thing. I took that for being my turn again. "Sorry about that, but this 'Heal the Sun' idea you're trying to cram down everyone's throats is…well, honestly, I feel like you've just stuffed five pounds of manure into my two-pound bag. I'm needing some help about now or things are really gonna get stinky!"

At that, the whole room busted out in hysterical crowing. Trimble was a pro and could handle most any situation in front of an audience…any situation except someone upstaging him. I was now officially in bonafide trouble.

The hair on the back of my neck was standing up like the moment right before lightning struck my house years ago. I knew without a doubt that something big and dangerous was coming my way. The laughter in the room died awkwardly. Everybody's eyes was now trained on Trimble, who continued to stare at me, but the grin was gone. It was replaced with a look of pure…no better word…ugliness. His guards continued holding weapons on our clan, but the gun holders was now ordered by the Master of Ceremonies to have all of the clan kneel with their fingers locked at the back of their necks. Any of them who tried to say anything or moved at all was reminded with a smart thump of a rifle butt in the back to stay in place and shut up.

My ties was cut and I too was pushed down and forced to kneel. I was ordered to turn and face out toward our clan. Trimble looked down on me and said in his most fatherly of tones, "I'm so terribly disappointed, Jason. I had such great plans for you."

"Well, one thing's for sure now," I said to Trimble. "You've got no power over temperature or thoughts. And here's one of my own ponderings for you. I hope it grabs you real good. Ain't nothing you got that we want."

"Life is too valuable to be wasted, my friend," Trimble said as he motioned for one of his people carrying what looked to be a.22-caliber pistol to come stand by me.

"No problem. You can shoot me in the head or any ol' place, I ain't turning," I stated with a calmness I couldn't and still can't explain, coming over me.

"Oh, I wouldn't dare to think that torturing you physically or ending your life would amount to anything—you're too much the man for that." With these words, Trimble gave another signal and Betty was ushered into the room and forced to kneel at my side.

"With all sincerity, Jason, we wanted so much for you to be a part of the greater good that is happening here and there is still a chance for that to happen."

Jonathan Trimble had mouthed this statement, speaking beyond me to our clan held captive and now kneeling before my eyes. The monologue sounded rehearsed, just like the phony prophet who spoke them. I peered over at Betty, who looked to be unharmed but tired and I winked at her. She kept staring at the floor in front of where she was kneeling. Apparently, she had caught my encouraging effort, for she smiled in spite of herself. I knew, no matter what, that we was going to be OK. His Voice had given me His own wink of a sort.

"Ain't a chance a'tall" I said.

Now Trimble walked around in front of me and got down on his knees too. He came right up in my face and said, "Do you realize that your god is not coming to your rescue? He can't, because He doesn't have a horse to ride in on. He doesn't finger a gun or threaten any weapon with which to erase me. He doesn't even have a court order to stop us because…Jason… He's not really out there! You must see that now. Look at the world! If God was really out there, He'd have fixed everything by now! I can fix things, though and with your help, I can do it faster and better."

I knew that this ranting egomaniac was probably not reachable, but there was a slew of his cronies who may be thinking the same thing I was—Jonathan Trimble was all about Jonathan Trimble. I prayed for His Voice to help my next words be good ones. I looked out beyond the man in front of me, beyond my own clan, to Trimble's. Maybe there was one more out there, just one would do—one who might hear and believe the words I would now speak.

"There was a man once who believed he could build a utopian place to live in. He was real good at building, actually great. Still, he had to force others to do his building for him by slave labor. He had to give up some things: a country, some people's lives, his family, other people's families. But in the end, Herod—who was known as 'the Great'—did build some incredible places to live. He finally died and you know what? So did everything he built."

I must have been talking good, because even Trimble seemed to be listening and wasn't stopping me. I pressed on.

"There was another man who lived about the same time as Mr. H. the Great. This man was a builder too and a great one as well. He also wanted to build something real special—the most special kingdom ever. Instead of forcing people to do his work for him, he invited them to learn how to build with him. Instead of sacrificing others, he sacrificed his own life out of true love. And before he was finished, he taught the others the most important words in the world—'Father in heaven; Your will be done'. That man died too, but because of what he'd done, he was given new life—forever as the Son of God. And all those who still want to help him build that special kingdom place can have that new life too."

There was a shift in the room right then and there—like the brains behind the faces was processing in high gear. I knew it wasn't my words that was working on them—it was the Spirit bringing the lesson home.

"Are you done with your little Bible story?" Trimble sounded real irritated. "Tell me, did your Jesus build this place? Did he tell you to come in without permission to burgle the resources of this place specifically built for another group? Is your God no respecter of property rights?"

He didn't wait for an answer. The self-proclaimed media messiah stood up once again, moved to Betty's other side and faced his audience. The guy with the pistol handed it across to his boss, who took it and nudged the gun's barrel into the soft indent of her right temple. He spoke once more to me. "Let's dispense with all the frilly faith-talk and superficial drivel."

Betty shuddered as I looked over at her. She asked, "Baby, we talked about this, right? No matter what we gotta do, it's for Him, not us." Staring out at the crowd in the room, she added, "I love you."

I'm not sure if she meant me or the whole place. I think she meant the latter and that was OK. I already knew what she felt about me. I also knew that His Voice had said everything was going to be fine, so I wasn't worked up at all. I just wanted Betty to have some comfort.

"Jason," Trimble spoke again facing the crowd. "No one need suffer today. I'll forget the whole affair if you'll simply pay homage to our efforts. We'll share our crops with you if you'll work them under our supervision. You can even have your worship services, as long as they don't interfere with our schedule. Nothing has to change at all."

In his last remark alone I just counted three real big changes. I knew he was feigning with the gun at Betty's head. He had to be. First, His Voice was filling me full of a peace that reminded me of my previous visit with Him. Second, Trimble must have known that if he started killing folks, that would alienate me and the clan more, not cause us to comply.

And then he spoke right to Betty, finally acknowledging her as a person and not my baggage. "So doesn't your book say something about humility in serving others? Why doesn't your husband humble himself to save you?"

"As I've seen it, people take these words and redefine them to mean other things—things they want the words to mean instead of what they was meant for." I could not have loved my bride any more than at that moment for the words she spoke at gunpoint.

"I'm going to give you another ten seconds to consider what would be best for everyone here." Jonathan T. was sounding mighty calm, but there was a definite sense of threat woven into the words. "Jason, you once told me that you bleed just like the next man, but are you prepared to sacrifice your wife's blood?"

I looked again at Betty, who closed her eyes and silently mouthed a prayer.

"Ten," began Trimble.

She turned her head my direction and said, "You're the greatest gift God's ever given me. You need to keep on being a gift to the others."

"Nine, eight…" Trimble was appearing to be kind by counting slow, but kept the gun barrel at her temple when Betty looked toward me. She turned and faced forward, closing her eyes again and a single tear dropped from her eye to her cheek.

"Seven, six…"

"Betty, you're the strongest, most beautiful person I know. You just keep being strong in God right now and…"

"Five, four…"

"…He's gonna take care of us," I finished.

"Three…"

My bride opened her eyes and looked my way again with those new sparkly eyes God had given her and she whispered, "I love you, Farm-boy…"

"Two…"

—then she sang in that meadowlark voice of hers for all to hear, "Jesus is my Lord and…"

"One."

The noise was deafening. Something hit my face and I tasted something metallic-like. Had I been shot? That would be a good thing. Instead, I saw

Betty's body slump lifelessly to the floor and realized I was tasting her blood that had spattered on me.

Trimble calmly shook his head and closed his eyes in what looked to be frustration. "Bring up another one," was his next words.

No one moved. I was still looking at Betty. She shouldn't have been there. I was sure of that. Any moment, God was going to have her sit up and say, "Fooled you!" But that didn't happen.

Trimble, meanwhile, was on to the next bullet-point of his agenda. "Someone bring up another of their clan. We have to teach them what's necessary for our mutual survival." He was sounding agitated now and still no one moved. Even in my stupefaction, I was seeing something real clearly. God was still working here and He was showing me in the faces of Trimble's group, that few, if any, had thought their leader would pull the trigger. As a matter of fact, as Betty's precious blood flowed out toward them, the guards all dropped their weapons and moved away toward the back of the room.

"I need a hand here!" Trimble's voice told all. His anger was over the whole room. This main cog was not used to having the gears jam up. Now he pointed his pistol at the man standing on my other side, the one who had brought it to him in the first place and ordered him, "I'm tired of repeating myself. I told you, bring up another!"

It's real hard to explain what happened after that. There was a scream— wasn't my scream, but it came out of my mouth. It was like one switch in me was turned off and another one turned on. All that peace left and something else lit up my insides. Not anger; that was old-school stuff. This was a new thing; powerful and alive. I would not, could not, let another soul in that room perish. The new power stopped time, but somehow, I could still move. Standing up, I turned toward Trimble, who had started the process of swinging the pistol back in my direction. Now he was frozen into a statue—everyone in the room except me was frozen too. My hands had been bound, but I spoke a word, just one.

"Off."

And the rope fell off, just like that. Then I used the new weapon God had just given me for something else. I looked straight at my adversary and said, "Sleep." Time turned back on and before he could finish the swing of his pistol toward me, Jonathan Trimble fell unconscious.

Now's where things got confusing: As soon as Trimble was out, I quickly went over to Betty. I'd like to say I was worried for our clan and how Trimble's people might react, but it would be a lie. Right then I had one thing on my "to-do list" based on one thought in my puny brain. *If I can put people to sleep, I can wake others up.* I know—it was selfish and quirky. I was apologizing to Jesus for the idea even as I was kneeling by my wife and trying to speak life back into her.

"Awake."

Nothing happened and I wondered if I had spent all my word-bullets or if maybe because I was gushing rivers again, maybe Jesus couldn't hear me clearly.

"Awake!" I tried again. I knew it could be done. I read several places in the Bible where people—even three-day-ol' dead people, even people besides my Savior—had risen from the dead.

But not this time: I turned Betty over and saw that the bullet had messed up the side of her head real bad. Strangest thing, though, her face wasn't hurt, her eyes was already closed like she knew and prepared for what was about to happen. And there was the most blissful smile ever on her lips. I gently kissed that smile and then stood up to face the others.

I wouldn't have believed it if I hadn't watched it happening. Trimble's group was kneeling with their hands in the air and some of our clan had stood up to collect the discarded weapons. Others in our group ran up to Betty's body and wrapped it in towels that someone else had fetched. Alice and other friends actually went to the kneelers and asked if they would let them pray for them. I heard words I never thought would come out of the kneeling group's mouths…all of them. Things like, "I've done terrible things, kill me now, I deserve it," and "Please forgive us," and, "I want to know Jesus."

The clan was praying with all of them and every one of them was giving their lives to the only life that mattered…just like Betty had done. Even the two miscreants who had followed Kendal and then became Trimble's toadies—even they was weeping and calling out to Jesus. That's when I heard His Voice, loud and clear, calling out to me.

"I told you it would be all right and it is."

And it was. Not the "all right" I thought it would be. It was His "all right". He needed Betty with Him and I realized I had made an awful selfish plea, so I cried out one more time. "I've asked a terrible thing, kill me now, I deserve it."

It was "Baby Ben," as we called him, who then did the most amazing of all. He came up to me and pulled me down to my knees as he too knelt. Then he spoke healing words—words that sang like Betty's voice from the heavens, to my heart and head.

"For God so loved the world and you, Jason, that He let His son be sacrificed for you and also for Betty—that all you need to do is believe in Him and be saved."

"I believe," I whimpered over and over again to Him who loved me that much.

And in the front of the room with Ben and me kneeled our clan and Trimble's clan, now one clan, all praising out the same words that pounded in our hearts.

"I believe, I believe, I believe…"

I couldn't read Jonathan Trimble's thoughts when he woke up tied to a chair, but I bet I could have come real close to guessing. Once his eyes opened, his face immediately advertised confidence. Then I saw a small sheen of sweat break out on his forehead signaling his real emotion—fear. Doubt and indecision played over his face and he tried to look back over his shoulder to see if there was now a gun pointed at his head.

"Don't believe in the Almighty?" I asked him. "I do and that may be a good thing for you right now. He's telling me to forgive you, to show you mercy."

Trimble faked bravado. "You don't need to do me any favors. Go ahead and get it over with."

I took by *it,* that he was ready for me to blow his brains out, like he had done to Betty. Maybe the old me would have—seems rightly so. The new me was looking at things real differently. Moving away from him to unblock his view, I watched as he took in the scene before him. All his people and ours was busy packing up inventory. They was all chummy and cooperative—like a family reunion. Some was still praying together off in corners of the Unity Hall and through the open door the voices from the nearby storage bay had to sound odd to his ears. "I baptize you in the name of the Father, the Son and the Spirit." Some of his people was walking back into the Unity Hall, drying themselves off with towels and then joining in the work at hand. The message was clear—God had paid us a visit.

This had an odd effect on the man tied to the chair. He no longer seemed to have the gift of leadership and persuasive communication. Instead, his words came out all hissing and poisonous. "You idiots. What are you thinking? God's going to save you from what is happening to the world? Is He going to wave his magic wand and make all the bad things go away?"

When their former honcho had come to, several of his close followers rushed over and began to explain their experience with him: how they had seen the Spirit's presence in the room and how, when they pronounced their genuine belief in Jesus, nothing else mattered. The outside world and what might happen to any of us didn't matter. Only His Voice mattered.

Of course, they was all talking to him at once and they was real excited, so I can almost understand why he too got excited and not so politely said, "Shut up! All of you!"

Everybody did too. Apparently Jonathan Trimble had one last audience, so he tried his best to deliver. "You too, Roxanne?"

The woman Betty had healed looked straight at the man and said, "Jonathan, please hear the message. It will save you!"

"I don't need saving! I was saving you, all of you. Don't you get it? We are on our own here and without strong, creative influence that sometimes requires difficult decisions, we are all going to die! We have to work together and stop seeking imaginary help from somewhere in outer space.

"Jason," he almost wept at me. "I'm sorry about your wife. Really I am. I know it had to hurt you, but I was trying to get your attention. I *had* to get your attention. Look, if you want to work alongside me—that's fine. We can be partners in this. I don't need seniority or control, but don't risk these people's lives based on some ancient voodoo. We all need to wake up to what's happening around us!"

Odd way of putting it, but I believe he was right on. Everyone in the room had woken up and had thrown away the voodoo. All had, except for Jonathan Trimble and his voodoo, that is. It was hilarious, him thinking he still had some kind of authority—offering me co-leadership and all. It wasn't his to offer and it wasn't mine to accept.

All of the folks in the room stared for a moment at Trimble, then most just shook their heads and went on with what they had been doing. Those who had come up to witness to him walked away, all except Roxanne, who kissed Trimble on the forehead and said, "God weeps for you, Jonathan."

Trimble disagreed. "There is no God!"

What Jonathan Trimble didn't know is that we was leaving; everyone, except maybe him. That was the part I had to explain to him now. He had settled down some and everyone else had left the room after bundling everything up as best they could. It was time for a heart-to-heart talk—just me and him.

"This has been a fine place, but it's time we head out. There's too much of a risk that others like you might be heading this way," I explained to him.

"Who is *we*?" I reckon Trimble was trying, with this question, to figure out who he had left on his side. This was not going to be pretty.

"Everyone. You're welcomed to join us. You'll be needing to wear one of the outdoor suits, though, doesn't seem to be much we can do about that."

"Where are you going to go?"

"We have an idea, but we're going to have to trust in…well, you'll just have to trust me, I guess." I wasn't about to blab that His Voice had very clearly told me we was to now find a way to complete the trip Preacher had started to Israel. Seemed crazy even to me—there was a lot of land and some oceans involved in the trip, but I was through saying "no" to the One who was always showing me what "yes" meant.

Trimble appeared to think through his options and then asked, "If I decide to stay, will you leave supplies?"

The group had talked about that and we all agreed; we couldn't just ditch the man at Ein Gedi to starve to death. We also couldn't hand him the lion's share. "We'll leave you three months' worth. That's the best we can do."

He nodded slowly and said, "Que sera, sera."

Fortunately, there was more of the special cargo-buggies like the ones Preacher and crew took with them. We loaded up as best we could and all forty of us assembled in the receiving compartment for a last briefing. I explained again the risks; that one group had already left and apparently had casualties. I told them that anyone could stay if they wanted, but that we couldn't guarantee Ein Gedi to be safe any longer. Everyone spoke out their desire to move on and to travel together. As a group they all asked me to lead them as God's representative. That addled me because I felt like I needed the most leading of all.

It was just before sunup. We all prayed for God's wisdom and for His will to be done. The original clan taught the new members a few traveling worship songs to help us get in the mood and then it was time. It took us a bit to all get out—just groups of five could enter the airlock at a time. There was no use causing Mr. Trimble any more distress by letting a bug or two accidentally sneak inside.

Once everyone was out, we stood for a moment to make sure the bugs wouldn't attack anyone. None appeared and that was a real good indicator that no one in our new upgraded clan, version 2.0, was a pretender. I looked up at the shielded observation window and waved, assuming that the last resident of Ein Gedi would be watching us go. But then came one more surprise.

His Voice prodded me to say a few parting words and that's all I could think of—a few. "Ein Gedi's been good for a while, but there's another place we're supposed to be. Heading out is risky, people in the world is dying all the time. But not many get to really live like…like Betty…and me. Like all y'all. Let's go where others are living like us, telling everybody we meet along the way about that kind of life and who gives it."

We were saying a farewell prayer when the outer hatch to the airlock opened and out walked a yellow HAZMAT suit. It could only be one person and he must have had something pretty high-sounding to say to come out as we was leaving. I remember at the time thinking to myself a saying my daddy once taught me—*Ignorant is a situation; stupid is a choice.*

Jonathan Trimble walked toward us and announced through his special speaker for everyone to hear. "There's still time for any of you to change your minds. I'm willing to forget the past and we can work this all out!"

Those was the last words I heard him speak, for at that moment, the bugs attacked. Not just a small swarm, more like a country-full. Some of us tried to run to his rescue, but before we could get to Trimble, he ran back to the airlock. It was a real bad idea as most of his attackers flew in with him. And then he made another bad choice, closing the hatch behind him.

Everyone had the same thought at once, running to the hatch to open it. The remaining bugs had their own ideas, threatening anyone trying to access the lock with a sting or a bite. Several of us tried anyway and paid the price. It only took one or two reminders for us to back away. It was obvious now what we was being told to do.

I had had real reservations about leaving Jonathan Trimble alone at Ein Gedi. Now it looked like he'd have plenty of company.

The Professions of Ilbani Midehina Acdah

Çıkmayan candan umit kesilmez:

Hope won't be cut from the soul that has not expired.

— *Kâzım Yetis*

By the God who corrected me and made me to look at life through the eyes of a dead man resurrected, I post these words. I have renounced my former life. I have died and my family with me. This is not a carnival trick to gain attention or power. This is fresh and good as it should be. Elohim Adonai has done it.

I am known as Ilbani Midehina Acdah, son of Denate Umble Acdah of the great house of Vytautas. But that lineage is of no longer of consequence. Nothing else but the return of the Messiah is important. Even the events of these days which I will recount, many of them dreadful and graphic, yet still they pale compared to the coming of our King who will soon set the chaos right.

By way of introduction, I am a merchant of sorts, born of one faith, converted to another and thus a potential heretic sought by some to persecute. Yet, because of my talents for trade across the hemispheres, I am welcomed and tolerated in most of the zones of fair Jerusalem, where I now choose to reside.

Why concentrate my commerce here? So many reasons, so blessed am I to have obeyed Elohim Adonai in His wisdom. But one thing as much as any other keeps me here. The mood of Jerusalem is like no other. I know this because I have traveled through New Asia, Africa and New Roma since the time of the disappearances. Here on Zion's steeple is kindled a community of hope, despite the dismal worldly condition.

I and my wife, Jende, who is of African/Lemba origin, came for sanctuary. We have enjoyed unusual prosperity and favor among all the peoples of the Holy City. This is now and will be forevermore, our hearts' home. As for what I will describe next, its telling pales to the actual experience of the events and the tangible dismay of my soul. Still, it must be said, so that others might understand what I cannot.

Today has been unusual from the beginning. Passover—*Pesach*: my first; many of the New Followers' first; and for some, their last. Dusty darkness and earth-traumas bombard our lives so that our remaining hope lay in the spiritual light that keeps us protected. But this day, the Spirit pours out: in the early afternoon, a sandstorm that has been torturing us ceases. The sun, which this city has not seen for a year or more, is a hazy emanation in the eastern sky, rising to warm all it touches. The tint of the sky is strange—more brown than anything. It makes me wonder about the oceans. As I understand from my studies, in the past, the expansive waters caused Earth's stratosphere to appear blue by reflection. Are the oceans now void of rich color, of life itself?

People in Jerusalem have flooded out of their dwellings as a rushing river after spring rains. The shining moment is a great joy to all: Jews, who are now referred to in New Israel as Yether'am—*the Remnant;* Christian *New Followers;* and Muslims alike. It seems we are 'sharing a special blessing of shalom, a fairytale *once-upon-a-time* episode that I know cannot last.

Remnants and most New Followers are taking advantage of the good weather to make ready for the traditional celebration. Of what celebration do I speak? It is the all about the amazing time when God acted through the prophet Moses to free His people from the bondage of Egypt. Typically, the Muslims respect or at least tolerate this moment, giving the participants a wide berth. For some reason, it is not the case today. Perhaps it is because of the press of the swelling crowds. Maybe it is resentment felt by many unbelievers who remember the disappearance of a great multitude from Satan's shackles. Whatever fire has been put to the water, it will take nothing more than one extra degree of disaster to bring the crowd to a boiling point.

And I see it unfold with the arrival of a caravan from the east. From beyond the Mount of Olives and through the *Kidron* they come: dusty and worn yet jubilant in their arrival. I myself remember the ascent to this great city and how it had stirred my own spirit. Many around me must be recalling their own entry experience, for as the haggard hobos process through the Jaffa Gate, New Followers and Remnants join in the chorus of Psalm 24:

> "Who shall ascend the hill of the LORD? And who shall stand in His holy place?
> He who has clean hands and a pure heart, who does not lift up his soul to what is false and does not swear deceitfully.
> "He will receive blessing from the LORD and righteousness from the God of his salvation. Such is the generation of those who seek Him, who seek the face of the God of Jacob.
> "Selah, Selah, Hallelujah!
> "Lift up your heads, O gates! And be lifted up, O ancient doors, that the King of glory may come in.
> "Who is this King of glory? The LORD, strong and mighty, the LORD, mighty in battle!
> "Lift up your heads, O gates! And lift them up, O ancient doors, that the King of glory may come in.
> "Who is this King of glory? The LORD of hosts, He is the King of glory!
> "Selah, Selah, Hallelujah, Amen."

The song within us swells and more join in, welcoming the journeymen and women to this sacred place. Not one of us apparently notices the increased agitation of the Islamists in the crowd. Even I, a convert from the former, am surprised by the gunshot, the clap of which ricochets through the open marketplace. We watch in horror as one of the riders, who appears to be of Indian or Pakistani origin, falls from the camel on which he is mounted.

Bewilderment ensues and contributes to what happens next. Those Arabs unsympathetic to faiths that do not recognize Muhammad as the prophet, pick up whatever solid objects they can find nearby—slag, bricks, anything with weight. They begin to throw them willfully at the caravan and at known Remnants and New Followers.

A rock collides with my shoulder and I have to take cover from the onslaught. From my vantage point behind a fruit stand, I watch in helpless fear as the heat of anger rises to a tempest. Everyone in the square—Muslims,

Remnants, New Followers—all react. It is impossible to tell assailer from assailed. I want to tend to those felled, but each time I try to leave the protection of the stand, a new barrage of missiles comes my way and I am forced back. The attack seems to go on unendingly, but is actually a few miserable minutes long. For such a short span of time, the tally of bloodied victims brought to the ground is deplorable.

Then a voice trumpets out from nowhere and everywhere. It is louder than the war cry of the attackers; louder still than the din of the injured.

"Dai!" *Stop!*

The behest rings through the marketplace with authority and indescribable force, conjuring with it a wind, more fearsome than the most titanic of sandstorms that stills all breath and results in instant docility. I have never experienced it in such magnitude before, but recognize immediately its source. The Ruach Ha'Kodesh, the Holy Spirit of Elohim Adonai, has been grieved. Its power is manifested in the form of a magnificent New Follower whom I recognize.

He is well-known in Jerusalem: Cherished mystic to some, pariah to others—a man who converted from Judaism to become the most dynamic of New Followers in the land. He is now called Brother Moses, once having been the most prominent rabbi in the land. He discontinued the title after recognizing Yeshua as Messiah, ceding that only the One deserves the honored banner. I have heard him speak before, exuding wisdom and a bright spirit indeed. He insists now on being called *Brother*.

After restraining the malevolence with his summons, Brother Moses walks to the center of the marketplace without anyone attempting to injure or impede his way. He is an imposing man whose garb might better fit that of an ancient prophet. A goatskin tunic—what some would call *sackcloth*—held together by a leather belt, cloaks his abundant body. His booming voice can be heard easily in the silence of the marketplace.

"Children of the Most High, what drives you to such hatred? What enslaves you to carry out this barbarism? Are we all not here to serve Him? Why do you who honor Him, kill those who also seek Him?"

I watch in amazement. The ground, the buildings and every bone in my body vibrate with the words. All people not hurt by the riot are brought to their knees by the tremor of his speaking.

"You will care for the injured, all of you. You will intern the dead and compensate the families of the perished, one and all of you. You will do this now and pray that the Most High God will not send you to damnation by stealing more than what you have stolen from Him!"

Then for an insufferable moment, I cannot take breath. I see everyone else also unable to inhale and I beg to HaShem—*The Name*—to forgive me. I concede I had succumbed to my fear and concern for my own safety rather than rushing to help the victims. I know my family will languish by my death—there is no younger brother to care for them.

Then my breath returns with a fire in it. Thankfulness and absolute awe to the One who can give and take life in an instant flies out of my mouth. "Adonai, Eloeinu—*Lord God*!" It is not just my cry at that moment, but the exclamation of all, save one, in the marketplace. One continues to clasp at his throat, his face turning more purple with each second passing.

Brother Moses comes to stand by this particular one and now we realize why. Next to the man lies a rifle. The Holy Man looks down at the offender and speaks with authority, as if inspired from the One Greater. "From dust you came and to dust you shall return. But not on this tragic day. On this day you will live with the agony of what you have done. Pray, before eternity's last call, that you discover the One True God, El Shaddi and enslave your destiny to Him!"

The man on the ground bellows his anguish, "Elahh, samikhni!" *God forgive me.* Welts form on his arms and face. Who knows what anguish must be going on inside of him. The man continues to weep in waves as if some terrible torture device is aggravating him. Brother Moses turns and roars to all of us. His voice contains incredible power—my own body now churns within. A vile red darkness appears before my eyes, hideous angry lightning bolts discharged at my ego with each denunciation from his mouth.

"You will live, all of you, but the time of repentance is now. You who already believe, search your heart for God's purpose in your life. Run to it with all your heart, for an evil is now present that will try to snatch away your joy. You who question or reject the Truth, turn back now. There is no excuse for your selfishness. Soon it will be too late to avoid the eternal excruciation of which this man beside me is experiencing but a prick."

Then the Brother's face and demeanor softens and I can feel warmth again. He reaches down with his hand to the man on the ground and beckons. "Trust in Yeshua, your redeemer and healer."

The man, still trembling as is the earth, slowly and pathetically raises his withered hand to meet that of his accuser's. As they touch, the ground stops shaking and I find myself also able to stand up. The man by Brother Moses straightens and there is no sign of welt or blemish on him whatsoever. He kisses The Brother's hand, grateful tears streaming from his eyes as he gushes, "Shukran, shukran, samikhni, shukran!" *Thank you, thank you, forgive me, thank you!*

Brother Moses is not done. His head suddenly turns toward the body of the man who was shot. He takes the hand of the one he has just healed and instructs, "Come with me."

The healed man reacts warily, but dares not disobey. The two walk across the cracked pavement to the body and for a long time both just stare at the victim. I cannot see The Brother's face from my vantage point, but from behind, I see his shoulders shuddering in great heaves. The man next to him has fallen again to his knees into the pool of blood that has formed around the corpse. I am crying too in great heaves for someone I know not and yet do. Somehow Brother Moses has connected us, for the entire collection of the living in the marketplace is mourning as one.

The Brother kneels as well, bending to kiss the forehead of the stricken. He has now turned a little my way so that I can see his lips moving. His body is rocking forward and back with the same motion I have witnessed of those in prayer at the Western Wall and in synagogues. After a long moment, he reaches over for something hooked in the rider's stiff hands. He patiently pries the fingers from the curiosity and takes it to his chest. Then he sings:

> "Ve-yish me-re-kha. Adonai, ye-va-re-khe-kha.
> Vi-chun-ne-ka e-ley-kha pa-nav Adonai ya'er.
> Sha-lom le-kha ve-ya-sem e-lay-kha pa-nav Adonai.
> Yi-sa Ra-tzon ye-hi ken."

> *May the Lord bless you and protect you.*
> *May the Lord shine and be gracious to you.*
> *May the Lord lift up His face to you and give to you peace.*
> *May it be His will.*

Then The Brother performs the strangest act of all. He turns to the shooter and hands him the package he has been stroking with his hands while pronouncing the benediction. "This is a holy testimonial, written by a new believer, a Hindu scholar who experienced near hell to make his pilgrimage to this city, who wrote his epistle so that all people may understand the power of God's benevolence. Can you read *devanagari*—Hindi script?"

The implicated one, kneeling in the blood of his fatality, fervently nods, but then seems to realize that a lie either way may cost him his life. He hesitates and then shakes his head shamefully.

The Brother smiles gravely. He lays his hand on the brow of the man and says, "Yes, you can."

At that simple statement, a puzzled look crosses the Arab's face. The Brother hands him the pages. The man receives them haltingly, looks to the eyes of the man standing over him and then to the runes before him. Turning the pages one by one, his eyes at first tear then brighten as he progresses to the last page. Here, he starts to read the Hindi script, transliterating publicly, hesitantly, in the universal language of English. He looks astonished, his voice cracking once, but then increasing in volume and confidence as he reads:

> "I know now what I have never known before. A peace I cannot explain, a home where I have never lived, but now know to be the sanctuary where I will dwell until I am called to heaven's gate. This is all I need to write. I have come from the bondage of worldly religious rituals to a place where I am one with a God who loves me so much, He would make Himself known to me (and anyone hungry for relationship with Him). He knows I am not able to love Him enough and so He does the loving, even loving to His death, even loving in Resurrection."

Not only can the shooter construe the strange language, he can speak and understand yet another foreign tongue. After reading, he states with no hesitation, so that the crowd hears clearly, "*Isa, il Tuhan*—Jesus, my Lord!"

I understand the declaration of testimony because of my own gift for tongues, but I do not know if others grasp what has just happened. To my amazement I watch all in the marketplace fall once more to their knees, this time of their own choice. I hear each of them, from all walks, all parts of the world—having come to this holy place for sanctuary—cry out in their own languages:

"Yeshuah, sh'Adonai."
"Gesu, mio signore."
"Jesus, my Lord."

Superseding the incredible fact that each is declaring their conviction, I can understand their utterances. Not just some—all of them! And they can understand one another, heedless of jargon. Delirium breaks out in the marketplace—everyone turns to those standing or kneeling next to them, regardless of nationality or bygone bias. The healthy minister to the injured; attacker bows to their prey; enemies become neighbors. There is conversation and hugging, handshaking and singing—all in unison, each in his or her own tongue. All comprehend that this is their pinnacle moment in life. Because of one man's death, they have been reborn and all in the crowd are jubilant. All but two, that is.

Brother Moses and the Arab stand within the crowd. I watch as they embrace and then kneel one last time. I see Brother Moses take some cloth he has in his pocket and use it to plug the wound in the Hindu's head. The Arab and the Jew then work together to remove the body from the blood pool on the street. The Brother removes his prayer shawl and uses it to wrap the body; the Arab also removes his own *keffiyeh* to join in the purpose. They begin to lift the inert body of the Indian man and lay it carefully over the back of the camel. Others nearby recognize what is happening and also come alongside the camel to assist—each one kissing their hands and transferring the kiss to the body on the animal. Brother Moses takes the reins of the camel and begins to lead it through the marketplace. The other mourners fall in behind, walking in solemn, silent respect for the fallen. Along the way, more and more people gravitate toward what is becoming a funeral procession to some distant location. Soon the din of praise changes—the entire crowd has been moved to silent prayer for their fallen brother whom they have just come to know.

We wind our way through the streets of Jerusalem, once the proudest of jewels on Earth, now known simply as a place of protection—refuge. Its walls, though strongly built, have been bombarded by enemies from outside and within. But the most damage has come from nature itself. Ever-increasing earthquakes and weather storms since the *Hvstr'ed Ytsyah Hmvnyt*, the Hidden Exodus of the First Christ Followers, have taken their toll. Tumbled buildings, blocked streets, gaping fissures and the crumbled walls themselves; all certify these to be the most dire times ever recorded. My description fails to encompass the desolation of the city and its inhabitants.

Our group's progress is frequently hampered; Brother Moses leads us ever up toward the anticipated destination.

Where there is no vision, the people perish.
—Solomon

We arrive from the western side upon the plateau where once stood a simple threshing floor made to separate wheat from chaff. Even before that use, it was understood to have been a special place, perhaps even the most special of places: some believe in ancient times that it was known as "Eden". In another time, at this same place, a great man whom YHWH loved, willingly offered his son as a sacrifice of total deference. YHWH cherished the offer, but instead of allowing the man's bloodline to be spilled to the earth, made a new covenant and designed a substitution by a mysterious plan conceived before the world began.

This location was once purchased and offered by an earthly king as a temple for tribute to YHWH, God of Israel. The son of this king constructed the First Temple and the *Ruach Ha'Kodesh*—the Holy Spirit of God—came to dwell there. Its foundations became an affront, a piece of choice meat dangled in the faces of enemies for generations to come. The walls of the Temple were toppled by the Babylonians, resurrected and then aggrandized as the Second Temple by Herod the Great, finally to be pulled down by the armies of ancient Rome.

Muslims later erected their own temple over the vestiges, alleging it as one of their monuments and the crusade to reclaim it for Israel continued until the Hidden Exodus when a great earthquake swallowed the Muslim structure entirely.

Without delay, the Jewish population surviving the cataclysm began a much more practical reconstruction—modeled after what once had been referred to as Solomon's Temple. The Muslim population of Jerusalem has tried in every way to damage the efforts. But their cause has been impaired since the Hidden Exodus, while the Remnants seemed to thrive amidst the adversity. The rebuilding effort has been overseen by the notorious Brother Moses, who is now leading our way to the summit. We approach the gigantic structure, which is still in the building process and my mind goes back to its planning. Brother Moses has been adamant that the Temple must not only meet the description laid out by the Prophet Ezekiel but that its architecture must be capable enough to defy the throws of the earth which seem to now be ever with us. Apparently The Brother has some additional scientific training that gives him skill to supervise such a task.

Because electric power has vanished, the work is slow and tedious. But Remnants and New Followers are inspired to offer whatever time they can give from their other duties to join in the project. I myself have picked up a hammer, hauled stone and stood watch over the ever-rising Tabernacle.

As we draw near, the New Temple priests come to greet us. There is a unique relationship among the administrants in this place. Brother Moses is widely honored because of his heritage as both Jew and New Follower. Because of the political and spiritual delicacies resulting from the priesthood of Israel being revitalized, neither the rabbis nor the new priests could agree on who was to be superior. So, The Brother and a well-respected priest known only as Eleazar have been given shared authority over the construction and the ever-increasing Temple duties. The remarkable thing about this Chief Priest is his physical features, which suggest he is of Iraqi Chaldean descent.

Although the Temple construction is progressing rapidly, I have noticed one predominant change in the structure. The sacrificial altar for the offerings is being constructed on tracks. For some reason it is movable!

I have wondered at the inclusion of an altar in this Third Temple. Do the priests actually plan to slaughter animals for presentation? Where will they get them? Due to all the havoc, cattle, sheep and goats are difficult to come by. Those who do steward them prize their milk and wool. Even the skins are venerated at death. How would the necessary and numerous burnt offerings mentioned in Leviticus be possible?

"Judaism has maintained prayers for the restoration of sacrifices that figure heavily into their liturgy."

I start a little at the remark, spoken from someone behind me. I turn to see Brother Moses smiling at me. I know him not, but his poise and warmth immediately wash away my surprise and discomfort of his engaging me. *How can he know about my mulling?*

"Even the Mishnah outlines sacrificial procedures to be rehearsed in readiness for the building." The Brother seems more intent on educating rather than explaining his abilities.

"Why is it necessary to reinstitute the sacrifices?" The question spills out of my mouth without an introduction.

"An excellent enquiry, Ilbani!"

H*e knows my name!* I know not whether to be concerned or comforted. For now my mind counsels instead, *Be silent!*

"Daniel 9:27 makes even more of the puzzle," Brother Moses enlightens me. And he quotes it in his rich Hebraic style.

> "'And he shall make a strong covenant with many for one week and for half of the week he shall put an end to sacrifice and offering. And on the wing of abominations shall come one who makes desolate, until the decreed end is poured out on the desolator.'

"If there are to be no sacrifices," Brother Moses asks, "how is the Man of Lawlessness to cease the sacrifices? And if there is no altar, how can he defile it?"

These are astounding questions for me to consider, but no less is the question on my heart: *How does he know my name!* It is a question that I do not ask outside of my own thoughts and so no answer is offered. Instead another voice enters in.

"Are you enlisting yet another *talmid*, Moshe?" the priest Eleazar greets The Brother. Perhaps now I will hear why we have come here.

"The Shalom of Elohim Adonai be with you, my kin," begins The Brother. They embrace in a way that demonstrates a bond beyond what formal duties require and Eleazar looks to the body on the camel.

"It is midafternoon in advent of the great feast of Passover. What would you have us do?" The implication is clear. The preparations for one of the great feasts of the year must be complete before sundown and much is left to do. Eleazar is wondering what the funeral of a man has to do with the Temple duties.

"You know our agreement and this"—The Brother gently touches the wrapped corpse draping the camel's back—"is one of those special ones."

Eleazar's impatience vanishes and he takes immediate action, assuming command and ordering some of the mourners, including Brother Moses, the Arab and me to help him carry the body up the stairway leading to the tabernacle. At the Outer Court entrance, which is still under construction, we halt.

From that moment on, I am restricted as a distant observer, according to the new commandments that govern the Temple. Four other priests appear from the Outer Court and effortlessly replace all who have helped carry the body. The only people allowed to enter with them are Brother Moses and Eleazar. As The Brother enters, he turns to me briefly and pantomimes that he wants me to wait where I am, watching and listening to everything within the holy structure. I think to myself, *Why does he want me, specifically, to stay? What purpose am I to serve?*

I watch as Eleazar directs the priests to lay the body on the table of sacrifice. *Certainly, they are not going to set a match to it!* Other priests bring oil and fresh linens along with jars I recognize as orthodox to the preservation of bodies. Now the team goes to work, rewrapping the body.

The Brother walks over to the newly erected support beams which are in place over the altar to support the yet-to-be constructed Temple roof. He chants an utterance with which New Followers and Remnants are both so familiar.

"Baruk ata Adonai Eloheinu, melekh ha'olam, me mattan pidyon", *Blessed are You Lord God, King of the Universe who gives redemption.*

Then The Brother proceeds with an additional eye-catching step. He had apparently recovered some of the victim's blood in yet another canister.

Climbing methodically through the scaffolding framing the side beams and the cap beam above the altar, the great man dips his fingers into the container and progressively smears the blood onto the two sides and top beam supporting the structure.

Everyone watching draws in a breath, recognizing the act from the Torah scriptures when Moses and the Israelites smeared the blood of innocent lambs around and above their doorframes to acknowledge to God, "Believers live here." The act in that ancient time protected those faithful from the Angel of Death that took the lives of the firstborn Egyptians. That was then, this is now. The new Moses, Brother Moses, unwraps the contemporary motive as one would a special gift or a storybook tale.

"Elohim Adonai, according to Your message through Isaiah: You are still creating and so in this period of tribulation, we ask You to reap the sum of Your martyrs: Jew and Gentile alike; not in death, but as newly alive with You. We see in the text which You revealed to Your prophet John, that the martyrs wait under the altar for Your deliverance to resurrection. So we on this day of Passover commit this martyr by name, Pasha was, to wait with others yet to be supplied. YHWH, we know that the souls to be offered within this tabernacle are not all of those who died for Your sake. The ones here represent an assemblage across time.

"We ask that You protect all of them and that You guard us who survive from the evil of this world. Into Your hands we commit the martyrs and our spirits—to Your purpose. Your will be done. Amen!"

While The Brother had been speaking, the priests had finished preparing the body for burial and now lay it on a wooden plank before the altar table. From cables engineered into the overhanging support beam, ropes are attached to the plank and then the body is carefully hoisted and swung over what I guess to be a compartment underneath the altar. Two priests take hold of other ropes on either side of the altar and slowly lower the body on the plank into the compartment.

It must be an abyssal cavity, for the lowering goes on for at least five minutes. What had Brother Moses said, "others yet to be supplied"? How many will it finally contain? Even from my skewed perspective of the space provided, I can fathom a vast area beneath the altar and the thought of how many martyrs might fill it depresses me.

In the age culminating with the Hidden Exodus, these acts I have described would not have happened in this way. The *tahara*—the bathing and dressing and anointing of the body for burial—has been an ancient, elaborate and sacred act. The *appointed ones* for this holy service would have been considered "unclean" for a period of time after the rites and Jews would have allowed someone who claimed Yeshua as Messiah neither entrance nor authority within the walls of the Temple in order to participate. A new day has come, however, bringing Remnants and New Followers into unity, to new understanding with new habits. There is even a phrase we use to brand the unlikely alliance: We are *Kin*.

I am beginning to understand my role in this ceremony. As a New Believer with knowledge of many languages, I am to be a scribe and translator of this new age in which we live. My small but satisfactory grasp of both Jewish and Gentile customs is somehow strategic to the task. Lord, I am not worthy of this duty, but the beseeching of Brother Moses convicts and compels me to obey. "Your will be done. Amen!"

God is good…His habit is to move in mystery, yet sometimes he permits us to think we see and understand him.

—Lew Wallace, Ben-Hur: A Tale of the Christ

As scribe, I know I should probably elaborate on my credentials. In the beginning of my writings, I mentioned that my title and heritage were no longer of import and it is still so. I hold no theological training or degrees. I have not had great visions sent from the Great I Am for my eyes only. I am prophetic only in what I have observed and do observe around me. But Ha'Shem has called me in this time to give verse to history. If nothing else, I am available to do so in obedience to Him.

I have been most despicable in my life before this time. I am from the country *Turkiyya*, which most had known before the Hidden Exodus as the Republic of Turkey. As a child and into my adult life I traveled with my father, a prominent merchant who traded in all of what was Western Europe, Eurasia and Africa. By this activity I assimilated many languages and learned the nuances of those who used them. I also became an unforgiving dealer in commerce. I was not prone to consider the true need or circumstance of my purchasers; my interest started and ended with the desire to sell for profit. My father taught me well and my accumulated fortune at the expense of others proves it.

As can happen by the Almighty's hand, I was made to see what I would not. It happened when I was negotiating trade in Zimbabwe, an impoverished area of Africa, but one with a population that has always attracted me. Why? It is still a question to me, perhaps because I share their dark-skinned palette; maybe because they are so proud of their freedom, their folklore and their choice of gods. However, one Zimbabwean attracted me most—Jende is her name and, as articulate as I am, I cannot explain how I fell in love with her. I am of Muslim decent; she is Christian. I was obsessed with my merchandising passion; she could only think of giving. I am stocky and unimpressive in my appearance; she is statuesque—tall and classic in beauty with a smile that would melt the ice of Mount Ararat were she to shine her face upon it. But of all the dichotomies between us, it was her attraction to me which puzzled me most.

I wanted so badly to wed her and she encouraged me, with a seemingly trite condition.

"We must first learn of God together," she said to me in her rich accent.

Learn of God? I knew Allah, blessed be his name. He was taught to me from infancy and I prayed my seven prayers daily without fail. But Jende persisted.

"What do you know of God?"

How simple, yet her question was a scalpel to my mores. I knew my laws and my rituals. I knew my obligations and the penalties for disobedience. What more was there to know? To be my bride, she would of course have to convert and there would be no debate.

"Show me Allah's love in Scripture and in the actions of the prophet Muhammad," she encouraged.

Ah, this I could do. I took valuable time that I ordinarily would not spend to research my case. I studied the interpretations of the Quran; I read the annals of the Great Prophet; I sought the wisdom of his imams. And to my utter amazement, the noble cause of godly love for a lesser being was not to be found in any of my inquiries.

"But what of it," I challenged back to her. "I am vaguely familiar with the Torah and tales of your god and know of no love there. Love is not for a god to show people, but for people to show their god."

She just smiled her warmth upon me, kissed my forehead and said, "Let me show you God's love." She read her scriptures to me—scripture I only thought I was familiar with. It spoke of a God who took a people out of bondage and relentlessly demonstrated mercy to them regardless of their ridiculous actions. Jende's God said to His people, "Love me as I love you, with all your heart and all your soul and all your strength."

Then she showed me the writings about the Prophet Isu, whom she spoke of as Jesus.

At first I was impatient, frustrated that this woman had more knowledge of and intimacy with her scriptures than had I. But patiently she encouraged me to read the book of John. She welcomed me to borrow her Bible and explained that she would return when I was prepared to discuss the question of love.

When she left that day, I felt insulted and frustrated, not understanding the gravity of her request. It was the very day that the world witnessed the weapon flung at the approaching singularity in space and that the great earthquake eliminated the magnificent Al-Aqsa Mosque, familiar to most as the Dome of the Rock. It was also the day that many whom I knew to be Christians disappeared from existence. And, of course, it was the last time I witnessed the miracle of electricity.

Even in the derangement over the next days, I was more concerned about Jende than the salvaging of my enterprises. As storms and mayhem increased, I searched feverishly for her to assure she was unharmed.

I found her in a shelter provided by the Zimbabwe government and she smiled at my arrival, though the world was coming apart.

"Do you have the answer?" These were her first words to greet me.

At first I did not understand her question and then realized: she was still waiting for me to read her book. I explained that I had not had the time to begin because of the awful circumstances affecting everyone.

"I will wait for you," she said in kind dismissal. She squeezed my hand, turned and walked away with nothing more said.

As chaotic as the times were with natural disasters and social collapse increasing by the day, I could not escape her question. *Do you have the answer?* Her voice chimed in my head and I became exasperated by her challenge. I should have been maintaining my fortune and positioning my advantage to increase my control. Instead I ignored the deterioration increasing around me each day. My obsession became finding a reply to her. I was determined to discover the flaws in her book. So I read John. I also read Matthew and the Acts of the Apostles. I became intrigued with the behavior and faith of Paul and then I was lured to the strangest book of all, Revelation.

I did not respond to Jende for another month. It was a time in hiding, reading, earnest reflection and, finally, prayer. And as the outside world fell apart, inside my life came together. I realized the true revelation—the love of God that I found in Jesus's teachings and example was the same love I knew to be in Jende's heart and smile. I came to understand that the love I had for her was actually the love I must have first for my God to then be shared with her.

I came to her on my knees, begging her to pray with me as I disowned all other passions besides that for my Lord and Savior, *Isu Masīḥ*—Jesus Messiah.

My next question to her had been festering in my mind the entire time I had been absent from her presence. Where was her family and why had not such a deserving Christian lady as she been raptured with the others who were now, to my understanding, with Isu?

She explained simply, "I was asked to stay."

The implications of her statement were stupefying. There could be only one who would ask such a thing and whom she would obey. She had forfeited the greatest honor—to be with her spiritual family in the presence of her Redeemer—and for what purpose?

She intuitively answered this unspoken question while smiling sadly, "I was to wait for you to confess your Lord."

My mind was reeling and so I asked her, choking back the tears, "What if I hadn't? What if I had refused to recognize the greatest miracle of all: a Savior who died on behalf of my sins and then was brought back to life that we might join his eternal kingdom?"

"But, that didn't happen, did it?"

No, it had not and so I loved her and the God she revealed to me, all the more.

Zimbabwe was ruinous and dismal. Besides the dismal economic and political conditions, a new virus was spreading in the land. It made Ebola look like a child's cough. This new ailment not only spread through the air and lived while the recipient died, it offered a strange scent that attracted every kind of creature to the decimated carcass. The animals and insects that gorged on the rotting flesh were then bagged and eaten by a starving population and any who consumed the poisoned carrion quickly succumbed to the disease and perished. Our country was dying and was not a place where we hoped to survive.

We dedicated ourselves to one another as husband and wife before Elohim Adonai and witnesses; then it became a matter of seeking a safe haven (if one even remained) somewhere in the world. We knew our call from the Creator was to forge a family, even in this most terrible of times and be witnesses to His plan.

After fasting and prayer, we understood our destination without doubt. Jerusalem! This would be no small journey, but with my knowledge of trade routes and with Elohim Adonai's protection, we found our new home. My connections from the previous life and what monies I was able to maintain served us well. We were able to foster a reputable trade business. Within our first year together, Jende gave birth to Jacquez, a noisy, squalling, but hearty boy. And just several days ago, my African queen informed me that I am to be a father yet again!

Why Elohim Adonai has blessed me so. It is a question only He can answer. I am grateful and desire to serve Him in whatever He requires, yet one thing still bewilders me. This morning during our prayers together, before going to the marketplace, I asked Jende's thoughts on the subject. "What is the difference between believers in this time and believers before the Hidden Exodus? Why did they get taken away while we remain?"

My bride took my hands in hers and poured upon me her great gift of wisdom. "I do not know the difference or why He separated the ages. That's why the Church is called one of the mysteries of God. I do know however, what we have in common with those before this Age of Affliction. Everyone, then and now, no matter how intelligent, well-spoken, or suitable, are born with a crippling void within them. They may or may not have actualized it; they may or may not have shared its presence with others. Still it exists as truth and there is one greater way to fill that void and light its darkness. We must help those who remain discover the Light of this world."

Until the events in the marketplace unfolded, I did not know how I would be of value to my Master in revealing His Light. But now, with the help of my wife, a converted rabbi and a martyr's passing, I see full well what I must do. I must be the scribe of these times for my Lord.

A voice cries: "In the wilderness prepare the way of the LORD; make straight in the desert a highway for our God. Every valley shall be lifted up and every mountain and hill be made low; the uneven ground shall become level and the rough places a plain.

And the glory of the LORD shall be revealed and all flesh shall see it together, for the mouth of the LORD has spoken."

A voice says, "Cry!" And I said, "What shall I cry?" All flesh is grass and all its beauty is like the flower of the field. The grass withers, the flower fades when the breath of the LORD blows on it; surely the people are grass.

The grass withers, the flower fades, but the word of our God will stand forever.

—Isaiah 40:3–8

Three days after that extraordinary Passover of triumph and tragedy, we are celebrating *Reshit Katzir*, the Feast of First Fruits. For Remnants, it is a celebration of the first crop from the spring harvest and possibly it was this third day after Passover when the Israelites crossed the Red Sea. For New Believers, it also is the day on which our Savior Yeshua, our First Fruit, passed through the sea of death, emerging victorious from the tomb.

And with the festivities, new miracles: an unsullied and cloudless day, the first since the months leading up to the Hidden Exodus. How sweet is Jerusalem. When contrasted with the reports I have heard from others now arriving daily from all reaches of the nether kingdoms, this place reveals itself as YHWH's sanctuary indeed. They have told me of the floods in some places, stifling heat and drought in others, even icy blizzards combined with volcanic ash, unending topographical upheavals and mayhem. Our hassles here seem trite in comparison, at least for now. Even the terrifying "devil bugs" we have heard about, which etch stings of unending dolor, do not come near us. Praise the One who makes well-being and creates chaos as He chooses. I decide to take advantage of the good conditions, going out to manage several arrangements with fellow merchants. This place is unusual in that way too. People here seem hopeful, willing to interact and conduct commerce, unlike what I have heard happening abroad.

How do I hear these things? By my communications system, of course; this is one of the ways in which I continue to prosper and apportion my prosperity with others. I have become a handler of carrier doves and it has made me a respected prince in the area.

Doves, you ask, not pigeons that in the past have seemed more reliable? A condition has been discovered across the new face of this world. Apparently pigeons have difficulty with the new magnetics that have occurred due to what most believe to have been a shifting of the north and south poles. Adding to that, the demon bugs that patrol the skies seem to have a discriminating dislike for pigeons, attacking them when the birds are in flight. Doves, on the other hand, have mastered the new conditions and appear to have immunity from the bugs' vengeance.

Few have been able to master the training of these wonderful birds. Fewer still can afford the cost of replacing any that are lost due to the harsh climate in the course of flight.

They have become crucial in conveying conditions and in conducting trade between the existing nations. What's more, no other method has yet become reliable. The creatures are incredibly intelligent and mostly able to survive the extremes. They provide an invaluable, if time–consuming, way to share information throughout the provinces.

I have just sent several messages to high-profile contacts in Samaria and am arranging a transfer of goods with a Jew near the Temple Mount. I catch sight of Brother Moses descending toward me from the area of the old pool of Bethsaida when someone behind me shouts his name.

"Moses Folzman, my teacher and brother!"

I turn to identify the caller and above me I hear The Brother holler, "Fitzgerald Elijah Hindeland, my *talmid*—my student! You have arrived!" Once the two names have been spoken,

there is an immediate reaction from the crowd. I hear many inquiring, "Moses? Elijah?" *Could this be the moment?* As a New Follower, I am aware of prophecy from the Revelation of John speaking of two witnesses for God coming to Jerusalem to deliver God's message and be His instruments of wrath. The Hebrew oral tradition suggests the prophets Moses and Elijah as the likely candidates, but these two—a former Jewish rabbi and a disheveled wanderer? It seems unlikely.

The newly arrived is an elderly but spry man with a bald head and white flowing beard that, in its growth describing a long passage of time to match his travels. The look in his eye suggests great acumen and a spirit that is not to be trifled with. And there is most definitely a physical connection between this one and Brother Moses. "Preacher," as I hear him being called by those who have arrived with him, sports a goatskin coat, similar to the Brother! His caravan looks haggard indeed; their bearded leader begins to detail their amazing journey for the benefit of Brother Moses and the rest of us.

"I am sorry for the delay in coming and for not arriving in time to share Passover—pardon my English—Pesach with you. The distance from Texas to here was made even greater by the bedlam along the way." The man spoke with a whimsical smile. Texas? He has journeyed from the former United States? What stories he must have! "Beginning seven long months ago, I gathered a congregation of seventy-two, more if you count those in the American South where we encouraged thousands to follow the Way. Some of those, I'm sure, will be coming this direction as well, but logistics, enemies and the bizarre physical world which we now combat are taking their toll. Amazingly, others bravely volunteered to permanently remain on the American mainland—now a desolate wasteland—serving as missionaries to the lost. They continue to encourage new relationships with Jesus, helping those saved to find some way of making transit to New Israel. We have lost twenty along the way. They were worthy Seconds— that is what we now call ourselves. Seconds are New Followers who have accepted Jesus as their Savior and are preparing for his second coming."

Here Preacher Elijah becomes hoarse with the emotion of someone who has lost loved ones to tragedy.

"Their bodies we could not leave behind. We have carried them across landmasses and an ocean. The steamship captain we hired was circumspect to bring them aboard, thinking them a bad omen. Fortunately, the superstitious can be bought and we set sail on a ship called the *Valiant*.

"Still, we were almost banished from our craft during the most violent cyclone I have ever experienced. It was God alone that prevented our demise. I was inspired to point out to the crew of the ship that under any other circumstances, their frail vessel would have already capsized and that perhaps it was specifically the prayers and the presence of us believers that were supporting the ship. We even suggested that if they were to pray with us to the One True God, He might still the waters. They became ecstatic in their assistance and true to His word, the storm abated with our kneeling to Him. That day, not only were all of us saved from certain physical death—a compliment of credible seamen became believers!"

The story was so compelling, so desirable to hear, that most in the outer court area of the Temple area, merchants—townspeople and itinerants alike—sat down to listen. Preacher Elijah's rhetoric was strong and repercussed throughout the square. Even the Temple construction workers ceased their hammering to take in the events.

"The *Valiant* was heavily battered, but survived to dock at Tangier for repairs and to barter for available sustenance. You cannot imagine the hunger and deprivation outside these walls. We had to deputize a constant guard for the ship. It was meager, yet the idea that it moved by steam and might transport others away made it sport for invasion. In fact, other ships had been hijacked or sacked for any precious articles. We learned of a larger freighter known as *Destiny* that had been bringing another group to Jerusalem. It had been badly damaged, its sailors and passengers marooned in Gibraltar. I searched for the stranded ones and found most working as laborers for a local leather craftsman. To my amazement, I knew many of them—some had been prominent members of the former United States government. But one I embraced as an old and trusted friend. If not by name, you will recognize him by his divested forte—the last President of the United States."

At that moment a man steps from behind Preacher Elijah and the crowd abruptly hushes. It is President Blueroad! He looks very gaunt and his dark flowing hair is more silvered in comparison to my old television memories. He still carries himself with the quiet dignity that brought him international acclaim. Beside him stands a familiar-looking younger woman—by her appearance, also of Native American background.

"Let me introduce you to Gregory Blueroad and his daughter, Ayita," says Preacher Elijah. "I have the pleasure of sharing with you their commitment to Jesus the Messiah—*Yeshua Ha'Mashiach!*"

At this proclamation there is cheering mixed with grumbling. There are many in Jerusalem who are New Followers, but also as many devout Remnants and Muslims who still will not yield to Jesus as Messiah. I am amazed that they all close their eyes at the referencing of the prophecy. The Hidden Exodus, which some call the Gathering-Up, was fulfilled three years ago during the New Year Festival of Rosh Hashanah or Yom Teruah, "the Day of Blowing". Regardless of belief or persuasion, the crowd is mesmerized by the storyteller's skill and by the notoriety of the new arrivals.

"Our ship's company and those from *Destiny* were able to mate equipment and parts from both ships," Preacher Elijah continues, "recommissioning the larger hulk and naming it *The Unity*. It was this boat that steamed us to Jaffa Port and from there we made our way up to you, oh Jerusalem our mother!"

At the mention of this respected label for the ancient city, all in the square uplift their voices again in a cheer. No one here denies the power of the place. Brother Moses takes advantage of his friend's arrival and quickly organizes another procession, this time away from the Temple, south past the old City of David and then west toward the area of the pool of Solomon to what had once been called the Essene Quarter. As we march, the Brother surprises me again by taking me quickly into his confidence, putting his immense right arm about my shoulders and pulling me toward him in a warm gesture.

"Have you been keeping records of these things?" he asks.

I nod and begin to explain what I have scribed so far, but he politely interrupts my description, continuing my apprenticeship. "I trust the Spirit is inspiring you, it is ordained that He be your guide. From now on stay close to this group that is forming. You must move your wife and child from your current dwelling and come to where I am about to show you."

There is so much meat to chew in what I have just been fed! How does Brother Moses know of my family and of our lodging? What new place is it that he would supply and how would this affect my merchantry? What is the purpose of keeping close with these people who are obviously much more prominent than I? At that moment The Brother also pulls in Preacher Elijah with his other arm and introduces us.

"Fitzgerald, you must watch after this one. He is our 'Luke'."

As Brother Moses says this, there is yet another disturbance ahead of us. Soldiers bearing uniforms from the government house known as Beit Aghion seem to come from every juncture, quickly and effectively surrounding us. Wisely, The Brother forewarns our column of followers to not provoke the authorities.

Other than blocking our way, there appears to be no ill intent and then suddenly, a path opens up before us. A man attired in an immaculate blue pinstriped suit comes through the break and reaches his right hand out, exclaiming, "Moses Folzman, Fiz Hindeland and, oh my word, Mr. President—what an opportunity it is to have you all in one place!"

"—And what an interesting moment in time for you to be here, Darius," Brother Moses replies. "*B'rachot v'Shalom—blessings and peace* be to everyone in this place."

His incantation almost sounds more like a warning than a pronouncement. It takes me a moment to realize who it is that has just greeted us, but The Brother has helped by uttering his first name. It is none other than Darius Mede, Premier of the Green Order Government. His reputation is that of a man with single-minded purpose. Prone to self-promotion, he took it upon himself to improve his own title. The Chairman begat himself "the Premier", after the Hidden Exodus left him as heir apparent to the peoples remaining in the world.

To have these powerful and influential thinkers all gathered here tells of a ticklish spiritual moment in the works. And I am somehow to relate these events framing them in YHWH's spiritual context? Lord, I pray for Your eyes and ears to be my eyes and ears that I may rightly emulate You in all that will happen.

> *For the enemy to be recognized and feared,*
> *he has to be in your home or on your doorstep.*
>
> —*Umberto Eco, The Prague Cemetery*

"I am so glad to have found you three. We have so much to catch up on. You must be my guests for dinner tonight at Beit Aghion."

The question of what the preeminent political figure in the world is doing in New Israel and why he would want to meet with these people at the Israeli prime minister's manor races through my mind. Darius Mede seems to have known the exact whereabouts of our group and the prominent intellects within its procession. It has always been said "Jerusalem has eyes within every wall," but why make this extreme effort to meet? I hope that someone will make sense of this conversation for me and Preacher Elijah does not disappoint.

"Your offer is kind, Darius. By the way, does your presence here have something to do with the meeting at the Knesset tomorrow regarding world order?"

"That and more. I know that you and I have not always seen eye to eye," Darius Mede says, "but we have always tried to find ways to work together to solve the difficult problems. It seems that providence calls us to join efforts once again."

Providence? I do not grasp his meaning. It seems to suggest luck and chance rather than transcendental interaction. The statement is not lost on my three confidants either and this time Brother Moses replies.

"Darius, we will pray about your kind offer. Of course, if Yahweh is in favor, we will participate in the discussions. Would there be anything else you'd like to discuss before we continue on our way?" The polite but abrupt tact of this man tells much of his character. There is little subtlety or guile in his action. Mede seems taken aback by the effrontery, but quickly recovers with a smiling counter.

"If you will excuse me, there is much I must do in preparation for our banquet. I'll have credentials waiting for your arrival." Darius Mede turns without further discussion and walks back the way he entered. With him, the small army withdraws and we are left to our foregoing course.

Preacher Elijah leans into Brother Moses and says, "He is ready to make his move, we need to prepare."

Brother Moses nods and motions for me to walk beside them. As we go, The Brother and Preacher Elijah banter, sharing stories and episodes in their lives that include laughter and remorse. At one point, after describing the conditions at a place in South South named after Ein Gedi here in Israel, Preacher Elijah confides to his friend, "As incredible as the time was, in a way, I'm glad to have gotten away from the smell of people and animals living in such tight quarters."

"Then maybe you will want to turn and run back, for you will not find the aroma here any better!" retorts Brother Moses.

The jovial interplay of the two men speaks to their rich humanity and joy for life. I find The Brother's arm pulling me close and I too catch the spirit of the moment. We are joined into an affinity that I've not experienced with anyone but You and Jende, Lord. What is it that You are preparing us for?

We round a corner and before us is the old Essene gate the ancient quarter beyond. The Brother says to me, "I will show you your new dwelling. You then immediately go gather your family and have them bring only the essentials. The rest will be provided."

The question must show on my face, for he answers without pause. "It will be safer for you here."

What a day it has been. First I was introduced to Preacher Elijah, then to Darius Mede. Next, I was instructed to bring my relations and possessions to the Old Essene Quarter with the suggestion that our lives might be in peril. This very same evening, I accompanied Brother Moses, Preacher Elijah and President Blueroad to Beit Aghion. There we broke bread with the elite leadership of this region and even of the world. The food was sumptuous and dessert even included particular favorites of mine, Bedouin coffee, macaroons and even dates. How the delicacies we were offered continue to be cultivated, I cannot fathom. During the meal, I heard the incredible news that the Prime Minister of Israel has abdicated all authority to Darius Mede and that Mede committed all funds and resources necessary to complete the Temple project in grand scale. Additionally, Mede heralded that he had negotiated with the countries surrounding New Israel a way to corral more land for the tiny state without warfare.

Not that the land is worth much under the circumstances—to the contrary, the surrounding territories have become a wasteland. Even so, I cannot in my wildest imagination conceive of how he was able to gain and offer these concessions. It will reshape and affect the entire region.

Mede added one caveat—more of a statement actually. He gloated that the newly combined territory would be known as Philistia, over which he has declared himself Supreme Magistrate. This is odd to me since, as the Premier of the Green Order Government, it would seem he had already assumed this authority.

Whether the new territory name or the expanded title and authority actually changed anything, mattered not. We were inside this man's domain. Brother Moses carefully chose his words indicating that as long as the Philistian effort did not inhibit the worship of YHWH, the name used to flag the realm was inconsequential. Mede visibly winced at the reply, but did not react otherwise.

During the meeting, I heard the New Followers and Remnants, represented by Brother Moses and Eleazar the priest, state their hopefulness that God will assist us in reclaiming the land. No one doubts their impartation. The cooperative agricultural efforts have been laudable, allowing all to benefit. Food and staples such as salt and fresh water are available to all.

Amazing, is it not, that the mountains of Samaria, under such terrible times and unstable conditions, are bearing rich harvests of grapes? The Jezreel and Jordan Valleys are also producing every sort of great crop. New Israel blossoms—even corn seed imported from the Americas is now becoming a cash crop; all of this a result of incredible brinksmanship between Philisti "Seculars", Muslims, Remnants and New Followers. God is working in the land and, according to Preacher Elijah; an unusual medley of weather conditions is protecting us from most of the catastrophes experienced by the rest of the world.

As I praise the One who allows these blessings, another large seismic tremor rocks us, punctuating the fact that YHWH is the God of reminders.

He reminds us now to quickly move to a nearby archway for protection. Fortunately, it is a short event that harms none.

"The heavens will reveal his iniquity and the earth will rise up against him." Brother Moses quotes the words of Elohim Adonai from the book of Job after the shaking stops and we continue toward the Essene Quarter.

It is befitting to mention that, in the preceding age, Israeli Prime Ministers had no ruling power, nor the authority to bequeath it to another as has just been done. In these difficult times, special sanctions have been granted to that office by the people, both over the government and the rabbinical council to make judgments and decisions to protect the country. The fact that such great control would be so quickly given up, even if it was to the most influential man of this age, speaks to the acuteness of the situation. The irony is not lost on us. The nation of New Israel has just tripled in size. As well; her enemies, at least for the moment, have become her supporters.

We must dare to think "unthinkable" thoughts. We must learn to explore all the options and possibilities that confront us in a complex and rapidly changing world. We must learn to welcome and not fear the voices of dissent. We must dare to think about "unthinkable things" because when things become unthinkable, thinking stops and action becomes mindless

— James William Fulbright, The Arrogance of Power

I have never been one to reason exceedingly, but now a discussion between Brother Moses and Eleazar is causing a great question to well up in my soul. We are all in a secluded location, having just finished a discussion about the events of the night. A question of how and when the Messiah might return has been posed.

"Return?" I can see Eleazar's smile from across the room and know that he is thirsty for *mishna*, the ancient art of debate among those seeking God's truth. I am curious, having heard great stories about this passionate method of seeking solidarity and suddenly find myself yearning for the learning experience. "Are you suggesting two separate reigns of Messiah?"

"Eleazar, there is but one Kingdom. Your question is a distraction to the real issue: What is so difficult about the idea of Yeshua as Messiah? Does he not fulfill all of the prophecies?" Brother Moses may not call himself a rabbi any longer, but he questions as one.

The Chief Priest does not back away from the argument. "I recognize that Yeshua was a profound prophet and teacher. He assuredly had messianic qualities, but you know well what causes rabbinical Jews to consider him illegitimate."

Even I am tempted to respond to Eleazar's commentary. It has been the ongoing contention between the Jews and believers in Yeshua since those days long ago when he walked the earth. But The Brother, possessing such unconventional qualifications, explains the dilemma better than anyone I have ever heard.

"Eleazar, you are a great man of the Spirit, yet you try to persuade others of a Messiah who is just a man of human heritage without eternal spiritual qualities? You would adopt the pharisaical mentality that Messiah is the *Conquering King* exclusively, as referenced in Amos 9 and Isaiah 61? What about his role as the Suffering Servant of Psalm 22 and Isaiah 53? Would you accept one prophecy and ignore another? Of course he is King; of course hs is the forsaken one who would combine his kingship with divine atonement for our rebelliousness.

"Would you ignore Isaiah 9:6 and Isaiah 42? Would you do away with one scripture to limit Yahweh rather than worship the awesome gift He has already provided—His sanctioned sacrifice in place of ours so that He may return in glory to unite with His people? Show me your scripture which is so great that it supersedes all other words from the very mouth of God!"

Eleazar smiles and nods while speaking. "I can give you many. But all can be wrapped into one: Deuteronomy 6.

"*Shemah—Hear O Israel, the Lord Your God is One—Echad.*

"Not three gods—One. Love Him."

Moses offers a warm smile as he replies, "A difficult concept for we mere humans to comprehend is the idea that God who is One can somehow be Three. Yet the Living God of the Hebrews and that of Christ followers is easily explained as One and Three, just as I can easily explain to you that I hear, see and feel things that all combine to make my perception of life, components united to make one entity."

And then as almost an afterthought, The Brother adds, "Why, you even said it yourself, Eleazar. There are many scriptures that Yahweh has given us all pointing to Echad. He himself demonstrates multiple characteristics, all One, yet each divergent throughout the Bible. Why cannot you see Him in each?"

"For the same reason I cannot see two appearances of the Messiah." Eleazar has taken us on a new rabbit trail.

Moses sighs and shakes his head slowly back and forth while he responds. "Whether Messiah's appearance will be a First Coming, a Second Coming, or a Third Coming, it is still a Coming. And of that coming Kingdom, Jesus was passionate! His passion was God's passion for His people and for His Earth. What are you passionate about, Eleazar? Tell me what your Messiah will be passionate about?"

I know these men to be trusted friends, but this place is not so friendly. The priest does not answer for a long while. Is he holding back his reply? Has he ever considered the question before him? It is unclear; his facial aspect and his posture betray nothing of his inner thoughts.

"As has been our pattern, I am afraid we will have to continue to agree to disagree," Eleazar finally states, choosing not to respond to the last posit.

"We will do no such thing!" Brother Moses is out of his chair and amazingly now kneels at the feet of the priest. "Two cannot walk together unless they are in agreement," he quotes from the prophet Amos. "Especially now, of all the time of times, we must sharpen iron with one another. Yahweh seeks unity…Echad…with His chosen, not confusion."

Finally, passion breaks free in Eleazar as he looks down at the man before him. There are tears in the eyes of both men. The priest nods his head and barely breathes, "Each of our peoples are about to face great persecution—we must find His strength in facing it together: Wise counsel, my brother; wise and difficult indeed."

"He has pulled together his alliances—there is no stopping Darius Mede now," says Brother Moses as we continue in the late evening back toward the Essene Quarter. "Why would he want to forecast his scheme so flagrantly? Surely Mede didn't glean we would cheer on his tyranny?"

"Have you looked up to the stars?" Preacher Elijah has his eyes to the heavens, squinting through one of his various filter lenses and seemingly oblivious to The Brother's question. It is a strange condition for a man who is typically lasered on the issues at hand. Now he gazes dreamily at the heavens as we walk and I become concerned he might trip and stumble or, as likely, by some spiritual means, start floating toward the cosmos he now admires.

"What? The stars you say? *Yeled*, you know I am the microphysicist. It is you who surpasses my knowledge of the cosmos. What is it you see other than the blue darkness caused by V4641?"

Had I heard correctly? Did Brother Moses just call his friend "child?" I would ask, but I want to hear Preacher Elijah's answer to The Brother's question.

"The other night, at Passover, was a blood-red moon—caused by a lunar eclipse. By my calculations, there will be three other such eclipses this year. And it appears that Jupiter is nearing a triple conjunction with Regulus and Venus. Do you know the last times such an escapade of events occurred?"

"There have been several, but most significantly during the time of the birth of Yeshua and also in the year of the Gathering-Up," replies Brother Moses immediately.

Preacher Elijah laughs out loud. "I thought you had not been listening when I first brought those instances to your attention."

"I even recall you footnoting that there were blood red moons in the year of Israel's independence in 1948 and also during the Six-Day Passover War of 1967," The Brother admits. "Do not be fooled by my seeming lack of interest in such interstellar manifestations. It is just that we have both learned, by our experience with Danny Adamson, that they are warnings of something to come, not results in and of themselves. When I hear of such things, I consider them signs and wonders pointing my attention to a greater purpose. We are in the middle of the New Advent."

Danny Adamson? The notorious physicist who predicted our current circumstances and then disappeared along with a third of Earth's population on the day of the Hidden Exodus? It would not surprise me if these two have some kind of relationship with that famous modern-day prophet.

Brother Moses now also peers up to the sky and then turns once more to question Preacher Elijah. "I understand why you are so fixed on the heavens. I have missed their beauty as well. Thanks be to Elohim Adonai for the great blessing of parting the clouds at least temporarily.

"And speaking of our new singularity neighbor, it seems to be smaller than I remember, at least by physical measurements."

Again Preacher Elijah laughs. "You truly are paying attention. Yes, another change is in the making. The time has come for the Watchmen to pray about revealing the new gifts God has given to us."

"The Watchmen?" Incredibly, the voice inquiring is my own. So many questions derived from their conversation resonated in my brain and somehow one has escaped through my lips. I am about to apologize for my impudence when both men turn and stare at me, each smiling brightly.

"Forgive us, Ilbani," Brother Moses says, again drawing me in with his arm. "You are right to be curious and indeed that is one of the gifts God has wired within you that we require. Please do not hesitate to ask anything of us. Then, scribe it with passion! You will authenticate one of the greatest moments in history and you must be fully aware of the physical and spiritual circumstances."

Under the wing of his confidence, I feel both a great honor and a large weight instantly upon my shoulders. The Brother then bids Fitzgerald Elijah, "*Talmiyd*, please explain about the Watchmen."

The physicist also sidles up to us and begins. "Watchmen, or *Tsâphâh*, have been used scripturally to depict those looking to the horizon in expectation of Godly action and also to warn of events great or evil approaching. These same lookouts, just like those in ancient times who stood watch over the gates of the protected cities, are now charged with guarding the treasures of the land, including its most sacred—the text itself. The duty falls on them to peer into the condition of the people of the land, alerting them as they veer off the path prescribed by their Creator.

"Another name you may recognize for these guardians is *Nâbîy'* or 'prophets'." Here he gestures to Brother Moses, "My teacher and I believe in the depths of our hearts that we have been given a duty from *El Shaddai*— God of mighty blessings. We have been called to be *Tsâphâh*."

"As I remember, the prophets of old were severely persecuted and even stoned to death for passing on Elohim Adonai's message." Why I am compelled to explain this to these two men, I cannot say for sure. I believe it is out of keen concern for their well-being.

"Bless you for your reminder," Preacher Elijah replies with a sad smile.

"It's time for the new offerings." It was Brother Moses who greeted me, in response to incessant knocking, when I opened my door the morning after First Fruits. His concerns for our next endeavor caused me to shudder.

The task had already been explained by Preacher Elijah. He revealed that there had been lives lost—twelve of the seventy-two had succumbed to various attacks by vigilantes and natural causes on their long journey. Four of these had been sent into a town to try to haggle for food. When it was learned the visitors were New Followers of Yeshua, the townspeople beheaded them and hung the bodies on dead trees outside their protective gates. The heads of all the victims were put in a burlap bag and buried beneath the trees.

Preacher Elijah explained that there was now great fear and irrationality in the world. Most were of the opinion that those who believed in the messianic promises actually caused the problems now plaguing the world. Preacher Elijah's group had had to salvage the bodies and heads under cover of night to avoid risk of the same fate.

With great effort, the bodies of all twelve martyrs were carried here and are now ready for rites. Preacher Elijah, Brother Moses and Eleazar all came to agreement that these were to receive the same honor as our departed brother Pasha and would be enshrined beneath the altar of the New Temple.

We have ported the bodies of the martyrs south from the Essene Quarter and are proceeding up the hill of the newly reconstructed and much broader David Street. We near the outer court of the Temple when another group of soldier police come out from seemingly nowhere and impede our progress. Darius Mede is not with this unit. Instead a very tall official, costumed in a ridiculously formal red robe bearing the Green Order Government insignia—*GOG*—walks to the front of the hindrance, pulls out a scroll and begins to read in very formal tones.

"By the authority granted to me by Darius Mede, Supreme Magistrate of Philistia, I respectfully order you to cease your intended action. The codes of the land strictly prohibit the burial of bodies of humans or animals near any urban areas. According to Healthcare Edict 277, all remains must be cremated at an approved facility under the supervision of..."

I watch as the man's droning is replaced by several burps, then a long belch and now by hiccups. The official himself and the troops behind him are all hiccupping. As this continues, the air becomes fouled with an odor more putrid than I have ever smelled before. It reeks of rotted matter and over-ripened feces. I manage not to puke, but see that very act elicited in all of troops and the official simultaneously. Frenzy breaks their ranks, some running to somehow escape this infernal torture, others seeking grates on the side of the road into which they continue to expel their rejectamenta.

The way before us is clear. Brother Moses, handkerchief to his mouth, gives a look to Preacher, who shrugs his shoulders. There is a glimmer of a smile on the physicist's face. The Brother motions for me and the others pushing the wagons containing the bodies to press on and he leads us the remainder of the way to the Temple gate.

The ceremony and burial of the Seconds were moving indeed and instead of impelling our spirits downward, the action seemed to uplift the whole city. Darius Mede dared not take punitive action as even the Muslims and Philisti Seculars—those with no religious convictions of any sort—reacted. The scandal had been spread of how the political authorities had attempted to interfere and how, miraculously, Brother Moses and Preacher Elijah had passed through their midst. The two were now seen by the populace as true holy men. It was obvious that YHWH was with them and they were not to be trifled with.

Now I am led by the two prophets to yet another unidentified meeting spot. Their reasoning is sound. Darius Mede and his inductees may at any time decide to impose sanctions on the faith-based natives—it is not necessary to give them an easy location in which to observe our activity. But even Brother Moses and Preacher Elijah seem surprised when we enter the location to find another large group that has recently arrived from the former United States. In tow, they have a number of pull-carts like those common to the members of Preacher Elijah's clan. And indeed there is immediate recognition between them all.

"Preacher!" a voice calls out. "Ah thought you was dead!" I was about to ask what language this man was speaking when Preacher cackles an introduction.

"Jason Billards, I am not yet in the ground and seeing you here makes me more alive! Child, when did you arrive? Where is Buckshot Betty?"

At this query, the younger man becomes downcast. He ambles up to Preacher Elijah, wraps his muscular arms about his bearded elder and whispers into his ear. I am close enough to hear a smattering of his tragedy but have difficulty translating Jason's strange accent. What I do understand is that this new group had undergone spiritual and physical attack and that a nemesis named Trimble executed the young man's wife. I also hear of physical and spiritual healings along with conversions; even many of the very people who had attacked this group were led to belief.

The two men hold each other a long time between moments of subdued prayer and tears. Others of Jason's group are also anxious to join the moment and Preacher Elijah's attention is ultimately drawn to a young redheaded woman, who, the whole time, has been trying to keep herself toward the back of the new clan. "Roxanne?" calls out Elijah.

Jason quickly begins a confidential discussion with the older man while the woman of interest, lavishly adorned with tattoos, seems to want to find an exit. The others in her party try to reassure her, but this makes her all the more anxious for escape.

"You have nothing to fear," Preacher Elijah again calls out as he walks to her. "Jason explained everything," he says, "and I am honored to call you my sister in the faith."

I cannot adequately describe the look of confusion mixed with relief that comes to her face, but the arms of Preacher Elijah pulling her into an embrace are too much for her to resist. She weeps in his arms while a black woman, who cradles a child in her arms, begins a song of praise. It is familiar and promptly picked up by all:

*I will praise You in the storm, I will lift my hands, because of who
You are, no matter where I am. Every tear I cry out, falls into Your
hands and though my heart is torn,
I will praise You in the storm.*

Too soon it seems, Preacher Elijah calls for us to discuss events yet to come, things that must be done, new tragedies and triumphs to prepare for.

It is *Shabbat*—Sabbath, the day of rest. Most Remnants in the city observe the command strictly. New Followers have taken a different approach, citing Ezekiel's teachings and Jesus's words to heart; the Sabbath is intended for man and should be desired, not legalized. Regardless of the debate, today appears one of rest for all. Even Brother Moses has taken leave from his habit of offering a lesson and has deferred to Preacher Elijah, who is helping us through sections of Ezekiel, especially the difficult visions offered at the beginning of the book. Our small house is packed with Seconds and some Remnants who are curious about this man's understanding of Scripture. He does not disappoint, his style being much like that of his rabbinic teacher, who sits, smiling and nodding approval, beside him.

Preacher has read the text mentioning the unusual apparitions, their bizarre appearance and their method of transportation. In the Hebraic way, instead of telling us the meaning, he asks us for our thoughts. "Are these hallucinations? Were the creatures true to form? Why do we not see such things in our time?"

The room buzzes with speculation and as with any dialogue of this type, many opinions are presented. Preacher Elijah is in no hurry to stop the intercourse and waits until everyone has had a chance to speak before he responds. "Great detail is offered by the priest Ezekiel. This is a man who, because of his training and upbringing, would not offer lightly such a radical account. The danger of that time was the same as it is today— making a god out of something ungodly.

I cannot believe that such a man of Yahweh—"

—Everyone in the room responds, "May His name be blessed."

Preacher Elijah smiles and continues, "—That such a man would embellish or reconstruct what he witnessed as reality. Would the vision be wild to him? Of course. Would the listeners in his day be any less skeptical? Perhaps more so! But there are commonalities between Ezekiel's time and ours that should not be ignored. By this astounding celestial appearance, God is demanding our attention. As we now look to the sky and see Him at work, so did they. And above it all, even above the vastness of space and time, the Voice of light and truth speaks. Speaks to whom? To us! Is that not more incredible than winged beings and flaming wheels? Why would the Maker of all things be concerned with a molecule such as me? Why would He want my response?"

I can hear individuals breathing in the room. No one has the answer. The man before us kneels and prays silently, allowing all of us to wrestle with the enormity of God's ways. Then Preacher Elijah offers an additional story.

"Two dear friends of mine, one a martyr, the other a gathered-one, shared a vision as eye-popping as Ezekiel's. They were able to track God's motion in the universe and discovered how the Almighty had designed certain physical particles to spark life, as we know it, into being. Though both had brilliant scientific minds, it was their faith that they sought to strengthen, not their brains. They became so…trusting of and intimate with, their Lord that both men began to emit a visible blue aura. Does that not sound as berserk as, say, a singularity transporting from one part of the galaxy to another? My friends thought it crazy, but they also recognized its source. They did not argue the absurdity, but chose to obey it."

No typical verbal exchange rises from our ranks. I am humbled into awed silence by the seeds being sown into my mind. And then with one question, Preacher Elijah pours life-giving water on his plantings. "So if this God of light and magnificent manifestations was to speak to me… and to you…were He to cause craziness in our lives to get our attention, to encourage a response…what would we…what *will* we do: doubt and reason away His presence, or accept completely His overwhelming power, abandoning all other gods and beliefs, to obey only Him?"

The weather cooperates for another seven weeks and then there arrives a reminder of the Creator's power. It is *Shavuot*—the day of Pentecost—when the ancient Israelites would celebrate the full harvest and when the *Ruach Ha'Kodesh*—the Holy Spirit—would indwell the New Followers of Messiah Jesus after his ascension. But today would not see those events celebrated.

From the great desert regions of the southeast came another sandstorm of blinding fury. Its ferocity caused everyone to bound for whatever scant fortification was nearby or perish in the ninety-kilometer-per-hour winds. Concurrently, a highly volatile front from the west came across the Mediterranean Sea, lifting unprecedented amounts of contaminated water containing red algae into the face of the sandstorm. The result of the meteorological collision was a mud hurricane that stalled directly over New Israel. Its finale had leveled the older, less stable buildings that endured slighter calamities.

After the squall has passed, Jerusalem and the whole territory finds itself entombed in great layers of muck—ochre in color, it reminds one of dried blood. I learn from heartier folk, who had found ways to navigate the sickly soup, that the crop fields of blessings I had so complimented are now in tatters. I am comforted only in knowing that, thankfully, forward-thinking overseers have filled local storehouses with grain, water and other perishables. But now we discover the root of Darius Mede's intent.

The wicked weather has kept most of Jerusalem's inhabitants from moving about the city until this day when the wind has subsided. I still have not ventured out, choosing instead to remain in our new apartment, working on my writings, appreciating precious time with my son Jacquez and Jende, who is nearing her term.

I hear familiar chitchat approaching from the outside and know that Brother Moses and Preacher Elijah are coming to pay a visit. I open the door before they even knock and cannot believe what is before me. The two prophets are so caked in red mud that they are barely recognizable. I am reminded of pictures I have seen of aborigines who purposely coat their skin in such stuff as protection from insects and as a sign of status. The men before me wear tired faces and do not apologize for their appearance. The Brother gets right to the point, as is his normal vein.

"Mede is delaying all delivery of food and replenishments to the city. We have been summoned to his quarters to discuss an arrangement of payment in trade for keeping what we worked so hard to procure."

Payment from those who had done the physical work to gather and harvest in the first place? Preacher Elijah suggested that Mede was using the circumstances in order to substantiate power. I could not argue and saw that the two of them expected me to join them to meet with the executive.

I have a thought and look over the shoulders of these two great men. They seem to understand the question in my observations and it is Brother Moses who responds. "Eleazar, as a co-administrator of our co-op, has decided it best not to join us. He has given us full authority to represent the interests of the Remnants on his behalf."

After kisses to my family, I insert another pen with extra writing paper into my traveling pack and follow my guides out the door, headed for Beit Aghion.

"Look, O Lord, for I am in distress; my stomach churns; my heart is wrung within me, because I have been very rebellious. In the street the sword bereaves; in the house it is like death.

"They heard my groaning, yet there is no one to comfort me. All my enemies have heard of my trouble; they are glad that you have done it. You have brought the day you announced; now let them be as I am.

"Let all their evildoing come before you and deal with them as you have dealt with me because of all my transgressions; for my groans are many and my heart is faint."

(Lamentations 1:20–22)

I am reminded again, where God is concerned, to expect the unexpected. A half-hour to forty-five-minute walk to the Prime Minister's manor takes us half the day to ply. Whole streets are sheathed in mud; the most familiar landmarks appear more like features described in some apocalyptic science fiction novel. We are delayed even more when we learn from a rescue squad that in one nearby street, people have been completely mummified in their homes.

Wading to the assist, what we encounter when we arrive at the collapse is dismal and surreal: mothers, holding crying babies, call out the names of other children who never answer. A husband speaks to a hand that sticks up at an odd angle out of the sludge. He must recognize the appendage as his wife's by the ring on the third finger. Instead of uncovering her body, he just keeps apologizing for not being with her, stroking the fingers, occasionally calling her name and humming a soft wistful melody.

There are many, many more, with few victories to be had in the slow-motion work as we espy body after body, literally digging with our bare hands, probing the mire and debris for any hint of life. We ruefully exhume them, knowing they will be reinterred in some generic grave by ultimatum of the Green Order Government.

Many who have survived stand in disheartened silence. Their homes, their families destroyed—no amount of encouragement or assistance moves them: Their bodies live, but within they have died.

In spite of the curses, blessings result. Sixteen are rescued with only minor injuries. Many more, however, suffocated in the tombs borne by nature's wrath and will never be excavated. By the time we help exhume the bodies and traverse the remainder of the way to Beit Aghion, the dim light that suggests sunset is evident in the western sky.

There is a further delay in meeting with Darius Mede because of our condition. We are living statues of clay and grime. I am actually concerned that if I do not keep moving, I might dry in the place I am standing and become a proverbial statement of architecture.

Mede is hospitable, offering us outlying rooms in which to bathe away the crust. Fresh clothing and food are also made available so that, when we meet with the leader, we all at least look the part of responsible dignitaries rather than filth-laden street vagrants.

"I'm so sorry to hear about your complications in getting here and I appreciate your wanting to meet in order to bargain the needs of the people."

Our complications? Bargain? I cannot rid the image from my mind's eye—the sunken stares of those who survived the mud avalanche. What will they now do?

Brother Moses bristles at Darius Mede's platitude and reciprocates. "Think not of our comfort, Darius. Your hospitality in lending us clean clothes is courteous, but all of our effort should now be convened on those left destitute from the recent storm. Of course, you will want especially to reach out to the families of those who perished."

"So many." Mede shakes his head mournfully. "I wish there was time to console them. Perhaps between us we can at least determine how much of the stored food and supplies should be allocated to this area and how much needs to be dispersed to other regions of the world."

"That will not be necessary," The Brother replies. The grain and other rations were produced with the hands of New Israel's workers and so it shall remain theirs. We will take care of the mud victims as well."

Darius Mede seems to consider this idea and then counters. "Maybe we should allow the people to make that decision. I have been speaking with the Philistia Administration and the various secular groups. All have decided that the bounty must be unselfishly shared."

"Unselfishly shared?" Preacher Elijah, who seems to have no love lost for the Premier, is out of his chair and leaning over the table, almost lunges with his reply. Mede's bodyguards are closing in to protect the Premier from any harm the eighty-something-year-old professor might present. There is no need for action as Preacher Elijah holds himself back.

Mede's face shows disappointment at the self-restraint and I hear snaring in his next articulation. "Fiz, my friend, in all our history together, you of all people should be well aware that policy must be agreed to and acted upon in complete agreement to the betterment of all—"

"I know nothing of the sort, we are beyond policy here," Preacher Elijah interrupts, not about to be trapped into a political discussion. "We just received a report that the whole Mediterranean sector is experiencing increasing volcanic activity, not just isolated eruptions but everywhere. Besides the immediate threat to lives, the dust and collateral from this activity will soon blanket the planet, causing a diminished ability for crop production, even inhibiting the ability for native plant life to produce oxygen.

"You know that animal and insect populations have already been decimated. Riots and anarchy escalates as you try for a power grab. These things are dire warnings of worse things to come and it is not something we can stop, but it is something we have prepared for. All you need to do is get out of the way."

By the time he has finished speaking, Preacher is amazingly calm, having released his own frustrations in the act. On the other hand, I notice a small twitch begin to attack Mede's left eyelid. *Is he about to order our execution?* I think it possible, but then another realization strikes me. *He does not know where we have stored the goods he wants to govern. Until he discovers the locations of our stash, we still have valuable to him.*

Brother Moses speaks to smooth those waters. "Darius, we appreciate your wanting to involve all parties. The two organizations you just attributed are no longer recognized as having authority over this issue. We have already sought the ratification of those who farm and those who have harvested. It is by their good graces that we have decision-making power in this matter. Praying for Yahweh's counsel on this has resulted in strong confidence that we are on the right path, so you have no need to concern yourself any longer with the matter."

There is an old Muslim saying, *Aley yetkelm awel yekhesr wely yetkelm balakheyr yerbh hel t'eref,* which roughly translates as "He who speaks first loses his crown".

Everyone in the room must be familiar with the adage because no one utters a word. The silence is electric—Mede looks sedate, but I watch as the twitch of his eyelid begins to escalate and he suddenly reaches to rub it vigorously. Brother Moses actually pulls out a small pocket Bible and begins silently reading. Preacher Elijah actually closes his eyes and…yes, I hear him snoring!

The waiting goes on for at least five minutes and finally Darius Mede, after containing his tick, concedes with a caveat. "Your position will be broadcast to all of the local and global leaders. I'm sure they will have strong opinions about your unwillingness."

Brother Moses looks up from his studies and responds, "If it were about sharing, then it would be a different matter, but we both know, Darius, that this is not about sharing. It is about control. Yahweh is directing us, who is directing you?"

This line of questioning does not seem to sit well with the Premier. His face visibly reddens and he takes a step toward us before accusing, "You religious zealots have no idea how you look to the world. You will not tolerate others, nor do you care for their improvement. You are hypocrites of the worst kind and I will apply the full force of my government upon you!"

Was it not just a week ago that this man had sung the praises of the Jewish and New Follower communities for our generous efforts? Something or someone has triggered his rage. Is it us or are other powers at work? Preacher Elijah opens his eyes and stares at Mede for a moment before speaking. "You serve your master well, Darius. But he is not ours and the One we all serve will answer you in due time. For the duration, you know what must happen and the peril of disobeying the will of disobeying God."

Mede's eyes seem to momentarily glaze over at the mention of the Most High and then a grin moves across his face. He actually sneers—a long, decidedly sinister sound coming from his mouth. He speaks, moving right up to Preacher Elijah's face, spitting caustic rhetoric. "If Satan existed, would he consider himself evil? Of course not! He would think himself doing good or better than the one he opposes. And that one you dullards call on for needs, the one you think is holy: does He consider himself holy? Well, of course he does…because you make Him so!"

Now the Premier walks past Moses, avoiding him for some reason and stares directly at me. I am suddenly ice-cold and pray for light to warm me as this man attacks. "Do you consider yourself evil? Oh, I know you can say the words, but does your inner being truly believe them? Or is your truth more along the lines of 'I'm a good person, my god recognizes and understands that I mean well'?

"Yet in your Bible, your so-called creator calls you evil. Even His boy-child says it!

'And if you then, though you are evil, know how to give good gifts…'"

My stomach is churning and I think soon I will eject my last meal onto the emperor of this world. Still God is working—I begin to feel a tranquility that overshadows this man's tirade. A characterization comes to my mind and comforts me: *False Prophet.*

Yet still he rails, "Do you consider yourself holy? Of course you do. What a hypocrite: because you have been taught to be by your contradicting god. All you have to do according to His is believe and suddenly you are not evil, you are as good as gold, no matter what you do from then on! How alluring and convenient for you."

He surveys me and I hold back a shudder, refusing to let his indignation cut me. His final allegation is indeed his truest and worst, "You are no holier than I."

"No, but my Savior Yeshua is." I have spoken. The reaction on Mede's face suggests he is as dumfounded as I am at my rebuttal.

"I believe there is just one remaining thing to discuss," Brother Moses rapidly interjects, not giving a moment's chance for Darius to respond. The big man steps between us to meet Mede face-to-face. The Premier looks startled and freezes in place as The Brother gently places his hands on both his shoulders and speaks in an emotional, nearly tearful whisper.

"Darius, we have walked so much history together, so much water has passed under the bridge. Events are taking place over which soon neither of us will have any influence. We were once united in our friendship. As long ago as that was, I ask you…beg you to reconsider your alliance. I had to do the same not long ago and came to a new determination about whom I recognize as my Master. I'd like to share with you more about why I did that and why it is imperative for you to do the same. May I pray with you?"

Mede nearly falls over backwards. His guards, who for some reason had not stopped Brother Moses's contact with the Premier, catch him and right the man. Darius Mede brushes at his immaculate suit as if it is covered in dust. His entourage tries to assist in that act as well, but he brushes them away like the infinitesimal matter on his outfit. He backs up against the nearest wall and continues wiping at his jacket as he speaks.

"I want no part of your superstitions. We no longer have the luxury of imagining a god who will swoop down and save us from our troubles. The world is my responsibility to lead and so I must be about the world's estate. You will be wise to understand that and not stand in my way. Regardless of our past work together, I will not tolerate any interference."

With that, Darius Mede escapes the room, still obsessed with his attire as he exits. His guards look first at us and next, with confused glance, at one another. Then they too leave by the same route, leaving us completely unattended.

"There is nothing more for us to do here," The Brother speaks cheerlessly and we let ourselves out through the front entrance.

The night is like most others; shrouded in cloud, filled with the sounds of the less fortunate, hoping in the darkness to scrounge one extra morsel of food carelessly discarded by some well-provided Philisti. There is unusual dampness in the air, abnormally high moisture pulled from the sea by the western wind still trailing after the mud storm. The mood is made heavier by it and by the moody silence of Brother Moses and Preacher Elijah. We are walking home after our encounter with Darius Mede and the typical encouragement these two provoke is noticeably absent.

"We have obeyed you, Yeshua. Can you provide any comfort? Any hope for this sullen time?" Brother Moses's voice is throaty and has difficulty cutting into the darkness.

"Faith, my *gadol awkh.*" Preacher Elijah has just honored his mentor with a great title—*elder brother*. A smile now starts to play on the physicist's face. "Remember when they called you Crazy Prophet? If that affront did not wear you down, why would you be so down after an effort so valiant as to offer redemption to the antichrist?"

Both men laugh and proclaim loudly together, "Praise Adonai!" Their words strike me in an odd way. Are they speaking metaphorically or do they truly believe that Darius Mede is the Devil's Spawn? I do not have a chance to ask the question, for immediately after they call out to their Lord, he answers. The breeze shifts suddenly from west to east and the warm blast of it absorbs all humidity from the atmosphere. I find it difficult to breathe.

I cannot easily explain the light I now see forming around my friends. It is a bluish glow that shapes and fills them. It lights the evening and I feel both a sense of warmth and fear. Preacher Elijah examines his hands and arms, then comments, "The Tau effect. Our neutrinos are shifting."

I have no idea to what he refers, but Brother Moses is equally inspired to speak. "The Ruach calls us. It is time."

Both men stare at the heavens for a time and then toward each other. The smiles return to their faces and they embrace strongly, holding on to one another as if it will be the last time for such intimacy. When they part, both are drying their eyes and Preacher Elijah offers one last chuckled comment. "I am so parched, I must confess that I miss my cold club soda!"

The blue glow lingers on and about them for a few moments longer and then fades. Without a word we continue walking back to my home while I try to grasp what has just happened. Neither man beside me offers any explanation.

To suppress free speech is a double wrong.
It violates the rights of the hearer
as well as those of the speaker.

—Frederick Douglass

According to recent municipal law, I am illegally writing these words. Has it actually been more than eight months since we walked away from Beit Aghion after the difficult quarrel with Darius Mede? So much has changed: Some things great, some terrifying.

It is not that I haven't been writing, but several weeks ago, some of Mede's local henchmen literally broke down the door to our home, ransacked the place and appropriated my most recent pages. I should explain how this came about.

After the strange happenings at Beit Aghion, the Spirit moved in some very unusual ways. One particular incident occurred at the beginning of the third month of the third year after the Gathering-Up. I was patching some damaged clay on the front of our family's quarters when a very tall and affable Ethiopian man walked by. He must have traveled a great distance for he appeared very road-worn. He slowed his pace as he caught sight of me and then stopped to watch my work. We struck up a conversation and I felt compelled to offer him shelter and food. As we spoke, Jande entered and it became very evident that there was a spiritual connection. By YHWH's provision we strengthened the young man and introduced him to the Watchman. He was then sent onward toward destiny that would help bring our Creator's plan into perfect clarity.

Another move of the Ruach occurred when the burial of martyrs became necessary under direction of Brother Moses and Eleazar. It was discovered that, included in the casualties from the mud hurricane, there had been Remnants and New Follower refugees whom Mede had exiled to that ghetto of Jerusalem. They had all been outspoken in their faith and actions, so it was decided to turn the tragedy of their loss into an honorarium for their service to YHWH. It was again the time of Pesach and the Feast of First Fruits (has more than a year actually passed since the arrival of Preacher Elijah and his South South clan? It hardly seems possible). The seasonal temperature had become very warm, yet, eerily, a cold wind increased around us during the burials, dark clouds billowing overhead, threatening more inclement weather to interfere with the dismal task. The weather held off long enough for us to finish the arduous task with a song of praise. It was an aged hymn of awe led by a Second called Luther Hine. He explained that the song had been composed by a relative of his long ago. Its haunting melody and message of its first two stanzas took us back to a time in a richly blessed world none of us would ever see again. We struggled to recall such things in our minds. But now, because of the gift of this tune, they are now permanently etched on our hearts:

O Lord my God, when I in awesome wonder
Consider all the worlds thy hands have made,
I see the stars, I hear the rolling thunder,
Thy power throughout the universe displayed:

Then sings my soul, my Savior God, to thee:
How great thou art! How great thou art!
Then sings my soul, my Savior God, to thee:
How great thou art! How great thou art!

When through the woods and forest glades I wander
And hear the birds sing sweetly in the trees,
When I look down from lofty mountain grandeur,
And hear the brook and feel the gentle breeze:

Then sings my soul, my Savior God, to thee:
How great thou art! How great thou art!
Then sings my soul, my Savior God, to thee:
How great thou art! How great thou art!

When we came to the third stanza a new message crept into the song. I feared that the Remnants would object, but instead they too let the words speak into their hearts…

And when I think that God, his Son not sparing,
Sent him to die, I scarce can take it in,
That on the cross, my burden gladly bearing,
He bled and died to take away my sin.

> *Then sings my soul, my Savior God, to thee:*
> *How great thou art! How great thou art!*
> *Then sings my soul, my Savior God, to thee:*
> *How great thou art! How great thou art!*

Upon singing the fourth stanza, all in the crowd joined hands and linked their voices in stronger praise as one. We all recognized the power of the vision. Whether those in the court, before the altar, venerated Jesus or another Messiah still to come, the inclusive bond of the words moved us toward hope. All were content to reprise the litany, exalting praises to YHWH for His ultimate gift:

When Christ shall come with shouts of acclamation
And take me home, what joy shall fill my heart!
Then I shall bow in humble adoration,
And there proclaim, My God, how great thou art!

Following Pesach, another storm hits; again a strange one with hail of enormous size crashing upon the earth. Fortunately, there were few additional deaths in the city as the population had seen the signs of impending foray and dashed into the underground tunnels built long ago by King Hezekiah. In that cramped, dark and wet place, someone once again began to sing the tune, "How Great Thou Art". It relayed throughout the tunnels and in the days following, many Remnants, Muslims and Philisti Seculars offered their lives to Messiah Jesus, saying that they could not stop the words (nor did they want to!) from singing into to their soul.

But other Remnants, Muslims and Seculars were not so moved. The day after the hail, when the extent of the damage to any remaining crops not obliterated by the red mud became known, a region-wide outcry began. By way of dove-messaging, the flak soon spread internationally. Brother Moses' and the priest Eleazar's decision to retain distribution rights for the supplies and edibles was fomenting jealousy among the indigent. Mede used the chaos as an excuse to release a special ordinance to control the media. He admonished that there was great danger in dissension of any kind and that our very survival depended on cohesion. Therefore, all public speeches and written correspondence must now be reviewed for acceptable content. This would even include religious ceremonies!

A ban on sincerely expressed religious observance? Restrictions on writing and freedom of speech? The Green Order Government as well as the local Philistia officials belittled such paranoia, stating that these were temporary measures and were not intended to prohibit such activities. The edicts were not meant as laws but intended to ensure order for the community. It was a brilliant way to silence not only dissenters but also reporters and prophets. Darius Mede knows well the history of Judaism and Christianity, how the "Word" was and, from its very origins until now, still is a living organ inseparable from the spiritual heart of YHWH's followers. He used the opportunity brought on by a few to control the many.

Hence my dilemma: When the Philistia authorities entered our home, it was clear what they were after and that I was now suspect. Fortunately, I was already suspicious, thanks to friendly ears in the Administration. I had taken the precaution of hiding segments of my histories in other locations. Also, friends made copies of my work for added safekeeping.

I was reviewing notes from many months of my work when we were invaded—all of that history is now wrested away. Those archived pages will need to be recreated when the opportunity offers. Thankfully, I had not divulged anything I believe was not already communally known, so no danger should come to us from the telling. Yet, according to the new laws, *any* telling is to be investigated for approval. Meaning I have to obtain permission from the bureaucrats before even considering picking up a pen.

I have solicited said permission and have been told that my case is under review. In the meantime, I cannot violate my God's calling and He has convicted me to write. There is no other authority that will stop me from fulfilling my service to Him.

And so an illicit summary of the circumstances and happenings must suffice. Finding the time and place for these writings is another matter. I am watched carefully. My friends have recommended that Jende and our children (yes, I am a father again—this time of a beautiful girl we have named Zeenajah!) move to another safer location. My heart breaks at being separated from them, but we all know it to be best. In their absence, I will try as best I can to recount the past and report the present to help us all prepare for YHWH's future plans.

As noted, Brother Moses, spokesman for the New Followers in New Israel and Eleazar, priest for the Remnants seeking Messiah, had been given authority by their respective groups for guardianship and allocation of the gathered goods prior to the devastating mud-storm. This united enterprise has changed us. All involved—Remnants, New Followers and any others who recognize the gist of these days and of our service—do not just call ourselves by the title; we have come to believe in our identity as Kin.

Since the Kin's cause flew in the face of Darius Mede's local governmental power grab and his broader authority as Premier of the Green Order Government, pressure was brought to bear. Sentiment was curried against the Kin by the government and that ill-will plausibly led to the dissatisfaction mentioned earlier.

But these actions had corollary effects. The Kin, by their conviction while undergoing persecution, became a powerful rallying banner for new converts. Additionally, because of the exceptional job of apportioning and the compassion demonstrated by this organization toward the population of all New Israel, most of the nonreligious factions actually empathized and supported the efforts of the group.

Therefore, the more the local authorities tried to characterize the Kin as a selfish splinter group, the more the country recognized the Philistia Administration to be hungry for power. This forced the non-committed factions to choose sides and, as popular as Mede was, he was having difficulty winning the argument. After all, things were working. The masses were being fed. Darius Mede and his supporters needed a rallying cry and some event that would tip the scales in their favor. It came in the form of another annihilating earthquake. This one affected all the world, ripping apart most of the infrastructure that remained. Tsunamis resulting from the tumult did not discriminate between classes, nationalities, beliefs, or conviction. Everyone, thinking everything had been lost, discovered there would be more with which to cope.

New Israel and Jerusalem were not spared. There were many deaths and much decimation. In fact, the new Temple was nearly completed when the quake hit. As cleverly as the structure had been built, it received great damage and the completion was yet again postponed for months.

In addition, the new virus that had first invaded Zimbabwe was spreading. Israel had yet to experience a case, but many speculated it was merely a matter of time before the pandemic would also affect us.

With these new crises affecting the surrounding territories, the confidence in the Kin was eroded. A new clarion for a better solution rang out. At this point, the Green Order Government pulled another deft move, somehow importing relief from another source and offering it to the New Israeli population in place of the Kin's stores.

"Thank you for your erstwhile generosity, but it is no longer necessary," dismissed Darius Mede. He suggested that the requirements for the people to participate in the Kin's program were too severe and that his all-encompassing government could now offer more and with less requirement.

We Kin knew it was a ruse and that no government on any scale, local or otherwise, could possibly maintain the necessary supply lines. But their immediate action in the face of disarray swayed the majority.

Regretfully, a splinter group of New Followers and Remnants endorsed the maneuver, encouraging the disadvantaged to browbeat Brother Moses and Preacher Elijah into handing over all control to the Philistia Administration.

I recall the day vividly when the two Watchmen responded. It was raining, misting actually. This was phenomenal, because this mist had been with us since the latest earthquake. It had gently soaked the soil and, by continuing, provided much-needed drinking water and new growth to the crops. When The Brother and Preacher received the notice, both men collapsed to the ground as if hit by some invisible force. I could actually sense a change as if all moisture was being sucked away and I suddenly became very thirsty. Before I could respond to their needs, the two gained their footing, but there was something different about them. They were glowing—an eerie blue haze could be seen around them and remains with them as I write this entry.

From that fateful day forward, not a drop of water has fallen from the sky; no dew is to be found: I have corroborated through my pigeon correspondence that it is the same throughout all the inhabited continents.

Darius Mede became unhinged by this change in events, crying out that somehow the two men, having access to some unknown sorcery, caused the worldwide drought. Neither man responded to the vilification, nor did they refute it. The nations, even New Israel, reacted with vehemence toward these two, once so favored.

Since that time, the two prophets and their associates continue to receive insults and physical rubble hurled at them. I myself have watched people attack the two, coming at them with guns, knives, even chemical bombs as we travel the streets of Jerusalem. The assailants close in on their targets, but before any injury can be attempted, either Brother Moses or Preacher Elijah will call out, "Jehovah!" and the attackers instantly crumple. Their skin appears cauterized as if the appellation itself engraves a hot wound. I have heard reports that anyone even defaming either man's character finds whatever water available turned to an undrinkable broth resembling blood.

To help protect the Watchmen, we started moving them about the city, having them stay several days in one house, several in another, to guard what little rest time and privacy they had. One night as they slept in our quarters, I heard Preacher Elijah and Brother Moses cry out simultaneously, "Kin, Israel, what have you done? Where is your faith?" Neither man awoke and I did not mention the incident to them in the morning. But from that time on, I prayed that God allow me, in some way, to help them carry the burden under which they labored.

Preacher Elijah's warnings regarding increased volcanic activity within and around the Mediterranean Sea went unheeded. Not that anything could have been done to stop eruptions or the physical destruction they would cause, but no plan was put forward, not even messages of alert were sent out to any of the potentially affected areas. So when Vesuvius and

Pompeii simultaneously blew beyond anything either had put forth in the last twenty-five hundred years, we were all put at risk.

A gargantuan tidal wave swept from Greece toward the northwest adjunct of Africa. Speeding at over 110 kilometers per hour, the monster rose to heights of 70 meters or more and within an hour, Tripoli and nearby coastal cities in Libya were no more. The mountains of northern Tunisia were instantly washed into islands of desolation. There was not time to ship remedies to the tsunami survivors before they starved into forgotten time. No refugees reached us, because there were no refuges to be had.

The ash cloud further tainted the planet's biosphere, in some places causing perpetual night, in others, choking populations with dust and noxious fumes. Even Israel, with the unusual spiritual protection it had enjoyed, is feeling the effects. Our ambition for replanting and reclaiming further harvests has been dashed by plummeting temperatures and lack of sunlight for any crop other than mushrooms—the last foodstuff that seems to still thrive.

And this brings us to the present day. The tension of the past months has stretched the tolerance of all the living. The intercontinental death toll is astronomical and strange new bacterial diseases cripple those remaining. Boils and sores will not heal. The anguish of the body affects the contentment of the personality, so tempers and passions are also exploding volcanic-like, without warning.

Thanks to the efforts of Darius Mede and his network, the blame for all of these maladies and for the starvation is being thrown at the feet of Brother Moses and Preacher Elijah. Because of this, the two of them, along with Eleazar, have called a meeting in another clandestine location. With great effort to avoid divulging the whereabouts, we have traveled by dark of night stashed in produce carts. Twelve, including myself, are in attendance and the mood is blacker than the evening.

"We have to go." It is Preacher Elijah speaking in response to a suggestion by one of the others. "It is the traditional station from which rabbis hone the people."

For most of their recent history, the Teaching Steps, leading from the Court of the Gentiles (made infamous when Yeshua overturned the tables there) up to the southern gates of the Temple mount, have been little more than a tourist stop. Now, with the reconstruction, the two Messianic leaders appear intent on reintroducing the steps as a place of exposition and tutelage, as they had originally been used.

"You would put them on the proverbial map again. I'm in agreement that the message has to be sent out, but averring your spiritual fidelity there will likely cause a powerful backlash." Eleazar says this while leaning back in a chair and stroking his curly beard. His concern for Brother Moses and Preacher Elijah is mutual to us all.

"Ah know we're supposed to make the Jews jealous and all that—no offence meant, Eleazar—but this might be taking the dog into the fight afore we know who else might be bringing a bigger dog, don't you think?" Jason, with his strange vernacular and stranger imagery, still makes his point. He has used Paul's letter to the Romans, chapter 11, as a strong argument. I'm becoming more and more impressed with this quiet young man's command of Scripture and wise counsel.

"We have to go!" Everyone looks at Preacher Elijah, who with his bare hand has just crushed the clay cup he has been drinking out of. He is trembling—it takes an uncomfortable moment for him to regain his composure and settle his breathing.

With effort, Brother Moses gets up from his reclined position and walks over directly behind his friend. He sits and begins rubbing the shoulders of the old professor, closes his eyes and I read on his lips an ancient prayer: *Elyone barak naw shamar shalom bene eber—May God bless you with the peace beyond understanding.* Then The Brother speaks a question out loud, "The dreams?"

Preacher Elijah nods his head and tears begin to trickle down his cheeks. He looks around the room, replying to the question as if he too is praying, "They are becoming more insistent. More…clear. We are about to be completed."

I do not know what visions torment this man, but my heart aches with him. Brother Moses motions for all of us to gather around the two of them. "Pray for strength," he implores, "pray for us all."

And so we do.

We have been discussing how to both communicate hope for the healing of the land and for God's people—what has been called from ancient days *Tov Shmuah* or the "Good News." This is no small order in a time when people are starving and dying of thirst. Since the blame is directed at our leaders, the two Watchmen, they have volunteered to reach out to the world, using the Teaching Steps as their platform.

They have even sent an inquiry to Darius Mede in the hopes of having his support to allow the discourse. I had little hope of a response, but to my amazement, Mede reacted positively and now plans are moving forward. The day chosen for the address is the Festival of *Shavuot*—Pentecost, the day of gathered harvest and thanksgiving.

"God's timing, to be sure," Preacher Elijah says. "This is the moment to prepare the world for provision far beyond what they are now experiencing."

I wheezed at his prediction and everyone turned to look at me, but it was Brother Moses who laughed wistfully and spoke to my obvious concern. "Yes, Ilbani, most will have the same reaction. How can a greater provision follow such horrible times? Many indeed already have condemned—judged Yahweh himself when in truth it is their very reactions that will bring the next events to a climax. You of all people must prepare for some of the most difficult detailing yet."

I have not slept all night. The day has come for Brother Moses and Preacher Elijah to edify us all, but I am angst with worry. Jende awoke from a terrible dream in the darkness. To her it was more—a vision. She had been in the street and without warning a giant rider on an equally sized red steed galloped upon her. She fell to the side just an instant prior to the horseman trampling her. She looked up to the face of the attacker as he passed and it was Darius Mede.

I tried to comfort her and did not append that, just moments before she was startled awake. I had imagined hearing the clatter of horse hooves outside our door.

*A peculiarity of our admiration for another is that it is
always looking for circumstances to justify itself.*

—Lew Wallace, Ben-Hur

I watch by the dim early morning light as people begin to trickle into the outer courtyard bordered by the mammoth wall built by King Herod. That structure's history is a story in and of itself.

Many think that when the Romans destroyed Jerusalem in AD 70, the western bulwark of the Temple was the lone structure not toppled. This is just a partial truth. Facing south, a rough and disproportional series of steps graduate to another wall that is also Herod's work. The blocks of stone on the extended wall are impressive in and of themselves, the least measuring ten cubic meters. During the original construction, these had actually been cut according to specifications at the quarry, miles to the east and then ported to this location. The skill of the masons was amazing; to this day not even a knife blade will slide between the perfectly fit, un-mortared brickwork.

To each side of the entry, there are cut cubicles called *mikvehs* fit into the ground for ritual bathing purposes. These were the same used by the pilgrims of Yeshua's day and before. Anyone approaching the Temple for worship, then and now, would be expected to be physically clean for fitness in presenting their spiritual offerings. The new waterworks would be a rousing sight to behold, but for the recent mud and earthquake events. The pools, intended to be translucent, are more like red-mud baths. As much as they are cleaned, all the more of the goo appears from the reoccurring catastrophes. And due to the recent drought, the mud has now dried in place. The baths speak to the problems beset on the Temple builders.

As for the steps themselves, the construction team did not skimp, laying polished white marble over the original plats. This was no small task, considering that Herod purposely had each of the twenty-seven steps on the eastern end and the thirty-one at the southern end set in odd depths, so that anyone coming up would have to look down and consider their trek carefully to avoid stumbling. Tradition suggests that the fifteen long steps were contoured that way to remind pilgrims of the fifteen psalms of ascent, which were sung as those travelers climbed to the Court of Israel.

Here, at the zenith, before the Huldah Gates leading into the Temple, stand Brother Moses and Preacher Elijah, ready to witness to the gathering crowd. They are easily recognized by their goatskin garments, which have distinguished them the entire time that I have known them. On the steps at their feet is a trove of twenty-four scribes, including myself, all poised with pen in hand to note what is about to be revealed. Each of these scribes has been provided with a bag containing unusual contents, which I will describe later. For now it is understood that these writers have proven their transcription accuracy by their history. It was thought that this dialogue would be much too meaningful to take a chance on error.

There is a noise like nothing I have heard before. It is obscene in the quiet of the morning: A hissing snake? A heated boiler in a kitchen ready to explode? Up from the old City of David slowly progresses an automobile—a dated model of what used to be called an SUV imported from the West! How is it possible? The grating noise and sight of the white-gray emissions make it rapidly clear to me. The truck is propelled by steam! I have not seen a vehicle under its own power since the time of the Hidden Exodus. I have never seen one functioning in this way!

And with the SUV, a parade—no, they are a security detail complete with uniforms, rifles and the visible confidence of implied authority. They clear the way of anyone who may obstruct the progress of the machine and warily scan the pathway for signs of a threat. Who would require such a production in these times?

Out of the vehicle steps the Premier's dame, the official steward of our terrestrial sphere, Brenda Anders. By the way she reacts to the crowds surrounding her, I'm of the impression she believes this assembly is for her honor. She waves to all directions, then motions for her guard to escort her toward the Teaching Steps. Behind me a voice calls out, "Mother?" I turn to see Roxanne, who stares in unbelief at Dame Anders. She then pivots and runs away from the approaching entourage, disappearing into a gathering of Ethiopians.

I bring my gaze back to watch in fascination as the detail takes a direct path for Brother Moses and Preacher Elijah, seemingly without a care as to the true purpose of this event. When she is upon the steps with us, Anders makes her own intent known.

"I'm glad I was able to find you…before he does. You have to believe me when I say you need to leave here immediately."

Neither The Brother nor The Preacher seems surprised or concerned by this warning. It is Elijah who replies warmly.

"Dame Anders, thank you for your concern. We have always shared your intense passion for the welfare of the planet. But our service to Yeshua is here at this moment."

Anders looks puzzled by this statement. "Do you expect me to believe that you can predict your future and that your god is somehow going to make this situation all right?"

"Belief is something you must wrestle with of your own volition," Elijah answers. "No one else can be involved in your grappling. As for what I expect, all I have left is my faith. Everything else of value has been stripped away and nothing I see now proves my faith misplaced."

Now I actually see fear and genuine concern in Brenda Anders's eyes. She comes in very close to the side of Preacher Elijah and almost whispers, "Fitzgerald, please, I've come here at great risk and have gone to a lot of effort to help you. I've even made arrangements for both of you to be given sanctuary in Babylon. I have the power to protect you there and an alliance between us is the best way to stand against Darius and his schemes.

"Please," she presses, looking around her as if for an imminent attack. "Come with me now or die a horrible death."

Preacher Elijah smiles sadly and tells her, "If we come with you, we will live a horrible life."

"You must believe me," Anders tries again.

Now Elijah speaks out to Anders and beyond to the entire gathering. "Am I to believe that you can protect me? I cannot! I cannot believe in any person's ability to protect me. Do you believe that I can harm you? Do not! You should not believe in any person's ability to harm you."

Brenda Anders has become clearly frustrated. "What, then, am I to believe in!"

"Believe in God. Believe in His plan." Then the Preacher does something I have never seen him do before. He leans over and kisses Dame Anders on the forehead. She shudders and her detail immediately starts to close in, but the woman holds up an unsteady hand to stop them.

"No," she orders in a quivering tremolo. Then, regaining her strength blurts again, "No!"

Brother Moses then speaks to the Dame, saying, "Grace and mercy are ours to ask but Yahweh's to give," and then both The Brother and Preacher Elijah place their hands on her head. They say together:

> "Adonai bless and keep you,
> "Adonai make His face shine upon you and be gracious to you,
> "Adonai lift up His countenance upon you and give you shalom."

The Premier's wife closes her eyes at the pronouncement and lets the words wash over her. She inhales and holds the blessing within. I see for the first time a placid smile on her lips. Then her head shakes back and forth discreetly, as if she is waking from a fantasy far away. She opens her eyes and the smile vanishes, along with the relaxed state that had pervaded her being.

"I tried to rescue you," she says, sounding very tired. "Don't forget I tried."

"We will remember," reply both men and then, more quickly than she entered, Brenda Anders leads her attendants back to her steam-mobile. With a smoggish snort, the beast chugs away, surrounded by the guards, who have difficulty keeping pace.

Apparently the news has traveled well and soon the entire area below, once known as the Women's Court, is sardined with people of all walks. There are even musicians leading the crowd in psalms of praise and the spirit of this place seems colossal in spite of the hardships experienced. For an exquisite moment, all sing and praise in chorus:

> I lift my eyes to the hills, where does my help come from?
> My help comes from the Lord, the maker of heaven and Earth.
> He will not let your foot be moved, He who keeps you does
> not slumber.

Behold, He who keeps Israel neither slumbers nor sleeps
The Lord is your keeper; the Lord is your shade at your right
hand.

The sun will not strike you by day nor the moon by night.

The Lord will keep you from all evil. He will keep your life.

The Lord will keep your coming and your going from this day
forward,

And forever more.

The singing goes on—The Brother and The Preacher seem satisfied to let the worship of YHWH continue. Eventually they signal for the musicians to finish their chanting; it is the former rabbi who begins the conversation. His homily is magnified and its sound bounced off the wall behind him, so that all below, even in the nearby City of David, can hear him.

"Elohim Adonai, *Lord God*, let the words of my mouth and the meditation of my heart be acceptable in Your sight, my Rock and my Redeemer. Let eyes be opened and ears be allowed to hear that Your will be done. Let all of us here and those who will receive this message later be obedient to You and You alone."

I hear him speaking in Hebrew, but, widely traveled as I am and having a gift for languages, I can hear a group of Koreans on the steps below us, amazed that The Brother knows their language. Another group a bit farther down quibble out loud at his skill with their Spanish idioms. Brother Moses continues with the message.

"We speak to the children of Israel and to all those grafted to the vine, in the name of the One God, Yahweh, who hungers for restoration of the land, His people and His kingdom on Earth.

"There has been death and tragedy, which some would even say has been God's doing. We are here to exclaim that nothing has changed from the time when the first of us rebelled. Not one jot or tittle has been excluded from the law and the prophets. Yes, the current calamities are God's doing, but it was our *causing* that provoked Him into correction. You know this to be true in your hearts. Your anger is dangerously misplaced if it is directed at the very One who has planned from the beginning to redirect our destiny. These next words, out of the mouths of His messengers, will be familiar to you, but they come with a new warning and opportunity."

Here Brother Moses pauses. He takes one hand of Preacher Elijah's in his. Both raise their arms high to appeal in shared voice:

"Repent, for the kingdom of God is at hand."

The people below them remain still and unreadable as fog. Preacher Elijah takes the lead. "Yes, the same song was sung by Moses in the wilderness and John the Baptist by the river. They and others like them have called for us to relent our will to the One. What has changed? All the great prophets have told us the Kingdom might come on any day. Why is this current moment crucial to you?"

There is murmuring in the crowd. These new-day prophets have snagged their attention. Preacher Elijah continues. "It is no surprise to any of us that many of our loved ones across the world are missing; their whereabouts, even their physical bodies, untraceable. Your governments and leaders give you unsatisfactory explanations; in your hearts, you cry out, 'Where have they gone, what have I done to deserve the desolation and loneliness I am feeling?'

"You know the answer, but it frightens you and it should not! Yahweh has provided one and only one way to repossess each and every child of His. He himself paid the debt we have incurred. As confused as you put on to be, you understand in your depths that the One True God creatively and wonderfully came to us, taking on human form."

The people are compelled by the oration and press in as one to take in every syllable, hungry to understand the meaning.

Brother Moses now questions, "But God is God! How could this happen? Is not the Messiah to be a Man-King like David? Surely you are asking right now, as I had to ask, 'How could one be fully man and fully God?' We, the created, would doubt the love and power of our Creator to perform such a miracle?

"We question how He could have walked with us, taught us how to recognize Him. We deny the possibility of God loving us enough to give Himself to be killed by the very ones He loved. By our denial and rebellion then, by our words and actions now, mankind killed Him and we continue to kill Him. All of us, even those who have not confided responsibility; we have tried to make His death a permanent thing, but we are unable to do this because He has risen from the dead! And with that resurrection, The God-Man instead killed the sin of any who call Him their Savior.

"Doubt no more that the God-Man has come; the absence of your loved ones is proof that we who remain missed his touch—missed the kiss of His grace to relieve our anguish!"

There is a flood of heartbreak. No words are heard beyond those of the prophets on the steps. Grief and mewling come back in response. Brother Moses and Preacher Elijah stop speaking for a moment to let the emotion distill. Then The Brother pulls his colleague close to his side and beckons with arms spread wide to include all before him,

"My soul magnifies the Lord and my Spirit cries out within me, for Yahweh has seen the humble condition of His servant. He is a God of second chances. He is the God of longsuffering to mend His creation! He yet desires for us to live in His spiritual Kingdom with Him. We are here to tell you the Kingdom is here. The time is not in the future but now! That Kingdom—the Kingdom of redemption—is now!"

"The Kingdom is now, the Kingdom is now, the Kingdom is now," chants the crowd. Their excitement carries the words on the wind and more people, from all parts of the city, gather in.

"The Kingdom is now," Preacher Elijah repeats when the din fades. "The Kingdom is where your loved ones have gone. And in the Kingdom of the returned God-Man lies our hope!"

In the crowd, one or two, then ten, now more, fall to their knees, crying out. Brother Moses responds to their imploring now rising in tenor, "I hear the names you are calling—Jihsu, Jesus, Messiah, they are all the same: *God is Salvation.* And there is one name He is called, that each of you know in your spirit—Yeshua! Sing it, let Him forgive you; but you must be willing to abandon all else you have thought precious to you, you must be ready to be changed! There is no more time to ponder your choices. Fall on your face at His feet."

And they do, all of them. Not one remains standing. The laments and songs become an open floodgate of nearly deafening unity:

"Yeshua, Lord, forgive us!"

The plea is bemoaned for uncounted minutes. The prophets have also fallen facedown to worship with all the believers. Finally, Brother Moses and Preacher Elijah stand again. The Brother gestures for silence. It is a long time before those on the ground quiet enough for him to be heard.

"There will be a day soon, when You will meet your Messiah face-to-face and with him, those who have already been raised up with Him. On that day the whole world will recognize Yeshua as Truth and will bow to him. But only those who are humbled, completely repentant and willingly obedient will be recognized by Him."

Preacher Elijah steps forward and adds, "That is the day we hope for, but today we must ready ourselves, prepare our houses and share the message you have received with every friend, every neighbor, every one you call family. Repent, the Kingdom is now!"

Again the crowd begins to sing, "The Kingdom is now, the Kingdom is now, the Kingdom is now!"

Brother Moses quiets the crowd once again and speaks. "There is still charity available to those who might believe and we are Yahweh's hands, Yahweh's feet to serve His desire. We have both physical and spiritual food and water to share with the world. It will not be by coercion from any government or other interest that God's gifts will be distributed. We have organized a chain across the nations by which to pass on what we can. We invite others to offer what they have as well.

"There will be no requirements set, no stipulation of adoration, even for Yeshua; any who choose to call him Lord must do so of free will, not by coercion. No worldly organization will direct these efforts, the ministration and love we offer have been freely given by a greater authority.

"As for your duty? It is the same as it has always been. As you are going, as you are feeding and serving the nations, make disciples, baptizing them in the name of the Father, the Son and the Spirit. Just as with Yahweh's people in past ages, there will still be persecution—more, in fact. This has not changed and will not change until the world is permanently changed.

"Some of you may have heard a term used to describe followers of Yeshua recently arrived from the former United States. They call themselves *Seconds*, those who, after the Hidden Exodus—or the Gathering-Up, as Westerners call it—have devoted themselves to The God-Man.

"God is a God of Seconds. Jacob was the second son, receiving the inheritance blessing in preference to Esau. Isaac received grace instead of Ishmael, Ephraim and other examples abound in the Scriptures. But most telling of all? When Adam chose to rebel, God offered the *Second Adam*—Yeshua Ha'Mashiach—Jesus—in a plan to redeem His creation.

"*Seconds* is a term that now describes you. There is no longer nationality or loyalty to family, to sect or race. Now there will be one proper centerpiece—the Son of God. By his death and resurrection, we have all become second sons of second chances.

"What happens to our freedom, then? Did we not say before that there will be no forced choice of belief? It is true! No one need believe in Yeshua as Savior, but for His reign as King upon Earth, there will be no refusal, there will be no other options."

At this, Brother Moses pauses and solemnly surveys the hearers. Then he walks down the steps to one of the muddy mikvehs and teases, "You who believe, now your witness begins!" At this, he produces a stone from a pouch within his robe. This he casually tosses into the muck and instantly the water becomes crystal clear—in that bath and in all of them. Captivation ripples over the crowd as the telling of the episode is dispatched and immediately new Seconds approach to be baptized.

Preacher Elijah walks over to the scribes, who all have been detailing these prophetic events. He reaches out his hand to me, inviting me to stand with him. When I am by his side, he puts his arm around my shoulder, looks into my eyes and speaks, "Child, it has been a great privilege to walk with you and to see these events through your eyes. Never cease to tell the very words of God as long as you have breath in your body and spirit in your heart." He directs his attention to the scribes still sitting and says, "It is time."

At this cue, we all take the special lightweight paper on which we have been noting these events, all writing one last note in multiple languages at the end:

Next year in Jerusalem!

Folding the paper, it is then inserted into finger-sized capsules saved for this occasion. These are attached to the feet of the birds we have brought with us in small cages, one for each of the scribes and then the seventy-seven doves are freed to seek their destinations—the nations of the world.

The sight of the fowl ascending and making their way outbound to parts unknown is a breathtaking vision of hope for those in the court and below. A cry rises from the mouths of all:

"Hallelujah! Hallelujah! Hallelujah."

When the praises subside, Preacher Elijah rejoins Brother Moses. They join hands and raise their arms again, with one voice offering another miraculous command, "The God who cleansed these pools offers one more sign of His forgiveness and loving-kindness. Let the earth be refreshed once again!"

And the heavens release a steady rain. I close my eyes and tilt my head up to let the liquid drench my face, its drops on my parched lips and thirsty mouth are perfect pleasure—the drought is no more. I look out at the crowd and all have naturally mimicked my act, the same expression of joy and peace reflecting on their faces.

The two prophets rejoin Gregory Blueroad, the Second called Jason and several other New Followers who now receive the people advancing toward the pools, asking their names and immersing each in the name of the Father, the Son and the Holy Spirit. Along with the bond of fellowship, encouragement is given to each of the newly baptized.

"There are many others who need to hear and receive the message. Go and find them."

The beneficiaries seem to flood from the waters out toward the city, unfazed by the downpour, to acclaim what has happened and yet still the crowd does not appear to diminish, obviously replenished by those who have heard from the witnesses sent out.

It is not for hours that the baptisms continue, but for the entire day, into the night, on to the next morning and on through the rest of the week. The rains have stopped, but not the work of those baptizing. They take no water or food, but continue to receive New Followers. The results are exhilarating, well beyond that of Jerusalem's population; the countryside and beyond must be sending in its lost. It is evident that this ministry will continue and I know I need not fear for the witnesses' health or for any of us; even the scribes seem oblivious to the heat of the day and the cold of the night. We record conversion miracles and exhibitions of incredible power. There are still the spiritually disturbed who come to attack the witnesses—those are struck down by a word from Brother Moses or Preacher Elijah; many of them, once exorcised of their demons, become converts themselves.

Daily, doves return and new messages of reclamation are flown out for the world to read. Only once, after seven days in front of the baths, does Brother Moses take a moment from his baptizing to kneel at my side.

He tells me, "Go with Eleazar to direct the deacons whom we chose. Tell them it is time to administer the rations to guarantee every one of the Seconds in New Israel has their portion. What is left beyond that should be distributed as best can be done to the children and widows of the remaining nations."

Then Brother Moses looks thoughtfully toward his partner. Elijah, who seems to read the big man's thoughts, pensively nods his head as he looks our way. The Brother turns his attention back to me and says, "In a compartment hidden in the ceiling of the place we have been meeting, you will find some instructions for you as well as some other very special documents. They are yours to protect now; guard them on the polished tablet of your heart. Soon our ministry will change forever and then you will be the Keeper to share them."

Eleazar and I walk in silence. I can tell he wants to say something, but we are almost at the entrance to the Essene Quarter before he speaks.

"Why is it that you and I are performing this duty?"

The idea that the Chief Priest of the Remnants would want my thoughts on this question bewilders me, but I answer what I know. "I am gifted to observe and notate. I was told to go with you, so I conjectured you were given the charge of directing the elders and I am to document."

"But I was told no more than you of the task at hand," Eleazar replies. "And even if I had been given more information, I am a priest, not an administrator. I do not recognize your Yeshua as Messiah, why would I be the choice of Rabbani Moses to accompany you?"

Accompany me? Suddenly I am thinking back in my mind to Brother Moses's last words. He did not elaborate to Eleazar, limiting the directive toward me, saying I was to follow the priest. I realize that The Brother has foreseen some mysterious thing involving the two of us.

One of his prayers spoken from Psalm 19 flashes in my mind as we walk:

Let the words of my mouth and the meditation of my heart be
acceptable to You, Oh God, my rock and my redeemer.

But what am I to tell this man beside me that he doesn't already know? All I can remember is the passage from Amos that Brother Moses had offered Eleazar earlier and so I speak it. "Can two walk together unless they are in agreement? Brother Moses said we are all now Seconds. Regardless of our differences, we both serve God and it appears now Yahweh is telling us we have a very short time remaining to seek unity."

Incredibly, I see tears welling in Eleazar's eyes and he nods as if I have spoken inconceivable wisdom. We enter the gate of the Essene Quarter, praying out loud our heart's desire, that the world may know that You, Adonai, are *Eloheinu Echad*—God Alone.

"We have been very carefully disseminating the food and water we have stored, not wanting them to be depleted too quickly. Now you are telling us that we should dispose of it all in one moment?"

This question comes from one of the New Followers who have been with Brother Moses from the time when he unveiled his own recognition of Yeshua as Messiah. Yacob is the young man's name. He has been a strong and endowed leader, having been commended as an elder to help meet the needs of the ever-increasing group of believers coming into Jerusalem. I had shared Brother Moses's words of disbursement with a group of twelve—six New Followers and six Remnants who have gathered along with myself, Eleazar, and a few other of the faithful. It has been thirty-seven days that the baptisms have continued since the "Pentecost of Seconds". This season is being called *Yom Tov Shmuah*, Days of Good News, with new converts descending on the city from all points of the globe. And here they remain. The increase of souls is taxing our ability to feed and provide to their limits.

"Perhaps we should not think of this as a depletion of resources," Eleazar intercedes. "Yahweh has always provided manna for His people, distributing enough for the day and for Shabbat." Now I understand why Brother Moses wanted him involved in this task with me. All those gathered in this small room respect him highly; his scriptural inference negates all selfish agendas.

There should be no need for further discussion; everyone knows what has to be done. But Roxanne interjects before we can move to our duties. "I've put all of you in danger. I didn't mean to."

She is barely out of her teenage years and the look of fright on her face gives her all the more the appearance of a child. "I…haven't told you…I haven't told anyone where I come from. I'm going to tell you now and then I'll leave. I know you'll want me to."

Ayita and Rachel have taken Roxanne under their wings since her arrival and now move to her side. "You will not be leaving anywhere without us," Rachel says in a reassuring tone.

"You may change your mind," the redheaded girl responds. "You see, my mother was very involved in a movement years back. It involved helping the governments of the world to bring awareness about changing climate conditions to the public. She became real outspoken about the whole thing."

"Your mother is Brenda Anders?" It is Eleazar who quickly draws the conclusion. His smile seems oddly out of place in the moment, but he says no more, leaving the question to be confirmed.

Ayita Blueroad takes Roxanne's hand and tries to encourage her. "We all have things from our past that we may not—"

"—You don't understand!" Roxanne interrupts with surprising anger. "My mother is not important. She was an idiot back then, just like she is now. She thought she could win the affection of my father by furthering his cause and when that didn't work, she…slept with him out of desperation."

The air in the room seems to stop. All seem to be having trouble processing the information just shared. No one says anything. No one has to. Roxanne's pain is not on account of her mother's notoriety, but because of her father's. Can it be, Lord? She is the child of Darius Mede? A sudden sense of urgency invades my spirit. The hair on my neck rises up and I can see that others in the room feel the change as well.

"Something terrible is happening," I spout. No sooner than it is spoken that there is a muffled pounding at the door to our location, but no password or any request for entry is offered: when the portal is cautiously opened, two people literally fall into our midst. One of the bodies that tumbles before us, I think I recognize. I say I think I recognize him only because the scalded flesh and smoking vapor emanating from him make identification sketchy at best. Is he Jason, the student of Preacher Elijah, who had also led his own group from Southern America across the ocean to New Israel? Yes, now I'm sure. The military ring still on his finger establishes him.

Jason attempts to speak, but all that comes from his mouth is a choking sound and he wheezes as if there is no oxygen in the room to be had. Then he exhales and breathes no more. The other man is even more badly roasted. His eyes are fixed open and I cannot tell if he is still of this world.

"Quickly, all of you, they are in need of immediate healing." It is Ayita, President Blueroad's daughter, who spoke and has moved to the injured. Laying her hands on them, she begins a plaintive chant of penitence. The others in the room except for Eleazar and two of the other Remnants gather to the cause. Then, the Head Priest himself pulls a flask of oil from a pocket of his *tallet* and moves to the men on the floor to anoint them—his devotees also coming close to intone a Psalm-cry for mercy from the Most High.

> Make haste, O God, to deliver me! O Lord, make haste to
>   help me!
> Let them be put to shame and confusion who seek my life! Let
>   them be turned back and brought to dishonor who delight
>   in my hurt!
> Let them turn back because of their shame who say, "Aha, Aha!"
> May all who seek you rejoice and be glad in you! May those
>   who love your salvation say evermore, "God is great!"
> But I am poor and needy; hasten to me, O God! You are my
>   help and my deliverer;
> O Lord, do not delay

Ayita begins a lilt in what I believe to be her native Cherokee. The two words I recognize—*Yeshua Adonai*. She then stands and holds her hands above us all, exhorting in English, "Jesus, Master of this place, if it be your will, heal your kin from ravaging by those who deny your power. Let them see and know that you are King and Healer of all." The clay oil lamps that dimly light the room suddenly brighten to the point where we have to close our eyes to avoid being blinded. At the same time there is a rushing of wind and I fear a fire will mutilate us. But just as quickly, the brilliance fades, the Ruach passes by and we are left in the quiet of shalom.

Incredibly, as my eyes adjust to the light, I see the two wounded men now encircled by the rest of our clan. Jason looks around and then guffaws, saying in his thick Southern tongue, "Don't that beat all. Lazarus just got brought back once. This be twice for me, praise Jasus!"

Praise Jesus indeed, for by the power of his name the healing of the two is complete and miraculous. I now recognize the other man as Luther Hine, the very same who gifted us with his ancestor's magnificent song, "How Great Thou Art". We learn that he is originally from Ireland. He was one of those assisting with the baptism procession along with Jason. Now they unfold what they experienced.

Sometime after Eleazar and I were sent on our mission, a cauldron of militia wearing the uniform of the Green Order Government appeared in such force that they were able to surround the entire baptismal locale by the Temple. An official from Mede's administration with a small army of his own then blockaded access to the mikvehs. Without introduction, the man used a megaphone to inform the crowd, "You are assembling without permission. Anyone who remains here after the next ten minutes will be liable to the full penalty of the law."

When he had made this proclamation, Brother Moses walked toward him with hands held halfway up, palms out in a gesture of peace. The man watched The Brother approach and, as he neared, gave a signal to the fifty or more soldiers who stood with him. Immediately, they belched their weapons at Brother Moses. The arsenal included automatic weapons, high-powered rifles, even flame-throwers and toxic liquid-gas emitters. All of the believers in the area, including my fellow scribes, watched in horror, frozen with disbelief as the aggression continued on The Brother.

Hysteria flared below the steps as those who had been waiting for baptism fled—fearing this same fate from the surrounding army. They had been told they had some time to disperse; however, Mede's forces must have interpreted the unrest as noncompliance and began to fire from all points onto the innocents. Luther tells us that blood wisped on the wind like a raining red mist.

Still on the Teaching Steps, the true hero of the moment was Preacher Elijah. He motivated the rest of the baptizers and the immediate crowd to quickly move up the steps toward the gates of the Temple—the most immediate location of protection. In order to give the group time to gain entrance, he distracted the soldiers by singing loudly while doing an odd sort of dance, west, away from the crowd. The weapons were turned away from Brother Moses and directed toward Elijah, who then released from inside the sleeve of his tunic one of the revelation bugs we had all come to know well. It zoomed straight for the attackers and gave time for Jason and Luther to open the large doors into the Temple Area. This allowed most of those who had been on the steps to reach sanctuary within the inner court of the Temple.

But the solution was temporary. Several of the soldiers managed to trap the bug in a container. Half of the attackers let loose their ammunition upon Preacher Elijah, who was now trapped against the Fatmid Tower wall. The other half loosed their fury on those escaping into the Temple. Jason and Luther were the last bastions remaining at the gates and were just closing the huge doors as fire and gas covered them. Even so, they managed to lock the doors before collapsing from their wounds.

How these two were able to retreat to us is a mystery. We know that designed into the Temple structure are tunnels for water transport, storage and safe passage in times of danger. We imagine that other believers, using the conduits to find their way to safety, must have recognized and aided the two in arriving to our location. We are all anxious to determine the conditions of the Outer Court and to see if any survivors are in need of care.

I have learned that Ayita's name means "First to Dance" in her native tongue and I now see its significance in relationship to how YHWH has gifted her. Other than my own enchanting Jende, I have not chanced upon a woman so strong in the Spirit and so confident in her ability to heal. She has not gone about bragging of her gifts, but just as her Savior did, she becomes immediately obedient to whatever need arises.

So now, instead of inquiring about her father, who obviously had also been ministering at the mikvehs, Ayita is the most vocal in organizing a detail to access the tunnels. The hope is to return to the site without interference from Mede's armies.

Jason warns that our adversaries may have already broken into the Temple structure and may at this moment be attempting to stalk and eliminate us. This concern does not deter any, including Eleazar, who is also worried about his people and the desecration of the Temple structure itself.

"Are not the Temple grounds already defiled by our unauthorized entrance?" asks Luther.

Eleazar pauses in thought and replies, "A wise prophet once said, '*Shabbat*, the Sabbath, was made for man, not man for the Shabbat.' There are numerous historical examples of the Inner Court of the Temple of YHWH serving also as a holy place of rest for His people when in the midst of chaos. It was He who provided your escape and He who expects all of us to defend that reverent place."

I say a silent prayer of thanksgiving for this man's wisdom as everyone in the room volunteers at once to make the trip. It is decided that a small group should make the first excursion, in case retribution awaits—there is no need to risk our entire assembly. Ultimately, it is Eleazar, a *sabra* called Rachel, Ayita Blueroad, myself, Jason and Luther (who are now, amazingly, fully recovered from their injuries) who are to return.

After a careful check of the surrounding streets, we slip out into the fast-approaching night, knowing that it may be our last journey on this Earth.

Surely it is not true blessedness to be free from sorrow
while there is sorrow and sin in the world;
sorrow is then a part of love,
and love does not seek to throw it off.

—*George Eliot*

No destructive apparatuses are brought with us as we know the foolishness of any attempt to outgun the enemy. Instead we carry what we know to be more capable weapons: the belt of truth; the breastplate of righteousness; hearts impatient to relate the Good News of Yeshua's imminent return; strong faith to slap down attacks of doubt; and a Bible. As we make our way to a concealed tunnel entrance, we pray together, unafraid of being discovered.

The journey is complex, winding and weaving in and out of friendly and sometimes unfriendly lairs of the city. Finally, we furtively knock on the door of a merchant known to be friendly to both Remnants and Seconds. Although we cannot see who is behind the door, we hear discreet movement indicating that someone on the other side is trying to determine our intent at this late hour of the night.

"It is Eleazar," the priest states quietly. His words are either our pass or our peril.

In another moment, the door opens, but we are not greeted by anyone. There is a small clay oil lamp on the table and by its dim light we see a door on the opposite wall of the small room before us. There is nothing else to do—we enter.

Proceeding, we arrive at the next door, which turns out to be a movable wall. Once beyond that threshold, Eleazar pulls on a lever that swings the entry tightly shut. He pulls the lever again, but nothing happens, suggesting this is an entry only, not an exit. There is light ahead, another oil lamp. We are being led to an unknown fate and I pray it is to Your glory that we proceed, Yeshua.

The passageway twists and turns, steps up and down, making the perception of distance a tangle. I cannot tell when we may be far underground or above as we weave our way through ancient structures and catacombs. Every hundred meters or so, another oil lamp leads us, but we never see our guide. Then we sink into water. We are likely in one of the nethermost couplings of the city, Hezekiah's tunnel. The air is pungent but not vile; there is a flow here working against us, so the going is slower. The oil lamps are now placed in brick insets along the way and we can sense an increase in temperature. Eventually we step out of the water and all of us smell distant smoke—an acrid incense of once living, now dead things.

There are no more lamps to be seen; we retrieve the last two and these are what we must depend on as the light to guide us to our final objective. The way is straight with no alternate avenues; the temperature continues to increase as we encounter what looks to be an exit or some new mystery.

The question of our destination is answered in another few minutes as we come to a dead end. In the dim flickering, Eleazar seems mesmerized with one place in the wall. He brings our attention to a symbol scratched into the brick. It would be difficult to spy if one were not intent on its discovery—the symbol ת for the letter *Tav*, the last letter of the Hebrew alphabet.

"I am the beginning and the end," quotes Ayita, "the Alpha and the Omega…"

"…the Aleph and the Tav," whispers Rachel.

Eleazar presses firmly on the brick with the marking and nothing happens. He stands puzzled for a moment, then smiles to himself, counts twenty-one bricks to the right and presses there. "Twenty-two letters from end to beginning," he chuckles quietly.

There is a clicking noise and then the frontage pivots, allowing passage to a new chamber. This one looks to be very old, with must and mold hitting our nostrils—garnish to the stifling haze increasingly billowing in front of us.

We quickly make our way in and seal the portal behind us, then walk a short hallway to a simple wooden door. I am the first to arrive here and look back to the others. All nod their heads and I push open the exit.

What confronts us is beyond comprehension. We have come out of the tunnel to find ourselves in the Kidron Valley just below Nehemiah's eastern wall line. By rough estimation, this puts us just under and very near the Teaching Steps. It is dawn, but the smoke is thick and further obscures an already clouded sun. What light does break through reveals absolute carnage—bodies all around us.

Mede's forces are not to be seen, apparently satisfied that no one, no organized effort, now exists to stand against them. I look at the way the bodies lay, appearing to have been shot point-blank and then pushed off the edge of the tiered ground above us. My first temptation is to search for survivors, but the oppressive silence, save for the crackling of still-burning bodies and buildings, speaks to the senselessness of this.

Everyone else in our group seems as numbed as I at the carnage. For a moment we stand amidst the mire and then there is another sound.

Lamenting and weeping, Eleazar leads us up the path that leads toward the Teaching Steps, carefully trying to avoid stepping on or over the dead. Often we have to stop while several of us pick up bodies, respectfully moving them to one side or the other—in some cases, having to stack several upon one another. I can hear each of my coworkers whispering prayers between shudders and more tears.

Ultimately we reach the plateau, but what greets us is worse than anything we might have envisioned. The body count is difficult to assess in the courtyard, because all are crisped so completely by some chemical means that they are mostly fused together into more of a charred lake. I am reminded of a time in my youth when I was taken on a trip into the bowels of a dormant volcano. There, I walked across the crater bed and it had an identical look to this moment, except for these countless bones sticking out of the sludge. The image of gloom in the aftermath of the mud-storm pales to this.

Dry bones. The phrase from Ezekiel comes grossly to mind. To punctuate the grizzly scene, there are gallows erected at the top of the Teaching Steps. Two bodies hang there. These have not been melted completely like the others, yet so disfigured are they that their identities are evident only by what remains of their goatskin coats. They are, of course, the beloved Brother Moses and Preacher Elijah.

I fall to my knees and cough up all that is within me. From somewhere outside of my vision, I hear a moaning that grows progressively into a riling scream.

"Adonai!" Somehow, adrift in my own somberness, I still recognize the heart-cry as the voice of Eleazar.

A forlorn Cherokee tribal eulogy recites through the courtyard. Ayita, in her own special way, recognizes the loss of her father. Each of those present mirror her mourning song. But soon we all realize there is a duty to be done—by Jewish standards we are inapt for the task as we are unclean, having touched blood and death. The books of Moses strictly prohibit ones such as us from approaching the altar of the Most High, but it is Eleazar who offers an amazing suggestion. "You non-Remnant Seconds, as sensitive as you are to Jewish formalities, have a foreign freedom by recognition of Yeshua as Messiah. By his blood you have been cleansed and so is it not fitting for you to confer this sacrifice?"

And so we do. We labor in disconsolate love to collect what we can of the martyrs, who are then joined in burial beneath the New Temple altar. The doors to the Temple had been unlocked from within, we know not by whom and at first the work was slow. There is no water for cleansing. There are no shrouds, not even swaddling for dressing the dead. Dejection and supplication are the wash with which we prepare the bodies. In this our Jewish brothers and sisters join. The song of our sorrow rides the wind beyond the Temple walls and soon others appear to assist. No one seems to fear for his or her own life; not a word is spoken about the horror around us.

I bend to awkwardly pick up a body and soon other pairs of hands assist. I look up and am surprised to see they belong to Eleazar himself. Looking around, I recognize many Remnants who are also about the work. Eleazar says to me, "Just as in the days when Moses listened to God give a new commandment, just as Yeshua spoke revelation that reshaped tradition, so we are being changed by YHWH in this new age by new understanding."

The burials go on through the night and into the darkness of early morning. Nearing dawn, as I help lower one more corpse into the Martyrs Pit, I notice a feature on the chiseled capstone that waits, a few feet away, to be hoisted to the nearly constructed roof of the Temple. It is an inscription in Hebrew: אבן העזר —Ebenezer, *stone of help*. I remember an English song that Jende sings to the children at night and now I offer the song to God and the people in this place so in need of help. My singing voice is not a pleasant thing and quickly, others who know the tune join in to straighten out the melody.

> Come, Thou Fount of every blessing, tune my heart to sing
>   Thy grace;
> Streams of mercy, never ceasing, call for songs of loudest praise.
> Teach me some melodious sonnet, sung by flaming tongues
>   above.
> Praise the mount! I'm fixed upon it, mount of Thy redeeming love.
> Sorrowing I shall be in spirit, till released from flesh and sin,
> Yet from what I do inherit, here Thy praises I'll begin;
> Here I raise my Ebenezer; here by Thy great help I've come;
> And I hope, by Thy good pleasure, safely to arrive at home.

There are more verses, but at this time, we have reclaimed all except for the bodies of Brother Moses and Preacher Elijah and the arduous task of freeing the two from their nooses causes a pause to our singing. Their swollen corpses do not give up their perches easily, but are finally freed, allowing us to prepare them for internment as best we are able.

When they are at last on the ground, we surround them and offer the last stanzas of the song as a choral prayer:

> O that day when freed from sinning, I shall see Thy lovely face;
> Clothed then in blood washed linen, how I'll sing Thy sovereign
> > grace;
> Come, my Lord, no longer tarry, take my ransomed soul away;
> Send Thine angels now to carry, me to realms of endless day.

There is a long silence after the song is done. The thoughts and emotions working in the minds and hearts gathered around the dais are individual mysteries. Suddenly Eleazar pronounces, "Leave them there."

I think, *he is tired and believes us to be also. He will direct us in a decorous service for them later.* But it is not to be. I soon realize that the priest intends to leave the bodies lying where they are and we are appalled at his insensitivity. We begin to refuse his request, when Ayita states, "He's right. Let the world see by their example what has been done here." Reluctantly, we prop the bodies against their hanging mast and so forsake the cherished men, moving attentively to the altar.

"Ashes to ashes, dust to dust." Some oil has been found and it is now poured over the rough-hewn table. Eleazar speaks a choked blessing over the now-closed tomb and when we have sung a last lamentation, he signals for me, Luther, Jason, Rachel and Ayita to come to his side.

"There is another task in which I would ask your assistance. It is far more dangerous than what you have just done—you will be at risk of losing your lives. Also, I know all of us are tired, but it cannot wait. You do not need to join me, but I would be blessed by your company."

"With artificial intelligence we are summoning the demon. In all those stories where there's the guy with the pentagram and the holy water, it's like—yeah, he's sure he can control the demon. Doesn't work out."

—*Elon Musk*

What is the task? It matters not. Our brother—a Second, as Brother Moses would call him—asks and we will not refuse. He leads our drained contingent back to, of all places, Beit Aghion, the domicile of Darius Mede and the hair on my arms and neck tingles with apprehension when the priest requests of the guards that we be permitted entry.

There is a long period (my guess is an hour) that we are made to wait. We pray with and for one another before an administrator comes out to the gate. Without a question to our purpose, he grants us access and leads us again to the room where I, Brother Moses and Preacher Elijah last grappled with the Premier of the Green Order Government. This time, there is no offer of food, water, much-needed rest, or even an opportunity to change garments. I am the first to be led into the chamber and there see Mede sitting in what can only be described as a throne. Once we are all escorted into the room, no other chairs are made available. It is evident that we are either to remain standing or sit on the floor. Regardless, Mede's roost is elevated so everyone is forced to look up at him to clarify our issue.

Eleazar wastes no time with parliamentary banter and goes right to the issue. "Why?"

Mede does not seem offended by the bluntness; indeed, his crooked smile reveals mild amusement. "Perhaps I should ask you the same thing. My men arrived to protect innocent civilians and keep order during an unauthorized assembly. Suddenly, there was an uprising when Mose…the usurper came at my people, obviously intending them harm with one of his magic tricks."

"That is not…" Lord God, the words are my own, out of my mouth before I can stop them. Adrenaline replaces my fatigue and I have taken a step forward, inspiring the guards in the room to pull weapons from their holsters. Eleazar calmly puts his left arm in front of me to stop any other motion or speech. There is a malevolent moment of tension until Darius Mede is assured that he is still in control and safe. He then puts up his arm and forces a laugh.

"Obviously no one in this room means harm to anyone else. I am sure we are all wanting to assuage this misunderstanding."

It is all I can do to keep still. I am *sure* I'm not the only one and I pray to You, Adonai, to cover all of us with Your peace that passes all understanding. It is now that a thought comes to me. *He is trying to goad us. He wants us to react, to give him validation for our destruction. He is scared of us!* Somehow the thought gives me comfort and quiets my soul.

Eleazar seems to understand the circumstances best of all and intercedes. "We have come neither for understanding nor for reconciliation. Yahweh will be the judge of all our works. I have come for one reason and bring these people as my witnesses. Before I reveal my purpose, I ask for your assurance that they be granted safe passage from this place regardless of the outcome of your and my discussion."

Mede seems to consider this for a long moment, as if he is Solomon himself determining the fate of his underlings. "Of course, they may leave here with my blessing. As for you, my long-lost brother, I am now more curious than ever as to your intent."

What has Mede just revealed? Brother? I am convinced the term is being used in an attempt to include himself as part of the brotherhood of mankind…until I more closely scrutinize each man's features: Mede is clean-shaven; Eleazar wears the beard and curls of the Hasidim. Their garb (one in an impeccably tailored business suit, the other in shoddy street clothes stained from the dismal task of burial) no longer distorts their similar build, height and…Adonai, their voices! They are not identical; Eleazar is obviously younger by ten years or more, but there is no doubt they are siblings!

All in the room come to the realization at nearly the same moment. Only Eleazar and Mede wear confidence on their faces. The rest of us, Mede's men included, exhibit unease.

Eleazar fills the chaotic silence. "We are not in control of the situation that has brought us to this point. Not I, not you, not one of us. It is Yahweh Himself who, in the beginning, spoke these days into being. It is, however, our choice of what we now do in this moment that is left to us."

Mede reaches over to a table beside him to grasp a glass of water. He takes a long drink, seeming to relish it and taunt our thirst at the same time. Placing the glass back on the table, he speaks. "Emptiness poured from a hollow urn. I heard such stuff from the goat-haired men before they began their insurrection. If you choose to continue in the same actions, defiling my Temple, considered holy to the world, then you too will be considered as a threat to our happiness."

"I now realize my choices in a new light," Eleazar continues as if he were speaking to another outside the room, outside of the world. "It was by Your will that the Temple has been rebuilt. It is to Your purpose that lives have been martyred—"

"It is a good time for you to recognize my authority in these things," Mede interrupts, mistaking the priest's invocation as being directed toward him.

Eleazar continues, unmoved by the interruption, "It is not You who defile our worship but we who enter Your presence who are broken and corrupt. And, Yahweh, You have sent messengers who have also been mentors to me, showing me the arrogance of my ways, helping to peel the scales from my eyes…"

Mede looks puzzled by the twist of deflection—the priest veering their exchange into a dialogue with God. He seeks to divert attention back in his favor. "And it is good that you recognize my message. Take heed of the lessons I am trying to share with you!"

"You offer repeated second chances up until the day of final judgment," Eleazar continues, "for mankind to experience Your grace and mercy. The Jewish people of old were bull-headed, resisting You as their Creator and in this time we are even more stubborn."

"Stubborn is a small description for what you are," Mede tee-hees.

"YHWH, I now recognize the work that You have put in place and I repent my resistance." Eleazar says the words as he falls to his knees, raising his hands and his eyes toward the heavens. "I cannot explain my disobedience—my actions were borne in pride and that was my fatal error. I had snubbed the signs of the One You sent and the one who now tries to commandeer His throne…"

I look to Mede and notice the same small twitch attacking his left eyelid that had developed when Brother Moses debased the man's authority. Eleazar presses forward. It is now obvious to everyone that he is petitioning the One True God.

"The two whom You sent to witness have spoken into my heart by their example and their own sacrifice. They spoke into me a *what-if.* What if there is no mortal man today who can save us through exemplary rule? What if, only by Your unmatchable power, one has already been sent who was both God and Man? What would that one's ministry look like? What if the God-Man taught us first what true surrender would look like and what if he promised then to return another time as conqueror, given authority by his own self-sacrifice? What would we call that *One?*"

Mede will not let the question be answered. In rage he orders, "Take him!" The guards react immediately, grabbing Eleazar, pulling him toward a side door. Mede's face is purple as he stares through the rest of us. Then he becomes white as chalk, thinking quickly of his next orders. "You, out before I change my mind," and he too exits through the same route.

Once again, our group is left without escort. Without word, we head for the main door of the throne-room. Before leaving, my eyes catch sight of a stack of papers in an open leather binder resting on the surface of a desk to the side of the room. Lord, I am not sure why, but I hear Your voice clearly in the moment. "Share them." I run to the desk, extricate the album and flee the premises. On our way back to the Essene Quarters, we walk quickly, but quietly, expecting at any moment to also be apprehended. A snip of Psalm 121, which the faithful had sung in the courtyard, continuously threads through my mind as we exit. *The Lord is your keeper.*

Brothers? Could it be? What must we all now do? There is confusion among us and more questions than answers—the relationship of Eleazar to Darius Mede being but one of the perplexing issues.

In our meeting, Mede had seemed to imply his ownership over the New Temple. Neither the government nor Darius Mede himself was ever involved in the funding or the construction of the building, so it suggests a spiritual coup is taking place. Then there is the question of how to aid Eleazar, who is most certainly now being tortured by his brother for his outspokenness.

There is little we can do at this moment; all are sapped, so we try to sleep. But in slumber, an unrelenting dream comes to me. The last words that Brother Moses spoke to me:

In a compartment hidden in the ceiling of the place we have been meeting, you will find some instructions for you as well as some other very special documents. They are yours to protect now. Guard them on the polished tablet of your heart. Soon our ministry will change forever and then you will be the Keeper to share them.

I awake after an hour and it seems everyone else has also had disturbing visions, now being fully alert. I ask for assistance to explore the suspended plaster. At first I cannot determine any unusual flaw secreted within its worn and cracked texture. But Jason finds a fissure that is actually less prominent and when pressed three times reveals a screened compartment. Therein we find a thick oilskin portfolio. As we peel the covering away, the first item to come out is an ordinary envelope addressed modestly: *Ilbani.*

I unseal the post to find within a letter written in ancient Latin, a troublesome lexicon, these days recognizable to few, besides myself. The choice of this language is obvious—protecting the information should it fall into the wrong hands. My eyes fall first on the signature at the closure of the page.

It is hard to read the text, not for its language but because I realize Brother Moses wrote this message knowing his soon-coming fate. I wipe my tears away and find strength in translating the text that I now read to the others:

Dearest Ilbani, my Talmid,

By now you understand the greatest campaign to be fought in this terrible new world you inhabit. Evil is amok and would have you think it is in control. This is not so! Yeshua will return soon, but there are still preparations that must be made before his triumphal reentry into Jerusalem. Part of that work is yours.

You have been given power and authority even greater than that of the prophets of old. That power began to emerge with your acceptance of Yeshua as your savior; it continued with the gift of discernment and writing that you have been given: It continues with your protection and dissemination of the documents that are now in your hands.

There is no need for me to further explain; they explain themselves and you will know what to do with their contents.

As for the group you now lead, I offer an additional gift in the words of an ancient follower of Yeshua:

> *"Here there is not Greek and Jew, circumcised and uncircumcised, barbarian, Scythian, slave, free; but Christ is all and in all.*

> *Put on then, as God's chosen ones, holy and beloved, compassionate hearts, kindness, humility, meekness and patience, bearing with one another and, if one has a complaint against another, forgiving each other; as the Lord has forgiven you, so you also must forgive.*

> *And above all these, put on love, which binds everything together in perfect harmony."*

These words are as true and precious for you as they were for believers before the Hidden Exodus. And that reminds me: you are probably all asking the same question I did about this new age, "What is changed, what then is different from the time before the Gathering-Up?"

Simply…you. You are a new creation. Before, your country, your culture and your religion defined you. Each of you pursued a different path toward or away from God. Now the lines have intersected. In the previous age, the Age of Pentecost, we were taught to corporately worship. Now, in the Age of Trumpets, worship will become a united front. All governments, all institutions, all political beliefs will dissolve. Not because one or the other is bad or good; they will vanish because, with the ascendancy of the God-Man, they become obsolete.

You Seconds are greater than any of us who obliged Yeshua Messiah in the last age. Why? As much persecution and trial as we faced before, it was nothing compared to what each of you have and will experience. YHWH has gifted you with far greater faith, strength and gifts than we ever had—frankly, because you will need it more. God has lifted His protection from this place for a short while so that your example, your singular and community demonstrations of faith, will become the greatest of all time.

And to encourage great testimony, to seek every opportunity to share one last time, the gospel of Yeshua's redemptive love, great leadership is necessary. Your ability, Ilbani, is proven not by your ego, but by your humility, your subordination. You have been chosen to lead by Him who taught us to follow.

Know that you have already found great favor. Now, as you are going and doing, use these tools I am giving you to make disciples of all nations, teaching them to obey Yeshua, the Word, just as he has taught you.

At the end of the letter, one line stands out from the rest because it is written in Hebrew…

Tchn hshlvm shl h sh'vvr chl hhvnh lhvt tch ch, vshmv shl shv'—
May the peace of YHWH that passes all understanding be with you, my brother, in the name of Yeshua.

Moshe

For a moment, none of us speak. Then Rachel moves to a backpack she had reclaimed from her quarters on the way to our meeting. Reaching in, she pulls out two loaves of bread and a bottle of wine and speaks serenely, "I have been saving this wine for some special occasion. The sun, though veiled, still infers that the noon hour is upon us, it is Shabbat—what could be more special? Let us show appreciation for what has been given to us by YHWH. Brother Ilbani, would you bless this meal."

We join hands and my voice breaks once as I begin, "Barukh atah Adonai, Eloheinu, melekh ha-olam borei p'ri hagafen…"—*Blessed are You Lord God, King of the Universe, who creates the fruit of the vine…*

After the meal and prayers, we remain seated on cushions; one oil lamp flickers in the center, helping the dim light of another thickly clouded day. I unfold the portfolio used to protect the papers we recovered from its hiding place. Some of the pages are written in Hindi script. I recognize this as the diary of Pasha Sumje, our recently martyred East-Indian brother. Two other portfolios are handed to me by the trembling hands of Ayita Blueroad and I see why.

One contains Preacher Elijah's notes detailing his journey to New Israel. Within the other...its front page speaks volumes about the contents, representing a time before this great pandemonium. My hands also quiver as I speak the title for all to hear. "The Journal of Daniel Adamson. Epilogue added by Fitzgerald E. Hindeland."

Ayita hands me two other items. One is a small canvas case. Within its felt lining are lenses and filters such as would attach to a telescope. "I've seen these before," I respond a little too excitedly. "They are Preacher Elijah's tools to study the heavens!"

The second item is a plastic zip-lock bag containing five identical wooden sticks. I recognize their past purpose—they were once used as holders for a child's frozen treat called popsicles. But only a few among us, Jason's clan of Seconds, seem to have any idea as to why the sticks have been saved. Jason himself reaches for the wooden strips and meticulously assembles them into a strange configuration. He then passes the handicraft over to me and suggests, "You might wanna look up what Danny had to say 'bout that."

And I definitely plan to, but first, I pick up and reexamine the bag in which all of the contents were contained. On its surface, there is indelible marker writing that reads:

To Fiz from Danny

"Will the journals explain how all of these testimonies came about?" asks Ayita.

"Oh, they will," responds Jason, they sure 'nuff will.

What we obtain too cheap, we esteem too lightly: it is dearness only that gives every thing its value. Heaven knows how to put a proper price upon its goods; and it would be strange indeed if so celestial an article as freedom should not be highly rated.

—Thomas Paine, The American Crisis

Eight refills of the lamp oil later, it is completed. We have all taken turns reading Pasha's testimony and then dug into Danny Adamson's history and, finally, the travels of Preacher Elijah. How enriching the details, how alive I now feel after reading prophecy unfolding.

Jason, usually the quietest of our clan, is the first to speak. "Ah need to tell you that there's other thangs stowed where Ah'm staying. We brought six typewriters and lots of ribbons from Ein Gedi. Preacher told me to keep it to my own-self 'till the right time. Guess this be that time. He said to tell you, 'spread the word'."

It's immediately apparent what he means. With my talent for languages, I'm to translate the pages before me into dialects for the world to receive. This charge excites me, but there is an even more immediate challenge on my heart. I look around at each of my companions and say, "Now that we know the truth about Darius Mede, it is imperative that we find some way to emancipate Eleazar."

"How?" ask Luther and Jason as one. The same question shows on everyone's face but for one…

"We needs inside help. Daniel Adamson's story tells of one person who might gives assistance." Rachel looks around the room after making this suggestion in her stilted English. She pauses and then makes a request. "Before we makes plan, would any know of fresh water near? Reading Daniel's words, I am come to decision and now I would to be baptized."

After a healthy discussion, it is decided to keep the rescue squad small to avoid drawing unnecessary curiosity. If our plan works, few will be needed to carry it out. If we fail, no unnecessary lives will be jeopardized.

We believe the two women Ayita Blueroad and Rachel are best suited for the task. One more is needed and I volunteer. Everyone else protests based on my new status: their leader, as deemed by Brother Moses's letter. I refuse their protection, arguing that I am most familiar with the layout of Beit Aghion and know many places to hide along our route if we are discovered. In the end, they unenthusiastically agree. "Besides," I quip, "who better to write the account of such an adventure once we return?"

We gather in a circle one last time to pray for exactly that outcome.

Our path involves immediate risk in that I need to recoup crucial materials for our plan to work and those items are safely kept by my wife Jende. By going to my family's location, I am risking their safety as well, but it must be done. Thankfully, it is dark and as best we can tell, no other eyes follow our movements. Jende is at the door immediately upon our coded knock. The three of us enter quickly and in whispers explain the plan. There is no grousing, no tears, just a nod and a very passionate, embarrassing kiss from Jende that I would have preferred in a more furtive moment. But time and privacy are short in these times; my friends understand and do not make sport of the affection with me later. We all carry with us the knowledge that these may be our final actions ahead of new life. What we also carry is hope and faith that YHWH's purpose be served with each step we are given.

She is not difficult to find. The newly modified vehicle is more than a convenience; it is also an icon of status, which she seems anxious to display. Early in the morning, from a vantage point on a hill that overlooks Beit Aghion, we see the gates open and the machine lurch to the streets, surrounded by guards trotting as best they can to keep up. Actually, the motorcade is a bit comical, but the challenge is evident before us. How do we win her attention while avoiding the wrath of Brenda Anders's protectors?

It was Ayita's suggestion we chose. She seems to have been given a special sensitivity to people's partialities. Based on our history, interests and beliefs, we tend to be individually piqued by different words, items, even smells. Ayita is confident she knows that which should beguile the Premier's Dame.

We ask once more for the Spirit's guidance and then head to a junction on David Street that we believe will be the predictable course for Anders. We are rewarded, for we hear the obnoxious steam engine announcing her approach. There are enough vendors and workers on the street in the early morning to make our presence inconspicuous, so that when her accompanying guards jog by, we move unpretentiously to the side with the others. But as the SUV draws beside us, Ayita pulls a cardboard sign from beneath the tallit she wears. The lettering is in English and is written large enough to see from inside the vehicle:

THANK YOU FOR LOVING OUR PLANET

The glass windows of the SUV are rolled up, the morning being a brisk one, but it is easy to see Dame Anders's eyes glance at the sign and then a smile form on her face. The SUV continues ahead and I begin to think we have failed when suddenly the contraption shudders to a halt. The guards, who were all positioned ahead of the truck, are unprepared for the stop and have continued to run ahead several yards. They look as surprised as we when the Premier's wife exits her smoking chariot and walks back our direction. I look around to see that, somehow, our clan and Brenda Anders's contingent are the only ones remaining on the street. I feel an immediate need to pray about the question on my mind. *How did the citizens disappear so quickly and what excited them so? Should we be disappearing too?*

"I have the damnedest time figuring out how to brake that monster," Anders says casually in English. Then, just in case she is not understood, she tries the same statement in Arabic and fails miserably. I have to stifle a laugh.

Her detail is now trotting back our way with their weapons at ready. Anders remains facing us, but speaks to stop their motion. The guards, unsure of the situation, slow, but continue to move toward us. The motion of their boots alerts her that her orders are not being followed and before she turns, I can see the look of wrath the Dame has prepared to give the soldiers. Apparently they know the look well, for when she faces them, without her having to say a word they stand immediately at rigid attention.

"That's better," she compliments in an equally casual tone, then walks directly up to Ayita. "Do you mean that," Anders asks, gesturing to the sign, "or are you looking for a handout?" By her cynical tone, I suspect we are not the first to compete for her approval.

Ayita smiles warmly, another gift YHWH has given, enabling her to relay an immediate sense of warmth and trust to others. "My heritage is Native American and our people always honor those who love the land."

Prior to the Hidden Exodus, Ayita Blueroad had been incessantly pursued by the media for her outspokenness on the planet coupled with her

Cherokee lineage and, of course, for being the president's daughter. Both she and her father favored a much lower profile for her work. The Dame of the Premier had been world-famous in her own right for originating the Green Government Coalition that had been instrumental in helping Darius Mede to coalesce his power. She might recognize Ayita through their communal cause and if so, the risk of our introduction turning provocative is tremendous. Still, the gambit is worthwhile; Ayita's tribal traditions are genuine and should attract empathy from Anders.

Sure enough, there is a pause in the conversation and the Dame narrows her eyes at the younger woman. "I…know you."

The guards grow immediately restless, as do the rest of us. All but Ayita, that is, who continues to speak warmly. "We share many of the same concerns and now, the pang of what has happened to our common home."

"OMG, Ayita Blueroad. I read your exposé on the suburban blight plaguing the Midwestern heartlands of America. It was…was…absolutely inspiring!" Without warning, Brenda Anders makes the extra step towards Ayita, embraces her and begins to blubber, "And your children's book, *The Silent Song of the Prairie Dog*…ohhhhhh!"

It was comical to watch this prominent woman blubber upon the shoulder of the Cherokee. Ayita does not shun Anders, graciously accepting the compliment. "You have…encouraged me as well." After allowing the elder to gather her composure, Ayita probes for our opportunity. "May I bare another cause that might be worthy of your consideration?"

"I would love to hear it! You have no idea how lonely I've been for someone like yourself who understands how we are now being punished by Mother Earth for our abuses!" The Dame is almost giddy now and Ayita allows the misrepresentation without correction.

"Thank you. It has to do with assertions I heard you make in the past about the plight of those who support a lifestyle in harmony with the land, at the expense of those who would take advantage of all resources." The wording is delicate and true, actually describing a very Hebraic drift of being firmly rooted in the land that is being embattled by dark forces.

"I would do anything I could to help those being persecuted for an environmental position," says Anders with almost patriotic flair. I find myself fascinated, listening to her filtering Ayita's request and described abuse through the prism of her own ethics. "Who is the suffering party?"

Ayita plays the final card. "Your husband's brother."

"My husb…Darius…has a brother?"

Praise You, Adonai, we could not have hoped for a better outcome. Brenda Anders has just discovered that she too has been kept in darkness.

Having read Danny Adamson's journal, our group had come to a suspicion that there was little love lost between the Premier and his wife-in-name-only. Besides their daughter, whom we now secretly harbor, there were probably a great many privacies each kept from the other and we had just illuminated one of the greatest. This had been the major jeopardy in our strategy for freeing Eleazar. We had already agreed to respect the request of Roxanne, who asked us not to reveal her presence in Jerusalem. Now that we have crossed this new hurdle, the unveiling of the sibling relations, both the stakes and the unpredictability of our success are intensified.

More than ever, I pray for the Spirit's participation and protection. Brenda Anders pulls us all in close and whispers conspiratorially, "There is more to this than you know." The once-proud CEO of the largest ecological think-tank and community action group in the world looks toward her protective guard that still stand in statue-like readiness. She catches the eye of one who appears to be her senior man and says, "It's time, Claymore."

Anders's senior lieutenant barks out, "Ten-six, sixty-six!" At this code, ten of the others fluidly arm their weapons and shoot the other six in the detail. We all recoil at the action and then cower, not knowing if we will be the next to be considered expendable.

"Oh, you poor dears," the Premier's Dame titters. "So innocent to reality! There will always be those loyal to one side of a cause or to another. I have vetted my guards carefully, but of course, my precious husband would want to keep a more careful eye out on my behalf. For a time his spies met a purpose, but…well, that purpose is fulfilled."

With schoolgirl animation strange to the circumstances, she now encourages us to our feet. "You are safe now, don't you see?"

I could not see it at all.

*Just because something doesn't do what you planned
it to do doesn't mean it's useless.*

—*Thomas A. Edison*

Brenda Anders is quite the enigma. She seems energized by this clandestine affair and has embraced us as her own. Yet not once does she ask for, nor does she apparently care to know, any of our names other than Ayita's. We have integrity, thanks to the president's daughter, but will that continue to be sufficient?

The Dame leads us directly back to Beit Aghion. She orders her guard to go ahead after they "clean up the mess" in the street and gives permission for Claymore to drive her steamer back; this way we have privacy for our next moves in this complicated game of chess.

The gates of the government house are opened for us without question when we arrive. Brenda leads the way, talking with us as if we are dignitaries being given a tour in the days when such luxuries were unremarkable. We are interrupted just before entering the compound by yet another moderate earthquake. "Good," Anders states. "They will be busy with the usual structural checks."

By "they," she must be referring to the security force that inhabits this place. As we enter Beit Aghion through a lesser side portal, my concern is that this is my fourth visit to this place. Because of my minimal status during each of the other encounters, I may be seen as either a friendly face or a wanted criminal: which one is yet to be determined. The looming question is, at this early hour, where is Darius Mede? How will the Dame explain our presence and will he recognize me? Adonai, please help me, help all of us be invisible.

"Now where would they hide someone they would not want me to find?" Brenda Anders says this out loud, but I believe it to be a question to herself.

"I believe I can help with that." Did I just open my mouth and speak? Everyone stops and looks at me. It is time to explain. "I was with Eleazar when he was subdued. The Premier and his guards left me and several others without escort when they took him from the throne…I mean the reception room. I was last to leave and saw into the hallway where they had taken him. They pressed on one of the walls and a passageway slid open."

"That would've been helpful information to have had when we began this little adventure, honey," Anders says, whimsically chastising me. The other "helpful information" I decide not to include is that Ayita and Rachel had been two of the others in the room and that I had also expropriated Darius Mede's classified chronicles in that same event—was that just yesterday?

We encounter no one else as the Dame leads us upstairs to the reception room, complete with its throne and the feel of an imperial chamber. She looks to me and I point to the door left of the unwieldy chair. All of us pass through and we examine the hallway beyond. The window at the end of the passage lets in just enough light to help search for a switch or button or some method to open the ulterior compartment.

"Click." Rachel has pushed on one of several tile inlays. The wall moves inward, allowing entry into a darkened recess beyond. "So many secrets," the Dame muses and reaches into a pocket in her pants to retrieve a flint spark spark cigarette lighter. "Nasty habit. I took it up after Darius and I…" Brenda appears to think her admission is too much and leaves the explanation unfinished. She ignites the device and its wavering flame leads us into the unknown.

No one, not a security person, administrator, Eleazar, or Mede himself are found in the vestibule. I look around nervously, expecting at any moment for someone to come in behind us to discover our unauthorized entry. Instead, there is another *"click,"* and the false wall moves back into its sealed slot. Immediately, chemical lights provide a strange red ambiance to what we now see as a small laboratory complete with various bottles on the shelved walls, a whiteboard filled with scribbled equations, gas jets for heating and a tank of liquid hydrogen. The room measures approximately ten meters by ten meters. Not overly large, but ample for any scientific efforts such as performed in most universities. The walls are constructed of some kind of burnished silvery substance. I touch it and it feels almost rubbery, but quite solid. I push in hard on a portion and it gives some to my effort, but immediately reverts back to its flattened form.

"Flexsteel," Brenda Anders answers without being asked. "Darius was a biochemist prior to his political liftoff. He has recently been reapplying those skills and I overheard him discussing this new discovery—a type of aluminum and steel compound with great strength and flexibility. I think he is trying to use it for building structures that ride out the relentless earthquakes."

I hope he succeeds, I catch myself thinking. Indeed, it would be a great advancement, even if the contrivance of Darius Mede. *But at what cost and to what dire purpose might he use the innovation?* I am actually not convinced the thought is my own, but it is a good one. Darius Mede has already proven his heart's intent. Even the best of inventions might be used by him for unthinkable darkness.

And as my thoughts race, my eyes also pinpoint one word written in large letters on a dry-erase board at the back of the room:

DIMONA

What interest might Darius Mede have with the highly inaccessible nuclear facility built by Israel in the 1960s? Word has spread that the core melted after the New Exodus and it would seem logical. Is he planning somehow to confiscate the radioactive material to use as a weapon? What other diabolical scheme does he have up his sleeve and how, without sophisticated power sources, would he be able to achieve his aims?

Now my mind makes several more connections. In our reading of Danny Adamson's journal and in listening to Brother Moses and Preacher Elijah's conversations, I didn't recall hearing the origins of their relationship with the Premier. But in Preacher Elijah's writings it became so powerfully evident. Darius Mede was in studies with them. Both Moses Folzman and Fitzgerald E. Hindeland had begun their scientific research careers right here in the land of Israel. It would stand to reason that Mede would have associated with him based on his chemical abilities. Another thought weaves its way from the depths into my consciousness. *Eleazar was a well-received university-trained Jewish priest...*

"...My word!"

"What's wrong?" Rachel and Brenda Anders ask simultaneously.

"Darius Mede is..." The realization won't come out of my mouth; I am too flabbergasted by what my mind is now telling me.

"Look, I don't understand what you are babbling about, but we need to be about getting out of here." Anders is all about efficiency in the moment and her criticism brings me back to the task at hand.

"But we haven't located Eleazar," I insist.

"That's because he doesn't really ex…" Just as the Dame is mouthing her denial of her husband's brother, a faint groaning, very human in pitch and tenor, emanates from the wall I had pressed on. The noise stops and I place the side of my head, ear flat, to the partition. The sound emits again and there is no doubt—a person is on the other side. The sound suggests whoever it is to be in poor repair.

"Quickly!" I have to say nothing else; everyone joins in trying to find the access point for freeing the prisoner. Where I have been pressing, there seems to be one area more flexible than any other. *Maybe Flexsteel has to set like concrete and this chunk has just been built up?* I have no idea if the thought is harebrained or just desperate, but there are no other options obvious. There is a sweeping broom in the corner; I latch on to it and push the pole end into the soft spot I have found. The wall material is resilient and will not break, but does flex dramatically, much like a strong plastic bag would from compression of a finger applied to it. The women join my efforts and search around for something else to break the seal.

Brenda Anders titters again and says, "Wait, why didn't I think of this before!" Again, from another pocket in what now I notice to be what we used to call "cargo pants," she extracts a leather sleeve that contains a bowie knife with a blade at least fifteen-centimeters in length. "A girl can't be too careful these days," she contends as she digs the point of the weapon into the wall where I am ponderously prodding.

There is an immediate pop and a hissing sound as the pressure between the two rooms equalizes. Our efforts are doubled as we hear choking and coughing from the other side. Once the seal is broken, the knife does the best work of cutting an aperture. Soon there is enough removed to allow me to enter into a small alcove big enough for perhaps two people. There is a body on the ground that I almost trip over. I cannot see much; the only available light is from the other room, but it is just enough to see that the person appears to be regaining consciousness and is stuttering for breath. There is no time to assess other injuries; I determine where the head and shoulders of the victim lay, bend down and lift, managing to get both of us back through the opening.

To our relief, in the light we discover it is indeed Eleazar and other than nearly suffocating in the alcove, he seems otherwise intact. It is then that I myself laugh tensely, thinking of a parallel Bible story. "Welcome back from your tomb, Lazarus!"

"I was not dead, but would have been soon were it not for you," the priest croaks.

After regaining some strength, we all quietly exit Beit Aghion without interference. "Where are the guards?" Ayita asks. "And what about the Premier?"

The Dame seems unconcerned. "Darius comes and goes at his whim." We are walking back up toward the Temple mount. As best I can figure, the most recent quake has caused the townspeople to flee the area, for we are the sole occupiers of the street. This also makes no sense to me; most residents to the area are now acclimated to the ongoing tremors; quickly and efficiently resuming activities of the day afterward. This earthquake was little more than a tremor—what would cause such an exodus?

Suddenly, Brenda Anders motions her guard to a halt; our progress is also stopped as they surround and face us as in a circular barricade. Their weapons are again at ready and I think, *It was always a ploy, she means to execute us here.*

Brenda asks nonchalantly, "What I'd like to know is why Darius would entomb his brother and why this man's rescue is so integral to you?"

I don't know why I feel compelled to answer; I am only one of our group. I do know that the way I acquaint the issue may have a huge impact on the response of Anders and her minions. Before I can reply, though, Eleazar assumes responsibility.

"I am the head priest for the Remnants," he responds in a raspy voice.

There is silence as the Premier's wife works through the association and implications in her mind. Her face changes from puzzlement, to astonishment, to something that looks like delighted surprise before she responds with an outbreak of outright cheerfulness that bounces through the empty alleyways. "Delicious," she finally manages. "Utterly delicious."

"Perhaps the irony is great, but I would caution that Darius Mede's plans, as I overheard before my premature…burial, do not suggest this is a time to delight in entertaining twists." Eleazar looks thoughtfully up the street as we all now hear a great cheering throng, the sound emanating from the direction of the Temple mount. "I believe I know your husband's whereabouts and his intentions. We should proceed to the altar area as quickly as possible."

Melodies are just honest. They can only be what they are. Words have the capacity for deception. They're all full of subtext and some of them are cliché and overused and vernacular. They're trick. All I can say is, words are tricky.

—Andrew Bird

We approach the Temple, coming up toward the Teaching Steps from the lower city. There are thousands here again and I am immediately concerned for their safety. We press through the crowd to see why they have been perpetually cheering.

As we draw closer, a thought intrudes. *It is the fortieth day following Pentecost* and I realize something both obscure yet hugely relevant to the moment. "Today is the Fast of Tammuz!" I say out loud. Eleazar turns to me with a dumbfounded look on his face, but says nothing. The implications are staggering to all of us, save perhaps the Dame. *We have come to the Temple on the Day of False Gods when the Israelites bowed down to the golden calf and the prophet Moses broke the tablets of the Ten Commandments.*

To our trepidation, Darius Mede stands at the doors that open into the inner court of the Temple. With him are fifty or so guards and assistants with air guns that they now use to fire loaves of bread and plastic bottles of water out over the crowd. As the projectiles arch and descend, the ravenous surge, all attempting to reach for the precious goods.

Where Mede acquired the highly prized plastic bottles is anyone's guess, but the outcome of this spectacle cannot be good. Each time the people in the outer court sway toward the bread and water, I hear a scream or the sickly snapping of bone. There is no concern for others—anyone too feeble to move with the crowd is trampled by the others rushing for pickings.

Wisely, Eleazar leads us to the east, circumventing the mayhem while still making progress toward the steps. Miraculously, it seems, in the press of the crowd, we find Jason and Luther with a group of other Seconds who also had heard of the commotion at the Temple. I am relieved to learn that Roxanne and my Jende are watching over the children at our quarters. I would not be well focused if they were in this company. Ultimately, we are all able to cluster at the bottom of the Eastern Steps, when the crowd is suddenly silenced. From our vantage point, we see the Premier, but he is facing southward and does not seem aware of our presence.

"It is washed." Eleazar is pointing to the courtyard floor and now we all see it. Though we had buried the bodies—*was that just three and a half days ago?*—we had no method for cleaning the blood and mutilation from the Temple grounds. Even with enough water, soap, shovels and labor, the undertaking would have been enormous. Yet before us the masses stand on a polished surface that glistens even in the murky light. Mede wants to impress and, other than the two bodies on the platform, has wiped away all reminders of his manslaughter.

Why I am drawn to the area, I cannot explain. But like the observation of the capstone, my eyes now rove to the cornerstone above and behind us at the junction of the southern and eastern walls. Written in Hebrew and then in Greek, I see:

יהושוע משיח / Ἰησοῦς Χριστός
Yeshua HaMashiac / Jesus Christ

That is the work of Brother Moses! How sublime the Father's dealings can be.

I have no time to announce the visible victory with the others for Darius Mede now makes himself known. He stands self-assured before his audience and says, "You have been lied to by those who said they would distribute their precious consumables fairly. If they were going to do so, would you not already have full stomachs?"

Another cheer goes up from the audience before him and Darius soaks in the praise.

"I promise you more where this came from. And also you will see the completion of a new and safer Jerusalem. I have been working hard on your behalf and the results are thrilling. I have designed for you a new material with which to build, strong and flexible enough to withstand the many earthquakes from below and the terrors that fall from the sky. Now together we can live in safety rather than the fear promoted by the religious fools who would have you believe a god is going to protect you. If a god were going to do that, why are we all in such dire straits?"

The crowd clamors their agreement and now Mede points toward the bodies of Brother Moses and Preacher Elijah. They still lie on the platform toward the Western Wall, but I can see they have been pelted with refuse. As I watch, others run up to spit on them and quickly flee into the crowd again.

Darius asks, "Where is the god of those two?" There is actual stadium laughter and my heart weeps at the rapid change of attitude of the supposed *faithful.* Darius looks thoughtful for a moment and then continues, "Those fanatics—I will not even bother to give them a name—limited the religious sects that may enter through these gates. Even that other extremist group that formerly dominated this locus, sworn enemies of the supposed 'chosen ones', they too put restrictions on those who could enter.

"But I say we are a tolerant collective. We should all be able to worship as we wish and do so peacefully together." Strangely, a smile crosses Mede's face and he offers, "I know! They were so insistent on burying their dead up here,"—at this he points toward the still-unfinished altar which can be seen through the open gates—"let us show them a new way. Let us deposit their bodies as well under that altar and then bury the altar itself. We will show them there is a new way to worship. I will lead you in discovering the power of corporate praise. I will demonstrate how following one strong man is the finest future for humanity."

Darius Mede waves his arms above his head and woos, "Follow me and I will give you renewed life!"

"We'll be needing that bigger dog we talked about, and now would be a good time for it to show up, Lord," Jason prays out loud.

I look over to see Brenda Anders shaking her head. The cheering of the crowd is deafening, so I can barely hear what she speaks now. "The arrogance of that ass!" And when I turn back, the mob has split and is rushing in two directions at once—some toward the platform of Moses and Elijah, the others toward the altar. Mede, protected by his minions, watches approvingly as the latter group reaches the altar, lifting it off its plinth and preparing to allow the bodies of our beloved leaders to be muscled in. Their conduct is insensitive and un-ceremonial, unlike our mourning of a few days before.

At this moment, a noise like I have heard but once before in my life—it is the same as when the Great Exodus occurred—rushes upon us and the Temple court on a hot wind. It carries with it the feel of searing fire and the stroke of a mother's loving touch all at once. The sound is the blast of a ram's horn, but from all directions; it vibrates to my bones and is accompanied by a blinding light whose source is unknown. I drop fearfully to my knees, unable to see and having marginal hearing. A name forms in my brain and the words tremble out of my mouth, "Ruach Ha, Kodesh"—the Holy Spirit of the Most High.

When my senses recover in a moment, I hear the gang nearest the execution platform suddenly cry out as one and I can see enough to discern them crawling, backing away from the disgraced effigies. The light is still strident, but I can now regard its source. The stage where Brother Moses and Preacher Elijah had been hung is now on fire. It is not a blaze as I have ever experienced, but more of a shimmering blue storm of light. I cannot explain it better. Lightning is within the fire and within the lightning… movement…small particles that grow and coalesce.

Music, there is no doubt, flows out from the Ruach. Its indescribable tones make me sob and laugh with no distinguishing between the two. Then both the light and the music erupt. I am again without sight or hearing for several minutes. My life is a question. My existence seems between two universes. Finally, images start to crystallize and a ringing appears faintly in my ears, turning to actual voices—familiar voices, voices that should not, cannot be.

"Kin, Israel, what have you done? Where is your faith?"

My eyes clear and there is no more doubt; upon the platform stand Brother Moses and Preacher Elijah. They glow with the same electric fire I saw before and seem completely physically restored. Even their tunics shimmer and seem new. The two now speak as one and in harmony—and there are other voices that speak with them. All unified: all so sumptuous, yet terrifying in tone.

"You are standing today, all of you, before the LORD your God: the heads of your tribes, your elders and your officers, all the men of Israel, your little ones, your wives and the sojourner who is in your camp, from the one who chops your wood to the one who draws your water, so that you may enter into the sworn covenant of the LORD your God, which the LORD your God is making with you today, that He may establish you today as His people and that He may be your God, as He promised you and as He swore to your fathers, to Abraham, to Isaac and to Jacob."

I recognize what is being spoken; Moshe's final descant in the wilderness. *Why are these words being offered to both the Remnants and to all in the courtyard who do not practice or recognize that faith?* The witnesses speak the rest of the scripture passage as if to answer my ruminations.

"It is not with you alone that I am making this sworn covenant, but with whoever is standing here with us before the LORD our God and with whoever is not with us today."

I want desperately to take in every syllable, but I finally have to close my eyes and cover my ears; the light is too bright, the voice too powerful, yet somehow washing me in unexplainable peace.

"Do not fear, my good friend." It is the voice of Brother Moses. I open my eyes briefly to see that the two are still firmly set on the fiery pulpit of their hanging, still castigating the crowd. But in my head, I hear the soothing bass voice of my mentor. He is speaking to me with a love that I want so much to hold but cannot quite touch.

"Our time here is short," he says to me. "The words I am sharing with those who have fallen away in doubt are not meant for you. But soon the persecution must increase even beyond this. I know it seems needless, but do not take the name of YHWH in vain. His purpose is without question. He asks only that you continue to obey."

I nod my head, still awash in tears and not able to reply.

"You and yours will be provided for. Unavoidably, however, you will also be bruised. It is the way, matter-of-factly, life will be. Stay in Jerusalem and lead His believers. Write down everything you experience and observe. As for what you have already recorded and the folios you were gifted from Beit Aghion, these must all be given to Eleazar, Jason and Luther. Those three must travel now for another purpose."

I force open my eyes again to see these three beside me; we have all dropped to our knees, as has the rest of those on the steps and in the outer court. The men just spoken of, however, are nodding in unison with me. *Somehow he is speaking to them as well.*

Now Brother Moses's voice booms aloud for all to hear. "Each of you has to conclude for yourself, the greatest question of all:

Who will triumph in the battle for the souls of mankind?"

I had other questions, but now they seem so small. From across the courtyard, I look to see the back of The Brother's hand moving and I feel his gentle touch stroking my bearded cheek! The experience is joy itself—in it I know God as if a newborn receiving my first breath. In that warmth, I hear a new voice, not meant for me, but directed at Brother Moses and Preacher Elijah.

"Come up here."

My eyes open once more, but I keep my ears covered, averting the cacophony of fear and awe from onlookers as the blue light surrounding the two prophets begins to swirl into a cloud. The cloud lifts them upward and the overcast skies suddenly clear to allow the blue figures lustrous passage into the evening sky. As they climb, another glow appears in the sky. It is the preternatural V4641: the Dark is no longer so. It begins to pulsate, as does the prophets' cloud, which, by way of its increasing distance, becomes a blue star that now races to meet the sympathetic pulse.

I move my gaze down from the heavens to see Jason, Eleazar and Luther also weeping uncontrollably. Ayita and Rachel are on their knees praying in their native languages. Brenda Anders, also kneeling on the pavement, looks around in absolute fear and confusion, blood seeping from both her ears. "I can't hear," she keeps repeating.

All of this might be considered strange; but stranger still, in the darkness of the night, I can see that each one in our party is glowing with a blue aura.

"That's gonna be a problem," Jason suggests.

And he is correct! It is the *Mark of Christ* upon us, which was first experienced by Danny Adamson and Brandon Lader years ago. It now serves to distinguish us from the rest of the crowd and immediately attracts the gaze of Darius Mede himself. He apparently realizes the opportunity to draw attention away from the ascension of the two witnesses. "Seize them! This is their doing," he brays in the hush of the moment.

The mob turns as one to the command of their leader and we are trapped. I begin to pray, knowing that the end is near and then another strong voice travels across the courts.

"Sleep!"

And they do! All those who meant us harm, the security detail, even Mede himself, drops to the pavement in apparent slumber. I look up from my knees to see Jason standing beside me, again with a prayer in his voice. "Thanks, Lord, needed that."

Suddenly we are all maniacally thrown into the air. The earth beneath me seems to disappear and then comes back to meet me ruthlessly. Building bricks, bodies and all untethered things fly unexplainably as the most powerful earthquake I have yet experienced tumbles the city. I have no time to react, dumbly watching one of the altar stones from the temple slant straight for me. I look up to see the brilliant light within the singularity above disappear and then my world too is darkness.

Darius Mede—Chronicle I

Revolution happens in tiny motions, niggling twists, incidental nudges, until its momentum cannot be ignored.

—*Darius Mede*

There is a strange solitude that comes with control. Some would call it loneliness because they fear the seduction of complete power. I have never in my life known that fear. One has to realize that control must be carefully grown and nurtured, never rapidly nabbed. Power gathered without planning is not truly owned; it is borrowed.

I have learned this through my own laborious calculations and a few failures, yes. But well I have learned it and now my methods have paid off. I choose to be complete in myself while others covet the collaboration and counsel of others. I have come to need no such distractions.

Perhaps it is ironic, then, that I write these words. Why are they necessary? I care little if anything for the opinions of men. Then again, I believe in educating those less capable. Perhaps one or two may be encouraged to learn my ways, join my efforts and ease my burden. The rest of humanity? Well, they may be taught to improve their plight by my edification and warnings.

Even I am confused due to the recent events that threaten a toppling of my empire; what must the underprivileged be going through? Superstitious fools across whine about God unleashing judgment. I know better. God… oh yes, I believe in such a beast…played a most unkind trick on this place. He waved his magic wand to percolate the soup of life into a boil and then went on permanent vacation.

And boil we do; because the soup has not had the cook to maintain and nurture the recipe! I grew bitter until I realized the soup must now congeal and take care of itself. Someone has to have the mettle to be the manager of that destiny and I am proud to don the mantle of that role.

Humanity, learn from my example and you will be in control indeed! Look at where religious causes have taken us. See how much we have been held back by those who would entreat us to carry them forward? The weak want their weakness—find strange comfort in it—and within its chains discover perversion of true power. They give control away, then demand it back, piteously claiming abuse at the hands of their pious rulers to whom they have relinquished control. It is a sycophantic relationship with the lesser sucking greedily from the tit of the greater: who then must always provide in order to be provided for.

I am familiar with the shadows and darkness lurking within all mankind. I am familiar with the lies of the heart and the insecurities of the mind. I have conceived a solution to our depravity and I will save even those who believe they are already saved.

I considered it a great setback when electrical power ceased to work. How was I to know that, by my own attempts to help mankind, some strange reaction would somehow interfere with the planet's magnetic polarity, thus creating an inability for any sort of electrical current to exist?

Who can blame me for the bold plan to alleviate the threat of that confounded micro-quasar that still behaves as if it had life? Ridiculous, of course—the thing is yet to be explained by a science yet to be understood.

We will again have power. I will not stop until the damage is undone. Meanwhile, there are other ways that we can harness our resources. After all, flame and water are still available. My people have already started manufacturing steam-powered vehicles and industrial engines that will restore at least a part of our once-magnificent societies. Now I must direct those same energies toward diminishing the chaos of communities and world government.

My plan involves both science and scheme. It will involve several great discoveries connected to the science we know still works. They were not destroyed by the incursion of the singularity.

For now, my creations and these pages must remain closely held—I dare not circulate the complete idea. My folk are too fragmented and confused to understand its good intent. Mankind must succeed and to do so, we must enhance its best qualities and eliminate its worst.

Perhaps electricity may never work again, but chemistry will prevail!

It still seems strange to me that people do not see why science breeds the best leadership. My own case and point: As a biochemical engineer, I had to learn the minute details of a single strand of DNA and also how any liquid or gaseous compound might affect another when in the same stratum. What a natural leap for me then to apply the same study to *Homo sapiens.* The ability to manipulate the plurality depends on familiarity with intricate customs and anticipation of personalities. I have trusted science implicitly, applying its lessons to the structure of everyday life and in doing so, my control has grown enormously.

My continued frustration has been in finding others well suited enough to carry out my plans. Even Brenda Anders—perhaps especially she—has fallen short, evidenced by her wasted vanity and craving for meaningful relationship.

Here I must take a mental detour and educate on the queer differences between blood-family and premeditated relationships. The example is my own: I was born into a household and am, by chemistry, a captive to that lineage until the heritage of the gene pool has been eradicated. My parents, my siblings—they grow up with me. We watch and learn one another's behavior, so the deficiencies and faults we might hide from one another are very few. It is worse with children—I have had that experience too. They grow up mimicking what they think the parent wants. They may even demonstrate supposed loyalty when asked to perform important tasks. But it is a hoax. Sooner or later they turn to their own devices and desires— blood be damned. They use the nuances of their genetic connection to play parent against parent, relative against relative. No, in my experience, devotion to the donors of one's sperm and egg is a lie.

When, however, I meet someone who is not born to my immediate family and choose to befriend them in relationship, we are already starting with an opaque past. Our separate histories include many indiscretions and failings we may or may not want to share. It allows me to be uninhibited in who I would become, by safely sharing my refined character that I desire for the world to see and respect. That is the better family, the more regal relationship. That is the bond I would rather invent—one that includes an admirable history that suits me rather than one requiring an involuntary breeding program.

How can one have a pure relationship with another until they first wipe clean the contamination of an unintended affiliation? To ennoble a genetic accident is to cradle failure to avoid the pursuit of success!

There will be no accidents in my breeding program and my efforts are bearing great success in spite of those who would stand in my way.

There is so much to do; this written account almost seems a waste of time. But as I glance back at my notation, it helps remind me of my purpose, the great accomplishments thus far and the challenges I must yet overcome.

The first and most complicated of my successes was the move from Geneva, now a ghost town made so by the newly erupted volcano in the nearby Alps. Where to go? There were few options: most everywhere was becoming hostile to humanity.

Then I intercepted a missive about one place, strange as it may seem, that is thriving—at least by today's standards. Of all places, it had to be Israel. At first I refused the idea and then a thought came to me. It had to do with one of my introductory logs where I mentioned finding ways to eliminate the worst qualities of mankind. But how can one do that while inferior ethnic groups continue to breed in and even boast of those defects—as if they are a treasure? Of course, I speak of the Jews: that stubborn and religiously petrified sect of squatters that refuse to know when they have become irrelevant.

I have learned from past experience, even from my own hapless history that I have gone to great efforts to expunge. From all of this I have discovered how obstinate are these nomads and so it has become part of my mission to minimize their influence. What better way to do so then to superintend their activities and correct their attempts to subvert a government that is actually to their benefit?

Being in contact with other leaders in that region, I have leveraged my control to an even greater extent and will now be able to subjugate from Jerusalem itself. Thus, tomorrow, the difficult but necessary journey to that pathetic region begins. It will be both a trial and a triumph, even for those who do not understand the goodness I intend for them. From that location I will re-create industry, improve orderliness and synthesize a new way for all to live as one. I will be their guide and their example.

Geneva, I do miss you. The beauty of Lac Leman, your pristine boulevards, the scent of pine everywhere mixing with the tantalizing aroma of raclette and rosti delectably served at so many sidewalk cafés. And the backdrop of the once-mighty Mount Blanc—the mind boggles at nature's power to reduce the highest of the Alps' peaks to a flattened heap. All of my pleasures are gone along with CERN, my nearly completed masterpiece.

But—not my plans, not my intellect. They survive! Perhaps the irony is in the fact that those who would see me destroyed have challenged me to new heights. Without the collapse electrical structure, without the particle accelerator we had built to discover and tame antimatter, I would not have considered chemical alternatives. Who but I would have thought to use nuclear waste to charge water particles in such a way as to have them accelerate? No one but I would be able to create a formula to control the glue of the universe in this manner. All it took was the discoveries at Dimona, along with my newfound workforce, to continue the great work.

Perhaps with the power I will soon harness, the ability to reshape matter and minds to my liking, Geneva and its perfect elegance will be restored.

These insolent people! I have been nothing but tolerant and generous with them since arriving and expositing my authority. Yet they seek trade-offs and continuation of their barbaric ways, including enshrining bodies near the center of the city beneath a crudely constructed sacrificial altar. I am aghast that these rustic colloquialisms still exist in a civilized, if somewhat chaotic, world.

I have committed myself to blotting out these mannerisms. Some education will be necessary, instructing them on how a modern society functions to the betterment of all. And, of course, they will resist. They always do.

The same mistakes will not be made here as has happened in the past. The Jews must not be seen as victims as my plan unfolds. For this reason I have connived temptation so great that they cannot but accept. And the acceptance will be their undoing. An opportunity has arisen allowing me to monopolize, by fiat, a vast region of land—offering it as a shared investment to bribe those corruptible hypocrites. I will offer this land for which they yearn so much. The price? Reverence to me. They will refuse, of course and thus look unbending in their ways. This appearance will then be easily used to sway their supporters away to my cause.

I know their leadership all too well; they will attempt to convince me of their good intentions. They may even make yet another attempt to invite me into their fold of religious nonsense. All of it will be to their demise.

An interesting side note: part of my historical past—an ugly blood connection, to be sure—has surfaced in this place. The other party has not spoken out and I have yet to decide the best way to deal with the problem.

She is the proverbial royal irritation! I speak of no other than that woman whom I consider my one true mistake. Why I acquiesced and formed an alliance with her in the first place, I have trouble reconciling. Of course, there was the factor of attracting her voluminous Green Government Coalition following to my own purposes. After winning them over, I should have more quickly and effectively distanced myself from her. Now she pesters, because of the lenience I bestowed on her as my primary mistress, to have her powerbase restored!

I have tried to distract her from her visions of grandeur—even devoting some of my scientific team's valuable time to building her a steam vehicle. It has been a ridiculous effort and has not diverted her from her disgruntled threats.

Whore Anders seems to believe that she is entitled to reigning authority, even ruling status of the land to the east recently haggled. Granted, she was helpful in the negotiations necessary to build the alliance that expanded the borders of Philistia, but she did so at my bidding! So what if her influence from her past has been an aid in swaying the proletariat and those lesser leaders of states in this region. It was still my idea to redefine power in this land and beyond, was it not?

Yet somehow she has connived with the corrupt ones in Old Iraq, now reborn again as beatific Babylon. It was to be my new palace headquarters once my plans have been completed in Jerusalem. That bitch, however, now purports it to be her enclave. She arrogantly states that I may present myself to the nations as the architect of this union, but unless I pronounce her prefect over Babylon, she will put in place a plan that will permanently cripple my alliances. She is even adroit enough to have anticipated my thoughts for eliminating her as a threat. At our once-a-week dinner together, she nagged that she had made arrangements with unnamed others to release information (highly damaging, I'm sure—she does have the access and the means to reveal my darker behavior) to the other world leaders as insurance, were anything unforeseen to happen to her.

Therefore, I must tread carefully and for the meantime allow her the title of Baroness of Babylon. It will be a token title of course, as my other plans will soon enough rob her of any real esteem. The people, even her allies, will thank me once they see how much more benevolently I will manage their welfare.

Postscript: I find it deliciously amusing that the likes of Brenda Anders finds my government's name and insignia to be offensive. It is especially ironic since I at first had chosen the name "Green Order Government" as a kind acknowledgment for her efforts: the membership of the Green Government Coalition constituted the initial support for my ascension.

Now she complains that I have attempted to steal her conceptual identity and tension has grown between us. Nevertheless, I have decided to stoke the fire of her frustration. The insignia for our great institution will be read as an acronym—GOG. Said reference will also not be lost on any who have managed to hide their precious Bibles from me. To them the insignia will serve as a fearful premonition based on obscure scriptural references alluding to a mighty power that will dominate their followers. Why not use it to my advantage? Why not inflate the trademark and use it to subdue any hope of rebellion?

Darius Mede—Chronicle II

Now you have seen what you cannot do; do you see what we can do?

—Darius Mede

The time has come to become more firm, especially with the Jews—and of those, notably two, who refuse to comply with my most simple requests. They are a part of my history I have wanted to forget and now I see that to do that, they must be used as an example to the rest.

It seems both a waste of my effort and at the same time a necessity to have them out of the way. I detest these menial diversions, knowing how much more I and my subordinates could be accomplishing if those two did not intentionally stand in the way of our progress.

While that plan is being orchestrated, I am finding other ways to structure global efficiency. Great strides are now being made to redesign the world credit structure. After all, what a ludicrous muddle is the exchange of paper as legal tender. How tiresome is the porting around of items with supposed value to trade; how obsolete the ferrying of heavy precious metals such as silver or gold for trade purposes. Do such items define wealth? It is by willingness to perform physical work or offer mental skills that one's true affluence can be measured.

Without electrical power, monetary transaction records are impractical. Besides, such systems of virtual accumulation have been more of a plague than a boon to the world's economy. Tradable assets must be stable and transferrable throughout the nations.

That is why a new form of currency will soon become the standard. It will be much more customized by region, based on the population's attributes, willingness to conform and attitudes. Each person will be assigned a code of prominence calculated through a formula. The numerical code will indicate to others how much of a contribution others are willing to offer. Of course, over time a worker may somehow improve or become less productive, but tracking such variations would be far too tedious. Therefore, the beginning assessment will remain a permanent hallmark. Harsh as it may sound, it is the most equitable and practical way to proceed.

The numerals will designate a class of citizenship and with that, permission to procure necessary items according to level. It will also allow access and egress to and from cities, regions and governmental audience.

At first I thought this might be construed to be too much like the Indian caste system of old. I am not dim-witted; we will not determine prestige based on lineage or cultural bias. Permanent, yes: but entirely idiosyncratic to the *one*.

How will counterfeit identities be avoided? My self-schooled skills have enabled me to become familiar with certain liquid compounds that, when precisely mixed and applied to the skin, will produce a brand. The affected skin is changed with little discomfort and the resulting numerical signature will be difficult, if not impossible, to alter.

I am excited about this international currency. Oh yes and where would be the best place to display this moniker so that none will be confused? Why, of course it would be most prominent on the forehead of each.

There is so much to do, so much to offer. Commoners cannot possibly appreciate exactly the extent of things being done on their behalf. No matter; it will become evident soon enough.

My research and formulation of the new building material I have called Flexsteel is completed. Allowing Jonathan Trimble's corporate engineers to use my pioneering formula for a government contract to construct a Catastrophic Event Protection Facility in the southern region of the former United States made all the difference. That experiment allowed me to refine the inventions which benefit us today—not only Flexsteel but also my specialized chemical lighting system and various other smaller accomplishments.

Within the confines of Beit Aghion, the foundations have been reinforced and walls made of the compound have been completed. According to the strength and durability tests, this structure and any containing the same designs will ride out any but the most catastrophic earthquake. I have framed a berth in which people can safely live and work even while the planet experiences great duress.

The profit of this invention will be astronomical. I have already designed my own status identifier. Perhaps I will allow it as an award for others to wear as well—a sign of attachment to my cause.

The digits I have picked are ironic indeed. During the archaic times of the last age, the "Age of Paradox", one superstitious cult had determined a numeric cryptograph that supposedly represented mankind. In their eyes it was a representation of corruption. I, on the other hand, grudge the idea that we are inherently flawed. We have demonstrated continuously the ability to expand and improve our conditions. So I instead glorify the number, which I will wear proudly on my forehead. Everyone who sees it will then fancy one for themselves, of course—understanding how valuable the imprint of 666 will be in terms of universal prominence.

I have been playing and an accident occurred—a very practical accident that will serve me well. I was in my small laboratory making adjustments to my Flexsteel formula when I intermixed a nitrogen compound with white phosphorus. The spontaneous combustion that resulted permanently maimed my clumsy assistant and singed my eyebrows. Regardless, using a new Flexsteel air-driven rifle I have devised, I was able to re-create the accident and direct the flames toward a specific target with amazing accuracy and energy efficiency. The benefit is that the compounds used require lighter and smaller storage tanks than traditional propane or acetylene. The high-pressure required to propel the gas is the quandary. Explosions and injuries to my forces will be the risk—one I am perfectly willing to take. This new weapon will help instill commensurate fear into any who might oppose me. I will regret if using it becomes necessary, but am comforted that the machinery is available for such occurrences.

Another strange episode has been reported to me: hail the size of basketballs—not here in Jerusalem, but in all other quadrants of the globe. This is just one more of the increasing aerial assaults that have taken the great cultural centers and cities from glory to ruin. It is all the more reason for us to manufacture and distribute Flexsteel to the ends of the earth as quickly as possible.

How this land escapes most of the convulsions is in itself a scientific confusion which I plan to research when there is adequate time. But now I am committed to working on my proudest accomplishment of all, a project so grand that it must be perfectly prepared. This chronicling and my scientific notes will be my guarded admission for the time being. There is a practical reason for divulging my work by this more vulnerable written method. My research records will not adequately define why I have seen the need for my many hours of exertion to this cause.

By the culmination of the Age of Paradox, science had leapfrogged the dreams of plebeians. In fact, that was part of the problem with the social order of that time. Everyone began to consider themselves entitled to cutting-edge conveniences. But no one wanted to disavow their religious impulses in trade, though these had been proven to be futile and unnecessary. The dimwitted public then lived a dualistic life, seeking gods to praise for their bounty, but denying the one true god— humanity itself.

I blame this double-minded lifestyle for not encouraging the scientific community to even greater feats. So, when the galaxy presented an implausible challenge to our continuance—the sudden appearance of the V4641 micro-quasar—most reacted with arcane behavior rather than increasing efforts to destroy or at least manage the threat. Instead of striving to conquer their adversary, many chose to worship its presence and thus perished by its hand. Simpletons one and all; such self-destructive nonsense will not be tolerated. It endangers us all.

The religious zealots have come unglued. At this moment, my informants tell me they are planning to carry through with the rally in front of their precious temple project. They obviously plan an overthrow of my lawful government; it is obvious by their consistent disregard for all of the regulations I have put in place to protect my federation. It is regretful that for this reason, a strategy has to be set in motion to remove them as a threat. Yet I also believe that by their demise, I will feel the satisfaction of revenge. After all, it was those two, Hindeland and Folzman, who thwarted me all the way in my ascension.

They have even attempted blackmail over our good intentions by refusing to relinquish control over their vast food stores. I have searched extensively for their warehouses to wrest the commodities from them to the benefit of the populace. But my enemies have hidden their provisions better than I would have suspected. It has become very clear to me that they will not cooperate with my efforts and therefore I will no longer tolerate theirs.

Come to think of it, it was also that baldheaded, self-righteous old fool who somehow managed to occupy and discover the workings of my protective stronghold in the former United States.

Apparently one of his lackeys was even able to somehow overpower my most prized asset, Jonathan Trimble. I am hopeful that Jonathan has managed to survive and will follow through with the plans we have made. It is annoying not to have heard from him—communication with that part of the planet is nearly impossible at this time.

I intend, if he succeeds and completes the journey here, to lend him some of my authority. I cannot possibly manage all of the duties necessary to fulfill my plans and who better to direct *Media Affiliations for the Green Order Government?* (Ha! The upstart Seconds will cringe doubly when they decipher this acronym.)

And that one who caused the inconvenience to my plan, the boy called Jason, will be taken care of as well, when my actions for Hindeland, Folzman and all their naive followers are implemented.

"Yom Tov Shmuah", they are calling it. I will teach them a lesson about Days of Good News. It has to be this way. Elimination of the superstitious mindset is the only way to rise above the mindset of misery. Names like *god* and *the devil* must be ejected from our vocabulary along with the names of those who brandish them like weapons of warfare.

The new name by which we will survive is not a weapon but a tool. It is a name that has existed from the beginning and will continue until nothing on this planet exists. It is a great name, it is Our name. *Mankind* is all that is, all that was and all that will be. And I am the One of Mankind who will show them the way!

The deed is done. In some ways I will miss those superstitious pugilists. They indeed kept me sharp. Great crowds had gathered to hear their words and those who heard were swayed. Regrettably, that necessitated that they too became casualties. Regardless, none of them remain a threat and their actions have given me an inspiration.

It was obvious that their god did not save them or truly help them in any way. But the crowds were still attracted. By what? The power of the place and the ceremony, naturally. The temple they were constructing, if completed with the proper intent, will endow its magistrate with a formidable degree of authority. It remains and they do not. I might as well integrate that symbol now to my purposes. In a strange way, I have my rivals to thank for elevating my position to unanticipated levels.

And once I am recognized as both the political and spiritual power of this place, there, of course, will be others that may challenge. The timing, then, to complete my greatest deed is crucial. All looks ready and so I can now divulge my designs, confident that the plan will soon unfold without interference.

Being privileged to have developed many scientific advances in the Age of Paradox, one study became more intriguing than any other—the idea of duplicating material from a biological organism.

Much had been accomplished in this arena prior to "the cataclysm". Animal tissue, even complete specimens, had been reproduced and much ground had been gained in the cloning of human tissue to use in repairing injuries. But due to ridiculous ethical complexities, no one had taken the audacious step of cloning an entire human being.

In this great New Age of Freedom, I have taken it upon myself to cross the boundary and have successfully replicated three individuals from their corpse-state. They are alive and are functioning well!

As these three demonstrate, there is still much work to be done. Although they respond to every charge I give them, there is a noticeable lack of initiative in their character—their behavior appearing somewhat mechanical. I have determined that until advancements can be made that will invigorate their psyche, these subjects will make an ideal laborer class for our improved society. More so, I continue my work at Dimona—benefiting from their expendability. They are, by their very nature, easily replicable. Considering it further, I may even continue replicating them in large quantities to meet the menial needs of humankind.

Note: A small setback. My test subjects have been displaying erratic behavior. Were I superstitious like the Jews, I would almost define it as demonic. Such nonsense; the issue can be corrected and I will put my efforts to it after the meeting I am about to have with the remaining rabble from the so-called resistance movement. These Seconds, as they call themselves, they are like fungus reproducing. Will I never be rid of them? They must be dealt with.

Letters of Luther Hine

To Ilbani of the Seconds in Jerusalem and to all those who now have and will, submit in every way for their faith, knowing that Jesus is our purpose and service—he is the One we wait for,

I pray this letter finds you well. I want to thank you for the gift of the doves you provided. They are allowing rapid communication between us. Your brief message at our last checkpoint suggests the birds are dependable! I will keep these reports and requests short—as you know, the birds can only carry so much payload.

We have also been able to trade messages with those regions we are heading toward—I am keeping specific geographical names out of these correspondences to avoid disclosing our ultimate destinations to unwanted eyes. For now, simple compass points should give you a good idea as to our whereabouts and progress.

As we discussed before our reluctant departure from you, Jason and his group will soon be splitting off from us and heading into the upper North to offer hope to those faithful followers. Rachel, I and the other Seconds with us are letting the Spirit guide us to the West. I long to visit my relatives and share with them the amazing miracles we have experienced.

I am amazed at the strength and resolve of Rachel; she has become the greatest gift beyond salvation that my Savior has ever provided. The marriage wedding ceremony was our shared vow that our service to our Lord Yeshua must always be first, even above our love for one another and He has honored us by His protection thus far. Thank you again for standing as my best man (especially considering you were still recovering from your wounds from the great earthquake) and for your and Jason's other most special gift, the typewriter. Once we arrive at our destination, we will use it as planned to copy the Word and the Book of Seconds to distribute light to a very dark world. I am confident that Eleazar will be using their machine to that same glorious purpose.

Speaking of light, the blue glow that radiates from all known Seconds has become both a boon and a cross. It is comforting to enter a town and catch a glimpse of a fellow Christ Follower by way of what we have come to call their *blue*. The problem is with our enemies. They too use the light to earmark and dog us. On one hand, we are now committed; there is no easy way to marginalize the intensity of the Mark of Christ. But then again, we have become easy objects of persecution. Thank God for our spiritual gifts—an example being a brother who has joined our travels. He has the ability to somehow shade the mind of unbelievers so that they cannot see our glowing. The effect is temporary and limited in distance, but it does help us to walk undetected through spiritually dangerous territories. Still, we take the extra precaution of wearing leather suits with hoods to mimic those who must protect themselves from the Revelation Bugs. We pray that you have secured similar gifts for protection and look forward to the time when we can again join in worship together.

For now, I must stop typing and prepare for the next leg of our journey. God be with you, Ilbani. May the shalom of Adonai Yeshua continue to complete you,

Luther

Friend Ilbani,

We pray that Ruach Ha'Kodesh continues to guard your hearts and your minds in the fairest city of all—the city we will once again call our home when Yeshua arrives.

I have to ask you first, because of the widespread rumors that have reached us this far away from you; is it true seven thousand was the final count of those lost in that last great quake there? How tragic and pointless, considering the power of the Most High to intervene if only the world's population would recognize Him, not just by name but by true belief in submissiveness to His Son.

As for our current journey, we are still in transit. The conditions outside of the Land are far more horrific. There are very few civilized areas and those that do exist are brutal places governed by Mede's thugs. Seconds are methodically chased and eliminated—hence the cryptic disposition of our location.

The Revelation Bugs, more hailstorms, earthquakes and other cataclysmic events continue to ravage the land and starve the people. We ask for your continued prayers, encouraging us to lead as many as possible to relationship with Messiah while we make strained progress toward our destination.

Eleazar and Ayita have traveled to the eastern mountains of the former priest's origins to reveal to his father and remaining family the heinous schemes orchestrated by his brother. He has also delivered the long-hoped-for package.

This message will be duplicated and sent by multiple methods to discourage others' intent on interfering with our communications.

> Grace and peace to you, my brother in the Messiah and to all Seconds in fair Jerusalem,

Luther

Greetings Ilbaini,

Praise Ha'Shem, we have your latest correspondence. I agree that we must make the connection between us more difficult for our enemies to track. Granted, they will still pursue, but at least we can seek ways to slow their efforts. Duplicates of our writings will be kept safe in hopes of forewarning future generations of the harsh realities under which we serve our Lord.

I have copied Eleazar on my messages and have received a note back from him. God has blessed his union with Ayita and she is with child! Please keep them in your prayers as well as all of the Seconds—we are receiving word of many such new births; God's hand is providing new seed for His future harvest!

Speaking of new life, Eleazar's father has confessed Yeshua as his Savior! All of their family in that country is now spreading the hope of the New Advent. They are also working diligently to undo the damage done to that region by Eleazar's brother. He is now being exposed for what he has suspired to become— the antithesis of Yeshua, Darius Mede hungers solely for the things of man.

On a bleaker note, we have lost three of our clan to infections and skirmishes with outlaws we have encountered during our travels. We have also received notice that one of Jason's clan has made the transition from life temporal to life eternal. Remember them all by name: Endeo, Joseph, Pavoli, JeongHyun—virtuous Seconds, one and all—and pray for their families who remain faithful.

Ilbani, be comforted in His name,

Luther

Greetings, Friend Ilbani,

Let me start this letter with a long overdue question. Have I apologized in the past for the tiny script of these notes? If not, please understand that we want to impart as much as possible in the small space allowed in order that it may be transported by the doves.

Getting to the point—some very wonderful news: Rachel, my spirited sabra, has given us a son! Had I told you she was pregnant! No, she had insisted on secrecy until this moment because of the enemy's ever-vigilant search for us. By YHWH's grace, our boy Jander Ilbani (after you, my friend!) will have a fighting chance.

And he will need it! We are now in the place I once called home. It is now an evil place inhabited by demons that have infested the bodies and cognition of people I once called friends. It is by my knowledge of their past that I can see the legions within them and so we have begun a ministry of exorcism. It is dangerous and incapacitating work—the unwanted spirits do not give up easily—but many have been reclaimed to Messiah, thanks be to His Spirit's presence.

More disturbing, however, are the rapidly increasing numbers of what we now call *bose spooks* or wicked ghosts. They are zombie-like creatures, seemingly normal in every way, human enough except for their complete lack of emotion. We have learned to avoid them carefully for they are bent on destruction, showing no hesitation in attacking and mutilating any Second who comes near. Fielder, a new follower, was lost to their menace, as was our dear young friend Ben (whom Jason sent with us). Please pray for the Spirit's protection over us.

Rachel, I and all our clan send greetings and the kiss of Messiah's love to you. As wretched as things appear, your hope is our hope—the King is soon-coming. All of this will pass and we will live as one with him—in this comfort we celebrate, knowing the enemy has already been defeated by the eternal plan of YHWH!

The dominion be Yeshua's now and forevermore,

Luther

P.S. I have not forgotten the other gift you provided, Danny Adamson's five sticks. I have been using them to teach any who will listen about the connecting love of God. You will also want to know that Eleazar assures the South South Tablet remains protected in Ayita's hands. Preacher Elijah was guided wisely by the Ruach when he charged her as its keeper.

EPILOGUE

This time, it is not his forehead that he dries, but his eyes. *Can this be?* Amos BenMadai asks himself as he sets the manuscript down once again.

Since his youngest son's return, a world he thought had become evil incarnate is suddenly full of promise. Forget the collapse of civilization; forget the devastation and death that seemed in control. God is alive! There is now no doubt. *My prodigal has returned and with him comes a message encrypted within another—God too has a son! The message, of course, is not new. It has been there all along; God, ancient and eternal has not changed. It is this old Jew who has become new!*

BenMadai is distracted a moment by another item on his desk—his carefully preserved Jewish calendar.

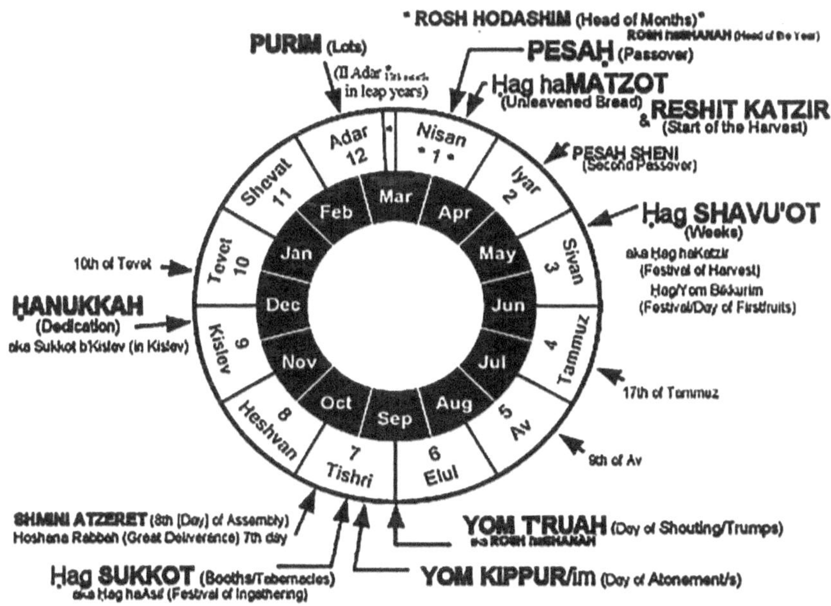

239

He makes a note on the chart, identifying today, the first full moon of the month of Nissan. It is Passover: an ironic moment to become new, to be humbly redeemed into true fellowship with YHWH.

—what a loathsome man I was. Next to the calendar, one more relic—a tarnished mirror—he picks it up and peers searchingly into the past of the grizzled façade reflected there.

Amos BenMadai, proud Jewish Social Services Manager in the Chaldean region of Iraq, had wanted to teach the world and its Creator how they had been created. Resentful of how mankind and their cobbled religion had abused him and trampled upon his dignity, he set forth to prove them all inferior. He would rebuke them, introducing a new and better way, starting with an example more prized than even his own. He would steer his own son Darius in the wise ways of Amos BenMadai.

The lesson was fearfully absorbed. Darius BenMadai soon became the teacher, revealing to his father not a beautifully crafted gem by his hands but instead an egocentric element which grew of its own greed. At the hand of his self-arrogant yet naive father, Darius discovered his own desire for control of anything not under his control. There was no limit to his lust and soon there was nothing, including his own father, that he did not treat as inanimate, undeserving of relationship. To Darius, who changed his surname to Mede in an effort to mask his disreputable Jewish roots, the world and its occupants became nothing more than an experiment to be shaped by his avarice.

As for the supposed instructor? Amos tried desperately to reverse the chain-reaction he had set in motion. But he was cursed to watch helplessly as his new lifeform morphed into the most subtle of monsters. The father its prey, discovered his son the beast, while in the process of being devoured. One of those whom the elder BenMadai saw quickly and frighteningly destroyed was Darius's own mother, the elegant Llana, who could not bear the rejection of her firstborn. The more she reached out for him in love, the more he derided her with casual, uncaring torture. In the end the flame of her love was easily extinguished by her offspring. It took one word—a change of name, to be precise. Darius started using his mother's first name instead of her matronly title. Then he unabashedly began mispronouncing her name. Instead of Llana, he referred to her as Yanaal, pronounced almost with the same inflections but meaning something quite different—*idiot.*

Within three weeks of the mocking, Llana BenMadai took her own life rather than have it sucked irreverently away by her son.

Darius left the remaining family to pursue his dreams of instituting his all-encompassing empire. It took several years of emotional recovery, but ultimately, Amos BenMadai committed himself to self-redemption for his inglorious undertaking. His efforts became singularly centered on the ardent upbringing of his younger son, Eleazar.

This time, the method would be quite different, with Amos questioning and listening rather than injecting and imposing. In this way, he learned his son's hopes and dreams. The teacher heard and responded to his student's interests and became a safe-harbor during times of doubt and fear. A new emotion grew between and within them—one neither had truly experienced before: Love. It shaped them both into a true family and that is when both became *echad*—one in the understanding of the other. Together they discovered the one thing they had desperately run from and now desperately desired in their life: God.

The elder encouraged the younger to learn discipline and refinement in Israel and it was there that Eleazar came under the influence of a dear old friend, Rabbi Moses Folzman. It was not long before Eleazar was recognized for his compassion and equal understanding of service before YHWH. A movement was afoot at that time to ordain a new priesthood system to be ready should the rebuilding of the third Jewish Temple become eminent and Eleazar was chosen by his peers to serve as the high priest. Amos prepared also to move to Jerusalem, to partake in the joy of his son's spiritual enlightenment. But that is when their world…everyone's world…fell into chaos.

The Hidden Exodus, the Gathering-Up—whatever it was called—kept son and father from being rejoined. And it caused one more ordeal in each of them—one last question tugging for an answer within both men: *Do I serve the right God and if so, what is He saying to me by means of these terrible times?*

The younger discovered the answer by the most serendipitous of means: a Jewish rabbi turned Christian convert who remained, after all others had vanished, to offer one final gospel message.

When Eleazar did return, the prodigal brought to his father two gifts. One was a new fire in his eyes that apprised the elder, *I have ascertained your answer.*

Now the younger has again taught the elder and the irony is not lost on Amos. *YHWH has always worked this way, in the past ages, in this one and in the ages to come.*

He notices that the pages of the new publications are starting to curl at the edges, having not yet been suitably bound. Looking around, he finds a great tool to be married to the task of "pressing". It is an ancient Bible given as a gift from a colleague, containing both the Tanakh—the Old Testament, as Eleazar now refers to it,—and the New Testament—the B'riyt Hadashah as Amos now calls it. "Father and son together," he muses out loud.

Placing the prized texts gently alongside the New Testimonies he has just read from Eleazar, Amos begins to consider the entirety of the history combined here on his desk: the beginning and the end…but not quite.

One more oracle: that is all he needs. Closing his eyes, the aged scholar reaches for his newfound Savior in prayer and is rewarded with an equally new gift.

"Tell." He speaks it out, testing it on his tongue, to hear out loud its authority spoken into him. "Tell." Yes, that is it. He will feed the message to others. They, all of us, can survive by the hope of this inspired purpose.

But what message is it that I am to tell, Lord? There is so much here to share and it must be fed to them lovingly, as it was fed to my son and to me.

BenMadai leafs back through the pages to a token that had captivated his heart. As he does so, another tremor shakes the small room, reminding him that the times are still perilous, the task ever the more imperative. Brushing away fragments that have fallen from the stucco onto the manuscript, the man reads the conversation again, translating mentally into his own language, letting the power of the words convict him as he works them through.

> "I serve no purpose at all, or didn't, until—"
> "Until you discovered life?"
> "I think it's more like realizing I was dead…really dead, not
> just my body. That's when everything began to change."
> "So you are a Second."

In the dim light, Amos BenMadai picks up the five flat wooden sticks his son had given him. He carefully assembles them into the odd configuration the younger BenMadai had taught, first making a cross with two sticks and then wedging together three other sticks to surround and contain the cross.

The old man smiles at the work of his hands which now glow radiant blue. He speaks out his heart at that moment to a God he knows shaped and guided those hands and who longs to love him more.

"Yes, that's a saying for it. I am a Second."

"Therefore, when you see the abomination of desolation,
spoken of by Daniel the prophet, standing in the holy place…
then let those who are in Judea flee to the mountains…For then
there will be great tribulation, such as has not been since the
beginning of the world until this time, no, nor ever shall be."

—Matthew 24:15–21

E N D

AUTHOR
MARK A. CORNELIUS

Mark A. Cornelius has authored numerous books, video productions, a journal ministry, musicals, and several podcast series.

His works include *RUT Management—Discovering Adventure in the Routine of Life, Believement—Breaking Through the Belief Barrier, Welfare Christianity, Thunder Buffalo Goes Home, Tomorrow's Bread, Marginalized, UnMeasuring—What if we are ALL Wrong?* and the popular fiction series *The Ruach Saga (including The Singularity, The Book of Seconds, Bronzeman, and War of the Lost Song).*

His books can be purchased at https://quantumdiscovery.net/shop/, and at www.RUTmanagement.com.

Amos 3:6-8, The Bible

Mark has authored other insights and blogs, all of which can be obtained on his website. You can experience Mark's passion for writing at **www.MarkCornelius.me.**

Catch Mark's podcasts at:

Watchmen podcast:

https://www.youtube.com/channel/UC3fA03AhXRh RZNhNyrEhgA

Mark My Words (Critical Thinking) podcast:

https://www.youtube.com/channel/UCR8Csunh9mJMOZHjT97NUZg

Travel with Mark at his blog: **www.DeepEndFaith.blogspot.com**, and dive into discussion on **E-mail: Markcwrites@gmail.com**, or Facebook: **https://www.facebook.com/Mark-My-Words-103741988034911.**

Join Mark in asking his ongoing journey question…

"What If?"

Looking forward to our journey together!

ILLUSTRATOR - SHAY CAVENDER was born in Nashville, Tennessee. She began her drawing career at a young age doodling and writing short comic strips. Her unique style specializes in animals both real and fantastical. Currently she is a student at the University of Tennessee at Martin as a Graphic Design major. She plays Trombone in the UTM Marching Skyhawk Band and aims to continue playing her instrument later in life despite her art-oriented career direction. Drawing and illustrating are her passions along with her love of animals including dogs and reindeer. In the future, Shay hopes to secure a profession that will utilize her distinctive talents.